RED MASS

A RED Agency Novel

Daniel Moler

friend TaraStar Barnett, for reviewing queries in a time of need; Tyler Stransky, the computer shaman, for being my technical problem solver; my sister Rachel, for always believing in me; and my guides and allies in the Unseen Realms, for *being* the source of my imagination even when I didn't notice you.

"Peoples of the Earth, you have all been poisoned."
--William Seward Burroughs II

"Culture is not your friend."
--Terence Kemp McKenna

1 - The Trial

The courtroom was stale. Walls made of pine or substitute thereof. The air full of an invisible mist, clouding the inexorable toxicity prevalent in every pore. Any ensuing reality outside of the courtroom was assuredly non-existent. Tree falls. No sound. No one, nothing there to receive it.

Gregor sweat as his vision began to swirl. He looked at his attorney, who twitched anxiously. Her attorney sauntered toward the stand, a short and obtuse-looking man. Graying mustache tickled his upper lip. Clearing his throat, he began:

"Mr. Samson, with reference to the Petitioner's Exhibit Number 52, that being the counseling records from Blue Star Family Services . . . you answered a series of questions about your past drug use as reported in these records. And again, that was LSD, cocaine, marijuana, opium, and heroin, et cetera, from 1999 to 2003. Is that correct?"

"Yes." Gregor answered quietly.

"That was as reported to them by you, not by Kathleen, correct?" The attorney motioned to her, sitting behind the Petitioner's table. Auburn hair and bone-colored skin. Eye shadow that fluttered like sarcophagus butterflies.

"How do you mean?" Gregor asked.

"This is your substance abuse, past and present."

"We filled it out together, Kathleen and I."

Her attorney's smile was contrived. "But you were aware this was being put down in these records and you agreed with it at that time. Is that correct?"

"Yes."

"You have now testified today in court under oath that this prior drug use was limited to what you call *experimentation*. Is that correct?"

"Yes."

"That you *only* tried LSD ten times?" The emphasis was cynical.

"Yes."

"And that you didn't ever try heroin, you got that confused with opium. Is that correct?"

"Yes." Gregor blushed at the embarrassment of that mistake. His mind was muddled then. Even worse now.

"Okay. Would you agree, though, that on . . . it says on the top of page 5, of Exhibit 52, in the integrated summary and recommended treatment plan paragraph . . . would you agree that in the last sentence of the first paragraph it says, 'Gregor used a lot of drugs in the past, but reported not any since being married to Kathleen.' Do you agree that it says that?"

"Uh huh."

The Judge leaned over with a creak and snaps in. His voice deep, shaking the witness stand. "Yes or No answer."

"Yes, she asked me to quit if I wanted to marry her. So, I did."

"Okay. So, is this the same as the *experimentation* . . . as you call it today?"

"Yes."

"Alright, so what was then using 'a lot of drugs in the past' is now called 'experimentation', is that your testimony?"

"Well, there was a lot of marijuana in college." A few chuckles from the audience. The Judge glares at them in annoyance.

"That's right? This says you, Gregor Samson, 'used a lot of drugs in the past.' Are you saying that's not true?"

"What exactly are you trying to ask?"

"I'm asking you if this is a true and accurate statement. That you, Gregor, used a lot of drugs in the past."

"More so I guess than the average person."

"Okay. So, a little bit more than just *experimentation*, correct?"

"Doesn't *everybody* experiment?" More chuckles from the audience. The Judge taps his gavel.

"My question to you is was it more than *experimentation*???" His arms stretch down the sides of his coat. Voice tense as an unturned fiddle.

"It was experimentation."

"Okay . . . *a lot* of experimentation, then, according to this exhibit?"

"If that's the way you want to look at it."

"Well, I'm asking you about what is in the record. This says you used a lot of drugs in the past. Do you agree with that or not?"

"I don't agree with that, no." Gregor felt a knot tighten.

"So this counselor that wrote this is incorrect?"

"She's incorrect in that particular statement, yes. She exaggerated."

"Is she also incorrect, then, on the next line where it says both you and Kathleen reported having been abused in the past by your parents?"

"She was talking about emotional abuse when it came to me."

"Okay. So, you weren't physically abused by your parents, but you were emotionally --"

"Emotionally, yes."

"By mother or father?"

Gregor paused in a quiet uncertainty. He needed a drink a drink of water . . . throat parched and thick. "Both. It happens to a lot of teenagers, doesn't it?"

They stood outside, smoking cigarettes like carnivorous fiends. Heat index close to 110°. Sweat splotch islands under the arms of Gregor's gray suit. The smoke twitched from his shaky hands in little iridescent curls. Mouth was so dry he could feel the bumps on his tongue. He and his friends crooned on the front steps of the courthouse, craning gargoyles ready to crack: Ramona, Lawrence, sister Lena, and his attorney Jezebel. She hovered two steps above the rest, Jezebel; her towering and haughty stature frightening to any creature of the law.

"What the fuck was that, Samson?" she bellowed. She could give two dried dogshits that Kathleen and her troupe were lounging at the gazebo across the walkway. Her voice carried the weight and slur of a drunken Dutch sailor.

"What's the problem?" Lena chimed in; her tendency to ring her bells wherever music wasn't welcome. However, Gregor had thought, the supportive effort would be appreciated. "He was side-swiped! That was a cold maneuver." Lena tends to think that her abilities at strategy allow her innocuous flexibilities to language. Reading the *Art of War* and playing *Risk* regularly sets her on the path of the Khan.

"Honestly, Jezebel," Gregor slid in front of Lena, quietly aiming to block any semblance of conversation Kathleen might overhear. "What am I supposed to do? Where were you in there?"

"I did what I could, Samson," she crossed her arms and glared down at him glumly.

Gregor scratched his nervous head. "Next time he starts asking me to cite exhibit records, maybe you could jump in and let him know that's out of scope."

"Who's the fucking legal counsel here, Samson???" Bellowing and haughty.

Lawrence stepped forward, stomping out his cigarette. "You are, Jezebel. You're the one getting paid here."

Jezebel loomed in uncomfortable dormancy. It seemed like her body shook in its own stillness, ready to implode. She kept her icy gaze locked onto Gregor's demure face. "You trying to lose your daughter? Fine by me, be an asshole on the stand. Try to make him and the court look stupid. After all, you're the one with experience, right? The rest is up to the Almighty now, anyway."

Jezebel stomped back into the courthouse in mushy shoes.

"Is she right?" Ramona asked. "You think you could lose?" Blonde hair refracted the aching sunlight. Gregor turned away and saw Kathleen and her mother walking back into the building. They looked over at him with machinated grins. He wanted to kill them. God, how he wanted to kill them! They sauntered in with a pretentious smell. Kathleen's mother waved smugly. They had this in the bag. This was their day to be had.

Lawrence patted Gregor on the shoulder. "Come on, let's go. Get this shit over with. Either way, drinks are on me tonight."

The Judge entered. Everyone did the "all rise" and then settled in to hear the final order. To Gregor, it was a verdict. *Am I or am I not a bad person? Am I or am I not a fiend? Can I or can I not be trusted with my child, because I had a little fun in college? Can I really be punished for things I did six years ago? Will they believe her lies?* He folded his hands, not necessarily to look calm, but to squeeze and strangle the white tension permeating the room like static.

He began. It took a while, voyaging through the exhibits and testimonies, picking out what he thought was pertinent. Weighing the evidence available to him.

After a torturous half an hour, he leaned forward in his chair. Gregor heard the leather squeak. The knot tightened, clogging his throat.

"I don't like to do this. It's not in the court's place to be able to parent a child. That's your job, mommy and daddy. And it's unfortunate that you can't put the child above your own misgivings and learn a collaborative approach. However, you've asked me to do this, to make a decision in the child's best interests, which parent the child shall reside with. I'm going to recommend that the child, Alice, reside with her mother. The child shall be in the joint legal care, custody, and control of the parents subject to the parenting schedule that I am setting forth here today.

"Part of this plan should consider the concern over some drug use. I'm not going to order any drug testing at this time, but I will allow the mother, if she feels there is a concern, to have the opportunity to request analysis from the father at any

5

time. If she has that concern, I can be contacted and I'd sign an order . . . I'm willing to do a follow-up and order some type of testing if she has a concern."

Her attorney stood up briefly. "Mrs. Samson would be fine with that."

"Well," the Judge adjusted himself and looked down to a notepad he was scribbling on. "Based on the evidence presented in this matter, the court feels that Alice would be in a more stable environment with her mother at this time."

The world spins.

Eddy flow into a concentrated vortex . . . down. Gregor felt the choke, feels the choke ever more. And, in that moment...

. . . something died.

22 - Not the Final Term

I am the Psycho-Shaman; the Product of the Bleed - air pushes on my chest, all story is the story of the child ripped from its Mother's breast . . .
>Matter Immaculate<

Mystery humbles . . .
. . . assimilation with ambiguity.

No more of the "I".

Never again.

2 - After the Fall

Alice, Kathleen, and I are walking along the streets of
New York City, holding hands. Vacation maybe. Sight-seeing.
The whole-suburban-family-gawking-at-the-sites thing. In awe
of the gargantuan metal spires looming above us, looking for
swinging superheroes. There was a man in spandex that did
appear dancing on air pockets. He somersaulted in the air above
us . . . twirled his leg in a cloud and we go "Oooh" and "Aaah."
People gathered around and we all laughed. Then, the air
pockets just below his fingers and toes began turning to ice. He
began slipping and falling: face racked with confusion and
despair. The crowds dispersed. Nobody looked back.

When I returned I snuck past the clerk into the back of
the store. I could not find water, only liquor. I tried to ask some
customers where the water was, but all I got were strange
mumbles and wavering eyes. They were all leaving, the market
was closing.

We went into a grocery market that was located in the
basement of a tenement building. Something about the clerk I
did not like, as if I knew him. I did not trust him. We bought
staple items and went back to our room, located in a Victorian
hotel off Broadway. Kathleen said we were out of water and I
should go back to the market. The city water was not safe to
drink. I didn't want to, but she forced me to go. I didn't
understand.

One fellow, whose physical traits are completely
unmemorable, featureless, decided to help me and show me
where a couple of bottles might be. He took me to a special
section of the market, in a back corner. There was a girl,
probably 18 years-old, with stark black hair that flowed straight
down her back. She wore a cashmere sweater with an emblem
on it I couldn't make out. I think I had a dream about her before,
about a year ago. She was a fortune teller dealing out Tarot
cards to me.

"I'm going to check you out, specially," she said. She grabbed a stack of black construction paper. While telling me, and the featureless man, a story about pumpkins and rabbits, she cut out one shape out of the entire stack. It looked aboriginal, dreadlocks, anthropomorphic face, something native rang to mind. Mind . . . do I have mind here? I told her, "Oh, this is one of **those** special check-outs." This was a fortune-telling. She told me to go to the back of the store. Just when I was ready to argue we were already there, I followed her pointed finger and saw that the 'back' was extended further than I had originally seen. The featureless man nodded. He stayed with her.

It was dark, stumbling over boxes and crates, shelves of olives and other pickled items. A dim light cast over a mural on a wall. It was a triptych. A wooden bench positioned in front. I sat and examined the paintings.

A sequential narrative in three parts. The first a medieval battle scene: knights in detailed bronze armor fighting barbarian hordes. An emphasis on one in particular, wearing a helmet ordained with silver dragon wings. He is skewering a bearded savage through the gut, a waterfall of blood pours into a pool of red in the snowy landscape. Next scene: the same knight, though he is alone, facing off against a mighty chimera with blood-stained claws. This time the knight has a javelin thrust into a foreleg of the beast. The chimera's lion head roared in pain. Its tail whipped around, tipped by a venomous serpent, snapping its maws at the side of the knight's torso. The bestial wail from his face matched his adversary's expression; both in throes--both in checkmate. The third: the same knight kneeling at a bedside. His face cannot be seen. On the bed lays the body of a beautiful woman with long auburn hair stretching past her feet. She is covered in cone flowers and lilacs. I don't assume, I just know she is dead.

This was a holy place, powerfully charged. One of the paintings is a doorway. It's up to me to choose. I stand up and pick one. I don't remember which one . . . hold my hand up, palm out; I walk through and everything becomes confused, sketchy. A *swirl of memories and visuals I don't understand. I am standing in an arctic landscape, glacier and mounds of white. The sky is gray and the wind is bitter, but not frozen. I feel metal underground, tingling beneath my feet. I think I can control it. I think I can maneuver it with my mind, by waving my hands around like a carnival magician. The ground shifts and rumbles. 'I think I will make a castle', I say as tiny fragments of minerals pop out of the ground and into the space around me. "I think I will make a castle so big . . . so big that the tallest tower could not even be seen with the eye." And I begin to assemble my masterpiece like a god with tinker toys.*

*   *   *   *   *

I remember the way I was.

I am awake now and I am, indeed, a bug.

No, I am an alien among hominids, paradoxically treated as a Neanderthal. They know I am here . . . they can see me; might as well be a cockroach scampering across the floor, pleading for rationality over the heel of a boot. I pray for desensitization in our communication.

They should learn cockroach, or alien. Maybe set up a translation methodology. An electrode network comprised of neuro-symbiotic arthropods with tentacle conductors for thought delivery. That would be easiest, probably.

Tap, tap.

Waking up, rebirth happens in seconds. Blink my eyes; suddenly someone else.

Tap, tap, tap.

Fingers grow numb after a while. Overtly artificial light blinks at a narrow frequency that causes palpitations in my lower left eyelid. The doctor calls it a twitch, I think it's a palpitation. Has something to do with the heart, I'm sure. Palpitations start at 150 MHz, I believe. I am still doing the research.

Tap, tap, tap, tap.

A light flickering at exactly the right frequency can send any animal brain into a hypnotic trance. One may feel it like paralysis, and time compresses and becomes extinct. 150 MHz and counting . . .

Tap, tap.

Fingers grow numb after a while and everyone needs a coffee break. Lock the desktop and the chair creaks metal as I sludge off to the break room. The environment would be sterile if it were actually clean, but dust cloaks the air in secret. No music, not even elevator. All around a grid-work sea of cubicles in a chorus of more tap, tap, tapping. Keyboard orchestra. I think I can see the windows from here.

Jena sits across the aisle. Overweight and smells like stale cheese crackers. She has hair on her cheeks and talks to her monitor as she writes code arbitrary applications that will never be used. A framed picture of a smirking David Boreanaz sits on her desk next to a collection of glossy gnome figurines.

Make my way to the coffee station. Doug hangs around the pot like it's an Irish pub in Westport. He has a Special Forces military background and spends his day on the phone drumming: "Echo, Bravo, Bravo, Alpha, Bravo." A button is pinned to his polo shirt that reads *It's Free*.

"Greg-ORE, my man," he slaps a calloused hand on my back. I cringe. "You got those grain reports ready yet? PM's gonna want those by tomorrow morning."

I pour an eighth of a pot of blackened tar into my stained cup. "They'll be finished by then," I tell him, eager to shuffle back to my private little cube.

"By the way," he continues, obviously unaware I am uninterested in pursuing further conversation. "Did you see the game last night? When're the Chiefs gonna be worth watchin', eh?"

"I've got to get to work," I maneuvered away.

Just in time . . . Paul and Manoj making their way over. Paul is a typical corpulent programmer. His face is wide and miserable. When he smiles it feels embarrassing. Manoj, on the other hand, is a chipper Indian who giggles like a schoolgirl. He is notorious for his incessant snorting every minute; management shuffles him from cube to cube every other month to satisfy complaints.

They are talking about the game, headed toward the coffee bar, toward Doug. They nod and say their good mornings to me, but I lower my head and move onward. I'm sure they'll swap stories with Doug about how many beers they chugged while the Chiefs were getting their asses handed to them. "I gotta finish those reports."

Sitting back down . . . CTRL + ALT + DELETE . . . Password: Alice0703 . . . skip the work and open a browser. I check my personal email and see what's happening.

Skittles4. That's Lena. A message checking up on me. Just seeing how I am. What's my state? Would like for me to come over for dinner, meet the new guy. She told me about him briefly before, over drinks at McCannon's. Older guy, she said. Works in law enforcement. Maybe I will meet her later, depending on how the day progresses.

godISsoGOOD. That's mom. Skip.

godISsoGOOD. Mom again. Skip.

BLOOM777. Here we go. click, open, the *WildPendulum* newsletter: *WildWire*.

Link number one: "*More research on the Mitchell-Hedges Crystal Skull -- radio waves recorded emanating from ancient artifacts.*"

Skip. Over-read on the crystal skull phenomenon, need a break.

Link number two: "*Li Qingyuan Sighting!*"

Click. Li Qingyuan, a legendary Chinese mystic, was reported to have lived for approximately two hundred and fifty years, his birth reported in 1677. This is attributed to his heightened enlightenment and strict herbal diet of Tibetan Goji berries. Some believe him to still be alive. His existence is well-documented. An intriguing sighting is a lecture he delivered at the University of Beijing earlier in the twentieth century. He was reported to have looked in his fifties. There have been recent reports of encounters with Li, tingling the nervous systems of the mystery-seeking crowds all over the globe. The link connects to an article on a supposed Li sighting in the Middle east; however it is written in Arabic.

I can't read Arabic.

Go back. Caption under the link states: "*WildPendulum.net seeking freelance translators. Will offer American currency.*" Move on.

Link number three: "*Found this the other night. Be cautious. Scan for monitoring.*"

Sounds intriguing enough. Click on the link . . . a few seconds and a page appears; a photograph of an archeological excavation taken from above. There are a few diggers shoveling and sweeping, a wooden plank laid across a massive hole. In the hole lays the intact remains of a gigantic human skeleton, must be ten times the size of the diggers in the pic. I know what this is. Text appears underneath the image:

"*This image surfaced on the Internet in 2002 . . .*" Blah, blah . . . I know the story. The image circulated around the net for a while as a cryptozoological urban legend until Worth1000.com came out and posed it as a hoax. According to Worth1000, the image was part of a Photoshop contest. I read on: "*The supposedly engineered conspiracy centered on the accidental discovery of skeletal remains of a phenomenal size in the Empty Quarter of the Arabian desert. The Saudis believed these to be the remains of the people of A'ad, giants mentioned in the Quran. These mysterious beings are also referenced in the Torah as the Nephilim, supposedly produced by the sexual union of the sons of Yahweh and the daughters of Adam. The Saudi military secured the entire area after the initial discovery and it has been kept secret ever since, no one was allowed entry except restricted personnel. The picture was supposedly taken by a helicopter flying overhead, just before the Saudis confiscated the site. The image generated a lot of buzz, but soon after Worth1000 came out with their by-line and speculation ceased.*

"However, we at WildPendulum.net have just recently acquired new information. In a manner worthy of unconventional secrecy, one of our WildPendulum.net reporters was recently contacted by an agent of unknown origin. Without going into unnecessary details, this stranger passed information on to us about this particular occurrence: included were photos and files of transactions made between Worth1000 and the Saudi military, as well as evidence that the Worth1000 contest never really existed. Hence, there is no author/artist for this 'Photoshop' photo. Included in the links below you will see scanned PDF images of billing transactions converting large sums of money from the House of Saud to Worth1000 CEO Alan Rowe's personal account. Could it be that the Saudi military paid Worth1000.com to lie about the production of this image engineered as part of a Photoshop contest? We asked our mysterious informer, whose most distinguishing characteristic was his bright red outfit, if this was indeed true when he handed the documents over. The only response we received was a cryptic phrase: 'The weird will always have a way.'"

I perk. *Bright red outfit.* Feel an itch in my cerebral cortex. Palpitations in the eye lid. I look over my shoulder. Jena is talking to her code. I hear Manoj snorting two aisles away. The perpetual momentum of tapping surround-sound. Other than that, no managers. No passers-by.

Reach into my backpack and pull out my journal— leather scrapbook. Lay it on my desk. I caress the letters pasted on the cover, cut from various magazines. In jarred, asynchronous forms they read *Akashic Memoir.* I flip it open and the first page, written in a heightened state of tardive dyskinesia and uncontrollable nausea, strewn in jagged ballpoint: "*A good citizen is an effectively paranoid one.*"

I open it further, rustling grate in the worn creases. My eyes scan the compilations of newspaper clippings, magazine articles, printed out Web pages, hand-written notes, and photographs. A torn piece of notebook paper, sloppily taped to the first page, my own handwriting: " . . . until 1950, when

President Truman took the advice of J. Edgar Hoover and implemented the contemptible and fanatical law, put into effect through emergency protocol three months later, the detention of radicals who were perceived as a political threat to the United States' agenda . . . pentacle crux in the war of ideas . . . history books tell Truman never followed through, but clandestine press shows otherwise, independent of capital influence . . ." I look on. Pictures of flying saucers, some circled in ink, some with scrawled post-it notes beside them. A newspaper article – a family murdered, all had lacerations on the back of the neck, no suspects. Another article, major headline, a study from the U.S. Geological Survey about pharmaceuticals found in tap water: including various tranquilizers, anti-depressants, antibiotics, estrogen replacements, chemotherapy agents, among others; over two hundred cases of hospitalized victims associated with this, a highlighted section about the deaths of four children. Flipping pages. Articles about 9/11. News items and notes on the Federal Reserve. Articles on various conflicts around the world, oil production, NASA, and more.

Then, I find it. A color photograph ripped out of some news magazine. April 16th, 2007. Seung-Hui Cho massacred 32 innocent students and professors at Virginia Polytechnic Institute and State University in Blacksburg, Virginia. The left side was tattered, but I had taped it down effectively. A crowd of students and news people are gathered on a perimeter; Emergency Medical Technicians bring out bodies from a stone building. I saved this particular photo because in the crowd, behind a jostled twenty-something girl screaming in tears, stands an individual wearing a single-breasted suit . . . in stark red.

Correlation and nascence ring in my mind . . . an interconnected state of lucid apprehension. To the desktop, I click on an icon and search for Bloom777 on IM. Hourglass turning upside over and over. Connected.

ME: "M, you there?"
BLOOM777: "Here. How you been D?"

He calls me *D* for some reason. Asked me to refer to him as *M* the first time we chatted.

ME: "Viable. Read your recent post. I have considerations to make."

BLOOM777: "How so?"

ME: "This informant of yours. Did you see him?"

BLOOM777: "One of my techies ran into him on the sidewalk, right before coming to work."

ME: "Have a description?"

BLOOM777: "Dark skin, possibly Afro-American male. Very fit. Red suit & black tie. Why?"

ME: "I'm coming up with something. I want your take."

BLOOM777: "For post? We've been through this, D. u need to iron out ur research."

ME: "No. Something new. An idea. Post it on your own, if u want."

BLOOM777: "Shoot. I don't have much time."

ME: "Men in Black. They have their role, not just UFO/alien shit. But, they're still there, in other news, right?"

BLOOM777: "Sometimes reported malignant. Sometimes not. What's ur news? A report?"

ME: "Your informant. Your guy in red. I've seen him before."

BLOOM777: "On the street?"

ME: "No. On stage. During phenomena. Sightings."

BLOOM777: "WTF???"

ME: "Not shitting u."

BLOOM777: "How many examples u have?"

ME: "One."

Long, unmotivated pause.

ME: "Maybe more."

BLOOM777: "Then get me more. It would be nice to have more than just an ID, figure a role/motive for each sighting. Otherwise there is nothing to report."

ME: "What do you think it is?"

BLOOM777: "To early to speculate, D. That's what separates legit theorists from the loonies."

ME: "Right."

BLOOM777: "My recent post is a strong piece of data for motive. Feel free to use it. After all, information is liberation. The only true freedom."

ME: "Right. Bye then."

BLOOM777: "Ta-ta for now."

Just remembered Ramona is coming over tonight. Making dinner. Must pick up teriyaki sauce.

There were people at the store who eyed me eerily. That was expected. I picked up what I needed and headed home. I skim the items in the plastic bag, hanging placebo bouncing off my knees as I walk, mental checklist to secure my ease:

- Herbal tea: Green. It helps me sleep at night.
- Orange Juice, 100% natural. For increased intake of Vitamin C.
- Cephalexin, 500mg. One tablet every night for staph infection on my right shin.
- Lorazepam (generic Ativan), 1 mg. One tablet every six hours as needed for stress.
- Day-Quil Liquicaps. Two caps every four hours for aches, fever, coughing, nasal congestion, and sore throat. I have adverse effects from Night-Quil, including erratic pulse.
- Ibuprofen, 200mg. Four to five tablets three times a day for fever reducer and pain reliever.
- Cough drops (Eucalyptus flavored), 6.5mg. Two drops every two hours, if needed (just in case).
- Teriyaki marinade, 15 fl oz.

I love walking where I go. Provides a chance of illumination encounter; lets the mind exchange with the quantum environment.

I hold myself in and hustle through the cacophony of bobbing heads milling about on the street. Two old ladies in knitted shawls sit on a bench and discuss the polluted air; they click their glasses and tip their hats to passersby. The aroma of sewage dances all around me. There is a bum on the sidewalk waving a cardboard sign written in black crayon: "SMILES ARE FREE." He is skinny, unshaven, and opens his mouth to reveal toothless violet gums. A mutt scampers between the legs of patrons, hoping to retrieve a discarded crumb. Signs for pubs, exotic restaurants, and variety shops populate the Westport area. The city is alive—I breathe her in and want to vomit. It is my home. Enter my inner space:

I speculate, an unwritten fondness . . . once running downtown to sell the ring (great cane fondue abhorrent) the sky is the home of the fish inboard. She is waiting, awake, say what thou wish.

Collectively collecting the clocks. Sickly, the seeker seeks the clown-man; giving the cane, killing the fan. We are all alive when we die.

Amen.

I am caught in Katmandu, I am seeing aliens all around. Shedding their skin they call to me (warning with red eyes to keep it under wraps). Too much overflow—they don't know me. My threat to reality is consolidating, my threat to reality could be real. I feel the invasion of the perceptions of ALL. Believe in NoThing despite the contrary to other belief there it is all a conspiracy nothing is real . . . there is a veil . . . a veil to everything, to ALL . . . can it be lifted to the fragrant block which under the crescent under the current we accept we think we know, but we don't. Because under this fabric—this hubris; it covers the True senses; what is actually going on? Nonsense, it seems. Absurdity. Philip K. Dick thinks the universe is insane. A mad child playing games. It is all illusion, this street I am on, this city, the business suit attired attorneys walking toward me are all not real, not part of the (parenthesis) (collective)?

Summarily, reason is a cognitive dissonance running to the beat of elephants . . . one foot on the side walk, two . . . running to the beat of elephants; thwart the distinct relationships we receive with the others that believe and this is the answer, my friend.

I love walking where I go – harder to track someone on foot than in a car.

Ramona fixed salmon. I made the pasta and we both helped with the salad. Turns out we didn't need the teriyaki. We were relatively quiet. We listened to Bauhaus during preparation and sat down at my two-person table. I ate very little. She cleaned her plate. I twirl my fork around a string of angel hair pasta and she asks about my well-being.

"Fine."

"What about Alice?" she presses.

"Let's not talk about that right now. How are you?"

"Work's good. I mean, you know . . . the kids are always great. We're getting plowed by legislation, so it's been hard on the teachers. I saw Terry yesterday."

"Terry."

She smiles. She has a crease on her forehead, makes my gut fly. She's a sweet girl, takes in cats off the street kind of thing, but I know where this is going. "He says '*Sic transit gloria mundi.*' He'd like to see you."

"He would like another customer, you mean." My fork clicks on the plate.

Ramona stands and walks over to my computer terminal. Her hand swipes across the three inch-thick layer of foil surrounding the monitor and CPU. FDA regulation 21 C.F.R. 1020.10 outlines the amount of harmful radiation emitted as a result of the electron beam's interaction with the aperture grille and phosphors. A clear plastic shield covers the screen.

"He means well. Look at this . . . and this . . ."

She sighs and motions to the corkboard above my desk, covered with pin-pricked newspaper clippings: a collection of obscure incidents and presidential appearances.

"Can't you see that we're just . . . *concerned*?"

I stay in my seat and turn to her. "I have concerns too. Have you been seeing lights everywhere? Mostly blue lights, sparks, streaks, and the like? I saw a disc of light over I-35 the other day. Twenty-five others reported the sighting to Channel 4, but they didn't air it. Why do you think that is?"

"Gregor, what are you going on about? I'm talking about your health," her voice leans a bit. When it leans, she's nearing a point of frustration. That's when I'll lose her; when I won't reach her.

"I've been seeing drops of water everywhere, where I shouldn't be seeing them. The drops have dry centers, like donuts. Does water do that? I saw one last week on my book . . . what was I reading? Oh yeah . . . *The Aquarian Conspiracy* by Marilyn Ferguson. And then earlier this week, on the bathroom floor at work. Except the dry part in the center was in the shape of a claw. The Inuit people—I think it's the Inuit—have a myth about the Claw People . . . anyway, it's reflective of initiatory experiences. It's very comparable to the modern day version of a panic attack."

"Are you having panic attacks again?"

I stop myself from answering. I was sensing the conversation was one-sided on both ends.

"Gregor," she walks over and places a hand on my shoulder. It is so soft. I look back down at my plate and swallow a forkful. "You know we're here to support you. You know this, we've made it perfectly clear. Beyond that, it's up to you to make your world better."

She picks up her hemp satchel, flings it over her shoulder, and makes for the door.

"I've got to get up early tomorrow. But, I'd like to see you this weekend. I'm not asking for a date, or anything. You don't have to go through that with me again. I'm just saying . . . time. Just some time, the two of us. Will that be okay?"

I shift in my seat. Should I stand up, saunter over, peck her on the cheek? What couples do? I don't, of course. I finish my glass of wine and sit for a few moments in silence, scratching the scruff on my jaw.

"I could probably do that, sure."

She smiles (that crease on her forehead) and exits. Soon after I sweep over to the door and lock the bolt and knob. Then, I reach to the ground and lift the thick grain of yarn, pull it back up to latch the hook on the end to loop above the frame. The other end runs through a system of eight pulleys which eventually lead to a conglomeration of old tin cans in the nearby coat closet. If anyone was to break the locks, they'd arrive to a concert of metallic racket loud enough to wake Tangiers. There are fourteen other such contraptions in the apartment, mostly around the windows. The one close to my bed actually shoots darts. One more thing to protect me. One more thing to separate me from her.

I realize how much I hate my sanity.

WWN Headline News

Commentator Jon O'Maley: " . . . and let me bring up some of these estimates on the bailout proposed by the administration for this major economic crisis. $20 billion for Grizzly Fern, $159 billion for Billie Rae and Billie Mac, $70 billion to bail out AGI, and an additional $148 billion dollars to address the ongoing mortgage meltdown. And here today we have Senator Spike Reed with us to discuss this issue. Senator Reed has been one of the lone outspoken critics of the administration—including a failed motion for impeachment last month—and says 'No' to the bailout. Senator . . ."

Senator Spike Reed: "Jon, it was not a failed motion, it was referred to Committee."

O'Maley: "Referred to Committee essentially means it was tabled and won't be bothered with, Senator."

Reed: "Not true, Jon. I made the motion for it to go to Committee."

O'Maley: "Okay, sure. Anyway, Senator, would you agree with the estimates?"

Reed: "Absolutely not. I have been sitting in these so-called bi-partisan sessions and the numbers run much higher. We're talking close to a *trillion* dollars, Jon! It's unbelievable! And it could go even higher, every day another financial institution is in trouble, they up the ante on how much will be given out."

O'Maley: "So what is your proposal, Senator? People are losing their homes . . ."

Reed: "Well, like I've said before, Jon, we've got to look at the root of our monetary system. There is no blame to be had here between Republicans and Democrats, the focus needs to be on the bankers, the lenders—"

O'Maley: "No blame, Mister Reed? Just last week, you yourself criticized the, and I quote, '. . . the fiscally irresponsible, de-regulating policies of the Republican administration led to this current blunder of staggering losses.' So, how can you say, Senator, that you now oppose the finger-pointing ideology of the Liberal leftists?"

Reed: "First of all, you are misquoting me because I was referring to the administration alone, and did not reference the Republican Party. I have many friends in the Republican Party that are real fiscal conservatives and I appreciate their positions. Second, we have to stop spending overseas, change our foreign policy. Look . . . I've been in the hearings with the Federal Reserve Chairman; me and ten other Senators addressed the declining value of the dollar. The Chairman says that's the Treasury's responsibility. How is that the Treasury's responsibility when the Federal Reserve is in charge of the money supply? If you increase the money supply, you decrease the value of currency. If you don't have stable currency, you won't have stable prices. Lowering interest rates, like he did six months ago, is only a band-aid for the bigger issue."

O'Maley: "And what's the bigger issue, Senator?"

Reed: "Well, we have to get rid of the Federal Reserve, for one thing—"

O'Maley: "Oh come on! Give me a break!"

Reed: "The Federal Reserve is a private, for-profit institution that has nothing to do with our govern—"

O'Maley: "Be serious! You're living in a fantasy land, Senator!"

Reed: "Let me finish, Jon. Let me finish! The Federal Reserve was created un-Constitutionally in 1913. It's a hybrid organization that was unilaterally voted for in an over-night Christmas break session with only three Congressmen present—"

O'Maley: "I don't want a history lesson, Senator. Answer the question please."

Reed: "I *am* answering your question, but you have got to understand your history—"

O'Maley: "No, I want to know what you plan on doing *now* in our current financial crisis. What happened in 1913 is irrelevant. What's your plan, Senator Reed?"

Reed: "Jon . . . it's *not* irrelevant. The Founders understood that runaway inflation and the continental dollar was devastating to the economy. Ben Franklin stated explicitly this is what the Revolutionary War was about. There is no authority in the U.S. Constitution authorizing a central bank. Now, why were the Founding Fathers so adamantly opposed to this? Nowadays, every President appoints directly to the Trilateral Commission and Council on Foreign Relations—"

O'Maley: "Okay, Senator, that's enough. If you're not going to answer the question then we can move on to—"

Reed: "Wait a minute, Jon. If you give me longer than thirty seconds here, I'll be able to answer your question—"

O'Maley: "No, no, it's the same leftist propaganda spouted by adolescent bloggers on the Internet and we don't want to hear it on this network. We try to run a fair and balanced program here."

Reed: "Very few people understand how currency is issued and the devaluation of—"

O'Maley: "Thank you, Senator. It was great to have you on. In a few minutes we'll take a look at pop singer Bobbi Dakota hitting the media spotlight with her new . . . *girlfriend*! We'll be right back after a word from our sponsors."

3 – Cold in Town

The hallway is dark. I am somewhere underground. The walls, floors, and ceiling are made of rusted steel and bolts. The air is stifling, breathing is like being smothered with a pillow. I am scared I will die.

A man (beast) walks up. He (it) is twelve feet tall and adorns the head of a shark. His teeth jut out in all directions and smiles at me like dinner. I find it appropriate he is wearing a three-piece suit, probably Armani. The tie is gray.

"It's about time," he grumbles, his voice an incinerator against the hollow echo of the hallway. He turns and walks, expects me to follow. What else can I do? If I go, I die. If I stay, I die alone.

When he walks the floors shake like they might give out. There is an eerie light up ahead. An ugly sick orange. As we near the source, I notice rusted sludge oozing out of the steel panels and bolts, a mechanical patchwork of illness. The light (?) is very near, though I cannot see because he (it) is so huge. We approach a small dog-sized opening. Part of the light is coming from inside. It is rocky in there, a cavern.

Suddenly, a bulge of humanly flesh whips out quickly. It is a mass of veins and muscle, part of a larger extremity that is on the other side of the wall. At the end a nubby hand and foot stick out and plant themselves on the ground. In the glob of corrugated skin I see an eye blink and stare at me. Pieces move and a voice comes out.

"Is he good? Hunky?" The thing asks the shark-man (thing).

"Sufficient," he (it) answers the thing. The mutant thing giggles (though not in any joyous way—more like the death gurgles of an obese tart asphyxiating on pudding and frogs) and scampers back into its hole.

We continue on. There are sounds of construction and screaming.

We come to another opening, though more like a horizontal window at eye level. The shark-man (thing) taps on the wall next to it. I look in, orange hued sickness massaging my face. The other side seems to be part of the same cavern the mutant thing came out of. Looking forward, there is a head growing out of the ground, veins tubing in and out of the rock like roots. The head had no lips, was staring at me, and screaming. Endlessly, endlessly screaming. It would not stop. I cower away from the window and the shark-man (thing) smiled even wider than he (it) already was. He (it) straightened his (its) tie and turned to continue down the hall.

I peered back through the window as we walked—in the direction we were headed—hoping to preview what was next on the other side. I saw a miniature railroad coming out of the far wall in the cavern and running into the hallway. As I moved on I noticed something rolling out of an opening, down the tracks to meet us.

After a couple of yards the shark-man (thing) turned and motioned to another opening in the wall. "Cremation of Care," his (its) voice rumbled under my feet, the walls crimped. "Effigy, my ass! Ha, ha, ha!!!"

I met the end of the tracks coming out of the opening. A flat-bed cart rolled to a stop. On it sat the plastic doll's head of an infant. Its left eye was missing, a slight crack underneath. From the dark a horde of beetles scuttled onto the cart and into the socket of the missing eye. Shark-man (thing) laughed like a badly done villain from a '60s comic book.

* * * * *

On the corner of Broadway and Southwest Boulevard, there is a claustrophobic whiff of grease and nicotine. It's Saturday and I tell Ramona to meet me at Town Topic. On the roof sits a pastel blue spike that points to the heavens in typical 1950's gloss and glamour; riveting neon letters that now tweak and jitter to the patrons below. Spider web phone lines hang over the building in layers as thick as this tiny diner's history. Will have to be careful of those.

Not the most romantic of getaways, but Ramona knows my style. She knows my style. I case the street. I told her to be here at 7:00pm, it is now 6:04pm. I need to be sure and scan for any followers before she arrives, don't want to endanger an innocent.

Make my way to the entrance. On the first Friday of every month, the galleries on the surrounding block open their latest exhibits to the public. The streets then are swarmed with vendors, musicians, and patrons crawling from show to show. After being pumped with enough liquor to tip a horse, the dazed bohemian scene usually squeeze themselves into the already crammed dining area: barely able to fit one Formica plastic counter and a few miniscule tables for sardine seating. First Friday was last week, so I am sure to avoid any such encounters.

The bell jingles dully as I push through the front door. The diner is half-full. See, I'm optimistic. Two women behind the counter grunt through the cigarettes dangling from glossy red, wrinkly lips. Both have slightly overweight, bulk stretching through stained aprons and hairnets. High school lunch ladies with an edge. Annoyed animals. When they look at their customers, they imagine homicide as a form of stress-relief. They pray for fewer customers, not more.

"Shiiit," one of them mumble in a smoker's drawl. She was referring to me. She makes brief eye contact and returns to flipping beef patties on a sizzling grill. They are known for their burgers here. Menu's on the wall behind the counter.

John Coltrane is playing on the jukebox.

I choose a spot at the counter and settle in. I leave an empty seat between me an older man reading the *The Kansas City Star*. I size him up: balding, soft hands, body shape of someone who sits at work all day. Should be safe. One of the women shuffles over. I look at her nametag: Loretta.

"Whattya want?" she grunts, cigarette trickling snowfall of ash on the floor.

"Coffee. I'll order food later. I'm waiting for someone."

A response isn't given or needed. Loretta plops down a saucer, brown-stained cup, and fills it with a pitcher of steamy tar. I love this place. I really do.

Sipping the wretched sludge, I pull out my journal and begin to write.

I think about Ramona. I can feel the oxytocin spurting from my pituitary gland and into the rest of my body; it is warm and full of rapid current . . . recent studies are finding this neurotransmitter is not just a maternal hormone, but is active in bonding, affection, and trust in mammalian relationships. When two people meet—when they reach that tipping point of exclusivity—oxytocin is released and overwhelms the neuroendocrine system. The entire body is stuck in a habitual, sexually charged acid trip. Oxytocin prevents you from thinking about anyone else – it stimulates infatuation, fascination, and even obsession. It can easily become dangerous, for it may take up to a year for the oxytocin to wear off to moderate levels of excretion. By then it may be too late and you will find the person you have been bedding for 12 months is someone you hate. It's a tricky thing, the human brain. I am working to consciously tame and mollify my oxytocin levels; don't want to walk into a trap blind. Work with Kundalini yogic breathing, particular focus on the Sahasrara chakra, has been helpful. This energy point focuses specifically on the pituitary gland and nervous system, thus being located at the crown of the head. Indeed, this is heavily related to Ajna—the third eye—but, my intention is distinctive at this time.

As I write, the bell jingles again. More like dinks. More "shiiits" from Loretta and her co-workers. Brewing in the doorway, a customer curiously scans the cascade of faded letters above the cookers. He grins. His features are sharp, pointed inside a smooth round head. Olive skin. He is small, maybe five feet tall. He is quite peculiar. Wrapped in a dark brown topcoat, he is even more peculiar since it is 96 Fahrenheit on an August evening. A bit aestival for heavy wear. His arms are crossed, hands tucked under armpits.

After a few minutes of intensely examining the menu, he walks over to a seat at the counter. The other side of the older man reading *The Star*. He grins still as Loretta shuffles over.

"You're a happy guy. Whattya want?"

"Loretta," his voice high and shrill, like the static of an old phonograph. "Please provide me with an order of charred cylindrical slice of ground beef, accompanied with processed milk slices and leaf strips. Yes, please." There is an eerie rhythmical quality to his tone—Bela Lugosi movies come to mind. I watch him intently.

Loretta is unimpressed. "Lissen, buddy. I ain't no caterer. You being a smart-ass? Wanna wait 'til next shift?"

Unwaveringly, the man grins and stares. It is bizarre, like he doesn't know what else to do. I notice how huge his eyes widen. And . . . how black they are! There is no iris! Dark pools filling the entire socket, and . . . they aren't blinking! His eyes are not blinking!

"I believe this particular assortment would be accommodating for energetic replenishment," he motions to the older man reading *The Star*. The plate under his newspaper is reduced to scraps, but Loretta gets the point.

"Chili-burger and fries," she notes and shuffles away. Flames on the grill flutter in a small grease-fire. Loretta and her co-worker mutter to each other, cursing us all under their collective breath. It seems nobody else notices the uncanny spectacle of this man who doesn't need to blink. Human beings blink at least once every two to ten seconds. I've been watching this oddity for almost five minutes now and he hasn't blinked once.

"I wouldn't fool around with these women, young man," the older man reading *The Star* leans over. "I know a guy who got a bloody nose for playing Bon Jovi five times in a row on the jukebox. One of them used a spatula. Name's George. And you are?"

There is a pause. The peculiar man grins and cocks his head.

"And I am . . ."

"What . . . is . . . your . . . name?" George puts down his paper, extends a hand. "It's okay, the wife and I volunteer in the group homes. I can tell you must be handicapped. Down syndrome?"

Is this guy blind? Insane? An unearthly oddity is staring him right in the face and he thinks it's a lost handicap! I begin to sift through the archive of my mind, all the cryptozoological phenomena I have studied . . .

"Ah," the peculiar man perks in his seat. "I am cold."

"You chilly, son?"

"My brand is Propit. And you are George." He just keeps grinning.

I scribble down the name in my journal quickly: *Propit*. Familiarity range of the periphery of my consciousness. I know this . . . where do I know this?

"Uh huh," George muses. "Must be Chinese. You kinda look Asian, maybe, no?"

Time continues. Time to think . . . feeling life around me moving, clicks of silverware, charred meat. Hiss of a match. Oh yes, rolling and breathing. Flowing fluid flourishing in the wake. Beyond the dream.

Where do I know that name? Next to me alien man with no eyes; they are all aliens, aren't they? Long ago I used to be one, didn't I? Used to be apart . . . disconnected from the living, from the minority. Disparate consciousness, and then . . .

Well, it all comes down to a punch. Why do we do things? Why go through the Motion, with the Current? All horse shit. So, I'm right here, before you and dumb. Extra dimensional and universal differentiations. Make a choice, go in a direction. These people, they all spiral going to and fro, there are bubbles traveling back and forth, there are islands with Ferris wheels thrusting with rockets along the bridges – between worlds, between minds . . . somewhere something breaks inside the mind. >>Crack<< and then what? Between worlds, between minds, there is something there. Something peripheral at the edge of Being. None of this makes sense. a job, economy, retirement, every Sunday . . . none of this a lick of rationality.

Now, the goal is mine: the Fortean way. Because the Hindus knew there was something; I may be dumb, but well-read. They knew about the Akashic Record, Heraclitus calls it the Logos . . . find that and find all knowledge. Then, I'll know. Then, this'll make sense. Won't it? The Greek philosophers' unity codex. But, all this will have to come later because I see this peculiar Propit character staring at me. His wide round, almond eyes are looking right at me! Shit! I look away and down to my journal.

Scribble, scribble, scribble, holy shit is he still looking at me? Look up, Gregor, take a look and see if he's . . . oh shit . . .

"Gotta go home to the Missus," George pulls on his tweed jacket and nods to me, eyes Propit wearily. "You watch out for yourself, kid."

Paralysis. Real and absolute immobility.

That is what happens to every one of us. I am sure of this. In one moment, a spike of ice impaling my body, courses through every nerve. I can see us all, everyone stiff, even the spiraling smoke from Loretta's cigarette – locks in a coiled helix phantasm. We each probably try to jump, scream, recoil in any way, but the enmity grip holds tight every fiber of every muscle.

Stunned, wrapped in a claw impossible to wriggle intuit form.

Do you know what true terror is? *I . . . can . . . not . . . move!* The truest opposite to freedom.

Propit, though, can move. Propit's round head turns, moves in and quietly opens his little bark-colored mouth next to George's ear. Crackle in the air, crumpled Styrofoam. Whispered words come muffled static: "Wake up, now . . . Liberation for 729 . . . 12, 3-dot-4 . . . 5 divide 22-dot-2 . . . 7-dot-43 . . . 8 . . . Liberation for 729 . . . wake up, now."

Slate of oil comes over my vision and memory no longer takes place. Is there a doctor in?

Blank.   Is there anybody there?   Blank.
Wait.
Where   do   the   spaces   fill   in?   Necromantic serenity   Olive skin, it wore sand-paper wraith alive . . . "it's October," he said. "Everyone thinks about death."
No.   It's August.
Not to be morbid, but fascination of a perverse recognition thereof imitates sworn oath of mitigated soil. Lake, wooded lake. Ensure when, if you say it again, you might get a headache.
Hello?   Why is it blank here?
Have you ever asked yourself that?
Just go along the redesign forum: from triangle to square inner length. Triangle square. Conqueror torn down by the Lotus flower, thrives and longitude down under more . . . speed can kill the brown; until the loving embrace petal cure, until the end of patriarchal litany.
This is about Gregor Samson. His failings and his dreams. This is about Alice Samson and the reverie in the sea.
Here I have no form.
Here whipped cream hold.
Gregor? Gregor come on . . .
Whip, whip it is all white but not.   Black and what not.
Gregor . . . wake up . . .
Do you ever dream of cocooning? Do you ever wait for the monarch reach?
Let's go, Gregor . .
. that's it . . .

And there she is. Right on time.
"Gregor, you okay? Give me a sign!"
I see the crease between the eyes, physical Ajna. It is pleasing to hear a response when calling for an answer.

"Hi," I tell Ramona.

"Good," she nods, squinting eyes in joyous relief. "Thank you, thank you. Are you okay? Can you see me? How many fingers? How many fingers? Count."

I look: see a display of peacock feather foray limbs. Lotus petals all lined up. Could be a thousand, could be infinite. They are all pink and red splotches at the end. Breathe. Sahasrara, breathe out. The crown. Whoever holds the kingdom holds the crown.

"Ffffffour?"

She shakes her head: that's what you would call trails. Speed of light incensed. Sahasrara damn! Focus is moot.

"Just like the others," gruff voice invades. Male. I look over. Yes, male. Uniform. Paramedic. Clean-cut goatee, mole on right cheek. "He'll be fine. Give him a few minutes to orient himself."

I am lifted up halfway. Must have been on the ground. Head is wobbly, can't keep it up straight—same with the seeing of all. Everything spins, everything trances. Paramedic leans in close and hollers in my ear, as if I am far away.

"YOU'LL BE FINE! EVERYTHING WILL BE DIZZY FOR A FEW MINUTES, BUT YOU'LL BE BACK ON YOUR FEET IN TEN! HELL OF A TRIP, HUH? HA HA HA HA HA HA HA HA!!!!"

God, damn him! Like a super-sonic gong! Horrible, horrible man! He slaps me on the back (red spot left to be sure) and leaves me in Ramona's grasp to fetch a coffee. Still in Town Topic. Everyone around me on the floor, shaking their heads, except a few EMTs offering wet towels and SOUND advice. Everyone discombobulated. Everyone groggy. Everyone . . . not everyone.

"Where's George?"

"Who?" Ramona tilts her head, golden rope falls over the eye.

"George," wave the hand. "George . . . the old guy . . . sitting next to me. Where is he? Everyone else is here but him." I wasn't expecting to see Propit.

"There's one guy who got taken away on a gurney," she points out. "You mean him?"

"Was he dead?"

She brushes her peacock feathers through my hair—oxytocin rumbling—through my hair in comfort. Mothering look in her concert eyes: "I don't know . . . it definitely looked like he wasn't responding."

I can't let go. I am choking and I can't let go. Time to push: there is a hole, dark rift, in the fabric of knowing; need, there is a defined need. Try to pry myself off the floor, vision spins merry-go-round. Propit and George, both strangers, both interconnected woven into my sphere of being. Why? Because there is no such thing as coincidence. THERE IS NO SUCH THING AS COINCIDENCE! Causally unrelated . . . bio-synaptic responses in the air—there is no better tool for the Fortean mind! There IS an underlying, conceptual pattern to all. Carl Jung calls it the acausal connecting principle, which denotes a cardinal framework for all events . . . life is nothing but a series of events, thus there is a fundamental anatomy to existence. A design? A directive? Too soon to tell. That's what the *Akashic Memoir* is for, to assimilate and correlate the data in some sort of standardized method.

She helps me up, but not without protest. A procession of 'be careful's and 'take it easy's and 'you should probably lay down's fluidly swish in and out of the atmospheric swirl. I understand. She cares. This is more than I can say for most, even myself. Though the annoyance is still present. She knows better. I have a commission. She *must* understand that, or there may be no room for her in the litany to follow.

Information needs its allies.

Now I am pushing through EMTs and police officers who don't seem to be doing much; crawling over wires connected to channel news cameras, capturing the mysterious event of twenty-some citizens concomitantly passing out in one of Kansas City's oldest hamburger joints to date. Make it okay! A stranger has appeared and a stranger is gone—for some reason this holds enough appeal to incite a pliers' grip on my lungs. I cannot breathe. I am twisting my head, wet bangs flick on my brow. A sign, any sign, of George. Need to talk to him. What happened to him? What did the non-blinking Propit (digging sourly into the amnesiac fields of my membrane) do? I don't see him. Ramona gets the hint. Good for her.

"You want me to talk to a cop or a paramedic, see if we can't find out what happened to this guy?" Ramona gingerly asks. May have gotten part of it, losing it now.

"No!" I snap. Then, lower the intensity. Can't draw attention. "No authorities! Can't be trusted."

"What then? How do we find out where he went?" She doesn't understand . . . she doesn't get the intricacies of living in a police state. A culture where the Authority answers to no authority; there are no checks and balances. Welcome to the 21st Century, where the leadership no longer serves the people—the people serve the leadership. They don't need our consent anymore (did they ever?): for war, for policy, even for elections. They got it. We work 40 plus hours a week to make $8.00 an hour while they take half and supplement their own salaries for working only 10 hours. And . . . there are billions of us with only a handful of *them*. That makes for a lot of dollars.

"We need to go see Lawrence."

Lawrence is one of the more odd characters in my sub-cast. Sharing my views of the anomalous canvas percolating throughout society, he has a slight bent in character than can prove to be hazardous. When his parents died in a freak accident six years ago, he inherited a mansion in the white collar suburbs of the Blue Valley district, on the Kansas side. Surrounded by telecommunications executives, lawyers, and Chiefs players, Lawrence is a lone entity in one of the wealthiest neighborhoods in the entire metropolitan area. He is a cancerous tumor among the grassy knolled backyards, white colored privacy fences, and mailboxes decorated with sunflowers and family names. After he moved in without grief or hesitation, he immediately turned the property into a fortified stronghold. You see, Lawrence believes World War II never ended, only the face of the enemy changed. Unfortunately, the enemy was at home, our own daddies. Lawrence is waiting for the military to come knocking on his door and drag him off to one of the many secret concentration camps that exist right here on American soil; he'll be ready, he's got an arsenal fit for another Waco or Wounded Knee (Part 2).

He's a good comrade in a tight spot.

We pull into the foyer drive and stop at the electronic cast-iron gate covered in Vinca and grapevine. There is a security camera staring at us above an intercom system. I know for certain there are two more we can't see. As well, if we were to enter without permission, a copious amount of custom-made TNT will detonate enough explosive impact to vaporize a tank. I neglect to inform Ramona, no need to heighten the stress of the current situation. She pushes the red button on the intercom console. We hear a swish of static and then a voice.

"Ramona Udell. Third child of the great Randall Udell, antiques dealer in a small remote Ozarkian town, named Pew. What brings you to my front door, lass?"

She leans her head out the window: "Lawrence, open the gate please."

"Why should I? Shouldn't you be entertaining our mutual friend-at-arms, Gregor Samson? What would distract you from such an occasion and bring you calling at my kingdom?"

I lean toward Ramona from the passenger seat, crouching down a bit so the camera can see me. "Lawrence, you prick. You need to re-align your cameras. If you can't see the shotgun, you're in big trouble."

"Fuck," he mutters under his breath. I imagine he is turning a radish hue, furious at himself for the misstep.

"Better us than the alternative," I tell him.

There is reluctance in his voice, disappointment: "Right. Dammit, come on in. I've got things to show you. Free the conspiracy!"

The gate eases open with a rustic scrape. The world is ever more prevalent without a sense of safety; it is when walking into the unreal that one is at home in the womb.

"So do I, man."

* * * * *

Wreck of nervous twitch or Two I AM this day
--There is SO much going on
I feel lost without my _____
My symbolical mechanisms are in
code or CODEX: can't recall the which
Just came from a place where it all comes together
AND then apart again (Black) magick crackling in the Air/over
there: where the Zombies walk in empty houses
and the Wives sing sad songs over
days THAT are no more . . .
if people could twirl, if people would just sing and then
we would not have to worry about dictators swinging from
gallows . . . there ARE dictators swinging from g-g-g-g-
gallows!!! turn on the TUBE and >>Click<<, double >>Click<<
on THE mouse.

We are living in a darkness of sick custard knee-drop
IN the thick melee principle that can usher in and distinguish the
quarantine of Below . . . the guy across from ME blinks and
SHRUGS. "Chaos is my KIND of structure," I say. I think he
understands while crunching on salad. Want to know your
heritage? Where you come from? Look at WHAT language you
speak. Look at who conquered YOU.
safeguard the correlation of the universal "I".
I am not above the (UN)known, I am the shaman of the
waking world.

4 – Incarceration

1964:

1 chance.

As the years go by, events become stories flat in the mind . . . images get manipulated over time . . . sketches over canvas. Illusory tricks play on hard-core facts. It is all perception. What has really happened is not in the history books. Reality is the eye witness account, what the weather was like on that day, the aroma of chicken soup on the pot, what she was wearing when it all happened. The stain on the wall. The ragtime on the player. It is all subjective, every bit of experience. No fact truly exists. Only holograms. Memories of memories.

Always remember the day.

There is a common phrase passed around the white-coats in D.C., especially during this time: "What the people don't know, won't hurt them." Sure it won't, but it will *enslave* them. Then, when the Truth finally has a chance to reveal itself, there is too much noise in this god-forsaken country to distract the masses from the nightmare of history.

Very few people ever get a chance to wake up from that. Every 1nce in a while, someone awakes from 1 nightmare into another.

"His logical conclusion, having weighed the matter and allowing for possible error?

. . . That it was a Utopia, there being no known method from the known to the unknown: an infinity . . . "

The rise of the 3rd Reich was the climactic machination of the Conspiracy, an orgasm of mass manipulation. Part of its undertaking was its demise and the waterfall of international chess that ensued afterward. In 1945, the CIA-predecessor Office of Strategic Services (OSS) executed Operation Paperclip. The Soviets had their own similar endeavor, but

America wanted to get its hands on the top Nazi scientists to use for their own means first.

Deputy of the Reich Health Leader, Kurt Blome, was 1 recipient of the U.S. effort to recruit the Nazi masterminds; an insidious underground effort camouflaged by the "bleaching" of their origins, the OSS' interests ascribed to the deadliest of Nazi militarist technology. In Nuremburg, Blome was tried and charged for experimenting on humans and practicing euthanasia at Dachau. He was saved from death by the Americans. In exchange for the acquittal, Blome was flown to Shangri-La (later named Camp David by President Eisenhower) where he revealed his repository of bacteriological warfare, as well as his experiments on Dachau prisoners with plague vaccines. Blome sparked America's interest in mass biological weaponry. As a result, Operation Paperclip segued into a throng of multiple clandestine projects that would begin the secret government's search for the ultimate weapon.

Blome's history was wiped clean. A few years later in 1951, he could be found working on chemical warfare agents as an employee of the U.S. Army Corps.

As journalist Jim Marrs 1nce stated: ". . . those who sincerely believe that conspiracies don't exist only benefit those who may be conspiring."

So Jonah pondered as the men in blue uniforms approached him and his brother. Neil was the first to notice, eyes glazed with that rotten awareness of futility. The sky was clear and brisk, crumpled brown leaves crunching under the officer's feet like a field of fortune cookies. Neil scratched at his afro. Jonah's grimace wavered somewhere between disbelief and disgust.

"Shit, you kidd'n me?" Neil hopped down from the stone wall and swooped up his basketball. "Can't even chill without Fuzz com'n an' interupt'n our business."

Jonah froze. Neil was always more compulsive; his courage bordered somewhere between tenacity and stupidity.

The officers were bulky, stalwart lions slowly inching in for the kill. Their predatory eyes were hidden in the shadows of their caps. They wanted Jonah and Neil to run. They wanted a chase. To them, this was a game. Jonah considered otherwise, recognizing safety in quiet and submissive stagnation.

"Just sit, man," he consoled Neil. "You act tough an' we gonna be in trouble."

"Fuck the pigs, man! We in trouble regardless!" Neil snarled. His chest puffed. His brow furrowed with intent to stare down the oncoming threat. He may have to submit his body, but he would not forego his spirit. There was no way Neil could let someone put him under the heel of their boot, no matter how powerful. It was both his charm and downfall. Jonah knew this, and grieved for the stubbornness of his brother; the same stubbornness that had cost him 2 expulsions and continuous throw-downs in the street. "We people too. We ain't bother'n no white people! Jus' shoot'n some hoops, man!"

Jonah was no clairvoyant; however in the '60s one does not need premonition when it comes to white cop encounters with black men. The engagement of questioning would soon turn into a quarrel of racial contention. But, it was too late to do anything about it. As Jonah crawled slowly toward Neil, an instinctual provocation triggered the animalistic synapses deep within the officers' nervous systems. It's all nature. 1 gorilla against another. The batons slipped nimbly out of their nooses. Purple-knuckled fists clenching and swinging. There is only so much you can do against metal truncheons and a badge. Just curl into a ball and hope your arms break instead of your head, not too many ribs broken. Snap, crack. The sound of slapping shovels against meat . . . it never escapes your head.

8 years later, African-American novelist Ishmael Reed would refer to this as the Atonist agenda. The oppression of black culture was rampant during this time of change. An integral part of the Conspiracy, any public figure that called for the equalization of rights was systematically removed from the

equation: John F. Kennedy, John Lennon, Martin Luther King, Jr., Patrice Èmery Lumumba, Robert F. Kennedy, Medgar Wiley Evers, as well as El-Hajj Malik El-Shabazz (aka Malcolm X) after his public commitment to unity. You stand up, you get knocked down. The centralization of power is imminent!

Jonah never got access to his brother, or any of his family. He never got to issue a phone call. Jonah never got a trial, or rights to an attorney. It was around the 20th day (he cannot remember; he lost count) of solitary confinement with a spattering of random beatings that he realized: I've been abducted! That is correct, Jonah. You will never get your life back again.

The Atonists have their success.

He remembers crying that day—or night—his face squished into his hands. He was remembering a day when Helena, that girl from Main and 5th all jazzed up and saucy as a flapper goddess, swung her hips down the sidewalk. She unfurled the aroma of jasmine and whiskey into the air. Her skirt short enough to make his Grandma choke. Clusters of jangling beads chiming to the rhythm of her saunter. Sweat seeped down his scalp, swamped under his arms.

"Hey girl," he hollers. How poetic, *Hey girl*!

It did not matter. She came anyway and his heart would pound a million miles per second, ready to burst and explode in its cursory want of her. Every day, every single day she walked past and he would remember. Staying up countless nights dreaming of Helena . . . was she a dancer? A singer? An artist? Did she Jes Grew on tables in midnight brothels? Again, it did not matter. She was an angel to blooming adolescents mowing lawns in the neighborhood.

She would look over, those dark brown pools in her eyes. Dimple smile with round lips.

"'Sup shugah," her melodious voice like a million harps ready to open the skies. Jonah never felt so dizzy. "I see ya everyday mow'n these lawns. What? Ya got your own bizness?"

"Yeah." Jonah froze, big-toothed smile . . . must have turned red.

"Boy, don't get all bashful on me! You call'd me ovah . . . whatchu want, babe?" She teased and poked at his stomach.

What *did* he want to say? All the nights he lied in bed dreaming about the venerable goddess floating by each morning and evening. Sweet meanderings of curling into her ribbon design and movement of joyful sadness. If passion could find a name, it would be hers.

Jonah swallows, licks dried lips.

"I . . .I want you to be more than a memory to me, Helena," he tells her.

She looks over and then in response . . . .

The cell door then opens.

Light blaring luminescent spears shatters his retinas! Footsteps come and grab him like menacing bulls and drag him away. Down the hallway . . . feet slumbering behind. He heaves, the air so much more full and fresh than in that concrete cave. Jonah coughs and looks up as his aggressors halt. A pale man in a dark suit scans him over, revulsion smeared over his smug face.

"Hmm, he'll do." And that was that.

This is where the Nazis come in . . . but first, some history for context.

In the Year of our Lord 1932, the U.S. Public Health Service (PHS) contracted with Tuskegee University to conduct a series of experiments. The objective was to study the effects of untreated Syphilis in human beings. Instead of wasting time with volunteers, the PHS decided unwitting human guinea pigs would be easier to manage. 400 poor black sharecroppers, to be precise.

The head of the PHS food chain for the Tuskegee project was one Oliver Wenger, a snarky Arkansan doctor specifically selected for his shrewd demeanor and moral ambiguity. He also had an uncanny knack for manipulation—particularly for lower-class men of color—so as to ensure their naïve cooperation. This Tuskegee experiment lasted for 40 years. During that time, 400 innocent men were coerced into signing away their rights and lives, only to suffer from highly infected rashes and lesions slowly eating away their skin, liver, bones . . . just observed, never treated. The effects of this particular strain of Syphilis were so severe the white-coats, with their clipboards and ballpoint pins, named it "The Black Lion." Most of them begged to renege on their initial agreements with Wenger. But, you must know the Atonist code of law: small print is superior. Never mind the cries of pain. The "Lion" roared!

Speaking of the nightmare of history . . .

Tragically, Eunice Rivers was their token black nurse, thrown in for good measure. A PR stunt. This sad specimen of a female was forced to be present in any known photograph or public event of the Tuskegee project—for the entire duration of the research—to avoid any possible indiscretions or claims of ethnic discrimination: "Look! We have us a negro nurse on staff! We *love* black people! We're one o' them! All's good here! Go back to your new cars and Tupperware parties!"

This was not an experiment on the effects of untreated syphilis . . . this was an experiment to see if they could get away with genocide right here on American soil! A man's ability to show power over another man; the silverback reigns supreme. The Atonist's grasp clutching the last strands of liberty. Ultimately, this is what Tuskegee was all about. The Conspiracy had to make sure that the rising tide of black culture, the Harlem Renaissance, could still be dispirited, moderated, and *controlled*!

When World War II ended, the perpetual struggle for power had reached unimaginable heights. The amount of power America had with the flick of a button sent the remaining powers into a frantic race to gain the upper hand. With the drop of the atomic bombs on Japan came the birth of new era of "black operations." In high school, you may have read about the race for space against the Soviets, but this was only a massive media illusion. The race for *mind control* was the *real* game of the Cold War arena. Operation Paperclip was the beginning.

There was no such context for Jonah as he was carted away like a cow in a trailer, down corkscrew highways to a location as dark as it was unknown.

"I'll be okay," he told Helena through shaky cement bars. She was miles, worlds away. And he knew—in his deepest, most remote deliberations—that to see her again was as unlikely as it was futile. Maybe another time, another world.

"I'll be alright."

Jonah had never taken to lying to himself before now.

5 – Heliocentric Transaction

Three weeks from today:

The man hands Marvin two dollar bills, squished, covered with lint. Marvin straightens them out with his short, stubby fingers. "Four cents is yer change. You wannit?"

The man shakes his head, sipping from the steaming Sytrofoam cup. "Keep it. Thanks." He likes Marvin, comes by almost every day when not working. Marvin wouldn't know him from anyone else. The man likes it that way.

Walks over to the newspaper stand: quarter in, click, opens it up and pulls out the bottom one of the stack. Plops it on top. Cover reads: *Death Toll 10,000 – Congress Does Nothing*. Hmm. He unfolds it and opens to section C3. A few articles on the local festivals and city council meetings . . . a note card. Handwritten with a No.2 pencil. It reads:

> *Assignment Number: 44-5k, 2*
> *Duration/Location: Rendezvous in 14 days' time to approximate longitudinal and latitudinal coordinates given in 2030 hours at communication point X-13.*
> *Contact/Client Name: "Jack." Henceforth, C.O. Copernicus shall be under the strict jurisdiction and supervision of said "Jack."*
> *Objective: Eliminate any known operating cells of terrorist organization known as the "RED Hand", in all its parts and manifestations. Only when objective is satisfied can C.O. be relieved of contact/client's jurisdiction and supervision.*

The man pulls out a lighter and burns the card and lets the wind take the ashes. Sipping coffee, he tucks the paper under his arm and walks down the sidewalk. Marvin's kiosk makes the best brew in town.

6 – At Home with the Vicar

Lawrence is, through and through, a Discordian. His most treasured item—besides a collection of south Asian dung beetle exoskeletons—is a first edition of the *Principia Discordia* (of which there are only five in existence). Written by Omar Khayyam Ravenburst and Malaclypse the Younger, the "Principles of Strife" was written during the apex of the civil revolution in the ever-relevant 1960's; flourishing as an underground society of absurdist fuck-offs commissioning dissent and chaos in the form of the Greek goddess Eris. Omar and Malaclypse responded to the hippie didacticism of love and harmonics with a lunatic fringe; validating the paranoiac fear of counter-culture freakism seeping in the hearts and minds of Sunday school teachers everywhere in the Western world. They were the excuse: the scapegoat. Want to illegalize marijuana? Point to the Discordian raping puppies on the sidewalk! Want to arrest a parade of black marchers? Reference a Discordian as evidence of a social threat!

If at all possible, I have made an attempt to avoid Discordians in the past . . . my reason being pure conspiracy. Incidentally, Omar Ravenburst's real name is Kerry Wendell Thornley, a Marine Corps reservist who once served in the same unit as Lee Harvey Oswald. Becoming close friends, they shared many ideological views, particularly on Orwellian philosophy. Kerry (rather, Omar) was entranced by the young and competent Oswald, who soon immigrated to the Soviet Union (assumedly under CIA payroll, though evidence is still being collected). Omar was intensely inspired by the soon-to-be so-be-it-called assassin of one of the greatest Presidents in America's short history. Additionally, I have reason to believe Omar and Malaclypse may have had something to do with the same circles Oswald had networked with and was manipulated by. It is every Fortean's wet fantasy to pinpoint this highly secretive alliance:

the Controllers, the Dominators, the Conquerors. In the words of Philip K. Dick: "The Empire never ended."

In essence, caution is essential! Discordians are known for their fickle tendencies and allegiances, which is why they make perfect mercenaries. Lawrence, however, is a reliable resource and good with guns (and plus, he has them). I have made an exception in his case.

His house (more so, his parents') is crested by an ornate decorative wall of brick masonry. The structure itself is old and fortified. Covered in mixed stone, Wallis Manor is a 1970s tribute to Georgian architecture – a perfect example of proportional balance and symmetry. Two chimneys protrude from a slanted side-gabled roof, horns on either side of the red-faced monolith surrounded by uncut fields of grass and sunflowers. I admire this place. In the mornings, white mist smothers the land, crawling out from a luminous creek hidden in outlying woods. It is magical and sometimes I come here to meditate on what is to come, or what I cannot see.

Lawrence answers the door: "Fnord!!! Grand and glory to Old Discordja!"

Ramona shifts uneasily. I nod hello. We enter into a foyer encased with neoclassical columns. Sneakers squawking across turquoise marble, we follow Lawrence to a nearby parlor . . . a tribute to Greek Revival—usually reserved for special guests. What makes us so special? The carpet maroon and gold in Baroque embroidery. A crystal chandelier tingles overhead, flickering – obviously electric. I squint away, weary of its basic unit of frequency. We sit down on out-of-place flannel couches, Lawrence on one side of scratched coffee table, Ramona and I sitting across from him. On the table is a silver tray with three glasses containing clear liquid, a half full bottle of Himbeergeist schnapps to the side. The drink of the yeti. I'm impressed and compliment him on his fruitfulness. Lawrence shuffles in the cushions. His hair is greasy and dark, curling into shiny ringlets down his face onto an unshaven chin. His eyes dart back and forth. He wears a t-shirt so tight we can see his skinny nipples squeezing through the stretched nylon. It is bright yellow with pink bubble gum words exclaiming: *Oscar Zeta Acosta Still Lives!* His jeans are just as tight, ripped at the ends. I notice dirt on his knee. He smirks, leans forward, and offers us the tray.

"I've been pilfering the amount," he motions. "Out of my own, of course . . . I can always save even for honorary allies and their minions."

Ramona waves a hand in refusal. "I don't do German. But, if you've got the fixings I'll go find myself some Irish cream, thank you." He looks hurt, but only for a moment.

"A lady is never rejected in my kingdom." Lawrence smiles as he and I grab a glass.

She wanders off to the kitchen to find her take. It won't be much. She is a moderate woman, never partaking in too much of anything. An asset and, at times, a liability. She will be a good reason to leave here soon. She doesn't like it here. Empty cardboard boxes line the walls.

"Well, what brings you home to daddy?" Lawrence sipped. "I have many wars to wage. Her Apple Corps is calling!"

I scoot to the edge of my seat, set down the glass. Take off my backpack and pull out the *Akashic Memoir*. "I'm on to something. Something that may be my ticket."

"Ah, your Kubla Khan . . . your ever-quest to Charles Fort's paradise," he chuckled. Lawrence is 6 foot 4 inches. When he chuckles it is deep and rumbles your spine. "When are you going to learn that Socratic crusades never end pretty. Take a look at Peter the Great of Russia . . . you really think he died of gangrene in his piss bag??? Ha, ha, ha!"

I relay the evening's experience, the whole play-by. His shaky eyes don't deviate from mine. He doesn't take any notes. Intent, he listens and fiddles his thumbs between nervous knees that bob back-and-forth. By the time I am wrapping up, Ramona comes back into the parlor with no drink, but a sandwich in hand.

"You have . . . no Bailey's," she munches between words. "You are . . . the source of evil. But . . . I found fixings for a snack. Got enough . . . bread . . . don't you?"

"You think twenty loaves is too much?"

"Sorry . . . forgot whose home I was in. I shouldn't ask . . . could lead to a hospital stay . . . or a night in jail. Don't mind me."

"What was the name again?" he goes back to me.

"Propit . . . something . . . I know I know it." I scratch and shake my head; my mind screaming at itself, lost child and a mother hollering on a cliff-side.

"You've had an anomalous encounter for sure," he stands, grabs the bottle of schnapps and motions for us to follow him. He has never been able to sit for very long.

We comply, gripping the *Akashic Memoir* tight to my body. Ramona pats me on the shoulder. Her look is disconcerting. She respects my friendship with Lawrence—and, she doesn't *hate* him—but, he makes her uncomfortable with his unpredictability and anarchistic nature. There is no telling where this night will lead: burning down billboards across I-70? Raiding Westport armed with water cannons filled with tomato juice and Populist campaign slogans? Buying a pile of snakes in the pet store and letting them lose in the movie theatre? All in the name of Eris. With Lawrence, there is no guarantee that we weren't going to have to run away from law enforcement tonight. He is a rabid beast, a renascent Macedonian expanding his borders.

We follow him through a dimly lit hallway, stamped with dreary paintings: Victorian Dukes and Duchesses with dreary faces. He opens a door at the end and trails down a flight of stairs. The basement is fully furnished; bright, full of pendant lighting. A few more couches, walls outlined with over-abundant bookshelves, papers and leaflets sticking out of dusty cob-webbed oak. Two computers set together, twin monitor arrangement; can't look for too long. A print of René Magritte's *A Treachery of Images* hangs on a wall. To the left is an open, walk-in closet (where the armory is) opposite another hallway leading to bedrooms and eventually an exit. There is a smell of incense, a type of musk. Brahms is delicately playing from the computer station, stacked with CDs and wiring components in a mass of deprecated hardware parts. Blinking Christmas lights cover the ceiling.

We sit down and drink more schnapps. Ramona finishes her sandwich. Bologna, I think, with mustard.

"I'm surprised you don't recognize the name, comrade. He must have really swiped your databanks clean." Lawrence peruses one of the shelves and pulls out a wrinkled paperback, tossing it on the couch next to me: *UFOs: Operation Trojan Horse* by John Keel, one of the preeminent Fortean investigators of our time. I've read the book before: premise of a non-human intelligence covertly propagating distinctive input into the masses through various supernatural events . . . an excellent work. The Trojan Horse is the subconscious mind, where information can be stored into deep pockets without conscious knowledge. Also authored *The Mothman Prophecies*, an inquiry into cryptozoology and the men in black phenomen--

. . . . wait .

. . .

"You said he called himself cold at first, didn't you?" Lawrence nods.

"What're you getting at?" Ramona asks, sitting down to flip through the book. Dust particles flit into the air. She sniffles. "What does anything tonight have to do with flying saucers?"

"It doesn't," I explain. "This is a common misconception. I open the *Akashic Memoir* and turn to a particular page in the middle: Potala Palace with its sloping walls on top of Mount Marpori, the once-home of the Dalai Lama. "Keel didn't attribute UFO activity with extraterrestrials from outer space. Neither did Carl Jung, for that matter, who considered UFO sightings to be a psychic event, irradiated from the collective consciousness."

"Tulpas," Lawrence breaks in.

"Right." I sit next to Ramona, showing her the picture of Potala Palace. Crease on her forehead deepens as she studies the image. "The Tibetan monks have advanced philosophies on human potential, the most prominent being that we're all made of energy. Like the field of sunflowers outside, a massive field of energy. That's what all this is, it encompasses everything: you, me, this house, other buildings, the grass, birds, toilet paper . . . everything. The Tibetans believe this field of energy can be manipulated, because our *thoughts* are energy too, right? So, if our thoughts are part of this same field, then they can be manifested, made *real*. That's a tulpa. It's an indication as to what UFOs may actually be, according to Jung and Keel."

"What does this have to do with today?" she asks, unconvinced. Lawrence walks over to one of his monitors, nudges the mouse out of screensaver, and begins to punch away at the keyboard. Tap, tap, tap. "You passed out at Town Topic. You met a weird looking guy. I'm not connecting here. . ."

"Wearing a dark topcoat, right?" Lawrence queries. Tap, tap, tap. "And very tan skin."

"You think he was a 'man in black'?" I ask.

"Thing is, there are different variations. Didn't you mention he called himself 'cold', before saying his name 'Propit'? Cold, Propit. Propit Cold."

"Indrid Cold", I remember. Indrid Cold, the odd stranger in Keel's investigations who appeared simultaneously with the Mothman in West Virginia in the mid-sixties, claimed to be from another world. Indrid was a benevolent character, spending his time with salesman Woodrow Derenberger chatting about life and accompanying him to other planes of existence. "He wasn't really one of *those* men in black, though. That entire encounter was about teaching Woodrow, not scaring him. The other men in black wanted to shut everyone up in the town about all the crazy shit that was going down. They were just as weird as Indrid, though."

Point Pleasant, West Virginia wasn't just experiencing freakish sightings of a flying man with red eyes known as the

Mothman, but was bombarded with legions of UFOs and other supernatural events. Indrid Cold was just one of many.

"Not Indrid," Lawrence agrees. "You're right. He wasn't terrorizing anyone. But, what's the deal here, between Indrid Cold and Propit Cold? Why here and now? This isn't Point Pleasant. This isn't 1966."

I know Lawrence will set me on a solid path, a thread to chase, but I can't trust his motivations. The crazy bastard is likely to want to cage a reward for any efforts he might contribute to. Plus, I have timed my associations with him, especially in his home. If we are here any longer than half an hour, our night is likely to be sucked into Discordian vortex of tomfoolery. Now that I have something to chew on, I may want to table the mystery and head back home with Ramona.

And then it hits me . . . .

One of the walls warp, closes in slightly—Wonderland sways in the twinkling colors of lights above my head. A zephyr flutter of acidic taste crackles in my mouth—the schnapps has washed down, now I savor the dissolving of electrodes on cool fire.

. . . my head swoons . . . other walls liquid . . .

"Gregor?" Ramona notices my vertigo face. Crease, her hand on my head, warm and soft, smooth touch.

Lawrence stands and walks into the armory: "How was that schnapps, comrade? Surprisingly psychedelic, isn't it?"

She looks over at him, addled; turns her head back over to me in an ever so slow grab of apprehension. She doesn't understand what is happening, poor thing. I do. I know what this is.

Lawrence has impregnated the schnapps with a mind-altering substance. I've been through this before . . . Ramona, though, will be in a panic. But, that's right . . . . she didn't drink the schnapps . . . good!

I look up at her nervously, words dripping from my mouth in molasses globules. "He . . . spiked my drink . . . with . . . something . . ."

"Not just yours," Lawrence hollers, strolls out of the armory wearing a purple robe, cape with stars and crescent moons, holding a rifle . . . one of his favorites, Marlin Model 1894C, carbine .357 Magnum. He calls it Enid. "I'm poppin' too! The whole bottle, kids. Lysergic acid diethylamide, along with my own little experimental mix of a few other items. I call it Ergo Surprise! Ha ha! Whooo! This stuff is starting to *hold*!"

Ramona's eyes widen in feline alarm. She is stuck. He has us trapped. Worse yet, she will have to undergo the next twelve hours sane. Dammit, Lawrence, you pig bastard! What the fuck are you up to?

Jaunt down a sidewalk of a very, very long stretch of road. A straight path as far as your eyes can see. No curves, twists or bends. End destination so far away, as you walk it feels like you are getting nowhere. The end still seems as far away as minutes, hours ago. Yet, you keep on walking (you can't help but not). Fixedly staring at the end horizon, it seems to stay as far away as ever. It never gets closer. Frustration rises slowly— erratic temperature—how long will this take? It is a *dud*? Your mind wanders. While your legs pump like mad dogs, your mind turns in on itself, shutting down the outside world; what would you rather be doing? Grocery list, play with your kid, alone with your woman. Suddenly . . . you wake up to the world around you and realize . . . you've arrived. You're here! In a suspension of time, you've overcome the arduous path with no end and didn't even realize it. It only took an eternity when you were *aware* of the journey, when you were focused on the destination instead of just enjoying the ride.

This is what it is like—normally—to wait for the effects of LSD to overcome your system. It creeps on you for the first hour, a dawdling spider you know it's there but can't quite feel . . . turn to your shoulder . . . and there it sits, staring you in the face, pestering you with its very percolating presence. Then, it leaps! Your serotonin gushes into a typhoon current, thrusting your consciousness into an entirely new mode of perceiving the world around you. Then, you know . . . *I am gone now.*

Again, this is what it is normally like.

Apparently, as I am discovering, the process is a bit more intense when you realize you have been thwarted . . . when you have been insidiously drugged by a mad Discordian in wizard's robes pointing a lever action, 18 inch barrel in your face. The frenzy of hysteria is rapid and bleeds warm panic through the nervous system. Luckily, I've had experience with this drug before. I should be okay, but Ramona is frightened. She doesn't need a Schedule I hallucinogen invading her spinal cord to know that she is in danger.

She tries to argue with Lawrence for a while until she realizes he is deadly crazy and serious: he is holding us captive; and, as much as he still considers us his friends, will not let us go until he has "completed his mission".

"Time to prepare for baptism,' he states coolly, beads of sweat trickling off his face like glitter rain. He puts on a new CD, a choir of malevolent angels bursting extravagantly on the speakers throughout the room; battering ram resonance: Carl Orff's *Carmina Burana*. Based off of the Wheel of Fortune, the goddess Fortuna, the opening scene *Fortuna Imperatrix Mundi* pounds into the psyche like heartbeat cocaine drums. Lawrence throws his arms and rifle victoriously in the air, schizophrenic composer drooling at the mouth. After *O Fortuna*, and *Fortune plango vulnera* begins, he walks out the door we had walked into, quoting from the *Principia Discordia*: "'Remember: King Kong died for your sins'."

Doors shuts >>CLICK<< must be locked.

We are prisoners.

While Ramona checks the collection of rooms and outer basement exit for openings and provisions (Lawrence locked the armory on the way out . . . . and his desktop) I listen to *Fortune plango vulnera* move soothingly into the eerily soft wavy voices in *Veris leta facies*. A haunting tenor cries out. I scan my environment . . .

The Treachery of Images inquisitively catches my sight, staring out at me – the smooth and subtle painting of a wooden pipe is nothing incredibly special to balk over, but the inscription below the pipe invades my mind: *Ceci n'est pas une pipe*: "This is not a pipe." In the early 20th Century, this statement shook the foundations of Newtonian thinking. If that is not a pipe, then what is it? Of course, it is really a *painting* of a pipe, a representation of what the viewer (i.e. – the eye, the eye's transmission through the optic nerve to the brain, the translation of information to interpret the object) deciphers as being a pipe. Pipe: actual three-dimensional object made of wood and is used for smoking tobacco or other herbal supplement. I am looking at a two-dimensional parchment with oils on it. This is, indeed, *not* a pipe. It is not even that . . . it is a print of an oil painting of a pipe. What is the difference between an object and a representation of an object? What is the difference between man and the representation of man? Same thing? No? How is a concept rendered or interpreted? When I watch clips of the war on television, am I really seeing what's there or just a symbol of what's there . . . begs questions . . . translation meaning, is our language nothing but symbols . . . like math . . . is consciousness just symbols, abstract integers . . .

. . . little theories we exchange with one another, bartering ideas we do . . . do we exchange the true idea? Magritte can't give us the objective pipe . . . so, are we perpetually stuck with a print of the image of a pipe, a representation of a representation; layers and layers of abstraction between the subtlest of communications . . . it is all depictions, silk-screen reality . . .

That is where we are, I think—the glutamate excites and releases itself in my cortex—just carbon copies of ideas bustling around and patenting sentience . . . I am this . . . I am that . . . I am a symbol . . . I am an idea . . . that is the truth.

That mars spider nestled on the shoulder, the old way of seeing fades away . . .

I believe I have slipped into the in-between now –

Surrender completely to the process . . . it is best for everyone. If I don't it'll be a bad trip . . . Christmas lights blip overhead computer board Las Vegas, reminds of a landscape in *The Crying of Lot 49* . . . giant caterpillar oozing up my back with millions of little thistle legs . . . loaded with perception, I say . . . pupils dilate . . . reach out and touch the nothing of pure energy, pure thought, thought, thought, thought . . .

Ramona and the shelves and the couches and the shag floor tattooed with moving glyphs and alien integers—glow in ultraviolet fluorescence as they in unison flow across the moving picture screen of vision . . . focus on one, make it out, but fades when I do . . . becoming in and out aware of form; the music emanates around me in vibrating centrifuges, fusing into everything as Ramona is unaware this nothing is alive this reality is alive and breathing us in and out and the It perpetuated by the momentum of this sound, of Orff's soprano who sounds tormented to be, to be . . . rumbling grove the music I watch rainbows of sound rushing through the space between bouncing off of the walls in ecclesiastical curvatures and geometrical limits of dimension exceeding dimension . . . the mind opening its maw letting in the boundary the pure data collected.

"Cccaaaaaannnn't fiiiiiinnnnddd a wayyyyy ooouuuuuuutt," Ramona signals in front of me open eyes blinking they are big and squint and small, crease straight up. She wiggles in motion and it makes me want to giggle; not the place for that now must watch her and take care. The freckles on her face trail into the air little speckles of moon dust create oasis islands of created more more more . . .

Directed by these forms, form used as instrumentalist devices a means of designing social and cultural directives—like Keel said—no, not just that designing the very means of perception when we are all conscious beings and the rocks too conscious of me and I, it can be controlled the tulpa way, manipulated, utilized, recycled, unlimited abundant energy . . . enslaved by form, Ramona is enslaved by form, she is trapped in a basement in the suburbs of Blue Valley . . . I am free, in the in-between, in a space where breath is able to move around, independent of the tangible material of consciousness . . . entire field of vision tattooed by kaleidoscope of flowing impressions and runes, all theory, all as real as the I . . .

      "Wwwhhhaaaattt arrrree weeeeee gooiiinnnggg too dooooo?"

                . . . I don't think she understands where I am .
. .

      . . . no more real than I am . . .

      I close my eyes to try focus onto Sahasrara, but the dark behind my eyes is flooded with floating, shape-shifting blobs . . . one covering my sight and enter walk through I am in a dark space with no form of color . . . I am standing, no longer on an earthly plane, in the place of my dreams . . . in a void of none, and three figures appear on a non-horizon and approach me without walking; they are as solid as my hand and it is terrifying; three figures, bipedal anthropomorphic creatures, all taller than I: one a beaver, one a squirrel, the final a rabbit. They are wearing Elizabethan regalia and dress, except the beaver covered in French bourgeois garb. The rabbit stands behind the others, cape overflowing, red eyes piercing at me . . . the squirrel and beaver seem intrigued to be close to me. The beaver lifts a mirror and squirrel waves a furry paw over it: look in and see a bed, much like mine, and I move in closer there are two bodies, rubbing against each other and wailing like wild animals, covered in sweat . . . look closer and shock grabs my gut and twists . . . dizzying wrench of unbelief . . . see Lawrence smacking his naked pelvis into Ramona, her legs wrapped around his neck, he is hollering like a bear and she is laughing and twisting his nipples; I tear myself away and tell the animal-men to go away and they shake their heads slowly. They do not speak, but I know they are telling somehow I need to see this and see more and it is for my own good because I am nothing and need to realize I am nothing and they ask me about my daughter, ask me how she's doing, and beaver asks me to look in the mirror (I see rabbit's red needle-point eyes) so I turn and run and try my best, try the best to open my eyes to escape what I can see, escape what is seen, unseen, experience is mutual holographic and stick . . .

     . . . open, where are we?   .

. . fire . . .

         time lapse . . .

         . . . flame open upon the black edges of negative space . . .

     Outside. We've been brought out, night dark, can't see much . . . middle-ground campfire we sit before, wrists are tied . . . Ramona next to me, tied . . . we're kneeling before a stump shimmering in campfire blaze and flicker, orange and yellow dance of Ramona's face, she looks at me . . . I see her eye come forward . . .

     "Gregor, can you hear me? We've got to get out of here." Her voice is succinct, maybe I am even-keel, maybe it was a mild dose, though never felt like this before, never felt so out of control and separate from all, centered in beyond . . . absolutes no longer apply . . . voice is spark consecrated, Lawrence appears before us costumed wizard pointed hat, the stars and crescents float out and warp around him like a Merlin robot and his eyes are bloodshot, hair wet and salty, sticking to his face and neck . . .

     "Come one, come all," he waves his rifle, shimmering steel in fire light, holding hands palm up to the heavens. "Are you human beings? Or cabbages in disguise? I, Cappo, the Iron-Clad Bumpkin of Persia, Ordained Priest of the Paratheo-anametamystikhood of Eris Esoteric, with the authority invested in me by the High Priest of It, Office of the Polyfather, the House of the Rising Podge; do herewith require of ye: are ye indeed cabbage or something?"

     "What the fuck?" I hear Ramona say.

     "The question is not answered. Are ye indeed cabbage or something? If ye cannot answer accordingly the question, that is too bad. Idiots of how! Are ye willing to become philosophically illuminized? Are ye?"

"Probably," I answer, spilling out unnoticeably.
Ramona quizzically turns to me.

"Ha! We are all unicorns anyway. I am Rasputin in the
Good Forever!!!" He grabs my collar and pulls me to my feet.
Peripherals swirl around and around, I don't feel myself here . . .
a molecule under water . . . he sputters in my face, I imagine: "I
am afraid, aren't you afraid? The whole world is filled with pain
and we are surrounded by injustices!!!! Look around you . . ."
He points the rifle in an arc, to the trees hovering around.
"Watch the societies fall who plunder and disguise themselves
with rubber masks. Don't you want my apple? Don't you want
my pain? My fear? Mothers hate their own sons, sons kill the
womb and take back the ether that is rightfully theirs!!!"

"Why're you doing this, Lawrence?" Ramona screams.
Rough outline . . . act one . . . introduction . . . meet Gregor,
literally nothing more to lose . . . divorced, hated by his wife,
feared by his daughter, all lies, all miserable lies and that is what
he—I—is made of . . . corruptible and incomprehensible tales . . .
thereof . . .

I slam my forehead into his   >>RED<<
            cantaloupe smack, a crunch bit, waves of
corrugation, fusion into extravagant burst   >>explosion!!! I
stumble to the ground, don't feel the impact . . . red covers my
eyes and everything is all numb, world of cotton: rush, rush,
rush, rush to the brain, hurt, hurt, hurt and slop the solid soft
numb . . . can't . . .

            . . . Ramona screams . . .
                        . . . Lawrence hollers
immutable, hoarse wail . . . Lawrence has a broken head.

Ramona runs over, feet aren't tied . . . not to me . . .
going for the rifle (smart girl) . . .

They are struggling over it . . . she is kicking . . . she is
lashing . . . he is trying to maintain, though holding his head
with bloodied hand, liquid maroon streaming through fingers
waterfall, pools below droplets . . . and I try to sit up and then . .
.

. . . form comes, *a* form, dizzying and fierce . . . it is all red, I wipe away the liquid from my eyes . . . wipe clean, head splitting . . .

. . . form comes down, dressed up and out of the dark, splitting out of the dark, out of nothing . . . red streak lightening . . . slams down on Lawrence, crushing . . . in a suit, form suit, jacket, and fist goes DOWN . . . smack on top of Lawrence and he is no longer moving, Ramona yelps excitedly and the rifle goes flying in the sky

. . the form is crouched in front of Ramona, I hear voices . . . wipe away, suit, red suit? Can't see all red, it is sticky . . .

Hand, red hand, comes before . . . suit, can't see eyes, dark sunglasses and head is still splitting, hard . . . dark glasses peering down at me and a friendly smile, hand extended . . . throw hand back, flinch, but consoling voice comes in, not Ramona's:

"It's okay," it tells me. "You're being rescued."

WWN Breaking News:

At least 25 people were killed and 54 injured in a bombing at a mosque in Yemen today, according to security sources. The Bin Allah mosque in Sanaa was in the middle of prayer when the blast was detonated. Local officials have cited the bomb was hidden in a car or motorcycle.

Shia rebellion leaders have denied responsibility for the attack. "We condemn this regrettable incident," stated Abdul Salman, a local cleric of the Shia authority. "We deny any role in this deliberate attack upon the people of Islam. It is not part of our approach to target any mosque or place of worship."

A spokesman for the Yemeni government says Abdul Salman and his movement want to overthrow the government and impose Shia religious law. Salman says they are defending their community from discrimination and what they call aggressive acts of a U.S.-backed regime.

Tensions are rising in Yemen since the car bomb attack on the U.S. Embassy last week, killing 18 people including 6 Americans. The U.S. blamed al-Qaeda ties for the attack, and the President made a statement that it was a reminder that the U.S. is at war: "The extremists who will murder innocent people to achieve their ideological objectives are on the move. We must take the fight to them."

The President said the U.S. Government wants to ensure the freedoms of democratic nations and promised aide and security to Yemen. "We are working with Yemen's government to increase our counter-terrorism activities to prevent more attacks from taking place. Democracy will be secure in the Middle East and around the world."

7 – Misanthrope

So then he approached Rosedale Arch. Snaking along
the concrete path up Mount Marty in a 2002 Maybach 57 –
rental, real leather interior, updated with satellite GPS and radio,
and all paid for by the client. A glistening charcoal streak, the
German engine barely made a hum as he eased to a stop on the
parking plateau.

This city, he muses, is all trees. It's a perfect mix of
jungle and concrete.

Inspired by the *Arc de Triomphe* in Paris, Rosedale
Arch was created and dedicated in 1924 as a memorial to World
War I veterans of the city. The park is small, sits on a ledge with
ancient trees and moss-covered rock walls. The Arch overlooks
the ozone haze of downtown tombstone finger skyscrapers
jutting out of the ground. It is enclosed by a black cast-iron
fence. He slams the door shut and grips leather case in right
hand. Finishing a cigarette, he stomps the butt into the ground
sparking ashes splatter around dead leaves.

Walking up slowly, the iron fence stands a head taller
than he, spiked spear ends. Facing each of the four directions are
a pair of nefarious dragon heads of Oriental design: gaping
mouths empty and waiting, grotesque moustache and beard
waving in non-existent wind, empty eyes seeing past the all.
They give wickedness to the memorial – no one is welcome
here. They are gargoyles rather than guardians.

After the Second World War, five figures in hoods
piled out of limousines and conjured ancient mystical rites at this
site. They meant to protect something, newly built, underground.
This place is cursed, he knows. Behind the eyes of normalcy,
dark things lurk in the shadows of the trees, through the eyes of
the iron serpents.

A gate at the south entrance. He walks over; was given
a key to the iron gate by his oversight. Open the lock. Inside the

memorial garden sits a human-sized stone slab stating gold letter names of the dead.

He scratches a receding hairline. Compelling item about the *Arc de Triomphe*, he muses, is an earlier design from Charles Ribart submitted before Napoleon's triumph. The monument was to be in the shape of an elephant, though included a spiral staircase leading to underground chambers. It was rejected, but the idea stuck with the elite.

All the important stuff takes place underground.

He walks over to the archway, typical Midwestern masonry. He touches hand against the inside of a pier, sliding across the textured stone surface. Guttural movement and grinding stone. An opening recedes and fades back. He walks through after a quick scan of the outdoors to make sure no one is looking. It closes behind him. Stone stairs lead below into a chthonic shaft. He makes his descent.

The tunnel opens into a cavern: he estimates anywhere between 18 to 20 meters in length, 15 meters wide, and the roof close to 12 meters high. Screaming. There are fluorescent lamps hanging high above, wires running through the stone wall, probably tapped into underground utility lines. Tables and crates everywhere in no organized fashion. Blood-curdling screams. Tools and implements populate the area in scattered messes: a pile of gas masks, rakes and picks hanging to the side, jars full of brownish liquids stacked on top of filing cabinets. He sees the source of the screams, near the back of the chamber. The figure is tall, well over six feet—domineering tower in a dead landscape. All in black, melding in and out of the shadows cast by the dim lights above. Long, raven hair greased down past mid-back. Hunched over an operating table. A man is strapped down, bruised, beaten, and bleeding; the shadow figure is crouched over him like a mad surgeon. The shadow figure has an implement in hand, wires tangling to a vibrating machine with a battery on top. There is abuzz coming from the device in the figure's hand, sparks fly, the man on the table wails in putrid agony.

The shadow figure does not look up from his experiment and speak. "You must be my assigned subordinate. Copernicus, is it?" His voice spikes and reverberates like gothic cathedral wind-chimes.

Copernicus takes a step out of the doorway, gripping the case in his sweaty hand. "You must be the client."

"Supervisor," the shadow figure pushes down. Buzz. Sparks. The man on the table weeps. "How're the little boys in Washington? Still dancing on skulls and playing with little girls?" Buzz. Sparks. AAAAARRRGGGGHHHH!!!!!!

"Likely," Copernicus replies. "What're you doin' to him?"

"Extracting information." Another buzz, a lick of flame, the man on the table chokes a bit, red splotches squirt onto his face. Eyes pop open wide in utter horror.

"Really?" Copernicus shifts uneasily, steps forward some more. "Because it looks to me like you're just waiting for someone to take a picture."

The shadow figure pauses, but does not turn around. "Are you insinuating that I am having a little *too* much fun?"

"Fun and intelligence shouldn't mix. Makes for bad brews."

Between seconds: he shimmers for a moment out of sight, appearing simultaneously face-to-face. Ghost-paste face etched out of shadow, smudge of high cheek bones that make epidermis sting. There is a scowl, face moves like cream clay in a fomenting drool of wolfish sheen. Eidolon air stretches out in dark, tentacle manes. The dark mass blocks the light from the ceiling fan. Between seconds: moving faster than thought. The shadow figure slams Copernicus into the cavern wall, face-to-face, has him penned. This thing, Copernicus knows, is inhuman and did not give any time for reaction. Tentacle manes have the arms and legs in a vice grip. He is confined. Pointed nostrils glide in close.

"I *enjoy* gathering information," spit dribbles from purple lips. His eyes: bulging and maniacal, mapped in red vines and a spec pupil; sickly bruised bags hanging skin underneath. Embryo death. "It is joyous. Like flowers in spring rain. Besides, do *not* forget who is in charge of this operation. Not even your little *boys* at the Agency can over-ride my authority. Do . . . not . . . forget."

Dark vice tightens. Around his ribs. Getting hard to breathe. Satisfy the client.

"Got it," he chirps. "Sir."

Instantaneously, shadow appendages go back and the figure is over at the table again. Wiry buzz. Sparks. Another hoarse wail. The shadow figure continues his torture, undisturbed. "I am Jack, by the way. Now . . . your superiors speak highly of you. I have asked for a man of experience. I believe in experience, don't you Copernicus? Any sap can read a book and develop a skill. A man with some years under his belt, however . . . *that* peaks an eyebrow on a resume, eh?"

The supernatural faculties of this creature were astonishing, but decades of this work kept Copernicus in check – he has seen many strange things himself. Survival now depended on keeping his cool. Copernicus breathes heavy, straightens his composure and comb-over. He recognizes a slight accent, a modified accent, to Jack's shattering, echo voice. Irish? British? This is a horrible man, Copernicus thinks. It bleeds into the room with haunting penumbra. His stomach lifts tight. He has handled these kinds of elements before; like Jack was saying, he's been around.

"Panama, Grenada, Bolivia, all kinds of work in those pesky little Latin American commie revolutions . . . even making your ace beginnings in Vietnam and Cambodia. Ah . . . those were some good ol' days, weren't they? So the question is, why here? Why do you think they stuffed you head-first into this mid-western shithole?"

"I wanted something local. I'm going domestic with age."

"Heh, heh." Ugly cackle. The man on the table cries, Jack is cutting into him with the device. "This is no easy assignment, Copernicus."

"I'm aware of that . . . sir."

"Good, because we have an entire organization to disassemble. You thought finding non-existent Al-Qaida cells in Baghdad was hard? Heh."

Copernicus walks up slowly to the table. The man strapped down *had* tan skin, covered now in an abstract painting of beatings and slicing, electrode black mark burns. Jack peers over at Copernicus and smiles, that clay face evilly showing sick amusement.

"Who is he?" Copernicus asks.

"One of *them*," evil grin moving in close. Jack wants admiration. "*Fucking terrorist!*"

"Can I try something?"

There is a pause. Copernicus unwraps layers of "Oh shits" in his head. He stands poised, firm. Jack, surprisingly, grins wider. Horrifically wider. He places the shocking device to the side. With casual eloquence he slides to the side and motions to the half-alive body on the table.

"By all means . . ."

Copernicus sighs. He sets the suitcase down, opens, and pulls out equipment for his work: two full plastic bags, tubing, syringe, and an infusion pump he sets at the man's head. Checking the bags and tubes for blockages, he connects them to the pump. He wraps a tourniquet around an arm, inserts a tiny catheter into a forearm vein; connects one of the tubes into the connector hub poking out of the thick skin. Repeats the same process on the other arm. He undoes a set of clamps on the tubes and turns on the pump with a whir.

"Time is tissue," Jack quips. He slowly oozes in the perimeter shadows, black sludge in swamp. "What exactly do you think you are doing?"

"Intravenous hook-up on both arms," Copernicus explains, setting a gauge on the pump. "If you just cut him up, all he's gonna focus on is his wounds, the pain. Put him out, or close to it. Don't give him anything to focus on. A heavy dose of pentothal, a heavy barbiturate. Sedate him with that. Then, this is where the other IV comes in . . . desoxyephedrine, a Schedule II stimulant. Maybe 10 milligrams, right when he's about to go under from the pentothal. It'll throw him into a fugue state. A sort of limbo he won't be able to make heads or tails of reality. The filter in the brain, usually blocking information, lifts. We should be able to get what we need . . . no problem."

"Is that so?" Jack floats onto a table and sits cross-legged. Shadow drapes around his body in a cloak. "Then . . . extract."

Copernicus waits for the man's face to grog, eyes lolling back and forth. In a stop-motion stream angst-ridden features melt into liquid cream. Eyelids begin to bob up and down, Copernicus flips a button on the pump and the desoxyephedrine flushes in. No iris populates the eye, just dark pools floating in a sea of white. The man asphyxiates, atrophies, and squints to the ceiling. His dark skin flushes.

The desoxyephedrine rapidly accelerates his system while still sedated. The effect is a muddled state between high and low, an in-between perception. Ethic and conviction no longer make sense. There is only awareness of being unaware. Limbo. The goofball effect.

"We call this the twilight zone," Copernicus kneels down to the man's face. "What is your name?"

"Hmmmmmmmmmm," the man hums.

"Come on, buddy. What's your name? I'm try'n to help ya out here."

"MmmmmmmmmmmmmMerchantttttt."

"Merchant?"

"Bah," Jack snarls. "That's a code name. Get something real out of him!"

"Merchant, huh?" Copernicus leans in closer, simultaneously upping the desoxyephedrine. "This guy is insane, he'll rip you to pieces. You gotta help me if you want me to help you. Who do you work with?"

"yyyYYYouu dddon'tt . . . . reallyyyy uuunnderstannndddd . . . dddoooo yyyoouuuu? yyYYoouu mmaayy bbeee fffucckkinggg mmmeee uuuppp . . . bbuttt . . . yyyooouuu wwwwonnn'ttt bbeeeee . . . gggetttiingggg aaannnythiiinngggg ooouuuutttttt . . . of mmmeee."

Surprised and bemused, Copernicus let up on the desoxyephedrine a bit. At least he was talking, astonishingly with much clarity. "Why's that, Merchant?"

Merchant closes his eyes very slowly and takes a deep breath. Veins bulging, popping, knuckles white; his system is on overdrive. But, Copernicus notices, he is somehow retaining focus. Somehow, this man is not letting up.

"Bbbbecause," Merchant blurts in an even tone, exerting an extraneous amount of effort to speak even one syllable. "IIII . . . . II'mm aa pppartt . . . of somethingggg bbbbigggggeerrrr th . . . . thhhannn yyyouuu cannn . . . iimagggginnnee. Tthingg isss . . . . yyyouu . . . yyou'rree aaa ppparttt of itttt too . . . . Yyouuu hhhavvvee justtt ffforgottennn ittt." He opens his eyes and smiles at Copernicus.

Copernicus does not have time to react. Dark-gloved fist thrashes onto Merchant's ribs with a resounding crack. A horrific shriek accompanied by blood speckles thrust into the air. Merchant cries in agony.

"You're my shit," Jack roars. "I am the Marquis de Sade and you are my whore, you fucking . . ."

"Jack! Jesus . . ." Copernicus throws his hands in frustration. Though Merchant is still moving, still yearning to tell more. Jack's fist in his gut wasn't stopping him!

"wwWWwwhaattt yyoouuuu wwilll seeeeeee," Merchant's eyes dark blots phasing into a slight vermillion. "Is tthatttt . . . ttthhheee PPpoppullll Vvvvuhhh iisss truueee . . . Ttthhee Wwwiieeerrrdd wwilll havvvee a . . . . . wwwWWaayyy . . . thhhe SssSstranggge wwwilll rrrremainnn ssssafffeeee . . . aaaAAand yyyouu . . . Jjjackkk of Hhheeeelsss . . . aaAAggentttt

off . . . tthhhhee ffFFFiiatt . . . . yyyoouu wwiilll havvvve to . . . .
cccommennce fffor . . . ppparrradigmmm sshhhhifft . . .
bbbecaussse rrrrRRRReeeEEEddDDDD is . . . . hhhere . . ."

"Popul what?" Copernicus began, thought interrupted
by Merchant's choking gurgles. Seconds between seconds, a
shadow appendage of Jack shapes in spear form and thrusts into
Merchant's throat . . . blood spills onto the floor and into a
rusted gutter.

"What? Hey! We were just getting somewhere . . ."

Jack eases back quietly, moving spectral toward the
only entrance/exit in the chamber. The darkness shapes him,
embraces him, symbiotic fluid coalescing into supernatural awe.
Skeletal voice creaks low in the dark: "The 19th Dynasty was the
best time for sorcererkind. Ramses the First started a trend. The
first edition of golems manifested on this dirt clod planet."

Jack reaches into the darkness of his . . . cloak? Coat?
Pasty hand pulls out a moss green piece and lays it on the
ground. A rock, standing up. Copernicus looks closer. It is a
statue of a man, a bald slave, about six inches high.

"*Shabti*, they called them. Summoning the dead into a
limestone figurine. Great for tilling fields, don't have to pay
them, whip them, feed them . . ." He curls fingers in the air
around it, puppeteer macabre, dark eyes gleefully expounding.
Ochre teeth show in a putrid sneer. "Bhag' dool shabati chol-
inth'ral bhag' a dool-purrr th'eeeel VUH!!!"

No glitter. No shiny glam or sparks. The figurine just
grew, slowly, no sound, into a six foot tall man. Russet with a
tinge of jade emanating off its skin. its eyes are hollow, broad
cheeks, void of life. It wears the same Egyptian garb as it did
before—animate, it turns its head slightly toward its master. The
thing is strong and ready to serve.

"There is nothing you understand, Washington-
monkey. You are my cat's paw, my whore. You should start
acting like it. Which means . . . don't *think*! Now," Jack glances
at the pool of blood squirming under the table. "Clean. Make

69

sure the blood is preserved. There are empty containers on the shelf."

Jack and the *shabti* exit the cave quietly.

Copernicus pulls out a cigarette and zippo. He lights it, smoke coursing in spirals through the dim light shrouding the barbaric scene. He has seen a lot in his day. With a sigh, he reaches over and shuts Merchant's dead eyes.

"I miss Marvin's coffee."

8 – The Sangria Topic

Sitting in some kind of train station . . . Union Station in the twenties, sitting in the north waiting room, elaborate décor walls stretch so high to a roof that isn't there. I am sitting. I hear numbers being called over an intercom. There are a few people with languid faces sitting around me on wooden benches. White haze blankets the area. A man approaches. He has a red moustache, comes with his son who is all smiley. The boy's hair is buzzed and red as well. He is maybe 10 years-old. They are both wearing forest green cashmeres and bark colored scarves. They walk past me to a middle-aged woman waiting a few seats down with some children. They are all red-headed. The man and his boy are smiling.

The man tells the woman: "See my boy? He's a good one. See how good he is?" The boy is proud, but also nervous. The woman is excited. The other kids could care less.

Then, the man hands his son over to the woman. I realize he is giving his son away, prickle anxiety around my neck. She is adopting him. For good. The man explains he and his wife cannot make it work between them, so they cannot afford to handle the child. The boy freaks, begins to cry mercilessly, pleading to his father to take him back home. The man walks away while his boy hollers hysterically. The woman holds onto him and hushes hum gingerly. I see a girl—the girl— with raven hair in a corner, dissecting the situation with atomic eyes. The one from the underground market.

Hushed, undone epiphany—forgotten someone else

    In the wake beyond the dream, wing deface ascends to the justly

The walls open, as they always do, and there the little boy in his frock, glasses so stream slip away and dissipate – they all disappear

There, in the open, a tip-top melody is heard echoing

A woodwind flute, and there out of the phase
something is prancing; one foot, two, one foot, two
The frock coat is still there (?)

* * * * *

The air outside is in disagreement with me. It is thick and making me choke, stale roll of yarn muffled onto the larynx. I hear the people singing, crying, laughing—all part of the vociferous din of the city that is mine. My city, my home. I belong here, curled before the blinking monitor with a wool blanket, stained tomato soup splotches. Out the window next to me: there are evangelists in the street below, hollering at passersby for repentance and chocolate almonds. A bicyclist speeds past waving a gun in their direction. The sun drips like mercury behind dense concrete tenements and skeletal branches; rays bleed through in persimmon strips, squeezing through the blinds and I reach up to closet them.

I've taken 4 milligrams of Ativan and I am starting to calm down.

Ramona didn't have much more to offer the Discordian incident recall than I. But she did help glue some pieces together while brewing hot tea and slicing a banana.

"Honestly, Gregor," she puts the slices on the outer rim of the saucer, around a steaming cup of chai. "I have no idea. One minute, I was wrestling Lawrence on the ground, the next this . . . person . . . whips in. Like a red streak. Smacked Lawrence down like he was nothing. They mumbled something to you and slipped away. So fast."

"In red," I muse. I log into my email, fingers weak, rickety. I was able to sleep most of the day, but I can still feel the dregs of the acid in my veins. Aftershocks course through my blood in werewolf reminder. Compose message. Begin to type, tap, tap, tap. "Red streak. Male or female?"

"I don't know."

"You don't know?"

"I'm telling you, as soon as the shock wore down and I was getting a handle on myself, I got woozy. Fell asleep. It was so fast, uncontrollable."

"You were drugged. But, not by Lawrence." I nod to her as she brings me the tea. Her eyes sweet and sincere. She pulls the blanket up over the back of my neck. Radical regale in plaintive evanescence. "Aerosol of some sort, I imagine. No side effects?"

"I feel like I slept."

She plops out on the couch, baby blue sleeve pulls back and I see birds – black silhouette tattoos flapping down slender forearm. She pulls out Vonnegut's *Player Piano* and continues reading. My copy, creased bottom right corner.

Bing. BLOOM777 responds to my call. Celebration.

"I still think we should call the police," she says while reading. I ignore her and involve myself fully into BLOOM777 chat.

BLOOM777: What can I do for you, D?

So, I lay it all out to him while Ramona enjoys Vonnegut's first dystopian masterpiece. She has The Shins playing in the background. I'm not so keen, but her quiet presence is a blanket.

Interlude: I deal in conspiracy theory. Baseline framework: it is the currency of causality; both the origin and destination of all knowledge. The more you know, the more terrifying it all is . . . consciousness creeps talon ache in the knowing. Occam's razor swing—is any of this real?

One of the most uncouth conspiracy theorists alive is an arthritic British paranoiac named David Icke. We are all freaks: Orwellain superstars like Jim Marrs, Bob Frissell, Alex Jones, Stewart Swerdlow. Icke, like many others, not only believes in a global conspiracy of world domination, but touts—what some consider—anecdotal research that indeed this world-conquering development is being executed by shape-shifting reptiles from a distant planet in a galaxy far, far away. These lizard people, Icke says, have already infiltrated the highest echelons of our international and local leaderships. For instance, you know our balding spectacled VP that grumbles in business-speak about how little it matters that hundreds of thousands of young people are dying overseas in illegal wars? Reptile. Queen Mum and her flowery hat squawking down around Buckingham Palace? Reptile. Thing is, Icke correlates bloodlines from these high-class citizens (the Morgans, the Rockefellers, the Bushes, and so on) as a lineage of hybrid-reptilian families that have been ruling the poor saps of this world through every major authoritative system in history: the Federal Reserve, the British Empire, the Roman Empire, the Egyptian Dynasties, and so forth. We have been slaves since the beginning of time.

We are slaves of time.

Although a true conspiracy theorist never discredits *any* idea, I am not one to immediately agree with the aliens-from-outer-space-controlling-everything theory. First of all, as stated earlier, anyone who is anyone in the UFO research community understands that all evidence points to a terrestrial event in origin. Not extraterrestrial. Second, there is no *one* organization controlling the planet. At least, not as far as I can tell. What is most frightening—and what I believe to be closer to the Truth— is that there is *no* control. We have these rich bastards in power, vying to maintain that power, but they have absolutely no fucking idea what they are doing. So, they fight among each other and have been doing so for centuries. The conspiracy is that they use the rest of us as tinker-toy pawns, wind-up automatons testing out their own little serpentine imaginations.

In a way, I guess, they are reptiles aren't they?

However, the Icke's idea does have some literal credence. There *are* covert societies in place with ties to governmental authorities: Skull & Bones, Freemasons, Order of the Dragon, and others. These people are for sure executing covert wars among people in an *attempt* to gain control. Most conspiracy theorists refer to the big bad of these secret fraternities as the Illuminati, but I refrain from this label due to its popularization of the term by Robert Shea and Robert Anton

Wilson. So far I prefer the use of the term, "Dominators." But that is subject to change when new evidence is collected.

Problem with conspiracy theory is, it doesn't take binary attributes into account. With a big bad must come an equalizing force to counter it. I have been detecting this equalizing force behind a veil of secrecy . . . in pictures, in dreams, always in the background, always a blip on the radar . . . my red man. In deep Fortean circles, there lies an even deeper secret that most in the Dominator culture or Illuminati fail to recognize . . . there is something out there . . . something on *our* side, something that believes in free information, a free humanity . . . something that believes in liberating us from slavery.

I describe my experience and theories to BLOOM777 with tonal movements of tapping keyboard fray. I describe my earlier catches of men in red coats discovered in magazines, news clips, a blip here and there.

ME: There are men in black. And there are men in red. And I have found them.

Long pause. I look over to Ramona. She is halfway through *Player Piano.*

"Are the front door traps set?" I ask her, twitching left foot.

"Yes," she turns a page. "Set them while you were sleeping. Knew it would help you rest better."

Bing. Turn back to the monitor. A response.

BLOOM777: You in the K.C. area, right?

Weird question. And so soon after a pause. Remember, the universe is insane. On the lamb from a renegade Discordian. Ex-wife hates me. My daughter . . . need to be careful. Need to be wary of who I slip information to.

However, if the universe is insane, then so am I.

ME: Yes.

BLOOM777: I'm doing a presentation at Unity Temple on the Plaza. Tuesday night at 7. Would love to meet you, discuss this.

ME: Sure. See you there.

BLOOM777: I understand. Trust me. I know. They are keeping the Weird safe.

Log off. Interesting.

We lay down together to sleep after I have changed a bandage on my leg. Vicious boil roiling in a sharp, bruising pain. Apply antibiotic ointment and take my medicine.

She curls her body around me from behind. Cradle lore entangle in the deep. She smells of lavender and it hurts inside. I think of Alice and it hurts even more. With bedside lamp I pilfer through *Akashic Memoir*. Pages of flying discs and lost fables coming to life. I read a page of Joseph Campbell torn out of *The Hero with a Thousand Faces*, pasted over an image of the Great Pyramid in Egypt: "The hero, whether god or goddess, man or woman, the figure in a myth or the dreamer of a dream, discovers and assimilates his opposite (his own unsuspected self) either by swallowing it or being swallowed [. . .] Then he finds that he and his opposite are not of differing species, but one flesh."

Lay back, close my eyes. Fall into Sahasrara space, in and out the air pulsate lungs. The Crown is not there; it's a progression to such, but that is the benefit to being sick in the head. Maybe if I move into Ajna, all can be. Ajna: the command. Ardhanarishvara, the primordial duality. All in the two. There is pulsing in the veins around my skull. All alive: rationale sense of dreaming . . . dream-time. Speculate on the animal-headed men .
. .

Affirm life: being versus non-being – pedagogical stages of life:

the way of the Path: Golden Alchemy
religion is the sociological paradigm of governmental control,

the Ways, plural
the primal mind wants to devour
the transcendent minds wants to fly

Skim the concepts: subject/object . . . no right or wrong. Cosmology is the new god, we are expanding, we are the universe (insane), we are star dust. We die; like an eye open for a second, so is our life/ out of context . . . into a new breed. The hero must achieve self-submission, fling out the correspondence: we are all similar.

Omnicentricity—solipcism

Life is shaped purely by our own imaginations . . . I am my own calendar, I am my own character I create. We are collective, there are no individuals. We are the shit of aliens, and they are our snot. Develop our own mythology. Develop our own insight. And, in the end, it will die with the others. It will all dissolve in the end. Shape the culture of the tribe – localized ideas.

When the Source is centered the law is broken. We must go back into our Dreams, this much can be learned from Discordian terror. We must go back into our Story, we must figure out how it is that we ended up HERE.

An "eye for an eye" is just a plea for proportionality; not a justification for vengeance.

To be serious, the answer to our origin is not in the books . . . it can be *justified* by research, yes . . . but *found* rediscovered in the realms of the deepest subconscious: deepest dreamtime,

deepest fear,

deepest innocence,
everything is sacred, everything is

folk

there is no hierarchy: you cannot rank me, Mr. President

the child is the source of mystery – ritual is a cosmic play

Why did we settle? Who was the bastard that invented agriculture? Was it evolution's hand? In the grand scheme of history we went from being wild and tribal and nomadic to tame and domestic overnight. Instant eye blink overnight.

Why?

Let us breed our prey; let us manufacture the slowest animal; better to have our food in a cage next door than having to chase them in the wild; the awe of our thinking, that we believed we could so easily shape the wild universe to our whims; what a novel turnaround: to plant a seed!

The promise of cultivation is the freedom of scarcity and the severity of life. The movement to domestication was bi-polar: the Age of the Goddess (the abundance of Earth) rivaling the Hunter takes a Secondary Role (the Era of the Masculine Herders).

Farming vs. Herding
Goddess vs. God
Cain vs. Abel
Tiamat vs. Jehovah
Isis vs. Osiris

Abundance, then = war. War becomes biologically intelligent when there is stuff tto accumulate. Without stuff, there is nothing to plunder.

THIS is the transition of Paleolithic (wo)man to Neolithic man. THIS is the transition of trauma. When THIS step was made we became a whole new species. War stems from the instinct to possess. But, to possess transcendence . . . can we war over a relationship with the Divine? Can we possess that?

Step toward divinity, the desire to have no desire – the Will to stay lost in the Labyrinth. The Modern Project > break free from the cage. The human experience is about completing the cycle of our history as a species; returning to the Earth, to death, Tiamat: the primordial ether.

we have no more roots
we are the lost people
fuck Gilgamesh, and his laws to

enslave the people

we are free, we are wild
let us wander in seas of chaos . . . red

abound

Tap, tap, tap.

Fingers grow numb again. Back at work; my spine is paralyzed in tight, knotted pain. Took 1,000 milligrams of Tylenol with Codeine earlier. Starting to take effect, but adrenaline has been pumping into my system at high levels since yesterday – recuperating from the Discordian's tricks. Left lower eye lid twitching with the palpitations, the fluorescent lights strain my vision ache.

Tap, tap, tap.

Jena leans over after kissing a picture of a shirtless David Boreanaz. She scratches hairy cheeks and blurbs in a globule whine. "Doug is looking for you," she pushes cracked glasses up her bulbous nose. "He wants those reports."

"Right," I answer grudgingly. Keep looking at the screen, maybe she will go away.

"Did you watch Crime Scene Hollywood last night?"

Don't answer. Just keep looking at the screen.

"Fred got voted off and Beth is in the final rounds. Isn't that cool? I was hoping Beth would go all the way. Next week she has to solve the Barlowe Murders against Steve and Roberta. That's going to be, like, totally woot!"

PleaseGodinHeavenmakethiswomangoawaysheisdrivin gmeinsane . . .

"Greg-ORE, my man," Doug creeps around the edge of my cube. Thank you, God! I will never forget! Although I quickly realize one hell has been interrupted by another. "How ya doin' buddy? Hey, I was just seein' if you got those reports ready yet?"

"Yes," I turn in my seat. He's wearing a shirt covered in Hawaiian-style flowers.

"You know it's Aloha Day, right?" I look over at Jena, who is wearing a lei. I look down at my attire, first time I notice today. Black polo, khaki cargo pants with a few small holes, brown tennis shoes (more holes). Doug smiles with teeth full of pineapple chunks. "Anyway, the chief wants to talk to you.

Something about those reports, I think. Might want to take a printout."

"Right now?" I push print and follow Doug's nod of confirmation.

Howard Rios is my boss and I have about as much respect for him as I do most people: little to none. Howard especially rates a little lower on my Scale of Acquiescence, indicating a pivotal role in maintaining Marx's division between the bourgeoisie and the proletariat in the working environment. Like most managerial positions, Howard has worked as hard or less to achieve a hefty six figure salary than I have at barely collecting $25,000 a year. All it takes is getting a one week certification in Project Management from a second-rate community college, and suddenly you are god over hundreds of lives. But, in the words of bad blog writers everywhere, I digress . . .

I grab the printout and walk to the oak door with gold-plated RIOS on it. Knock once.

"Come on in," his Styrofoam voice warps through the door.

Walk in. There are tinted paintings of buffalo hanging on each wall. A giant window opens behind Rios' desk, looking down upon the insects crawling from shop to shop at Country Club Plaza. Sit down. Refrain from inner commentary at the pink tie wrapped noose around his thick, stubby neck. He is tan. His teeth sparkling white and he shows them obviously while smacking his mint-flavored gum.

"Hey Gregor, how are you doing today?" He smiles a salesman's smile and I feel like this conversation is not going to be about my reports on inventory numbers for wheat trading throughout three states. He's got raptor written all over him. I glance at his gold rings and sparkling watch.

"It's Monday," I assure him I am not susceptible to lame flattery.

"Ah, yes, the Monday blues," he chuckles as if we're chums. He reaches into the top drawer of his dust-free pine freshener desk and pulls out a piece of paper. He hands it to me and his tone becomes spuriously sympathetic. "Unfortunately, I may not be helpful in that area."

I take it from him and read like I have no idea what it could be:

> *Mr. Samson,*
> *The Kansas City Trade Bureau regrets to inform you that your position as Data Entry Specialist will be terminated in precisely two weeks (i.e. – 10 working days). We at the KCTB hold the highest expectations for our employees, as our mainstay of hard red winter wheat futures represents the bulk of wheat production in the United States. If even one of our employees cannot meet these expectations (as outlined in the KCTB Employee Handbook) we are forced to take disciplinary action.*
> *Therefore, because of your continual absences and neglect of job function, we must terminate your employment. Please turn in your badge and security clearance on your final day of employment at KCTB. We wish you the best of luck in your future career.*
> *Sincerely,*
> *Howard Rios, PM Operations*

I look up at him and he smiles again. Why is everybody always smiling around here? I think of Propit Cold.

"What does 'neglect of job function' mean? I've done everything I've ever been asked to do, and in a timely manner."

"Ah," Howard blinks nervously. He folds his hands across his desk. There are no papers, no folders, no pens, no signs of work. "Security informs us of your internet meanderings. Too much time surfing, not enough working."

"But I get everything done," I'm not trying to sound desperate, just lay out a simple fact. "And do you know how many other people spend their entire day playing games and blogging? People more important than me?"

"Well, that's no longer your concern, Gregor. We will certainly look into that, but in the meantime our position remains as it is. I wish you the best of luck in the future."

I think of about a million ways I could leap across the desk and push him out the window onto pedestrians below, body splattering against hot, noon cement. I think about how much I hate this game, this succession for the illusion of success. What does he attempt to accomplish with that twelve-karat watch and thousand dollar shoes? In the meantime, there are hobos below sprouting Shakespeare in dumpsters. He doesn't even know they exist; they are morlocks and the ultra-forgotten. I think of a million different things as I sit for the two seconds before getting back up to go to my cube. I look around this endless sea of tapping zombies and gray grids of symmetry and I want to vomit.

This is what we do before we die. This is our identity.

CSCAN

THE GENTLEMAN FROM IDAHO, MR. REED, TAKES THE FLOOR:

"Mr. Speaker I come to the floor to discuss the proposed economic bailout of the leading financial institutions on Wall Street. This is the largest fundamental change in our Nation's history, financially and maybe overall. So far, my constituents and I have been cut out of the proceedings regarding this supposed bill and have been called unpatriotic for not expressing initial support. Mr. Speaker, I have been thrown out of more meetings in this Capitol in the last 24 hours, than I have in my entire 15 year career in this Senate. Mr. Speaker, there are meetings taking place behind closed doors in one of the most monumental changes to the American people since the Great Depression. These negotiations are not taking place within the public arena. What is going on, Mr. Speaker? What is going on, Mr. President? As declared by you, Mr. Speaker, we are being threatened with Marshal Law, the sanctity of the democratic process, if we do not stay here and do what it takes to pass this bill. Mr. Speaker, you cannot *make* the American people pass a law they do not want to pass. Mr. President, I have gotten more response from the American people in the past 24 hours than I have my entire career. The American people *do not* want this bill to pass! This bailout is, in itself, a golden parachute for multi-billion dollar corporate executives who have spent the past eight years, under the de-regulation policies of this administration, and the one preceding it, sucking the American people dry. Mr. Speaker, Mr. President, the American people are losing more jobs every day. Homes continue to be foreclosed at an exponential rate. Gas prices continue to rise, along with food, and energy costs, gouging the middle class wallet. Four wars with no end in sight, American troops dying every day. There is no room for the average American to maneuver, Mr. Speaker.

And just today, *just* today, Mr. Speaker, the President has stationed an active military unit inside the United States to serve as an 'On-Call Federal Response' in case of an emergency. In essence, in case this bill does not pass. This unit is training for domestic operations only, to deal with civil unrest and crowd control to subdue unruly or dangerous individuals. Mr. Speaker, the President of the United States is holding the Senate and the American people *hostage*! Mr. Speaker, what has happened to our democracy? Mr. Speaker, the President and his cronies may get on prime time TV and tell the world we are traitors to the American people for not passing this bill. But Mr. Speaker, the American people have told us to stand firm. No bill will pass this Senate until the U.S. Government agrees to bail out Main Street, Mr. President. Let's get back to the drawing board. Let's stop putting country first, and put the *people* of this country first instead."

9 – Incarceration, Part 2

1964:

He was dragged down the hall like a fucking animal.

He was in chains. And they were laughing at him. Laughing! The air was sterile cold, floor like insides of a freezer. They stopped him in front of a steel door. 1 of the orderlies opens with a set of keys, creaking, haunting.

The room is the size of 3 bathtubs. Maybe 2. A cot and a toilet. That was it. No windows, no sink, no blankets, no pillows. Absolutely nothing. They tossed him down, smacking the concrete floor of the cell, discarded lumber. Just as cold as the hallway floor. He hears distant screaming: down the hall? In his head? The spit, it lands in his eye. Words like "nigger" and "chimp" are thrown at him like stones. With a crick, the steel door slams shut. There is a slit in the door that can be opened form the hallway only. He assumes, he knows, that that little slit will be his only connection to the outside world for a long, long time. That little tiny window he had no control over opening. Only they did. *They* are in control. Always *them*.

He cried that night, and many nights after, like he was 8 years-old again. No, like he was 3.

Night . . . day . . . the minutes and hours rolled into each other, bumping ambiguity with reality. There was no time, except the circadian rhythm of 1 meal slid through the window per day. Day? Seemed like a day. Long enough to make the hunger ache with so much pain that there was no pleasure in eating what little he was given. A stale roll, most of the time half-covered in mold. Some putrid broth, half spilled by the shoving motion of the orderly as it is passed through the slit on the floor; his only access to any liquids as well, licking the dirty floor for every last drop.

It must have been 2 weeks. Pure solitary confinement. Never spoken to. No baths. No walks. The toilet stopped up and nobody came to fix it despite his calls for help; his own filth pouring out onto the floor, confining him to the island of his cot. Now, he couldn't even stand, pace . . . sitting, curled, waiting and smelling his own funk. Soon, the need for hunger, the need for release causing him to step into his own shit and piss to release himself into an already-overflowed commode. Part of the liquids drained into a half-clogged drain in the center of the cell, but not enough to keep from filling the room with utter wretch.

Jonah had no place to go but inside, deep within--the intrinsic nature of perception his only salve. Torture, he thought, pure torture. Humans are social creatures. We need other people and things and animals and the sun . . . anyone who ever wants to tout the importance of individuality is full of shit. Life without Stuff is death, a death where shitting and breathing are your only companions.

It must have been the 2 week mark. Finally, much to the shock of Jonah's atrophied nervous system, an orderly unlocked the door. The waft of air rushing in was beyond any sort of heaven he could have imagined. Life pumped itself quietly and subtly back into his weakened frame. Relief painted itself soothingly across his face in bliss.

"Whatchyoo smilin' at nigger?" the orderly smacked a blow of hard knuckles into Jonah's jaw. Pieces of teeth crumbled onto the floor with blood, trickling delicately into the puddles of piss.

Chained and gagged, too weak to struggle, he was pulled into the hallway. The weeks of adjusting to the darkness of his cell made the light too bright for discerning any surroundings. He was thrown into a tiled room, stripped bare, and showered with a fire hose. The hose was turned off; he lay on the floor dripping, shivering. The hum of the air conditioning was pumping a rabid chill over his trembling skin. A woman walked up to him, dressed completely in white, an apron and rubber gloves. She pulled a pair of scissors from the apron pocket. Her glare pierces Jonah with the coldest eyes. Orderlies sloshed over to restrain his naked body as the woman cut his hair and beard. After some trimming, she brought out a razor and buzzed him down to a brown sheen. The fire hose came on again, thrusting a venomous force onto his frail frame, curled into a fetal position and dreaming of a life that was only a dream. The hose turned off and they brought him no towels. He sat on the shower floor until he had drip-dried in the chilled air. Then, they brought him some white scrubs and told him to dress. He did so obediently.

After being escorted down a maze of hallways, through a series of secure doors requiring eye scans and ID cards, Jonah found himself seated on a steel chair sitting in front of a steel table in a tiled room—all white—cold concrete floor on his bare feet, a giant mirror covering one wall. He knew they were watching from the other side.

A door opened. A man walked through. Middle-aged, receding hairline striped with white. Glasses arching over a hooked nose. A soft build, formed by years of sitting in front of a computer or a microscope, fed well enough in a life of luxury Jonah would not even be able to imagine. His name was Dr. Harris Isbell.

Isbell's face winced at Jonah. He pushed his spectacles up the bridge of his nose and laid a clipboard on the table before Jonah. The paper was blank. Isbell clicked his ink pen incessantly.

"So," he began. "Look where you found yourself."

Jonah did not know how to answer. A lump of fear curled into his throat, clogging any ability to respond. Fear spider-crawled up his spine in a new way . . . a fear unlike he had yet to encounter during this traumatic experience. A tingling fear one would feel in the basement of a haunted house, or foggy graveyard at night. A suffocating clasp on your stomach retarding all reasonable sense of logic or bearing.

Isbell looked down on him with casual indifference, arms crossed.

"You have been selected because you are expendable. The goal of the human is a race to succeed. There are those that drive this success and those that are the assembled parts which make up the car to be driven. I represent those that propel the process of this success. I drive the car. You, however, exist solely for the purpose of serving my needs. You are merely a part of the car: a tire, an axle, an air filter, a seat, a pedal. I will use you in any way I see fit. At times this use may indeed exploit your humanity, but that is your plight--your *job*--to endure. This does not dilute your significance. This merely dilutes your role."

Isbell began pacing back and forth, introspective.

"You see, despite what you may be inclined to perceive through your stay here, I love you. You are a part in the great human experiment. The manifest destiny of consciousness awaits us; the threshold of all knowledge! *Homo sapien* is on the cusp of a superior leap on the evolutionary ladder, and we will do so on the backs of those like you who are too weak to continue. *Ubermensch* is waiting. And you will get me there. You are my child and I will *keep* you that way. You and the others."

"Others?" Jonah managed to sputter the question quietly. The 1st word he had spoken in what felt like an eternity.

Isbell looked to him squarely, eyes of inertia.

"The botched."

*   *   *   *   *

Domination during the 1960s was a full-time occupation.

Project MK-ULTRA, the protégé of operations BLUEBIRD and ARTICHOKE, was the Central Intelligence Agency's most extensive foray into the realm of psychoactive chemicals and their effects on human subjects. MK-ULTRA had a few primary objectives, the 1st and foremost being the possible discovery of the ultimate truth serum for intelligence gathering during interrogations. As soon as Sandoz laboratories released knowledge of lysergic acid diethlamide-25 to the scientific community, the CIA, KGB, and all other interested parties honed in on the drug's potential. At the time, it was the most potent substance they had ever encountered. *Too* potent, it would seem . . . it was an unpredictable agent causing legendary tales that would spin out of the Agency's tangled web of operations for decades. Though the psychotherapeutic possibilities did not escape them, LSD was—and still is—1 of the most powerful tools to explore the subconscious mind, an uncharted territory that had been eluding psychology and psychiatry for centuries. However, the CIA is not invested in helping people work out their personal problems.

The 2nd objective of MK-ULTRA was mind control. Their research evolved into strategies for gaining advantage over the enemy and civilian populations by, purely, fucking them up. They also toyed with the idea of making super-soldiers. The top tactical approach was this scenario:

Imagine, you, in the jungles of Cambodia. Through an encounter with Charlie you capture a Viet Cong sympathizer. You bring your POW back to base camp. Instead of spending hours, maybe days or even weeks, to retrieve information out of the prisoner, you just inject him with a dose of acid and send him back home. Then, theoretically, a particular trigger in the mind of the ex-prisoner could be activated; either sending him on a suicidal killing spree or on an intelligence-gathering mission for the Agency.

Public documentation would indicate the CIA (or DOD, for that matter) would never get to this point, that MK-ULTRA was a complete failure. In fact, the best way to cover up the activities of a secret intelligence agency is to act like you are complete screw-ups, invent for yourselves a history of complete failures and quagmires so the public will be able to sleep comfortably.

It was at this time the Agency enlisted doctor after doctor with the help of the Public Health System to officially sanction its practices. The PHS funneled endless amounts of money to MK-ULTRA's program: do whatever you please, was their motto, so long as you are just gathering data; the more data you accumulate, the more we can analyze the overall influence of the thing called *acid*. What could it do? What were its effects? Its potential? Despite the example given, this operation took place right here within our American borders, the home turf, and *we* were the subjects.

We the People.

10 – And Synchronicity . . .

The room: stars in the clouds and mountains . . .
enclosed space, roots all around, jutting out of black dirt
surround

  A small, round woman in stitched animal skins her hair
is wild her skin the color of the dirt surround/she has white paint
on her face: covering the brow, stripes on cheeks, one strip on
the pudgy chin. She is squatting on the floor handling maize,
placing batches of it into a bowl. She begins to speak without
looking at me; she knows . . . I know, her name is Mother,
Mother Wakanabe. Her language is guttural, with clicks and
chokes, but I know what she is saying:

  "I am expecting you. My family brought you here. You
want to know the cycle, then watch as I split." She begins to
break the maize in half with her thick hands. Click, choke, click.
"Heh. The road you take, and make an end. We here, in the
place of no exit, no return. Life in the below, eyes adjust in the
dark. You want a counter-part? Grease-trapper? Soil-trapper?"

  As she explains, images of two cards appear in the air.
One on top a man standing on the clouds. The one on the
bottom, a man in goggles, with a shovel, standing in a cavern.
The man from the top card leaps out of the card space and down
into the bottom card. The man in the bottom card digs his way to
the top card. They repeat the cycle over and over.

  "Heh, heh. The lives with the switch. Like scales. Are
you the here, now? Heh, heh."

  She stands and looks at me for the first time. She is two
heads shorter than I. Her eyes are like a mother's. In a blink we
are in the middle of a wooden stadium, full of Indians. She
laughs (at me, with me?) and raises her arms. The audience
whoops and hollers – they love her. She is giving them a show.
But, what?

  Then, again, it starts: a tip-top melody echoing
Hallway in a wall, flooding out

A woodwind flute, and there out of the wall
something is prancing; one foot, two, one foot, two
The frock coat is still there, a figure is dancing
The flute melody is soma to the crowd, Mother
Wakanabe nudges me toward the sound . . . look, and it may be
true . . .

* * * * *

Lena calls, wants to hook up. Gotta meet my new man, she says. He's older, she reminds me, so don't be freaked out. In his fifties. Don't be freaked out. Lives out of town, in for the weekend. Works in law enforcement. Don't be freaked. I am always freaked. I told her Ramona and I are already planning to go watch Bloom777 present at Unity tonight. She said she would drop by, told me to give mom a call, and hung up.

Give mom a call . . . she knows I won't.

Ramona and I look up who is actually speaking at the Temple. If this is no sham, Bloom777 is one Jonah Mulligan. *M* for Mulligan. I find no other information pilfering through search engines, except as a noted Owner and Webmaster at *WildPendulum.net*. He is giving an hour lecture on "The Mystic Path and Animalism". My interest is, of course, ingrained.

I, of course, catch the off-chance conjunction of Bloom777 (Jonah Mulligan) suddenly, somehow coming to my town (of all the others in the country) to speak in the midst of all of this nonsense: with UFOs in the sky and supernatural entities on the prowl. Best friends spiking me with psychedelic drugs. But, my sensibilities will never allow me to *not* follow coincidence, replete with copious curiosity.

Currently . . . this is more important than anything. This may indeed *be* everything.

Unity Temple stands on the corner of Jefferson and 47th, on the other side of the Plaza from where I work . . . did work. It is a religious institution known for its liberality in all aspects of religious institutionalism. They are notorious in the

Christian community for ordaining gays as ministers and taking part in Zen meditations in their church services. I feel fairly comfortable here. Opened since 1948, it is one of the oldest buildings in the area. The sanctuary reminds me of a gothic chapel, a vivid stained-glass bible glowing overhead. Below that, a walled sculpture of the Egyptian winged sun, an attribute of the god Horus.

We sneak in, door slamming, in the back of the sanctuary. A few glaring eyes as we tip-toe to a rusted seat. Mulligan is already speaking, standing on the stage with a laptop, a projector laminating dusty light on a screen behind him.

The screen is black with white text populating its empty space. It reads: "'On the quiet church whence there streamed forth at times upon the stillness the voice of prayer to her who is in her pure radiance a beacon ever to the storm-crossed heart of man, Mary, star of the sea.' – James Joyce, *Ulysses*"

He is a locust, covered in layers of coats and scarves, and fingerless gloves; they shuffle in silent rhythm as he shifts back and forth. They look worn, unchanged for weeks. Black skin complimented by a ghostly beard, twirling like smoke off his chin. Gleaming spectacles rest on a rotund nose. He has a rasp to his voice with a geriatric texture. He is talking about ancient architecture. Flicks the laptop.

The new slide shows a Central American motif: ornate frame surrounds the image, decorated with geometric glyphs. In the center a man looks to be crouched on his back, bending slightly forward. He dons the headdress and gear of a kaleidoscopic priest. Beneath him a platform that, in Aztecan design and closer inspection, looks like the crazed maw of something vicious – leviathan horrid.

Mulligan continues: "This, people, is the exalted ruler of the city of Palenque. He is Pacal the Great. His kingdom was responsible for some of the most magnificent works of art and architecture in Mayan civilization during the 7th Century, as you can plainly see by the elaborate décor on this relief. Stare hard.

You are looking at a depiction of the lid on Pacal's tomb, found in the Temple of Inscriptions. A vortex, you must know, if there ever was one."

Okay, so . . . *Mayan*, not Aztecan. Can't get them all right.

He lifts a laser pointer from the podium and scans it across the glyphs in the upper half of the image. "These symbols are generally interpreted as the sun, moon, and stars. Many archeologists . . . many *pseudo*-archeologists . . . junkies . . . use this particular image of Pacal to prove that the Mayans were descended from the stars. This configuration below Pacal . . ." flits the laser to the platform in the lower half ". . . is most commonly misconstrued as the possibility of a flying vessel of some sort, a *spaceship*. Launching this mad king into the painful innards of the galaxy . . . an ancient astronaut! Like hell, I say! They like to think the advanced science and architecture of the Mayans comes from outer space. Bullshit. Grey theories are contraband material, made of trash. This platform Pacal's on is a *serpent*, the mouth of a giant snake. This is a typical shamanic symbol, everyone. The *cosmic* serpent . . . a symbol not just in Central and South American indigenous cosmologies, but in tribal cultures around the world. The serpent, the frog . . . . they all represent the underworld, the world of Other: the spirit world! What the Incans would call *Ukhu Pacha*. Pacal was a great sorcerer-king, so this assumption has great merit.

"So, the question needs to be asked: How does this apply to me? What can a junky do with this? What understanding can someone gain from learning about this type of symbolism prevalent in indigenous societies?"

Flick on the laptop, the slideshow goes to an image of a Faberge silhouette in meditative position: a person within a person within a person, until it centers to a small minute point. Rainbow color spectrum covers the outside figure.

"Now . . . we measly Westerners have a skewed vision of the underworld. Most generally we think of it as a type of inferno, a place of punishment. In fact, it is the world of the *shaman* we are discussing. Call it the underworld . . . inner landscape . . . it's all the same. Who cares? It's all language. The aborigines call it dreamtime. The path of the shaman is universally clear. It is the esoteric route where the shaman gets their powers to heal, to shapeshift. The Mayans call the road to this underworld *Xibalba be*. It is the road that is most important, not the underworld itself. This is the path to the world of spirits. Pacal wasn't the first to discover *Xibalba be*. It was Hunahpu, First Father of the Mayan creation myth, father of the Hero Twins . . . Hunahpu, the first shaman. Hunahpu paved the way for all who were to follow the *Xibalba be* in the years to come . . . the Shaman's Path."

Flip on the laptop, image of an ancient cave painting. Seen it before; a flat-faced, bearded deer perched on a rock. Mulligan waves a giddy hand in the air.

"Ah, now *this* is exciting! Junkies ought to appreciate this! Dubbed 'The Sorcerer' in the Trois-Frères cave system in Ariège, France. We can trace this marvelous work about 17,000 years back. God-damn beautiful, isn't it? This is one of the earliest recordings of a therianthrope we've seen, the merging of human and animal form. See the long, wizard-like beard? The feet and hands a blend of human and lion? With the exception of the owl eyes, the very human face? It is very common for Paleolithic cave art to mimic therianthropic qualities. What archeologists are beginning to agree on is that these therianthropes, particularly The Sorcerer of Trois-Frères, are recordings of shamans in action: transformation from man to animal, entering the world of Nature. *Xibalba be*. It is this amalgamation into the animal mind . . . this exotic state . . . that gives the shaman his power. It is a *true* transformation, for he is no longer a man. He is *sha*man, beyond a man. He belongs to the *natural* world . . . no more the *civilized* world."

The animal headed men – when Lawrence spiked me full of acid a couple of days ago. They came to me . . . as guides, albeit erroneous ones. I lean forward in my seat. Diligence.

An audience member raises their hand, an older lady in a pastel azure dress with a matching hat. Her hands were gloved.

"Yes ma'am," Jonah nods.

"Mr. Mulligan, are there traces of these th-ther . . . an . . throp—"

"Therianthropes?" he corrected.

"Yes, *those* things. Are there traces of them later on in history, rather than just the cave times?"

"You mean the Upper Paleolithic, ma'am. . . and yes, there are. Fast forward in history we see various gods in this man/animal hybrid form, such as Ra and Anubis. American Indians tell of the skin-walkers, a shaman with more lycanthropic qualities. One of my favorites, actually, is the *lemures* of Classical Roman mythology. The lemures are called "spirits of the night", supernatural human/animal beings with large eyes that wandered into the villages from the wilderness. This is actually where the lemur primate received its name, truth be told. Old mystics used to speculate if the lemur was actually an evolutionary offspring of the lemures. Lemurs, as well as their cousin the Indri, are known for their bulbous eyes and wailing cries at night, just like the lemures.

"And then, there is also P'an Hu of Chinese legend . . ."

"Did he really just say *Indri*?" Ramona leans over and whispers. Absolute certainty! *Indri*, but close enough. The certainty of absolutes, resonation manifests and I have a reason of Being in the moment. We wait patiently as Jonah Mulligan finishes his rap.

The line isn't terribly long. We wait in the corner, under a plastic palm tree covered in yellow ribbon. Ramona tries to hold my hand, but I complain of being too sweaty. She tries, I know she does. We hear toilets flushing in the background.

Mulligan tires of the few people that are vying for discussion and continued on to the refreshments: coffee, punch, and tofu cakes that made an obese janitor vomit after he snuck one. I approach Mulligan nervously, hands gripping backpack straps in a white knuckle collapse.

"Bloom777?" I ask.

"Ah," eyes brighten and he extends a hand. He shakes with a nectar flow. "You must be D. Yeah?"

"Gregor, actually. That was a decent spiel in there."

"Just a little ditty I dug up from a few years back when I used to do university tours. The ones who don't want information alive have influences everywhere . . . the Enterprise. . . even in our educational institutions. It's a shame, really. I really like college kids. Ripe minds, open and flowing like water." He flits a glance up to the winged sun. Files his laptop into a hemp satchel. "Now, it's venues of alternative spiritualities. That's fine, though, right? Brain's a brain, that's what I say. We all junkies! Heh, heh!"

"Hello," Ramona nudges in.

"Greetings, lady," Jonah bows in a gentlemanly manner. "And who might you be?"

I explain: "Oh, this is Ramona."

"I'm Gregor's girlfriend."

"Most definitely you are," he pats her on the shoulder like an old dad from a sitcom. "Radiance can tame a wild mind, such as my Dedalus here."

"Your who?" Your who?

"Now, it's a pleasure to meet you both, but could we find a more private location for a discussion I've been meaning to have with you?" His eyes burrow into me, no interest in chit-chat. "I don't trust any place I've been at for longer than half an hour. Thirty minutes, boy, that's what you have to remember. After that, you might as well hand yourself over on a silver platter."

"Well," I stumble. "There's that coffee house on 39th that's always—"

"Gregor!!!"

I turn to meet the interruption. It's Lena. She is bubbling with youth, wrapping her arms around me in a squeeze.

I almost forgot she was coming; overly-absorbed. I *did* forget. She is an interruption – I have too much to discern.

"So glad we could make it," she beams. Her hair is done up and silver lining around her eyes with blush cheeks. "I want you to meet my new man. Benjamin, this is Gregor, my brother. Gregor, Benjamin. He's Norwegian."

"Only by heritage." He steps up. Older man, light hair high up on the brow. Old man athletic build, close to six feet. Rough, creased face and periscope eyes. He is well fitted too, dress shirt and slacks – maybe weary of his own success: a wrinkle here and there, top button undone, sleeves rolled up. A strong arm comes out with a hand to greet me.

"Hello, nice to finally meet you." It's an even voice. Kind, but even. I smell ash and bourbon on his breath. We shake. His hand is calloused, a rock trying desperately to make motion. He smirks. It seems hard for him, to inch his mouth upward. His face is lined like dried-up river clay.

"Yes," I agree. "Nice to finally meet you too."

Lena motions to Ramona, kindly manner in a sweet embrace. "And this is Ramona—"

"Well," butts in Mulligan. "This is as *obvious* as obvious can get!"

"Excuse me," Lena retorts. "Who's this?"

"I think your boyfriend knows *goddamn* certain well *who* I am, along with everyone else." Mulligan hugs his satchel close and inches backward.

Benjamin waves his hands in defensive gesture: "Look . . . uh, I can leave, if this isn't cool."

"Hella-right you can leave, Nova Gestapo detritus!!! Go on back to Contessa de Vile's chamber of dirty secrets!" Mulligan throws his arms in the air silver back fashion, stomping at Benjamin's ground. His layers of clothing flutter around him in multiple wings.

"Gregor, who the hell *is* this guy?" Lena stands in front of Benjamin. Mulligan spews uncertain panic into the air.

I move in to calm him, the rabid beast flailing in schizophrenic fear: "Hey . . . Jonah . . . calm down . . . what's the matter?"

"Look at him," he maniacally points at Benjamin. Wild eyes. "Look what side he's play'n! You can't tell??? Jesus Heroditus Christos, Dedalus! What's aching your ills, boy? Call 'em out when you see 'em! You should know a Nova scent by now! Dominator, boy! DOMINATOR!!!"

Christ, I can't think. This is one of those pluralist moments, tugging between two spheres of influence. Mind: what the fuck is the old coot talking about? Break him down. Don't let some asshole off the street lay in to your own sister and her company like that. Take this hobo in and let them strap him to a bed and pump him full of morphine and elephant shock treatments. Other: *oh shit*! I know what he's saying – there's one of the Elite's own right here in front of me, scoping me out, fucking my sister. The very Dominators I spend every waking moment barricading myself from. Who do you trust? Mind? Ether? Brain? Spirit? One uses logic, the other made out of the stuff of underneath not yet measured by the scientific method. Everything is determinable by these two values: 1 and 0. The Jains call this dialectical dilemma *anekāntavāda*, a multiplicity of perspective which can't be held to any singular truth. How do you weigh this? How do you cope with inevitable ineffability?

Then, the universe says sod to hesitation when it wants something out of you, reaches down with a grubby hand and takes hold—splitting way that Mulligan takes hold and doesn't let go. His strength is astonishing! I can't break free. Fist closed around my collar and I am being pulled away, dragged to a place against my will – this is starting to become habit. He moves so fast their wide eyes fade into hazy blips. They are frozen in shock.

"Gregor!" Ramona hollers.

The cry of the damsel fades, I am the one in distress. I have been kidnapped by a raging lunatic that is the king of conspiracy theorists. He speeds out the door, throws me into a white unmarked van (the calling sign of either revolt or plumbing) For some reason, all I can do is follow limply along. Is it submission? Curiosity, mainly. He turns on the van with a grumble, slams on the gas and drives me through the Plaza on a Monday night singing "Go Tell 'em on the Mountain!"

11 – Ferrules Rendezvous (or Tipping Point)

It's very simple what happens next: *the veil finally lifts.*

"New rules," he roars, throwing the steering wheel left then right. "We gonna visit the junky gonna get you a better know-how!" Van comes to a screeching halt, look out the window. St. Luke's hospital, a health conglomerate with offices and facilities all over the metro. A parking garage off J.C. Nichols Parkway, the entire block seems to be under construction and I am bombarded with yellow streamers, torn up concrete, orange barrels giving warnings.

"Don't like these systems," he says.

I default to the laziest option: go with it. If I fight the bastard and take off now, I have a few miles to get back to Ramona and Lena and still deal with the possibility that Benjamin may in fact be Dominator scum. Find out what this is about, then contact Lena and Ramona. Find out if they're okay. Rescue . . . yeah . . . an unhinged Dick Tracy . . . sure thing. Bottom line, find out what this is about. Always the bottom line.

"Room 315" he says, in resolute pose. "I'll man the vehicle, Dedalus." Who is the fucking guy? There's no shrug about this. Follow the dominos. Follow the white . . .

I saunter through the entrance – nothing going on here – dodging gray patients in wheelchairs and frantic nurses fighting disease. St. Luke's is connected to the University, so there are oblivious students wandering around in scrubs trying to find people of authority (gotta know what dose to give 'em doctor, yellow stuff is coming out) looking forlorn in the endless white hallways. The air is sterile and stale. I take the elevator to the third floor with an old lady in a nightgown who is smiling at the floor. She mumbles something about flowers as the doors ooze open with a ping. Another hallway revealed, just as frantic and white. I pour out and look for 315. Bump into a few nurses and it doesn't take very long.

Stare at the plastic room number plaque. Stomach clenches. Whoa! Is that *fear*? No, a Tarot Fool . . . edge of a cliff, one foot on, one foot off. *One foot, two, one foot, two.* Imagine what the Fool must be feeling, teetering on the edge of a free fall, on the edge of the bitter unknown?

Breathe, one two . . .

First bed is a man somewhere in his eighties. He smells of urine and has not shaved in weeks. He eyes me coldly, bangs his call button against bed side-rail and screams, "Nurse! Nurse! I'm in pain! I'm in pain! Gimmie a drip! For the love of hillbilly Jesus, gimmie a drip! Nurse!!!"

Stunned, no time to respond to the berserker yelping . . . a portly woman with kitten-covered scrubs and long red nails waddles in behind me.

"Jus' a minute, Mr. Lewis. Jus' a minute. Damn!"

Her massive bottom sways in mushy teeter-totter over to the man's IV and begins to push buttons on the regulating panel.

"I don't want *yer* fat-ass! I want the REAL nurse! NURSE!!!!"

"Now, shaddup now, Mr. Lewis! That' no way ta treat someone try'n ta help yo' self," she suggests patronizingly. She suddenly notices me for the first time. "Oh! Hello shugah! I didn't see you come in. Can I do someth'n for ya?" Her teeth shine with gold fillings.

"I'm . . . I'm here to see . . ."

I look over to the next bed and I see him. Glucose fusion in topographical form. Inept, head rolled back, fully unconscious. I recognize him instantly from Saturday . . . the man sitting next to me from *Town Topic*! George! There is conspiracy afoot!

"I'm here to see *him*, Mr. Stransky."

"Well, he's right over there in Bed Two, honey. I'll get Mr. Lewis' morphine a'goin' so's he won't be bother'n you all. Out like a light!"

"Thanks," I wave and walk to the other side of the room.

"Just push tha' button on tha' bedside if you needs anythins, okay baby?"

He lies there transfigured as a pariah. A plethora of tubes and wires unfurling from beeping machines insert themselves into his arms, nose, penis, and mouth. What god could be so willing to make mortality so cruel? His make of environment a dark pool comprised of complex instruments and devices of torture, keeping the spark of life just that . . . a spark. Swirl in the vortex of black tech. I feel stupid. What's happening here? What am I supposed to be doing? I can't speak to someone with a tube the size of a boa sticking out of his throat. George's eyes flicker from side to side between Mr. Lewis and the window. Can he even see me? What exactly is happening to him? Think about getting the nurse and finding out what is going on behind those twitching eyes, but need to keep low and off the radar. If the Dominators are out, then everything I have ever speculated is true.

And that is terrifying.

"Mr. Stransky, can you hear me?" Stupid. What's he supposed to do? Blink twice for yes? A hovering pause floats into the air with his name on it. The machines seem to stop blinking. Breath stops floating.

"He cannot, if the option is to receive your sound." Turn! Source from the corner – say a thanksgiving prayer – there is the other (O) in the dark, illuminating like a spook light in oddest angle of the room – fitting out – it is the small yellowish man, grinning with wide lemur eyes like the surreal character from Keel's story – Propit Cold, smiling at me. I don't feel threatened, oddly; though I position myself as an edged cat. Propit is here!

"What's going on?" I ask him point-blank, jump to the shot.

He is so still I wonder if he's even real, some static image formed by the dim lampshade lightening. Then, the mouth moves again: "His sound is off. I am in the process, past, of vibrating him to be so again. I am got it on again. See? There are more."

"Off, you mean, he . . . he's a vegetable. And, what are you, anyway?"

"Answer cannot be forthcoming in yet," he grins.

"Is that so? You have to give me a cryptic riddle to do crosswords over, is that it?"

"Not riddles to be feasible," he nods toward the door. "We two of us are engaged in yes, in confrontation first."

I look and, no shitting, some burly Middle Eastern brute is hovering in the threshold, wearing a tunic piece with hieroglyphics on the skirt. Not shitting! There is an emerald pigment to his skin, eyes are completely empty though he stares at me, through, into me. He towers, sloped forehead touching the top of the doorway. My mammalian senses are driving fully a force inside my blood, adrenal glands extract – fight or flight kicks in – oxygen and glucose thrive in my brain. Muscles tightening. He might as well be a wolf – more a bear – eyeing a threat, ready to eradicate. Hands form at his sides as if he had claws. Ready to spring.

And then, an explosive red . . . streak, throws the brute to the side in the hallway.   Slamming and crashes. Peer back over to the corner and Propit is gone. Not alone for long, squishing of heels gets my attention and something has entered the room. Spin and it's . . . the red . . . the red man . . . -er, woman. It's a woman. Athletic build, medium height. Single-breasted suit coat and pants, all in a deep venetian red. Blouse and boots in black, matching color shades covering soft apricot face and sepia hair cropping down to her pointed chin. She walks to me in sage elegance. Extends a hand.

"Gregor Samson, I'm here to rescue you," she quips. "Again."

Can't even find a compulsion to deny that. We skitter out into the hallway. On one side, near the elevators, the massive, sinewy brute is inching up from a hell of a knock-down. She did *that*? Shaking stars from its head, it looks up directly at us in a new face of intense fury. Nurses and patients are scattering away, screaming, aware of the violence on hand.

"Move," the woman in red points in the opposite direction. At the end of the hallway, the emergency stairs. "Run!"

I race down the hall, her directly behind me – away from the massive Middle Easterner that I can now feel stomping toward us in a sprint – *feel* – the floor shakes and feet are unsteady. Fear gnarls its mangy claws around my intestines. I push forward, each foot pumping, straining harder and faster than the other.

Through my peripherals I watch the woman in red behind me – every few steps she grabs an extraneous object (a syringe on a cart, a clipboard hanging from a patient's door) and turns them into functional missile projectiles. Syringe shoots like a bullet out from her wrist, clipboard a shot put – the skill and precision – turning these miscellaneous objects into lethal weapons! The syringe needle sticks into the brute's blank eye. There is no blood. He does not flinch. The clipboard chucks into his muscular deltoid. Again no blood. He barrels forward, unnoticing. A few other items dart from her hands as she swiftly trails behind me, while the whopping giant deflects them like solid rock. I see her pull out a round object from her jacket – look closer – it's a fucking *grenade*! She pulls the pin and lever releases.

"Jump down the stairs!" She cries out to me. "NOW!!!"

Before I even have a chance to act on the directive, she pushes me down the emergency stairwell. In a millisecond free-fall, my elbow is the first thing to impact the concrete steps. A propulsion of air thrusts itself against me and maelstrom lunges my body further down the flight of stairs – ears go numb – searing explosion rips throughout the narrow corridor. My body tumbles helplessly to the bottom, two flights. The woman in red's body must have taken the brunt of the effect, we land in a heap – like limp marionettes. Smoke and dust linger everywhere

– there are screams from above and all around, alarms and sprinklers are going off. Spray of distilled water drenches us from above – she raises her head, moaning slightly.

"I hate using those things," she wiggles her head slightly and pushes herself up, offering a hand to me for assistance. I accept. "Time to go."

Out of the shambles of wall a hazy form inches through dripping dust clouds – the brute leans against broken brick and looks out beyond the explosive fog. Half of his head completely gone, but no blood or skeletal structure – insides parallel to the rock wall beside, a mass of greenish stone crumbling into pebbles scattering onto the stairs. He limps slowly to the staircase.

"That's a *thing*," I point in confounded astonishment. "And it's still alive."

"It's a *shabti*. Fuck . . . I know who's in town now," she states coldly. She reaches into her jacket and pulls out another grenade. Looks at me through black shades and nudges me to the lobby door. "Go."

The explosion shoots me through the door, into the lobby. Elbows scraped, feel salt on my lip. Shards of concrete, drywall, and dust spew out onto the tiled floor. My ears ringing – senses discombobulated, incessant buzz. People are running around, screaming, frantically racing out the front door – panicked sheep in a horde, tripping over each other, shoving down the cripples. Hands grab me and pull me up with exceptional strength, the woman in red brushes a blot of muddy dust off my backpack. "Fun, right?" she chuckles. "That should've done it."

"Hold it," a steel barrel is in my face. Portly security guard is shaking, sweat beads speckling his face. His legs are spread apart in action movie stance – I look over at woman in red, she is completely still. "Don't move, you degenerate shits, or I'll pump you with 9 millimeter Parabellum bitches! Understand?!?!?"

"Of course," woman in red calmly answers. I am crazed and scared like hell of sitting in a jail cell for guilt by association. As I'm about to shit myself from panic – a cloud of sand puffs into the air and red flips my eyes, pulls me away quicker than reflexes. Choking and gagging, when her red arm uncovers my face, the security guard is on the ground, pterodactyl scream, clawing at his eyes in pure ferocity – the gun is kicked away. Jonah stands behind him in his wild coats and patches, pouring a stream of the sand into a velvet pouch and stuffs it into one of his many layers.

"Make haste, Dedalus," he elbows me and winks. "'*Dublin's burning! Dublin's burning! On fire, on fire!*' Ha, ha!" He darts to a hallway in the lobby leading to the parking garage. People still piling outside and gathering in confused crowds on the sidewalk out front, on their cell phones, probably calling emergency dispatchers. Calling the authorities.

The woman in red turns to me with a charming smirk. "Want to join the Insurgency, don't you?" And takes off after Jonah. It doesn't take me a moment to think about it and follow. History is a nightmare. Time to wake up.

WWN Headline Hour

Commentator Jon O'Maley: ". . . according to the U.N. report, the death toll is rising. And now, we go to our hot topic, the moment everybody has been waiting for . . . our exclusive interview with America's favorite pop star! Success for this young sweetheart has been booming with her latest album release: 'Rump Me, Boop'. It's hit the top of the charts nationwide, even making record sales in Japan. Ladies and gentlemen, Bobbi Dakota!"

Bobbi Dakota: "Thanks Jon!"

O'Maley: "Now, Bobbi . . . the question everybody is waiting for . . . a *girl*friend?"

Dakota: "Ha, ha! That's right, Jon. I feel like a person is a person no matter how they are on the outside, knowwhatImean? Like, I believe in a person's *soul*, yaknow? Just because she's a girl doesn't mean I can't find, like, my one true person to be with, right?"

O'Maley: "So, where did this come from? Were you naturally this way, even though you were dating Kevin Florentino of the N-Street Boyz last year? Or, did you just wake up one day and say, 'Hey, I think I'll give girls a try'?"

Dakota: "You know, it was kinda, like, an evolution thing, right? So, I've always had this *connection*, with the female gender, yaknow? Girl power, ha! But, seriously, like there's this deep . . . connection, youknowwhatImean? And, you know, with all the craziness that went down with Kevin, which godblessmyfansIloveyoucouldn'thavemadeitthroughwithoutallof you which was kinda crazy, and . . . you know, Zeff and I just kinda clicked."

O'Maley: "Zeff Maxima, the star of 'Everyone's Friend'?"

Dakota: "Right. We met each other, um, when I did that single 'Love Cares' for one of their episodes. I visited the set and she was, like, *so* sweet, youknow? We just, like, totally hit off like best buds and then, you know, it just grew into something more."

O'Maley: "Now, being America's favorite singer, 75% of your fan base belongs to the conservative Christian sector of the country. There is a rising concern among analysts that there may be some discontent considering you are now engaged in a lesbian relationship. Do you have anything to say about this? Anything you want to say to your fans?"

Dakota: "Absolutely, Jon. I want everyone to know that, you know, it's not gay, really, to be lesbian. And, like, my pastor has cleared this and everything, because it's just in the Bible about gay guys. So, like, women, it's okay. So, I just want everyone to know, right, all of my adoring fans whoIabsolutelyloveyouarethebest that, like, Jesus Christ is totally my Savior. I am, like, *so* dedicated to my faith and, like, love going to church and stuff. So, I just want everybody to know that, right?"

O'Maley: "Bobbi . . . wait, I can call you Bobbi right?"
Dakota: "Absolutely Jon!"

O'Maley: "Great, thanks . . . Bobbi there's a lot of turmoil going on the world, as I'm sure you know. The wars in Yemen, Pakistan, Iraq, and Syria. The sub-prime mortgage crisis, people losing their homes. Fans want to know how you feel about our current situation."

Dakota: "Okay, first and foremost, I want people to know that, like, I am just like everybody else, knowwhatImean? I am, like, totally just an average girl and, like, totally just live a normal life. I have friends and family, like anyone else, youknow? So, I want people to know, right, that I feel their pain. Like, I know what you're going through. That's why I hope, like, you know, my music can help inspire people, you know? Bring 'em outta tough times. And also, like the wars and stuff? Like, this is *the greatest* country in the world! I mean, there is no other country that, like, has the freedoms we do. And, I am so totally for supporting our President, because, like, right now is when he needs us to support him when he's trying to, like, protect us from people who hate us just because, you know, we're free and . . . and have music and cheeseburgers and baseball and stuff. I mean, these terrorists hate us for this, so like, I totally respect our servicemen and women and, like, we totally need to be supporting our President and the decisions he's making to keep us from harm, so, like, another 9-11 doesn't happen again."

O'Maley: "So true. By the way, Bobbi, I love the song on your new album, 'Rump, Rump, Rump Me Up'. That song is so *ill*."

Dakota: "Oh yeah, 'Rump me twice, Rump me thrice, I gotta gotta gotta, boom boom, rump me all the way baaaabbbyyy.' That song was inspired by a really deep committed relationship I had with an L.A. gang member in 6th Grade."

O'Maley: "Well, it's awfully inspiring, I love it. Bobbi Dakota, I want to thank you for coming on here and chatting with us. You've definitely brightened up our day!"

Dakota: "Thank you Jon!"

O'Maley: "Bobbi Dakota, you can catch her new album in stores everywhere and available for download on the internet. Coming up next . . . College Sex Orgies: Should they be allowed? Coming up next after a word from our sponsors."

12 – Atelier Y

The drive from the hospital is a carnival asylum. I'm a bit confused.

"I'm a bit confused," I tell them.

Mulligan, the mad Ahab, is grappling the steering wheel, veering in and out of traffic at fanatical speeds. He runs stoplight after stoplight; I watch behind, heart drum beats pounding, waiting for the howling sirens of the heat locking on to our scent. His eyes are bloodshot and fanatic.

"Don't worry," the woman in red assures. I am sitting in the back with her as she lounges in nonchalance. "The heat's already on our sniff. Rest assured . . . you're an enemy combatant now."

We escape the city streets and bullet onto the interstate. Mulligan slows to seventy and we coast down 435 listening to "Send Me No Wine" from Moody Blues' *On the Threshold of a Dream* on a cassette tape. Mulligan sings along.

I look at the red woman in bewilderment: "What happened to the guard?"

She looks behind us. "Axe. A necrotoxin I developed for Jonah's use. The sandy composition comes from mixing it with silicon dioxide, of course. Very effective deterrent."

"Will he be okay?"

"It quickly devours living cells wherever the silica touches, which is why you see Jonah wearing gloves in August. The rate of the toxin is rapid and violent, it's quite painful. Whether he'll survive or not . . . well, he's in a hospital isn't he?"

"I have a problem with that. He's an innocent. Just doing his job."

"You have a problem with that? An innocent?" Calloused tone. "He's wearing a *badge*. This is a *war*, Gregor Samson. Nothing personal against him, but *war is war*. We have a mission and he was in our way."

"And that rock thing?"

"Oh, that? A golem, an ancient automaton. That was nothing. Speaking of which . . . Jonah, Spring-heeled Jack's here! We gotta call in Aztalan and get the whole damn armada into K.C.!"

"Christ in Baghdad," Jonah sputters over the dashboard, hopping on the edge of his seat. "You shitt'n me? Means we got NO time!"

"What do you mean mission," I squeeze myself into a crunch, hugging my backpack and its contents. Grasping my bearings and my own little reality. I feel my limbs trembling, not just from the van, but from the trauma ensued from the action behind us. "What mission?"

"You'll see," she turns coolly ahead to watch the highway before us. "The name is Darwin, by the way. Pleased to meet you."

"Yeah, likewise."

The undulating hum of the engine throttles into a roar, the entire vehicle reverberates from Jacob's sudden acceleration . . . I assume due to the news of the *shabti* and what this Darwin calls "Spring-heeled Jack." We turn off onto 87th Street and swing a right on Hillcrest. We approach a sight of remote antiquity, the deadland block of Bannister. A circus of consumerist paradise in the 1980s, Bannister Mall and the surrounding area was the number one place to be for shopping and entertainment from hundreds of miles around. For the secluded Midwest, it was an alien world of fantasy candy: Musicland, KB Toys, Mr. Bulky's, Orange Julius, Saturday Matinee, Big Al's, and on and on. It was enough to make any seven year-old swoon with elation; I remember it fondly.

Now . . . the residents of the area weren't prepared for the inner city migration and rise in crime. White Flight began. The surrounding rural areas blossomed with outdoor shopping plazas and west coast monopolies – the white people moved out. Urban families made intense efforts to move their children further away from the inner city, in hopes their little progeny wouldn't be infested with erratic gang culture. But, little did they understand that Reagonomics is a one-way street. When the middle class moves out so do the jobs – when the jobs go away, the payday loans and liquor stores move in. It's a poverty effect – a rapid sociological infection. What was a childhood metropolis became a dilapidated wasteland of sheer and utter desolation. Couple of years ago, the city voted to close the Mall completely – now it is a monolith structure hugging the plateau over the interstate, boarded and electrically shut down . . . it reminds the world, passing by on the highway below, just how far a once-fine community had slipped away so quickly.

The adjacent areas surrounding the Mall are just as desolate. What used to be shopping plazas and supercenters is now nothing but a collection of skeletal buildings, monuments to a dead culture. The surrounding hotels, once sporting modern American nuclear family tourists with cameras and matching t-shirts, now have hourly rates.

We pull into a parking lot, tufts of grass sprouting up out of aged cracks in the worn concrete. Mulligan speeds toward the long, brown two-story manse that used to be the Mall proper, the lot ringing around the building like an anesthetic moat – he whips the van into a small express tunnel on the side. An old merchandise pick-up for a department store.

A garage ahead, Mulligan pushes an opener on his sun visor and it rises. He sludges in and the door wiggles jaggedly down behind us. Van off – they pile out and I follow.

Mulligan slaps me on the back like a pirate: "Come on, Dedalus."

Through a small storage area, we enter the inner halls of the department store. Clothes racks everywhere, most of them bare – a few dangling articles hanging forlorn like old toilet paper on autumn trees. An acrid smell, dry and pungent – the sewer must have backed up at some point, calcifying over the summer. Pieces of paper – credit tape, receipts, flyers – litter the ground in a mosaic of rubbish; we skitter around until we make our way out of the store and into the mall itself.

The inner sanctum of the mall is divested, barren – huge skylights overhead pour natural light into the hallways, dust circling in the emitted rays – abandoned stores, caged and aphotic – benches lining the hallway, mediums replete with jungles of plastic dust-covered plants. We rush past lifeless escalators frozen in a better time – eerie silence. This place is haunted with shattered memories, a forbidden landscape neglected and destitute. Bannister Mall is a graveyard.

We enter a utility closet and shut it behind us, Mulligan motions to the wall on the other side of the cramped space. The paneling opens into another, darker corridor. We go in and Darwin closes the paneling behind us. We follow a set of spiraling stairs down into the darkness. A small tuff of light splits the dark below.

"Home," Darwin states.

Bottom of the staircase ends at a small doorway, pale blue light emanating. We step through to a large commodious space – dimly lit by the bluish light from some computer monitors and other equipment on the other side of the area. Illuminating flickering disorienting. It is a cavern, split into two main cul-de-sacs: one to my left, the other straight ahead (source of the flickering monitors). The walls are covered in wires, piping, and ducts spider-webbing to the monitors. To my right, a florid velvet curtain – another room possibly behind it – directly in front of the curtain sits a few suede couches and mattresses covered in books and blankets.

"I need some thorazine," Mulligan stomps into the chamber at the left.

"Welcome to Atelier Y, Gregor," Darwin walks into the antechamber, empties her pockets on a nearby table. "Prominent RED safe house for the K.C. Metro area. My sanctuary."

"Am I being kidnapped?" Despite my swirling confusion, I already calculated the answer to this question. However, my curiosity needs to be quelled – it is a good way to stimulate conversation.

"Ha!" Mulligan shuffles forward, with a syringe in hand. He eloquently takes off his outer three jackets and holds them aloft with a Shakespearean expression. "'*Mulligan is stripped of his garments*'. The Dubliner gives me voice." He drops them to the floor and plops down onto a couch, dust flecking in the air. He is much skinnier without all the layers. He rolls up a cashmere sweater to a thin, veiny forearm. He pulls out a tourniquet and begins to tie. "You aint' bein' kidnapped, junky. You bein' recruited."

"Into what exactly?"

"Into RED," Darwin leans against a puffy chair, springs bulging from its cushion. "You discovered us, Gregor. Not many people are able to see through the cracks, where we hide. Because of that, we want to offer you a position. There needs to be a counter to the Nova Enterprise. That's what we do."

"Hold on . . . *nova*! That's what you called my sister's boyfriend, Bloom . . . -er, Jonah."

Mulligan sticks a needle in a bulging vein, plunger ooze down the barrel clear liquid. His eyes flutter: "That's right . . . can't you see?"

"See what? What's Benjamin got to do with any of this?"

Darwin unties her boots, slips them off. "This guy . . . 'Benjamin' . . . works for the Enterprise. You call them the Dominators, the Elite. Jonah's referring to the writer William S. Burroughs' Nova terminology. RED refers to *them* as such."

The immediacy of the moment curls into aboulia apprehension. I must have stumbled, or flushed – Darwin steps forward and places a reassuring hand on me.

"It's okay. He's just a contractor. CIA. Probably just watching at this point, a walking surveillance camera. Most likely, he was there for Jonah. But, through casually unrelated events coalescing simultaneously in a single event . . . here you are."

"Not completely unrelated. *I* was there for Jonah."

Mulligan leans back on the couch, eyes closed, gone limp: "Aye . . . junkies! They found a weak spot. Two birds, one stone. I shoulda ripped his head open and served punch!"

"So, Lena and Ramona, I gotta call them."

Darwin shakes her head vehemently. "No! Phones, emails aren't safe. They'll find us. And we already have Jack on our tail. He'll catch our scent soon . . . we're going to need to relocate soon."

I'm not satisfied with that answer, but I let it slide for now. Since they are offering so much information, I'll keep baiting. Darwin walks over to the monitor lighting. I stand there with Mulligan near unconscious.

"So, who's this Jack character then?" I ask.

His head pops up, eyes Propit-wide. "Ha, ha! Isn't that a ripe, ripe one?" He chuckles, flings himself up, throws an arm around me in comrade fashion and ushers me to the room on the left. The chamber is smaller than the foyer, full of book cases with stacks of books on the floor – a table sits on the edge covered in maps and blueprints. Mulligan saunters over to the table and reaches behind it, pulling out a cylinder tank from an entire row. He picks up a mask and hose attached, placing the oral-nasal plastic mask over his face – twists the pressure gauge on the tank – checking the flow meter and tapping it, he smiles a great sigh. "That's the shit!"

"What's that?"

"Oxygen, what else? Old junky like me . . . all that excitement's gonna kill me dead." Breathes in, out. Breathes in, out. Heave. "So, Jack . . . Spring-heeled Jack. Boy, if you ain't shakin' in your shit then you're as ignorant as any of the other fucking zombies in this city. Spring-heeled Jack is direct from the Nova Police, an Agent of the Enterprise. Like a RED Agent. He ain't much of the mortal stock . . . practitioner of the Other, though, you know? Really bad, bad Arts."

"You mean supernatural? You and Darwin, you guys are . . ."

Mulligan, heaving: "No, no! Well, *she's* an Agent. I ain't. Jus' try'n to help. An ally. I came into town when you started noticin' certain things, when we been chatt'n. You found RED, boy, so I had to intervene and find out was going on. Ain't nobody notice a RED Agent unless someth'n big going down. You in the Underground now, boy. *Xibalba be*. Heh, hehe!"

"So, what's Spring-heeled Jack up to? Is he the boss of the *shabti* at the hospital? Is he after us?"

Mulligan flings the tank over his shoulder: "Let's go find out, Dedalus." Why does he keep calling me that? He walks to the larger cavern and I follow – to the light emitting monitors. As we get closer, the light reveals what I couldn't see from the foyer: a massive machine, nothing like I have ever seen before. Despite a work-bench and spare metal parts to the side, all of the wires and piping center into the amazing contraption. Polar parts, smaller and resembling miniature computer stations, sit on either side of one larger central component – looks like an alien nuclear generator from a 1940's science fiction film: upper portions replete with monitors creating the majority of the light in the entire cave, newsreels, internet pages, images of home movies, even cartoons; lower portions resemble buzzing lights and circuit boards amalgamated together in a mechanized world I could never understand. At the very center of the machine sits a pocket with a seat, inner walls of the pod glowing with chartreuse fluorescence.

Darwin sits in the seat, cross-legged on the chair in a meditative position. Her head is covered by an automated helmet – bleeping with video game chirps – connected to accordion hoses trailing into the larger machine.

"Already they have covered their mess," she says.

Jonah points to a screen above: a news clip of the St. Luke's hospital scene, emergency vehicles, people crying, smoke columns wafting into the city skyline. News man with carpet toupee screaming about the (in)humanity of it all.

I stare at the insectoid helmet on her head. "What is all this?"

"I call her Mahamaya. My own attempt at a Connection Machine mock-up of a miniaturized matrioshka brain run with nanoscale computronium, to put it simply. She's a model Class C-type stellar engine I manufactured on a molecular level. Instead of solar energy as fuel, I use morphic resonances and magnetic fields. She powers the entire place, Atelier Y. She is also its *mind*."

"Like, *my* morphic field? Auras, you mean?"

"Not particularly, no. Time is no factor for Mahamaya, more so even than me. She feeds from electro-magnetic imprints from the past. Lately, she's inhaling out of 1764, when the Spanish had control of the area. Still fairly wild. Lots of natural energy."

Mulligan inhales deeply: "It's a shamanic super-computer, boy. Connecting to the internet of *consciousness*."

"Back to the subject at hand," Darwin does not share Mulligan's buoyancy. "Homeland Security has been notified. Their dubbing our confrontation and appearance as a terrorist attack on the United States. The President will be making a statement soon. The population will be distracted. An acuminous increase in fear and anxiety. We can expect sudden and erratic Defense legislation and psychological break – Nova warfare at its most potent. Plus, that bastard Jack is in town and most likely sniffing us out. I can't take him alone. We need Aztalan."

"Then by the shitless gods, woman," Mulligan stomps. "Call 'em!"

"Only through Mahamaya, but I need you two to step away and give me a moment."

"Wait," I interrupt. "So, they're saying *we* attacked the hospital?"

"Absolutely," she answers with casual certainty. "That's what they do, Gregor."

"I don't understand . . . what are we going to do? What about Lena and Ramona? What about—" Delineation of the I in check. Delineation of the I in check. When you feel that thing crawling up your brain stem in handcuff tickle, seize a canister of oxygen from a raging Neanderthal and inhale like you've never inhaled before.

—Alice, she is

Get a grip, remember medicine is in my bag. Have my backpack. Pull out and pop a Lorazepam. Ease it down, plenty of saliva.

Mulligan pats my back. "Get a grip, Dedalus! *'History is a nightmare'*, boy. Time to wake up!"

Didn't I just say that?

Darwin sits there in her mantis helm of Christmas light spectacle, a wicked Hindi goddess of disco and illuminated acid: "He's right, Gregor. You wanted the veil to be lifted. Now it's here. Get ready for it. The Nova Enterprise, the Dominator Elite controlling and dominating this planet, wants to declare war. Well, they have it. And we will deliver. They think *that's* a terrorist attack? Just wait, Gregor Samson. RED is garnering itself – we will open their arteries and they will bleed red. This is an assault of mediocrity, on the ordinary. The Way of the Weird is upon us! Commence for Paradigm Shift!"

Radioactive ceremonies with monkeys. Heeding the call . . . magick, serpents, and spies. Heeding the call of the delineation of the I – in CHECK.

Welcome to the 21st Century Boston Tea Party.

This nation needs a neurological facelift.

13 – Gregor Samson Pushes Himself

Gregor Samson pushes himself up and out of the dilapidated couch, with its broken springs and pulverous stench. He couldn't stay asleep. It's hard to relax in the furor of hysteria. He cranes his head and scans the underground sanctum of the secret revolutionary organization that calls itself RED. Mulligan is splayed on a mattress nearby – his rugged breathing supported by a cylinder tank and tubing pumping oxygen into his aging lungs, his chest rising and falling like heaving tectonics. Darwin is nowhere to be seen – said she was going out.

So, he gets up, wanders around examining the lair below a ghost mall. Mechanized trinkets and obtuse wiring – miniature alcoves decorated with tin signs and bullet belts – cylinder tanks full of nitrus oxide and hydrogen – gas masks – and bookshelves with a variety of rare works: *Vorlesungen über neure Geometrie* by Moritz Pasch, *Operation* Chaos by Poul Anderson, a few graphic novel volumes of *The Invisibles* by Grant Morrison, *Phädon, or About Soul's Immortality* by Moses Mendelssohn, *On Future Motive Power* by Nikola Tesla, and *Enochia Tweaks* by Dorian Spare. He is entranced by how crinkled and yellowed they are.

He's drawn to the velvet curtain on his right. Walks over, glances at Mulligan to make sure he is sleeping, pulls open the hefty fabric and walks through.

Ultraviolet lighting lines the ceiling of a long, narrow corridor – by far the largest chamber in what Darwin calls Atelier Y. Plants of all varieties populate the sides, steaming ambrosial scents – basil and dill and cone flowers and lemon grass – an entire greenhouse of flora and vegetation under the ground with UV lights buzzing above. Gregor scratches his head . . . *how*?

He pulls out his phone, quick dial to Ramona. Phone to ear, he strolls through the subterranean botanical garden. It rings. It rings.

Pick up.

Ramona: "Gregor?"

Gregor: "Hi. You guys okay?"

Ramona: "Gregor, where are you? What's going on?"

Gregor: "Is Lena there? You guys okay?"

Ramona: "Her and Benjamin are here. We're at my apartment wondering what happened to you . . . did that guy kidnap you? What's going on?"

Gregor: "No, I'm fine. I'm fine. He didn't . . . that was just . . . so, Benjamin's still there?"

Ramona: "Yeah, he really freaked on poor Benjamin! Nice way for someone to be introduced to our group, huh? What was his deal, is he crazy?"

Gregor: "He's *still* with you guys?"

Ramona: "Yes, Gregor. What's wrong? He and Lena are sitting on the couch having a cigarette. We were going to call the police if we didn't hear from you by morning."

Gregor: "Listen, Ramona. Don't trust him. Don't talk to him."

Ramona: "What?"

Gregor: "Just listen, please. Look . . . there's some stuff happening. Have you seen the news?"

Ramona: "You mean the hospital? Gregor, what's going—."

Gregor: "Just . . . please . . . all of this stuff. Alice, Lawrence attacking us, the red . . . just, you need to get away from this Benjamin guy. He's not what he seems, at least . . . I think. Ask him to go home, have Lena stay with you, until I can figure out what's going on here. I'll call you when I figure out what to do, okay?"

Ramona: "Gregor, this is crazy. What are you talking about?"

Gregor: "*Please*, just trust me! Okay? Just trust me!"

Ramona: "Okay . . . fine. I will. Okay, I'll do it. But, will you please come by tomorrow and tell us what's going on?"

Gregor: "I'll . . . I can't promise . . . I'll try."

Ramona: "I love you, Gregor. I really do. Your sister does too. We worry about you."

Gregor: "I'll be in touch."

Click the button—hang up.

Quick dial to Kathleen. Phone to the ear, he rubs his fingers on a lamb's ear leaf. It rings. It rings. It rings. It rings. It rings. It rings. It rings. It rings.

Pick up.

Kathleen: "Umph . . . h-hello?"

Gregor: "Hey. It's me."

Kathleen: "Who?"

Gregor: "Me . . . Gregor."

Kathleen: "What the . . . Gregor? You . . . you realize it's after *midnight*?"

Gregor: "Is it? Oh, I uh—"

Kathleen: "What the hell do you want?"

Gregor: "Um, sorry . . . I didn't realize it was that late."

Kathleen: "Some people gotta work in the morning."

Gregor: "Right, yeah . . . I know. Sorry, I just . . . I wanted . . . is Alice there?"

Kathleen: "*What*?"

Gregor: "Alice . . . is she there? I just . . . you know—"

Kathleen: "Are you *kidding* me? Don't you know she's *seven years-old*? Do you even *think* she'd be up right now on a *Tuesday night*? What fucking world do you *live* in?"

Gregor: "Um . . . I wanna . . . I wanna talk to her. Just talk. I know it's late and—"

Kathleen: "Damn right it's late and I'll be damned if *my* daughter's gonna get woken up in the middle of the night to talk to some swept-up baby-daddy!"

Gregor: "Kathy, I pay my support . . . it's enough you deprive me of my weekends, all I want is to just—"

Kathleen: "Ha! Right, you wanna make issue out of weekends? Wanna go to back to court? I got me ten witnesses that say you've had the opportunity to spend time with Alice and then gave it up to—"

Gregor: "That's bullshit and you know it! You wanna talk about court? It's called joint *legal* custody . . . I'll use my legal right to come down there and pick her up—"

Kathleen: "Go ahead and try it, asshole! You'll have another restraining order on your ass in a second and police knocking on your door asking about the bruises on my neck! Don't forget Jeremy's dad is a cop—"

Gregor: "Yeah, how's he like fathering *my* child? Does it irk him to know *I'm* the one who knocked you up and not him?"

Kathleen: . . . silence . . .

Gregor: "I just want to talk to my daughter. I know it's late, I've had kind of an emergency—"

Kathleen: "Fuck you. Just so you know, she calls him 'daddy' now. He rocks her to sleep every night, because *she* wants him to."

There is a sickness inside every one of us, festers and eats away at deep parts inside the marrow and red blood cells affects the very fabric of the life we hold so dear. Something fatal and chronic. Something full of shameful flavors and filled with stifling throttle going down.

Gregor: "You fucking whore . . ."

Kathleen (laughs): "You're still *so* emotionally involved. You just *so* wish it was *you* sticking your shit into me every night and not some muscle-bound *cock* that makes *twice* your salary, don't you? It's too bad, isn't it?"

Click the button – hang up. Shaking, asphyxiation. He needs some medicine. Quietly he downs more pills than he should, walks back out to the front antechamber. Mulligan is still asleep. Darwin is still nowhere to be found.

Quietly.

Quietly he snuggles into the shabby sofa, curls into a fetal position and closes his eyes. He thinks about Sahasrara for a second and then thinks "fuck it". He thinks instead, quietly, of his mother's warm breast and a rocking chair, baseball covered curtains, whippoorwills outside the window, and euphonious humming to old hymnals from a distant time.

He falls away.

The Soma Patch™

You know when you feel the weight of depression: you may feel anxiety, exhaustion, or even hopelessness.

Whatever you do you feel lonely, unloved, as you watch life being lived by others on the other side of that foggy window.

Things just don't feel like they used to.

You are not alone; depression is a disease, affecting over 20 million Americans each year. Depression occurs from a natural imbalance of chemicals exchanged between nerve cells in the brain.

You shouldn't have to feel different.

The Soma Patch™ works to restore this imbalance in your brain. Its artificially systemic neurotransmitters promote this restoration faster and easier than other leading anti-depressants. Unlike other leading anti-depressants, the Soma Patch™ is for everyone.*

You can feel like a part of society again. You feel a part of the whole.

The Soma Patch™, where the machine of body is #1.

Although Soma Patch™ is for everyone, pregnant women should be aware of coughing, vomiting, and the possibility of miscarriage. Children under 15 should be aware of consistent nightmares, fatigue, and symptoms of homicidal rage. If you are taking natural vitamin supplements, be aware of excessive and uncontrollable diarrhea. Consult your local doctor or pharmaceutical representative if these or other side effects occur.

14 – Ego Stigmata

Three other people and I are involved in a crime. We are holding guns to the heads of sleeping people. We are being chased by the police. Running. Get captured. Beaten, amnesiac handcuffs; sitting in confinement and I am alone. Bombs. Going off. Find the opportunity to escape and we are wanted, we split up.

I am taking refuge with some girl, long raven hair and suede. She helps me disguise myself and dresses me in a type of translucent plastic armor plasters it in pieces onto my skin, they are red and in the shape of flames. I am hopping roofs naked with plastic flames on my body.

Oh way and how this being nonsense is horrendous

proximate genus
specific difference
YHWH   OHM

breathe the Universe in to life – the invisible supports the invisible

A tree on an island in deep space, sparkling glitter floating like fireflies, it splits and opens – a man spills out stringy long scraggly hair and beard and a frock coat, looks like Ian Anderson and he says: "Hey, kid! Have you walked through the waking tree today?" And pulls out a flute and starts playing, the tones are reverberating inside of me tell me to celebrate my cognition – under the illusion of being in control, under the illusion of being in control, under the illusion of being . . .

* * * * *

"We are in a state of crisis. *Humanity*, we. It exists because there is no more capital to be gained from the exploitation of natural, spiritual, or social resources. We are out of ideas. There is nothing more to sell. Our planetary homeland has been butchered and is almost beyond repair. Every facet of our cultural heritage has been copyrighted. Our human relationships have deteriorated – we can no longer adequately express feelings and emotions beyond our consumer identity.

"There are places beyond 'developed' civilizations where this is realized. And in these societies there are pockets of resistance. Civilization calls this resistance 'terror' and, yes, there are those that seek the path that supports that falsity. It is possible, though, to fight back with the ideals of justice and liberty behind one's action. For, what happens when there is nothing left to sell, nothing left to take? What then? They will have our souls, our very spirit – and they will market them and charge interest and we will all be broke, homeless, and without a place to rest when we die. Do you understand?"

This is what I wake up to – Darwin perched like a gargoyle on the sofa, staring into me, droning in seismic wave mantras. She crouches over me in strike position. My eyes are puffy, full of crust.

"It's all about personality. If it can be thought, it can be done. Otherwise, the thoughts couldn't exist. That's how consciousness works, that's how the Universal Wave manifests itself. All from one thing. Tap into that, tap into all."

I sit up, shake off the sleep. "Really . . . can you give me a minute or two?"

"There is no time. No time to dawdle. No time at all. It doesn't exist. Your true power, truer than anything that can be given to you, is now. This moment."

"How long have you been going at this? While I've been sleeping?"

"Of course. Your brain will assimilate it anyway. Osmosis works as good as anything." She hops off the couch and nudges me toward Mahamaya. We pass by Mulligan sitting at a cracked dinner table off to the side eating instant oatmeal. He waves and munches.

We stand in front of the monitors together and she looks like a cyberpunk superhero scanning for trouble. She is still wearing red; sort of a trademark for the brand, I wager.

"Look," she points. WWN screen. The President of the United States is walking out of the oval office and to a podium at the White House. His face pasty, perfectly toned. I see a blemish of make-up on his collar. He braces the stand with both hands and addresses a volume of cameras and microphones before him:

"Good morning. I come before the American people today with distressing news. Last night, at approximately 10 o'clock in the evening, a hospital in Kansas City, Missouri, was the target of a fatal and cowardly terrorist attack within U.S. borders. Unfortunately, this target was successful on the part of the terrorists, claiming 16 lives, including patients and guards on duty. As well, twenty-two others were wounded. This is a terrible tragedy and the United States is ready to respond. Authorities are on the scene, tending to the wounded and gathering intelligence. Our hearts and prayers go out to all the families of the victims of this vicious crime.

"We have reason to believe this attack on innocent civilians was implemented by a domestic cell of terrorists operating within the United States. This cell, we believe, is strongly linked to Al-Qaeda. This is a shocking reminder that our freedoms are under attack by religious extremists, and these extremists will be hunted down and dealt with by the *fullest* force of the law. I ask the American people to be diligent. We *cannot* let the terrorists win. Keep an eye out for suspicious activity and report it to your local authorities. We are doing everything we can to ensure the safety of the American people. We will do whatever it takes to bring these criminals to justice. I've just met with Mr. Burnham at the Federal Bureau of Investigation and he assures me that they will be working around the clock, tapping every resource, to find out how this disaster happened on our own soil.

"This is America. We believe in *peace* and *freedom* and *liberty*. We *will* protect these God-given rights, and we *will* promote these ideals across the globe. Again, we are reminded of the justification of the wars in Iraq and Afghanistan, among others. We *must* fight the terrorists on *their* soil, so they cannot come to ours. Any resistance to the fight against terrorism will be met with consequence. Now is the time for patriotism, not ambivalence or questioning. We *must* come together, through *bipartisan* efforts, as *one* people. Standing *united* against those who would harm us because we are *free*.

"Now, I know this comes at a time when our economy is on the brink of catastrophe. Americans are worried. Believe me, I *feel* your pain. But, I urge *all* Americans to remain vigilant. Patience is needed. We are a nation of *greatness*. We *will* pull through, because that is what Americans *do*. We pull up our sleeves and do what it takes. I *believe* in America. Above all, I believe in the American *people*. There is *no* greater source for good in the world.

"God bless you all."

He nods. There's a smirk on his face. A racket of cameras clicking, bulbs flashing, and raised hands. He points to someone in the front row.

"Jessica."

"Mr. President, a few days ago apparently there was an incident in Kansas City where a group of people were knocked unconscious simultaneously in a restaurant downtown, leading to one hospitalization. There's speculation this may possibly have been an incident of a supposed chemical attack. Is there any connection between this incident and the bombing at St. Luke's hospital?"

"Uh, that's a good question. Thank you. Uh . . . that was a part of the discussion between Mr. Burnham and I, and it was a *good* discussion. I'm grateful for his advice. Now, they *are* looking into that, gathering intelligence. I couldn't say for sure. But, it's *definitely* a possibility. All I can say for now, until we know for *sure*, is that the good men and women of the

Bureau are on the ground and gathering intelligence. Until we gather all of the intelligence, look at it, and make some decisions, we're not going to jump to any conclusions. But, it is a *possibility*. It's a factor to consider."

Darwin claps. "Ha! You see that? Propit's gone south! Made it on the morning show! You see that, Jonah?"

He shuffles up, scarfing oat clumps out of a bowl – clumps in his bristled beard. "That there's a tragic kingdom if I ever did see one."

"Wait," I halt the conversation to a dead-stop. "You guys know about Propit?"

"Of course we know Propit," Mulligan sputters oats into the air. Darwin and I back away an inch. "He's one of the Other, boy. We work for his kind. We follow his lead. That's why I took you to St. Luke's, Dedalus, 'cause Propit requested to meet ya . . . he's got someth'n to say. We just didn't know *Jack* would be there . . . and with a *shabti* too! *Dammit!*"

"Who the hell is this Jack guy? You want me in on this I got to know who the hell we're dealing with here."

"Spring-heeled Jack," Darwin interjects. She glowers in malaise. "One way or another, you've heard of him. English urban legend from the 1800's. Reported as a dark, devilish creature that conducted misdeeds at night and could leap incredible distances. The subject of a plethora of Penny Dreadfuls. It was only mild attacks on the populace that made public record. Most of those antics were just Jack having a thrill. What he's *really* known for, in our circles, was kept in the highest confidence by the Royal Family."

"Bad, bad," Mulligan shakes his head. "Kinda like how Propit is to RED, but for the Nova Mob. Bad as they get. One of the most efficient killers ever known."

"Well if he's so efficient then why was Darwin able to take down one of his henchmen, this *shabti*, so quickly . . . relatively?"

Darwin walks over to a keyboard. Sits and punches away. Numerical figures appear on a screen next to WWN. "He was toying with us, Gregor. Like a cat. He was most likely close by, studying us. Which makes us vulnerable. At the moment, he has us pegged."

"So, he's . . . a hundred years old or so?"

"More than that," Darwin shakes her head. Tap, tap. "He's from an old stock that you would be unable to comprehend at the moment. He's had many other appearances over the years: the Ripper, the Gasser of Mattoon, even manifesting in Mother Goose's world as Jack Be Nimble. Don't be fooled, he's evil and dangerous. Aztalan is aware of our situation and would like for us to reconnoiter there as soon as possible."

"Right, but about Propit—"

"All in time," Darwin interrupts and walks away from Mahamaya's terminal. She slowly makes her way across the cavern and disappears behind the velvet curtain. I thought there *was no* time. I look over at Jonah and he masticates with a smile.

"Fun, isn't it?"

We linger for a few minutes, watching more footage of the President chuckling and reporters expressing themselves in front of the camera – scrolling words about terror threat levels across the bottom – the Dow index is dropping, dropping. Finally, after a banking commercial that knows how to make us all happy, Darwin reappears. She approaches with a small wooden bowl in hand, full with a pile of some rather plain-looking, but very green leaves.

"Sit," she says to me.

I hesitate slightly, but then head for the dinner table.

"No," she corrects me adamantly. "In Mahamaya."

"Are you joking?"

No, she wasn't. I follow her lead and walk over to the glowing metal pod in the center of the behemoth machine. There – a little stool where the mantis helmet sits with blinking lights, chirping at me, goading me, daring me to step into this pulp fiction anomaly. I pick it up, careful of the wires and tubing trailing to the ceiling of the miniature capsule. I sit down and set the helmet on my lap. The inner walls glow with pearly iridescence. I feel a slight charge waft through my body.

"Okay," I say. "What now?"

"Put it on."

Okay. Right. Put it on. Here goes . . .

Slip on Mahamaya's helm and the ommatidium visor covers my vision. Surge of charge heightens and I become a battery – not uneasy, not altered – I am aware and conscious, but feel a slight pull of myself upward.

"Now open your mouth," she says. I comply. She places a bundle of the leaves into my mouth. "Now chew. Keep chewing and do not swallow. Let the juices soak into your mouth. And breathe. In, out."

So, I begin to chew and chew, the taste is somewhat repugnant . . . a sour dirt, a miniscule tinge of mint somewhere in the mix. I chew and chew, with each bite and rumination comes a breath inhaled, a breath exhaled. The flow of the air exacting a current inside of my body, creating a pattern, creating a code . . . and I am being read, Mahamaya is reading me! I feel her tugging me into her, tapping over my breathwork like Braille. She is translating me . . . and waiting, waiting for . . . the leaves.

Rumination, the juices gush in my mouth, dirt pungent . . . bite by bite . . . gagging motion, reflex stagger . . .

"Go with it," I hear Darwin. "Let it take you."

I am being drugged, again. Hands become torrid, heart is pounding furiously. Necromantic euphoria enveloping me, Mahamaya is quickening her pace to pull me in . . .

Almost there, she says on edge of thought. Mahamaya is speaking to me.

You will shoot like a rocket. Feel comfortable in the nothingness.

A disc appears, horns sprout from the top. Green flashing. Perception is not warping. This is not regular – such as LSD or other experiences – consciousness is warping; consciousness itself, manifested as the reality around me, manifested as itself, consciousness is skewing and twisting. Panic, heart racing beat beat beat faster. Darwin and Mulligan are slipping away – not going into another room slipping away . . . I am exiting the entire time-space location they are in.

Yes, here you go.

Consciousness around me is manifest. Segregates into walls and levels, it compresses from above, compacting down onto me. Crackle, a sound . . . one little sound . . . is that Darwin? Mulligan? Am I still in the cavern with them? crackle crackle crackle CRACKLES across the room in solidified resonance. The pod is crushing in – I am being squeezed out of it, oozed out like spaghetti tubing into Mahamaya's database . . . the old reality collapsing, I am gone from it.

gone from it – into her

"Hello?"

Welcome Gregor, you have come to suckle at my teat. Sample the chicken cordon bleu, it's simply mouth-watering.

(m)outh – bite, bite, always – panic fade . . . there is no more of that. picture of a leaf – sensibilities of an unfolding before my vision: I look before me to see and learn what is being taught.

didgeridoo pulverizations resound around, I feel inside the humming conical shapes sing into the amorphous space . . . in it; globules of sludgy liquid essence – there are faces coming in and out of the muck, so tangible, so fluid. hum didgeridoo presence on machine churning life essence, churning reality into an intricate whole. I am reminded of me who I am, me of past experience . . . every experience, every thing that happens, imprints. Imprint = another layer. visually, it manifests: every second – every quanta – of every person's memory is imprinted onto one's retinas, onto the fabric of reality (*Imgaine it as a fabric*)

every   single   memory

this means reality is nothing but stacks and stacks of memory, layers and layers of imprints . . . every time one takes a mind-altering substance, undergoes a life-changing experience, an altered-state of mind, makes for a MAJOR imprint . . . a very powerful and potent impression or signature on the psyche, soul, id . . .

This same thing does not fail to include Post Traumatic Stress Disorder.

One foot, two. One foot . . . that Ian Anderson flute-playing character . . .

. . . the cashmere sweater girl with the raven hair, she is shuffling her cards, Fate cards to be . . .

. . . affecting (infecting) the ability to disintegrate relationships through fear and anxiety.

I watch these stacks, these layers of impressions and imprints, flow into long cords. Long, flowing tentacles warping and tangling in and out of each other – one person per tentacle, shipman – when the tentacles make contact, it is two disparate imprints interacting at those particular points . . . . *that is the nature of relationships of all kinds. between humans. between rocks. between galaxies. between dust particles.* sometimes the imprint on one part of a tentacle – one form of consciousness – interacts with an imprint on another part of a separate tentacle, it may not mesh well (much like the PTSD) . . . this impression is more like an explosion, it sends a shockwave throughout the tentacle, a reverberation affecting all of the other imprints. this may cause discourse among the other imprints, in effect interactions with other tentacles (people) –

Growing.

Get pulled back, my self flows away from the tentacled moment, see the whole world, a network of tentacles octopus flow and mingling like underwater plants in ocean of cosmic mesh, very ends of some reaching the globe above, globe of pure substance they all are trying to reach, though sometimes not able. That was the point, reach the prefect roof of roundness above us: Logos. It cannot really be classified, except through the concept of unity. *Because in essence, Gregor, we are all it, we are all cords and tentacles reaching for the great unifying body that is one thing. This is the great thing you are shown. Łichii' hashtaał!*

floating with me and then the serpent, we belong to the stars

This, I watch, is the origin of RED. The Universe is still trying to figure out what it wants; the Universe is not an object; the Universe is an event; we are a part of that event, an expression; a revelation is a shattering; you cannot see a god and live; TRUTH shatters us.

And you will need to know about Hilbert soon, reserve your room at the Grand Hotel.

Spectroscopy is how we gather the majority of all known information we have gathered from the Universe – prism language – the measuring of light, what is RED? color = differing wavelengths and frequencies of the electromagnetic wave (+) particle called "light" . . . wavelength (λ) = crest separation; frequency ($\sqrt{}$) = number of times per second a crest passes a fixed point . . . *visible* light is only a small fraction of the entire electromagnetic spectrum . . . light is independent of the speed of its viewer . . . Beware, here be dragons! Uncharted territory looms on the horizon! *You're physical brain is trying to warn you. I am equipped for RED Agent consciousness. You have not yet taken the maninkari larva. You are _one hundred_ percent capable of brain dysfunction if I do not reintegrate causality sectors to 2.0 and then tonality tech to approximately - 144B22. Hear. me. scream.*

YYAAAAAAAAAAAARRRRRGGGHHHH!!!!!!!!!

Light is everything. The sun is worthy to be worshipped. It is our source of life. It feeds us, warms us, blankets us. We drink its nectar and dance with vigor. We are boiling pots of protons, neutrons, and electrons. I see the particles before me in myth. Not only are we able to theoretically understand the Universe back to its first second of being, but we can actually calculate as far back as 10 to the -43 power seconds . . . . heron of origin . . . what we are, infinitesimally small . . . 10 to the -43 power . . . what we need is a paradigm shift.

I AM THE PARADIGM SHIFT OF THE WORLD

there is a way in which our participation in reality draws forth reality . . . hence, the rebellion, someone's got to fight back. someone's got to fight against the monster of conformity.

Strange new colors abide – the President does not understand the precedent of the people . . . it was . . .

We were always around, embodying and materializing in all forms of R . . . E . . . D . . .; we were always around. Solidified in modern form during the latest revolt – the 1960's, and now the war has been officially declared and the Nova Enterprise is so close to winning to mass control to complete order and function for all and – WE CAN'T HAVE THAT, SONNY!

There is a particular bone to pick – I am in your dreams . . . spit.

Reality is only a metaphor for what really exists. A mask. What really is, you can only conceptualize through limited perceptions and observations (matter and tools). You can only understand what you conceptualize, not what really exists. The strings resonate in your essence . . . . everything has a vibration . . . all part of the same orchestra . . . let the DREAMS flood and unfold – awake you must be in the universal sleep, the dream of the giant.

The sleeping giant . . . BEEP . . . BEEP . . . woken, shock-trauma, by two airplanes . . . BEEP . . . BEEP . . . PTSD of the nation, PTSD of the world . . . BEEP . . . BEEP . . .

BEEP   BEEP

BEEP

BEEP . . . slips off the twinkling helm, Mulligan is in my face with mad Mongol eyes . . . BEEP, BEEP. What is that?

"What is that?"

BEEP, BEEP, BEEP.

"Dedalus, boy! Time is time, and the time is now to go!" Yellow teeth with oat chips stuck between. Mahamaya ripped away from me and he drags me out of the pod, reeling onto the floor. Equilibrium is no-state, I cannot sense the where of I may be. BEEP. "Sorry, boy. Emergency release, eject! Eject!"

BEEP, BEEP.

"What . . . what's happening?" Red lights blinking BEEP on and BEEP off. Darwin at the screens, looking at security monitors. "What—"

"I do apologize for that, Gregor," Darwin, points to hazy black-and-white image on a screen. A dark mass of shadow flowing down corridor of the mall. "We have an interruption."

"Jack," Mulligan explains. "Shit-fire! We gotta go!"

Mulligan helps me up, throws my arm around his shoulder, and we hobble toward the curtain space. Darwin runs to the entrance, kneels over, shifting something – she skitters away swiftly.

"This'll stall him," she hollers. "Run, run, run, run!"

Rush through the curtain, into the garden and foliage is whipping past. Mulligan is carrying most all of my weight, he is stronger than he looks. At the back of the corridor, an elephantine air unit, twin mattress, tables with vials and test tubes, another rugged bookshelf, and a steel door. Must be where Darwin resides. There are duffel bags and backpacks – along with my own – sitting next to the door.

TTHHOOOOOOMMMM!!!!!

Sonic vibration under feet, walls shake, bits of rocks fall to the ground. The curtain swishes. She set a device, a charge . . . and then I realize in jolting dismay.

"Mahamaya!"

"She's okay," Darwin consoles me. "I just blew the stairwell. Blast door's keeping it out there. Smell that? It's a napalm derivative. It should keep burning long enough for us to make our escape." She grabs a tote bag full of plant stems, vegetables, and hemp sacks – opens the steel door.

"Everybody carries something," Mulligan still has to assist me. He and Darwin pile on the bags and we all have straps over shoulders and backs, gripping as many as we can. Walk through the steel door and Darwin shuts it behind us. Concrete bathroom and shower, a rusted drain flowing to the middle. She walks to the opposite side and pushes her hand at the bottom of the wall. A small trap door opens, into the spaghetti skew, we walk into a corridor so small we have to crouch down – walking with 90° angle. Bumps and scrapes against the rock wall. I can't see; rely on Mulligan to lead me through the dark. We are scurrying cockroaches for what seems like almost half an hour, my legs sore and feet throb with needle sting. Mulligan is panting heavy. Darwin close behind, quiet as a ninja. Every minute or so a mumble of encouragement: "Keep moving", "We're doing good", or "That's it, we're almost there."

Soon, the corridor ends.

"What now?" Mulligan ponders, exasperated.

"Look and see," Darwin punches up and a hole opens above us, speckled light rays pouring down eye squint. She leaps up and out with no trouble. Hand reaches down, pulls me up. I crawl for a bit. Mind still dazed, but coming to. Look around. Inside an old gas station. Shoddy décor from the fifties, broken shards of debris all over the place. She helps Mulligan out and they walk to a garage where sits a whitewashed Winnebago – chipped paint splotches covered in Dalmatian speckles. She pulls out a set of keys and Mulligan whips open the garage door. I scuffle over slowly, leveraging my balance.

"Ready for a road trip, Dedalus?" Mulligan plops me into the front passenger seat. "You got shot gun!"

"Where're we going?" I ask Darwin as she helps put the bags in back.

"Where else," she answers. "To Aztalan . . . Wisconsin."

"No, wait," I struggle, maneuvering my way through Mulligan's arms. "Ramona . . . Lena . . . they're in danger! I've gotta help them!"

"No worries on that, junky," Mulligan steps a pace back, stalwart, and opens one of his many coats. Inside hangs an array of submachine gunnery the likes of which I have never seen before this close. I recognize two of them as Uzis and another bigger automatic rifle I don't recognize, replete with bullet chains, clips, and some grenades for good measure. I ease slowly in reverse back into the passenger seat.

"I got this," Mulligan snickers. "Someone's got to stay behind and work on this case. Your girls are safe with me. I'll find 'em and bring 'em home. You focus on what you're to become, boy!"

Darwin embraces him tightly and whispers a goodbye into his ear.

"Blessings, brother," she tells him and climbs into the driver seat.

"Y'all take care now," he hollers as Darwin turns on the ignition and we roll out of the garage. "'*He may not suffer their memory to grow dim, let them be as though they had not been and all but persuade himself that they were not or at least were otherwise*!!!'"

We head for the highway in a slow rumble, trying not to attract attention. It is morning. My mind is peddling over and over with thoughts from Mahamaya . . . intense concern for Ramona . . . and Lena.

"What's he saying," I ask Darwin, fast food chains and gas stations roll by in threadbare smog. "It sounds like he's quoting from something half the time."

"James Joyce," she answers curtly. "*Ulysses*, specifically."

"Any reason why?"

"That's his story."

I grimace at the obscurity of her answer. I try again to get *something* answered.

"So, we're going to Wisconsin. To . . . Azz . . . uh . . . tuh . . . lan, right? What for exactly?"

For the first time since I've known her she beams with a radiant smile, takes her attention off the road, and looks at me through her shades square into my own eyes. "For Initiation!"

15 – We Are All Insane

They walk across the beaten terrace of corrugated railing until they reach apartment C2. The heat is sweltering, even at 10:00 in the morning. A strong musk is in the air making it difficult to breathe. A dog barks in an alley two stories below. Ramona kneels down, saffron hair falling over eyelids shutting away the cloudless light. She pulls out a hair pin from her hemp satchel, straightens it, pulls out another, and does the same. Tongue sticking out the side of her mouth, she inserts them into the door knob lock.

"Better duck," she suggests. "With no key to work the cylinder, we're bound to set the trap."

"Trap?" Lena crouches down behind her. She pulls her purse in tight to her chest and gazes to the nearby apartments in a fleeting moment of paranoia. "Did you just say *trap*?"

"Don't worry. I've done this hundreds of times."

"Speaking of which, where exactly did you learn how to break-and-enter?"

"Dad taught his little girl sweet tricks. My family has a sort of . . . history of deviancy, I guess. Now, shhh . . . ." Ramona twists her wrists, pulling repeatedly on one of the pins with a severe jabbing motion. SCRAPE, SCRAPE, SCRAPE, SCRAPE . . . Click!

"Brilliant," she sighs in relief and turns to Lena intently. "Now, I'm going to open this slowly. Stay down until I say 'clear.' Got it?"

"Right," Lena concurs. She tucks herself into turtle form. Ramona eases the knob to the right and, crouching, swings the door open.

Tink! Lever activates a switch. Snap! Cord unwinds, pulleys ignite around foyer corridor. Rrrrooooooooooollllllllllllll. Sucks into a propulsion mechanism across the doorway. FWOT! Object launches from mechanism. fwap fwap fwap FWAP FWAP FWAP fwap fwap fwap. Flutters overhead, a bundle of plastic; unfurls with weights on its ends. Lands twenty feet past on the concrete terrace. Willowed thump.

"Netgun," Ramona smirks over to Lena. "Saran wrap and pool balls. Slaps around an intruder's face . . . stalls and suffocates them long enough so you can gain an advantage."

"But, what about—"

"Hold up," she reaches over the threshold and lifts a strand of yarn from a hook, lets it go and run through another system of pulleys. "Home-made alarm, we don't want to draw *too* much attention. All's clear now."

They slip in and shut the door silently, carefully behind them.

"I can't believe you've never been here before," Ramona locks the door and walks to the living the room. She throws her hemp sack on the couch.

Lena walks into the nearby kitchen. The sink is stacked full of dishes covered in crusted bits of food. "Um, since the trial . . . he always wanted to meet in third-party locations. It was like he was scared of me coming over here. Looks like he was scared of *anyone* coming over, period."

Ramona walks over to the foil-covered computer and turns on the power. "I'm going to see if I can find out who this Bloom guy is."

Lena follows after making a pit-stop in the kitchen, glass of orange juice in hand. She sits down on the couch and pilfers through stacks of papers and notebooks on the coffee table.

"Do you think he's okay? I mean, I know Gregor usually hangs out with psychos, but that guy looked really out of it."

"He called me late last night," Ramona perks as the CPU hums to life. The user login appears and she types in *GregorSamsa*. She pauses, considering the password field. "He . . . was okay, but he just . . . he had some concerns. And frankly, so do I."

"Like what?"

Ramona breaks from the screen and turns to her. "Like, how much *do* you know Benjamin? You've had an on-line relationship for two weeks? Is that enough to come see you from the East coast?"

"He has *family* here! Besides, we've been talking for *three* weeks and he's a *cop*! I've seen his badge and everything! He's completely fine. That guy last night just went totally nuts is all. You should be used to episodes like that hanging around Gregor."

"Trust me, I'm used to it," a bitterness taints her mouth with all-too-recent memories of Saturday night. Ramona turns back around to face the screen. Password . . . password . . . with moderate enthusiasm she types in *Ramona*. Wrong. Denied. "But, I trust Gregor when he's worried about something. He has a way of connecting the dots when I can't even *see* the dots. Plus, with Lawrence's freak-out and this red person floating around . . . a lot's happened in the past few days and we need to be wary. I'm just saying, look out for yourself. You still don't *know* this guy." *Ramona123*. Wrong. Denied again.

"Oh don't worry about me. Benjamin's great. Notice last night how much of a gentleman he was? He totally understood the situation, made sure we got home okay, and then took off without being too pushy. Class! That's why I usually like 'em older. More mature." She flips through a notebook filled with journal entries of news releases from the Associated Press. They are all catalogued by a sophisticated numerical system she cannot understand. She plops it back down on the coffee table and looks around, bored. "Hey . . . why doesn't he have any pictures of Alice up? Or, *any* pictures for that matter!"

"Of course! Why didn't I think of that?" Ramona types *Alice*. Wrong. Denied. *AliceSamson*. Wrong. Denied again. *Alice123*. Wrong again. "What's Alice's birthday? July right?"

"July 3rd. Why?" Lena sips the orange juice.

"Right," she types *Alice 0703*. Right! Access granted. "Yes, I'm in! Thanks!"

Lena straightens up, flips her hair back. "So, what exactly are you going to look for?"

"Gregor IM'd with this guy before, Bloom777. Jonah Mulligan. I'm just going to look up his chat history, see if we can get a better grasp of what's going on or where Gregor might be. Hope he hasn't deleted any of his recent stuff yet."

"You're kinda dangerous, you know," Lena chuckles. "You seem all sweet natured at first, but then you with your tattooed self, breaking into your boyfriend's apartment and hacking into his computer . . . you're kind of a punk, aren't you?"

Ramona flips around the screen with the mouse. "He's gotta accept that we're even in a relationship before I can call him my boyfriend. Of course, I *did* introduce myself as his girlfriend last night. I think he turned pale!"

"Whatever," Lena stands and looks over Ramona's shoulder. "I know my brother. He's totally smitten and doesn't even know it."

"He doesn't *want* to know it."

Ramona finds the message history in the internet browser. "There we go, BLOOM777." She clicks. Window pops up of a chat stream and they rummage through Gregor's chat history with BLOOM777; diving through loops of conversations about recent UFO activity, yeti sightings, signs of the apocalypse, and local haunting.

Someone is watching you from behind.

"Nothing much more than we already know," Ramona sighs. "Except, wait a minute . . ." She opens a particular stream. Lena leans over her shoulder to read along:

GS: I would hate to have to relate this to the men in black phenomena. The Will Smith franchise killed any serious discussion that could be had about it.

BLOOM777: All franchises kill ideas. That is what they are meant to do. It is how they are designed.

GS: Speaking of which, I lost my job today. I can't help but think for a reason. The conspiracy grows. I have no doubt the Dominators have a hand in it.

BLOOM777: They know more than you may want them to. Operatives are everywhere. Does your boss have gold teeth?

GS: ????? :/ Not that I know of. I never checked. Why?

BLOOM777: No matter. Just come to my gig tonight at Unity. The RED coats will be explained. You will get your answers soon. As long as you are willing to go all the way. How much do you care about knowledge? The Truth?

GS: RED. R.E.D. An acronym, you think?

BLOOM777: How much do you care, D?

GS: It is everything.

BLOOM777: Are you sure? This may change your whole world. ARE YOU SURE? This is the pursuit of Truth! CAPITAL T!!!

GS: It is the only thing that seems real. It is all I have anymore.

Ramona's gut sinks. She flits a finger across the black birds on her wrist. She recalls the day she was inspired to get her tattoo. The memory begins to wrap itself around her like a writhing anaconda when Lena yelps behind her.

"He lost his *job*?" Lena blurts. "I didn't know that!"

"Neither did I," Ramona states, though she figured something like that was up when she met up with Gregor last night; he was a pretty easy read to her.

"I can't believe this! Benjamin was right!"

Ramona peers over, confusion draping her face. "*Right*?!? What are you talking about?"

"Benjamin was right . . . about what Gregor's been involved in. And now, especially after him disappearing and the hospital attack last night. He was right!"

"Lena, what the HELL are you talking about?"

"Let me clarify," the voice comes from the hallway leading to the front door. Ramona jumps and turns.

Entering the room quietly, Benjamin's older, stately frame saunters in and sits casually on the couch. His demeanor is congenial. His tone measured. Dead wars wrinkle around his eyes, large calloused hands still feeling the cold of armaments. He has an unlit cigarette dangling from chapped lips.

"Hello," throwing one leg over the other, he causally lights the cigarette with a Zippo. Ramona notices a peace sign marked on the side of the metal casing. "How are you lovely ladies this hot morning? The humidity here is god-awful!"

Ramona turns and adjusts in her seat. Her gut churns with the innuendo of how uneasy of a scenario this has become. She is compelled to spring out the front door, a cat ready to pounce. "How did you . . . what . . . what's going on here?"

Benjamin lifts his hips to reach into his back pocket. His jeans old and worn, shirt un-ironed. he pulls out a badge and lays it carefully on the coffee table. A presidential seal braces the front, the words "Central Intelligence Agency" bordering the eagle. The government-issued stamp shines on top of Gregor's notebooks as an ominous reminder of the phone warning she received late last night.

"I have a few questions for you, Ramona."

Ramona glares at Lena. "What the *hell* did you do? Gregor's your *brother!*"

"Look . . . if he's involved in . . ." Lena stammers, hand nervously clutching her forearm, biting her lip.

"He isn't involved in anything!" Ramona hollers. She wants to run, but she is frozen in rage. She fights back a compelling urge to hit Lena. Lena has always . . . seemingly . . . been so supportive of Gregor, but now? How could she have sold him out?

Benjamin leans forward. Smoke trickles around his blonde brow. "Have you seen the news, Ms. Udell? The hospital bombing?"

Ramona juts out of her chair. She is standing over the coffee table, face maroon frenzy. "Of course! But, Gregor wasn't involved in that! He can barely step outside without having a panic attack, let alone taking part in something like *that*."

Benjamin takes a calm puff of his cigarette and blows a ring of smoke. "The Associated Press just made a release this morning. Gregor is a suspect in the bombing. He's involved with a terrorist organization, and we need your help to find him . . . find *them*, rather. Your country needs you."

"Christ, my *country*!" Ramona laughs mockingly. "Lena, you actually *believe* this guy? Come on, you know Gregor isn't capable of something like that! I'm around him almost every day. How did you end up with this spook?"

Lena lowers her head. Ramona notices how pitiful she looks. Did she even *want* to answer? Did she even care?

Ramona glowers at Benjamin. "You asshole! How do you know Gregor was involved? You saw it last night. You were there. Gregor was kidnapped!"

"By this man, right?" Benjamin pulls out a photo from his shirt pocket and lays it above the badge. It is a police mug shot of Mulligan, Bloom777. Ramona's chest twists into a knot. "And I am sure you recognize this, right?" He lays down another photo. It is fuzzy, but Ramona can make it out: a city back-drop, an alley, garbage can, all contrasted by a red haze – some sort of figure – streaking across the view like a red strip of light. "We need all the information you can give us. Gregor is sucked into something here; there may still be a chance to save him."

Ramona stands quietly for a moment, her stare painfully piercing into Benjamin. "I think I've already made my stance quite clear, thank you."

"So be it," Benjamin rises and places a hand gingerly on Lena's shoulder. "Thanks for getting us in. We couldn't have done it without you. Or rather *you*, Mrs. Wilcox."

He glances at Lena.

"Wait . . . what? *Wilcox*?" Ramona stutters. "What are you talking about? And who's '*us*'?"

The room growls into a thunder – the monitor on the desk trembling foil, the notebooks and photos on the coffee table flutter onto the floor. Uniformed men and women barrel into the apartment and scour the place with plastic gloves, tape, and metal detectors. Boots trample unvacuumed carpet, dust flits brown clouds into the air. Some gather up Gregor's notebooks, others push Ramona out of the way and begin the process of taking apart the CPU and monitor, and the rest charge into the bedroom to overturn the mattress and rip apart the closet. Huffs and whoops are exchanged back and forth between them.

"What's going on here?" Ramona steps back. Every molecule in her body screams at her to run again, but now she can't. It is too late. She is trapped in this nightmare.

A uniformed officer walks into the living room. He is young, younger than Ramona even. He looks at the girls querulously, sweat beads on his face. He stands attention in front of Benjamin and salutes.

"Agent Copernicus, the perimeter is secure."

16 – More Numbers

Margaret holds the key timorously. She holds it in her hand. It feels safe there. She holds the key and looks at the door. The door is closed. Good. She is glad that it is closed. And it is locked too, which is important. Very important. She grasps it tightly against her breast. Only one copy; that is all there needs to be. She squeezes it until her hands turn white.

Margaret walks into the kitchen, clutching the key. She looks at the pantry. It has no door. She took it off many years ago. Pantries don't need doors, *houses* need doors. She looks at the cans of soup, cans of beans, boxes of cereal and oats. She lifts her right hand from the key. That's okay, because the *left* hand still has it. The left hand holds it secure. Safety. She lifts her right hand and picks up a bag of bread. Bread is good, definitely; nothing wrong with that. She carries it over to the toaster. She doesn't need to let go of the key with her left hand because there is no twisty on the bag of bread. Mom came over and helped her with that two days ago, whenever she picked up groceries for her. Mom opened all of the boxes and bags and left them open, so it wouldn't take two hands to use them. Mom is good that way. Still takes care of her little girl even though her little girl is all grown up. Thank you, Mom! Margaret loves Mom. Mom is very good to her. However, not even Mom has a key. Only Margaret has *the* key. Mom would just have to understand that. Margaret believes she does understand.

She places the bag on the counter and pulls out two pieces, placing them into the toaster; as she does the telephoned rings.

"Aagh," she yelps. The hair rises on the goose-bumps that speckle her body. Margaret hates it when the phone rings. The phone is too loud. How would she be able to hear if someone was trying to get through the door, or through a window?

She can't have a cell phone, though; only a landline. You can't put landlines on vibrate, but landlines are safer. Safer for the head.

It rings again.

Margaret cringes. She inches forward, hoping to answer it before it is too late. Maybe it is Mom.

Another ring.

"Shut up, please" Margaret whispers. She inches closer still. She is just reaching for the phone whenever the answering machine triggers, springs to life, and picks up the phone call.

Hi . . . um, this is Margaret. I . . . can't come to the phone now. Please leave a message . . . and I'll call you back. Okay . . . thanks. Bye.

A loud beep.

Margie, sweetie! Hi, it's Mom! Good morning! Just call'n to check up on you, sweetie-pie. Hope you're doin' well. Do you need anything? Papa's goin' to work in about an hour and I'll be at the church. You remember Sherie and the girls are having that Bible study this week. You're welcome to come, if you like. Just call my cell if you want me to swing by and get you. Those things are so neato, aren't they? Still trying to figure out the whole text thing, hee hee! I think you would feel better if you got one. Anyway, you have the church office number too, on your refrigerator.

Margaret looks on the fridge door. It is closed. She wishes it could be open. But she sees the only piece of paper on it, stuck with heart-shaped and cross magnets. The church, Antioch Christian Church: 913-532-6671. Got it.

Well, I love you and hope you have a good day. Try to get out and take a walk, it's supposed to be nice, will you? Love you, sweetie. Bye, bye.

She makes two kissing noises and hangs up. The number "1" appears on the answering machine screen. The toast pops up with a finish and her heart leaps. Margaret clutches the key tighter against her chest. One bit of noise after another . . . not good. Not a good start to the day. But, that's okay. Breathe deeply. Just like what Dr. Hancock says. Move forward. Breathe. Big breath: in . . . hold . . . out. Sigh. Good.

She reaches over to the cabinet with her right hand to get a plate. Her left hand squeezes the key. The cabinets have no doors, of course. She picks up a plate and moves to the toaster. Placing the pieces of toast onto the plate, she picks it up with her right hand, and walks over to the eat-in dining table. The table is in the center of the kitchen, away from the window. Margaret doesn't like the window.

Margaret sits down. Her left hand never leaves its position from her breast. She reaches for a piece of toast. Corner of her eye.

In her peripheral vision something lingers . . . in the window! She gasps! Face! Deep face! Eyes! Big huge eyes! Intruder!!!

"Aaaagh," Margaret screams, falling back off the chair, hitting the floor. Her head smacks against the tile. Damn! Get up! Fast! Get composure! Get steady! Get to the phone! Call the police! 9-1-1! 9-1-1!

She looks around, looks at the window.

Nothing.

Everything is okay. Nothing at all. Nothing there. The window is empty. Just the neighbors' house. Rosalyn's flower garden. All serene. All okay.

What was that? Have the key. Holding it tight, the left hand. She picks up the chair with her right hand. Just a mind trick? Yes, must be a mind trick. Doctor Hancock said she would have mind tricks. Comes with the territory. Got to learn to distinguish what is a mind trick and what is real. Margaret breathes. Picking up the chair, the right hand. Setting the chair straight. Margaret looks out the window again. Nothing. It is all clear. It is okay. Nothing there. Nothing at all. Just Rosalyn's flower garden. Pretty tulips and lilacs.

The phone rings. Again!

Margaret doesn't yelp this time, but her heart pounds. She feels it pulses beneath her left hand. Margaret closes her eyes and holds the key tight. Damn it, damn it, damn it. Damn it all to hell! Why God? Why not just a few moments of peace?

The phone rings again.

Need to get it. Margaret hurries over and picks up the phone with her right hand, left hand clutching the key in a hot sweat.

"Mom," she answers the phone in a broken voice. "I really don't wanna go today, okay?"

"Margaret Young?" the voice on the other line states. It is an unfamiliar voice, high and melodic. "Margaret Young?" It asks again. It sounds like an old record player Margaret had when she was a child.

An unfamiliar voice. Margaret feels a lump rise in her throat. She can't talk. She clutches the key, white knuckles on her left hand. Her palms sweat more, key is slipping, a cold chill shivers up her calves. Then, she hears clicks in the receiver. Odd paced clicks, like someone is tapping a stick on concrete. The clicks hasten and steadily melt into Margaret's head. Margaret feels cold. The clicks melt into Margaret's thinking, her thoughts becoming clicks themselves. As this happens, Margaret can feel the panic rise. A pressure on her chest. Heavy, heavy weight. But, she cannot move! Margaret is unable to move! She is frozen in place. Margaret tries to speak, but no words come out. Her lips do not even part.

The clicks on the line cease. Margaret screams inside of herself. Screams and screams. She wants to be let go. She wants to move. Then, the voice comes back in the phone, a stifled static.

"Reach Margaret . . . 15 . . . 32.4 . . . 2.2 divide 5 . . . 7.4 . . . x55 . . . 8.8 . . . 23."

Blank slate.

Flash: White covers all. Inside. Margaret loses herself. Going inside deep. No, no, no, NO!!! Like a stream of waking, back farther. Deep in the past, just around the corner. Deep inside: Why did she trust him? She thought they were friends. He was such a nice guy. What is happening? He had such a darling smile. Such a gentleman. That little boy look. What is happening? Why am I reliving this? Full speed, static everywhere like noise, noise, NOISE!!! He was a friend. So, she made a copy for him. She was so clumsy. Always had a habit of locking herself out. Always had to find ways of breaking in. Or call a locksmith and spend a hundred dollars. It was so embarrassing. He was a great guy, how could she ever know? Why am I watching this again? Come home . . . after a revival . . . and he's sitting there on my couch. He's sitting there! On my couch! Why is he in MY home? Sitting in the dark, waiting for me. He moves so fast, shuts the door. I'm so confused. Duct tape over my mouth. He's so strong! Static, more. Rays of light flashing here and there. Very white. Deep inside. No, no, NO!!! Stop, please!!! This is *my* home! He was so nice! And now he's hurting me! God, why is he hurting me! Can't scream, can't SCREAM!!!! STOP!!!! White rays of lights, streaming and streaming and becoming a tunnel of void. Void. White out. Completely inert. Gone. Empty. Completely empty. Completely alone. No numbers, number in her head.

None. She lies on the floor. Her eyes roll to the back of her head. The phone dangles from its cord, tone beeping over and over. She is breathing, steadily. But, the numbers are gone. No more playing in her head.

It will be later in the day that Mom will figure out that Margaret hasn't checked in. Mom will call the authorities and they will knock on her door. Eventually, they will bust it down and find her on the kitchen floor. Mom will cry. Papa will hold his little girl. The authorities will tell her that Margaret is still alive. Margaret is still there, somewhere inside. But, she is unresponsive.

Margaret has been freed. Inside, she is smiling now. Propit's making his rounds . . .

SMEX:

Want to know who is who on SoulMateExchange.com?
Ordinary people . . .
From all walks of life . . .
Looking . . .
For some change . . .
For someone to EXchange!

SoulMateExchange.com: where you don't have to be stuck with the same thing, over and over and over again, for all eternity. Where you can borrow a little bit of someone else's happiness too.

SoulMateExchange.com: where people matter, but only for a little while! Only $99.99 start-up fee, including a free consultation with one of our qualified Exchange Experts. Find out if your match can be somebody else's.

SoulMateExchange.com: where we believe in fickle love. Visit us at www.SoulMateExchange.com.

Hard currency no longer applies. All major credit cards accepted. SoulMateExchange.com is not responsible for lost or stolen soul mates, excessive vomiting, instantaneous revelations that current spouse or significant other is not your soul mate, death of a soul mate during exchange, or any other incidents that could construe SoulMateExchange.com as being responsible for any hardship or trauma occurring from exchange of designated soul mates. For full list of improbable grievances call our automated customer service line at 1-800-433-SMEX (7639).

17 – From Jack's Perspective

Sniff. Sniff. The pestiferous odor of soot and ammonium nitrate. Charring streaks of detritus splay across the walls in Jackson Pollock explosions – crawl over charcoal debris, the smoke curling around form in liquid I feel I, I. Bestial affect in tune, effect. I feel, I the form of me dancing with the grayness vapor – I am vapor – it's grayness. Forming in I.

Sniff . . . . sniff, sniff.

They are gone, liquid mouth the three of them, they have gone: two males and one female. The boy is there. Farther away. Crawl down to bottom of the corridor, staircase shattered in explosion . . . blast door intact, hinges hanging barely. I, I feel myself extend in propulsion dark form punch swing . . . feel the I, I and

SMASH!!!!

Again . . .

SMASH!!!! Again . . . SMASH!!!! SMASH!!!!

Crash, down it goes. Door no more. Explosion enough to weaken the I of me to sink in. The darkened I, bloodshot propulsion. Creep through opening in to the foyer of cavernous hideout . . . admire the underground tactics. Sniff . . . sniff.

Nothing much here: books, primitive weaponry, a gaggle of plants I aim to defecate on, and . . . a prodigiously advanced piece of technology that is aware of my presence. Focus wave in . . . source of light in this place, the waves are all forming into it. Sucking it into it. Ghosts, from a plane of ecto-essence concretized . . . from a nearby highway, I – they wander in skeletal waste, not ghosts – memories, ones wanting to be forgotten (not I). Old settlers, native ancestors – imprints, memories. They are attracted to it, like magnets . . . needing and feeding two opposing forces to create – just that, create.

Create – nexus.

Erghgh . . . it pulls them in. Tries on me, the I. I can see, the I. I can see them going into it, minutely diminutive and down to levels of singularity. No polarity. Into single units enough for the machine to feed upon, fuel upon. It notices me and it is unhappy, to I.

How, intruder!

"I am no more an intruder than you are," I tell it, tell it good, I. "You mean to what . . . negotiate me out of your destruction?"

You cannot destroy me. You can only destroy that which is material. That is your weakness, Jack of Wanderers.

"Ah, you know my true name, do you? That is a rather dangerous responsibility to have. Know then that your existence will surely be licked between my teeth."

Again, you have misunderstood, Jack Blue Note. You can implement your death on machinations which convert my essence into translation, but my essence is not contained. I will be here, and elsewhere, while you sweat over the disassembly of metal wires and plastic tubing.

"I don't suppose you will point me in the direction of my victims; it never hurts to ask. They will die, you know . . . protect them all you want, I will rape every one of them while I slowly slit their throats and drink their blood. All three of them. And then, because you have annoyed me, I intend to do the same with their loved ones right in front of their eyes. You may watch from your ether plane. I know you will cry. When you do, I will feel it, and I will piss on your memory."

You come from a classical age, Jack. That is a dying time, a new one will soon manifest. You will not even be able to comprehend its unfolding. You are sad, creature. Your people are gone. You are so sad, in fact, that I shall not remember you when the new time arises.

No in, think I – crawl in and move the form in and out, my dark shadow form self, around, coalesce into I, of myself out and I . . . coalesce – I am a shutter in depth – ignore the mists, convulse thyself in I, and discharge – EXPOUND!

The darkness mandibles of I shatter out in jet thrust cords, a bust firework display of pure obsidian sludge of I, I am

the sludge of I the obsidian wreckkk! Out – CRASH!!!!
SHATTER!!!! – decimation abound! In mind of I, I hear
screaming. In mind of I, it is nice. The I enjoy the suffering of
external the sentience. I am beyond the death of idea, my pet.
Pull the wires, shatter monitors, shards of glass and
electromagnetic components and cathode ray splinters . . . I . . .
and it . . . conquer, I have.

I see the memories of spirits scatter.

Surrounded in my artful mess. Swirl my coat of black
back in, I – bring in the forms and they flow into I. Settle. Unfurl
and lift shadow cloak off of dark, lay it on nearby mass of
rubble: the remains of my enemy. I am white beneath. Complete
in my purity and iridescence, standing now naked, I. Cool air
brisk through my bare ass, shaven genitals; goose-bump teeter
across prickly, of I, epidermal surface.

You . . . have not . . . killed me . . .

"I never kill. I merely propel circumstance closer to the
grease vat of fate." In blackness cloak I pull out technological
mechanism with minute numbers, push and place to ear.
Cellular, the monkeys call them. I extend arms in ballerina
grace, I love my naked I.

*You have . . . only injured . . . parts . . . the whole . . .
still exists . . .*

"Quiet, I'm on the phone." It rings a few times only,
notice. A pick up, his crackle comes on and gurgles.

"Progress," says he. Impatient and callous, as I. Better,
I.

"Great poetry never gives you what you please at first.
Though there are always enough nuggets to keep the audience in
rhythm."

"What are you saying, you despicable fiend?"

"I have infiltrated their Atelier, so we have invaded
their home. But there are no chickens in the roost. They fled
when seeing the wolf coming. But, I can smell . . . they can't."

"And what of Copernicus? Is he proving valuable?"

"He is en route, yes. Doing as told for now. Pre-planning always works best. The pitiful monkeys call it 'four corner offense' in their slug games. I call it 'Jack-be-Quick'."

"Your theatrics get in my way. I only use you because it is required to fulfill the Mass. Is Merchant's body ready for pick-up?"

Better, I. Admiration and loathing for the same man. Eyes of mine squint in hate. "Yes."

"Then, run amuck. We have what we need for implementation. But, *get that recruit into custody*! We need to understand the whole of their process. Got it?"

"Perfectly." I hang up and toss the contraption to the side, breaks across the landscape of scraps this thing is.

You know . . . you have given me . . . knowledge . . . of your dealings . . . Jack . . .

"I have *teased* you, nothing more. Part of my way."

Do you . . . consider yourself . . . so cunning . . .

"Hmph," little jolt of chortle, I. Walk around the cavern . . . I examining the schema of their safehousing, the schema of the RED. "You know, that is a pleasantry of reminiscence." I walk, bare feet on cave floor, end of my mane tickling my back, the only part of me in shadow, is I. "One of my beginnings is in Irish origin, yes. That was a time, several centuries ago."

Large velvet curtain. Sniff, sniff. Basil, lemon grass, dill . . . entheogens, muster must get rid, I know. "I lived in a village, nobody liked me. Not at all. And that was good. Because I didn't like them."

Pull back the curtain. Sniff. Aromas deluge. Entheogens here, yes. Enemy of the State. Enemy of I. "One day, they sent the Devil after me. To send me away. Forever."

No . . . you must not . . . system's error . . . operational status defunct . . . No . . . warning . . .

Sniff. Sniff. There they are, yes. Wide array, quite the selection for the leap-minded: kava, tabernanthe iboga, datura, mimosa hostiles, reed canary grass, salvia divinorum, mandrake, amanita mascaria . . . even some cactus! Walk up to them, ever slowly I. "But, the Devil was not so smart. Was he? Not theirs, anyway. He asked me for one final request, as Devils do in the olden ways. I asked for an apple."

Stand in front of them. Shoulder width legs apart. Here I am, I. "The most magickal of fruit. The feast of fairy tales. Foolishly, the Devil climbed a nearby tree in search of one. Before the dope realized it was an oak, I had surrounded the base with crucifixes."

Piss.......piss I do on the RED criminal's vegetation – her shamanic brews, do I.

NNNNNNOOOOOOOO!!!!!! Malfunction!!!!! WARNING!!!!! Please . . . NNOOOOO!!!!!

Steam rise and the greens melt in a sludge of tar. My waste is poison, is. I am, poison, am I. "I trapped the bastard. Forced him to grant me immunity. I tricked the Devil, you see. You are just a machine."

I am . . . more . . . more than . . . I am . . . organic . . .

"And I am killing your connection. After that, I was given an ember in a turnip to light my way through the rest of the world's end. I left that lunacy to the Irish. Now, once a year the Western world remembers me with sliced pumpkins in autumn. I hate pumpkins."

They wilt and melt and the air is filled with my stink, not theirs, I. Love. Deep, deep inside myself, other than the machine I hear more screams . . . dying them, the ones inside the green . . . makes pores prickle on my bare scrotum and ass. Love, I, the death of it. Lick, purple tongue, on my lips and indulge in ecstatic luxury massacre.

Stop . . . please . . . can't . . . please . . .

Empty. Damn. Sniff. Sniff, sniff, sniff. Ahh . . . better the smell of I, than the vegetation of invisibles. Empty is the place of this once called life, I am it, I. "Complete, my pet. Don't worry. I won't make it last much longer."

18 – Enemy Combatant

Just outside of the city limits Darwin pulls the van over in a frantic rush and races to the edge of the highway ditch to vomit.

I rush to meet her. She heaves and heaves, misery painting her once perfectly composed face. Sweat drips from her cheeks, spittle from her chin into a pool of yellowish bile. I want to place a hand on her for comfort, but Darwin is the kind of person you think twice about touching without invitation.

"What's going on?" I ask tentatively. "You okay?"

She plops down on her knees, holding her gut. She looks up into the sky and sobs.

"M . . .Mahamaya," she whimpers. For a second, I imagine what she must have been like as a little girl. Like Alice. "Mahamaya . . ."

"What about Mahamaya?"

"Dead," she wails. "I can feel it! He *killed* her! Jack killed her! That fucking bastard!"

I inch forward and with moderate hesitation lay a hand on her shoulder. To my relief, she doesn't even notice. "But, it was just a computer."

Bad move.

She turns to me slowly. I can feel red eyes piercing me through her dark shades. I might have comforted her wrongly. I release my hand and back away a step.

"No, Gregor. *She* is more than that. She has a *consciousness*. You saw the plants on the way out?"

"Yes." I respond modestly.

"Together they were integrated on a subatomic level, amalgamating into a collective consciousness which functioned as Mahamaya's user interface. They . . . *she* . . . is real and alive. Just as we are."

"Was . . ."

"Excuse me?" she stands, apparently the conversation is drawing her away from her grief.

"You're saying 'is alive', but she's dead, so . . ."

"Yes," Darwin wipes her mouth and brushes off the green grass smudges from her red pants, suddenly reconfiguring her composure. "Well, Mahamaya as she was known to me is dead. She exists, still, out there . . . in the nether, in *the* Collective. But, I had an influential bond with her current incarnation, which is why you see my present state of physical suffering. We were . . . *likened* to each other."

"I . . . I wasn't trying to be unsympathetic or anything. I was just trying to talk you through, is all."

"I know," she slaps me on the back and marches back to the Winnebago. "You did good. Come on! We have no time and a long drive. Let's hit it."

I'm a little frazzled by the display, but follow her and climb back in. We travel out of the city on Interstate 35 north toward Des Moines. Once we pass the northland suburbs, the carbon copy housing turns to forest and farmland – rolling hills of green crops crashing waves through the window of the van. They whip past in row after row after row, so fast it becomes a blur of mesh. Only the occasional silo breaks the emerald tide monotony.

I glance in the back seat at the boxes and bags of supplies and weapons. I'm not expert but it looks like a few pistols, semi-automatics, and blades of all sizes. Gut churns with the forethought of expectancy to use one of those! Lawrence would be excited. Lawrence: the Discordian traitor. What the hell does he have to do with all of this? Look over to Darwin who is now calm and focused at the wheel. Does she ever sleep? Does she ever feel fatigue? There is an uncanny kinesthesia about her being, on an edge far superior to my own thinking. At the moment—I have no doubt—she is tasting a totally different world than I am. She (and, I assume RED Agents in general) has some sort of supernatural propensity. Her remarkable abilities during the hospital conflict with Jack's pawn more than proved that. Red jacket glare.

My physical body is surprisingly relaxed, given that we have just escaped the death clutches of a malevolent urban legend monster. Must have been whatever plant that was given to me during my experience with Mahamaya. In fact, I can *feel* it is the plant.

We drive for a while. With time comes thought. With thought comes questions, connections, correlations, and more questions. My first worries, of course, land on Ramona and Lena. Are they safe? Was my call effective? How is Jonah going to find them and take care of them? I need to find out more about Benjamin and what his agenda is. How is he associated with . . . who are they anyway? The Dominators? The Nova Enterprise? Something bigger? My thoughts stray to Propit. George Stransky. What's the connection? Am I involved in all of this because I was in the wrong place at the wrong time? Did I just happen to be at Town Topic when some alien weirdo decided to undo Stransky's mind? But, this goes back further doesn't it? Because Lena had been seeing Benjamin for what . . . a few weeks now? At least? And again . . . Lawrence! Who are these people? My kidnapper/rescuer has me in mind to join her cause – for what? What does RED do exactly? What does it stand for, both literally and metaphorically?

Time flies by the grass going by, I decide to ask Darwin about—

So, her voice breaks through the clamorous rattle of the engine. "Tell me a story."

"Excuse me?"

"A story, Gregor. About you. Standard RED protocol. A story . . . tell me."

"What do you mean? What kind of story?"

"You. Anything. Anything at all."

That can mean a lot of things, right? What to pick from: the pathology of childhood, the discontentment between Mom and I, the aspirations of a very long time ago . . . falling in love .

.. falling out . . . finding desperation and disparateness. What to pull out? How does one represent?

"I have an idea," she says, obviously sensing my hesitation. "Your journal, that scrapbook you carry around with you. If you're shy, why don't you just give me a ditty out of there?"

Why not? So, I reach into my backpack – the clunking up and down motion of the 70 mile per hour road – pull out the leather-bound book, jagged lettered title *Akashic Memoir*. I flip through a few pages, flutter from a bigfoot article to a piece I wrote on George Orwell's *1984*. Finally, I settle on some segments of news clippings from various newspapers, with a tiny summation I had jotted down on a restaurant napkin covered in coffee stains. Reminiscent, I begin to read my writing aloud:

"Nayirah is another element in the obvious Dominator plot. A 15 year-old girl from Kuwait, during the first Gulf War. In 1991 she testified to Congress and brought public attention to the situation in the Middle East. Her testimony escalated popular support for America's intervention of Saddam Hussein's invasion of Kuwait. The story was spun well, as she laid out to Congress stories of Iraqi soldiers tossing babies out of their incubators and watching them slowly die. Immediately the Iraqi Republican Guard was painted as a horde of monsters, demons that needed to be exorcised. Amnesty International backed her testimony.

"Then, further investigation after the start of the war revealed holes in Nayirah's story. Amnesty reneged their endorsement. After Bush senior's full-fledged oil war with the American population's stamp of approval, Nayirah's true identity was revealed. By this time, nobody gave a damn. The story broke the headlines for barely an hour.

"Who was the little innocent village-girl survivor of Iraqi oppression named Nayirah? Nayirah Al-Sabah, daughter of Kuwaiti ambassador to the United States of America, Saud bin Nasir Al-Sabah. Human rights groups all over the world jumped out onto the global network to uncover the true

incubator story: it was all a fabrication! Completely untrue!
Though these same human rights groups were flogged by the
media and labeled as unpatriotic, liberal-interest groups. The
media wanted *the war. It was the best thing for business, they*
discovered. This was the blooming lotus of the media war crave.
Ratings were beyond perceived numbers. Instead of turning the
tube to their favorite sitcoms, everyone in America was sitting
down with their families and TV dinners watching Baghdad in
night vision: gunners shooting into the sky, glowing pellets
raining upside down in the skies above the city like a bad Atari
game. It was simply brilliant. Hollywood could never have
simulated that kind of excitement on film. The nationalistic
mantras were fostered: 'Kill those fucking towel-heads!' 'Death
to the camel-fuckers!' 'Bomb those sand-niggers!' There was a
renewed fervor in the patriotic spirit, a thirst to win.

"Digging deeper, little Nayirah's testimony was
prepped by a private company called Hill & Knowlton, a public
relations outfit under the employ of particular sectors of
business and politics. Years later, one of their biggest clients
happened to be Enron, so it may be easy to make an assumption
on the ethical methodology of this company. They also
accomplished the testimonial preparation for Jessica Lynch, the
hero girl from the second Iraq War, the American Invasion.
George Junior needed to perpetuate popular support during the
occupation, so no better way to inspire a war than to have
yourself a true American hero story. Everyone loves a G.I.Jane!
Especially a cute, blonde one seemingly kidnapped by rabid
dog-like Arabs. Of course, Jessica herself later came out and
admitted to the exaggerated fabrications produced by the
Administration and media outlet about her incarceration. It is
all part of the grand scheme, the war of ideas. It's not about
winning territory anymore, like the Monguls or Macedonians.
It's about fighting over our own minds now. And I will not have
it. I will not submit."

Okay . . . it was a *few* napkins. I close my book quietly and put it back into my bag. Watch the green roll by, rolling, rolling.

"Very good," Darwin responds. "I like that you are keeping a record of the truth. When did you start it?"

"After my divorce. Well, after my . . . trial."

"You lost. It must have cemented your understanding of what it means to embrace truth and recognize conspiracy. You also understand now we are born of the dirt. Directly from the Earth's womb. This is something you learned after your trial, after you broke, correct?"

"I learned that, sure. I especially got taught a lesson this morning, from your really cute and spontaneous wake-up call. I really appreciate the head's up, by the way . . . been meaning to make a habit out of regularly being drugged without notice. What did you give me? I've never experienced anything like that."

"The Sage of Seers. Made by Mazatec shamans from Oaxaca, Mexico. Some of our allies. It is the access code into Mahamaya – the access code for Mahamaya into you. It's a deprogramming tool."

"Deprogramming? Like a computer?"

"We all are computers. The Nova method is a systemic program overloading the reality framework. The Diviner's Sage is an entheogen, a virus disrupting the program. It dissolves boundaries. Boundaries are what fight against us, keep us fighting with each other. You needed some unlocking before Aztalan."

"Is that what this Jack guy's trying to stop? And Propit? My deprogramming?"

Darwin snickers. Odd to see her switch so candidly from light to stern and back. "No, Propit is with us. Propit is not the problem. Jack is the thorn, a presence in this play that . . . well, we don't know what his game is yet. We have theories, but nothing terribly convincing. Jack caught your scent. We know how, but not why."

Chilled memories of Propit's large eyes and paralytic stare shutter through my elbows. "Is he like Jack? Another monster from European mythology or something?"

"No. Propit is Maninkari."

She doesn't have to take her eyes off the road to see the puzzled look on my face. She can feel the awkward bewilderment in the air.

"Maninkari are who we represent, Gregor. We are at war with the Dominator culture. The RED Agency was established as an embassy of sorts . . . ambassadors for the Maninkari, which in turn represent the Overmind. Through exploitation and abuse – what is generally called *progress* – human culture has severed its connection to the natural world. There is a mirror effect – what we do to the outer world reflects our own internal conflict – or, is it the other way around?

"We fail to understand the implications of what we have wrought upon our world. Humankind has grown into a society distinguished by its reliance on commodities. There is only value in the acquirement of *stuff*; it is the cosmology of the times. In the ages of the archaic, our children were raised with the currency of the gods, campfire nights, and the wisdom of the stars. Now, our children are being taught 'the commercial' from the media god every day. Our children are being bombarded 480 times more per week by commercial culture than they are by direct face-to-face parenting. We are in a dim cave, but there is something . . . something outside the cave. It is calling to us, to come out. Breathe fresh air. Stretch our legs. Bathe in the sun.

"It is the Maninkari calling. R.E.D is the enforcement for them on the material plane. We defend the Maninkari's cause. Terence McKenna called what we do the 'Archaic Revival.' I see it more as security for the true homeland. McKenna was a good friend of the Agency and the Maninkari; an ethnobotanist who passed a few years back. We have allies, like Mulligan and McKenna. Scientists, mystics, poets, people from all walks of life. Do you understand?"

I do not have time to answer. She immediately pulls off the highway and onto a side road. I don't catch the highway name, but it is only two lanes. Within a hundred yards she stops at a gas station called *Gus' Gas Pit*. There was a small sign underneath the title, drawn crudely with black paint:

"GASOLINE, BARBEQUE RIBS, BAIT AND TACKLE, ART GALLERY, ARCADE, AND SANCTUARY (WE DO WEDDINGS AND FUNERALS)!!!!"

The van comes to a screeching halt. Darwin opens her door.

"Come on, it's prepay," she motions for me to follow her and I do.

We saunter through the parking lot up to the shoddy building that is Gus', there are a couple of old trucks: both Dodges carrying heavy loads of lumber, gas tanks, water coolers, and guns. I see a pair of antlers sticking out of one bed. We pass by a rusted Thunderbird, covered in dried cranberries, somehow looks as if they were stuck to the coating of what little paint was left on the body.

We enter through a screen door broken on its hinges. The entryway is narrow and covered in sun-bleached brochures of lodges and campsites. A few feet in and the corridor opens into a larger store area: refrigerated beverages, snack foods, tourist trinkets, t-shirts, buttons, paper weights, and Bibles. I follow Darwin to the counter where a display of chrome Jesus reliefs are on sale for half-off. A pudgy man sits on the other side, fish-eyed lenses behind a freckled, acne splattered face. Dandruff spills from greasy hair in speckles all over a black t-shirt with an American flag waving on his round belly. The words "These Colors Don't Run" display across his chest in glittered font. A golden cross with diamonds strings around his neck. Darwin looks over at me and grins.

"Look at this place! I bet Jonah would be shitting himself right about now, wouldn't he?"

"Please," the pudge behind the counter squeals in high-pitched zealousness. "No profanity in the *Gas Stop*. This is a place of the Lord. We have a right to refuse service to those who don't serve the community."

"Ah, yes, citizenship first! Hold yourself, boy," Darwin shifts a hand inside her coat pocket. "We're just paying for gas, is all. Thirty bucks on pump . . . what is it? I can't see . . ."

Pudge boy looks over a stand of adult magazines next to the window, viewing the pump number the van is parked next to. His eyes squint. "I think it's pump, uh, three. Yeah . . . three. But I don't think you got any gas yet—"

He turns back around and is face-to-face with a Glock pistol. Pudge's eyes narrow behind those large lenses resting on his fat nose.

"What the fuck?" I back up, lungs surging into my throat. What the hell is she doing?

"Whoa, whoa now . . . take anything you want," pudgy immediately begins to shake and sweat. "Anything you want! I swear, no trouble. I won't call the cops! Promise!"

"I know you won't, Jeffrey," Darwin states coolly. Jeffrey . . . I know Jeffrey. Why does that name ring a charm inside? One, step, two.

"How . . . how do you know my name?" Jeffrey whimpers.

"What's going on?" I ask Darwin, as stunned as Jeffrey. Do I know him? I don't recognize him. At all. But, that name . . .

"What we got here, Dedalus," Darwin refers to me with the same moniker Jonah has been. She keeps the pistol's barrel aimed at Jeffrey as she inches slowly around to the back of the counter, shuffling past a display of beef jerky. "This is a man that I am going to *love* to terrify!"

She grabs Jeffrey's collar with her other hand and throws him over the counter, into a stand of Roy Orbison cassette tapes on sale for 99 cents each. Her strength! The plastic cassette covers crash – multiple gong splinters onto the tiled floor. Jeffrey scrambles to his knees, howling in pain. He weeps and curls fetal-like, ready to be kicked, beaten, or shot.

"Come on," I step between Jeffrey and Darwin as she hops over the counter. "Seriously. Put the gun away. I'll pay for the gas. This guy's just working a shift, he doesn't deserve this shit. What's up with you?"

"This *guy*," Darwin moves me aside easily. She kneels down, places the cold barrel square on Jeffrey's neck. Jeffrey is gurgling the Lord's Prayer in tears. "This guy is a deacon at the Farm Road 80 Baptist Church. This guy never misses a prayer meeting, do you Jeffrey? This guy gives money to the plate, don't you big guy?"

"HOW THE HELL DO YOU KNOW MY NAME?????" Jeffrey screams, driven mad by the surreality of the scenario before him.

I am patting the air in a calming motion. I am just as confused as Jeffrey, though less scared. I've had enough happen the past day to fuck my mind-set for months. "What're we doing here? Let's just go."

"That's the thing, Dedalus," she looks over. I can almost see burning eyes through her dark shades, red road veins. Other than that, her composure is perfectly calm. "We're where we need to be right now. Always here. Always the present moment. This is the beginning of you becoming you."

Oxygen and glucose shoot into my brain and muscles, feel ready to leap, ready to flee – norepinephrine release will cause me to hallucinate if I don't manage my epinephrine levels. How to? Energy center . . . align . . .

"This weak sapling," she stands, walks over to me, and . . . no shit! She places the gun into my cold, shivering hand. The handle is warm from her palm. "This pathetic fool is a volunteer for his church. Youth group. He's raped three children, Dedalus. And he's threatened to kill them if they tell. Can you imagine, Dedalus? You have a daughter. Can you imagine being a little innocent stripped and beaten of what makes you pure, and strong-armed into keeping it a secret for fear of your life? Can you imagine the *horror*?"

"How . . . how do you know?" I inquire. Anxiety swirls in my head, clouding perception.

"Like a good soldier," she eyes a nearby aisle of candy bars. "I do my research. We're still in mine and Merchant's *ayllu*, our local jurisdiction. We keep tabs on all the fuckups we can. You never know when we'll need to blackmail someone for information or . . ." She looks over at me. "Training exercises."

I look at Jeffrey. He's looking up at me, like a sniveling mutt. His eyes, round circles around rat irises and bulging whites. I look deep. And I can see . . . I can see in him. He's not pleading for innocence! He's pleading for . . . mercy! He wants mercy! Darwin is right! This man knows he is owned, that he has been caught . . . the look on his face! That licentious, sheepishly remorseful look! He is guilty . . .

So, I am standing there. With a weeping child molester at my feet. And a loaded gun in my hand. And no one around to stop me.

What to do?

I raise the Glock, that tool of power and force and death, I raise it into the air and aim it right at Jeffrey's depraved face. That ugly, abhorrent thing called Jeffrey. There is a second, no . . . not even a second that I think maybe Darwin is lying. Maybe she is blowing smoke up my ass. But, all I have to do is lock into those evil, deranged eyes, weeping like a pathetic creature born out of slime . . . those nervous twitches telling so much truth, telling me exactly what he did to those children. And telling me to have pity, to forgive him.

Fuck you, Jeffrey. Go to hell.

"Now, Dedalus," Darwin interrupts my reverie. She is opening a pack of candy and munching on a chocolate bar. I can smell the sweet cocoa in the air, coalescing with Jeffrey's weak sweat. "I know what you want to do. And who's to say he does or doesn't deserve it? Screw it, right? What's one less pedophile in the world? But, think about why he is here, Dedalus. Think about the cause. We can't leave a trail for the wolf to follow. We can't just leave a giant bloody mess that says, 'Yes, Jack, we were here. Thanks for dropping by.' Can we?"

I can't say a thing. I keep my sights right on this stupid creature groveling on the floor below me. Hate boils alive in my heart!

"So, how do we solve this enigma?" she asks.

I understand what she is trying to say. Deep inside a seed spawns roots. There is one form of currency that has always been more powerful than gold or drugs . . . and that is information. Darwin—as a RED Agent—keeps tabs on all the local flavor, finding all the nasty skeletons in the closets and exposing them at the right times. It's a way of making her, making RED, making *us,* invisible. We can force this fucker to forget we ever existed.

"Alright," I extend my arm, finger softly rubbing tempted by the cold trigger. "Stand up."

"Excuse me?" Jeffrey whines.

"Stand. Like a man would. Or are you a puppy?" I increase my grip, cold steel becomes warm with venom. Darwin has moved over to the refrigerated drinks and is picking out a juice. Jeffrey braces his knees, shaking, convulsing with the purity of fright, trying to push himself off the pile of broken plastic cases. "Come on, puppy."

"W-wh-what are you g-g-going to d-d-do to me?" He is starting to drool. Pathetic. A zombie edging itself out of the ground. He can't straighten himself; crooning over like a wailing old man. I want to spit on him.

So, I did. I spit right in his face.

And he cries some more. My spittle dribbles off his glasses and nose like molasses. Jeffrey, the violator of innocence.

I walk up, grab him by the wrist, and place the barrel of the gun into his palm. He is too horrified with his own mortality to struggle, to repel. I smile. He tries to look away, but I meet his gaze with the same beaming grin.

"Is this it?" I ask him eagerly. "Is this the hand you use to touch them? Huh? Is it?"

"I-I-I-g-g-g-g-g . . ." he can't say a thing.

"Sounds like puppy needs momma," Darwin is downing a bottle of grape juice, and then spits it out over an aisle of condoms. "Ugck! That's goddamn *disgusting* is what it is!!! How past the expiration is this???"

"P-p-p-please G-g-g-god sss-ss-ssave m-m-mme," Jeffrey stutters, his other hand is covering his filthy crotch. Splotches of wet bespatter the area. I laugh.

"God saves children, Jeffrey, not you. You are nothing. You have no soul. You have no magic. You suck out all the magic, make it all go away. You're a vampire, Jeffrey, an infinite vacuum. There is nothing inside of you. You are empty. That's why you have to fill that void with narcotics like patriotism and God and reality TV shows, because the nothingness scares you. But, those things aren't enough are they? Because narcotics beg more narcotics, don't they? After all that, you're still nothing, and you know it. So, because you're weak, because you are absolutely subhuman in every way, you are jealous of the kiddies around you because *they* have it. They've got what you want and you hate them for it. You despise them. So, instead of sucking it up and living with your own despair and shit like a decent human being, you decide to take it away from them. You take away their magic because you hate them, because you *can*. But, mostly, because you hate *yourself.* And that, Jeffrey, is why I hate you. That is why I want to kill you . . . right now."

My tone is surprisingly steady, unwavering. I am tapping into something inside I never knew was there. Something deep. Something always present; more me than me. An absolute place of pure stone wall. Vindication.

He is forming a puddle of sickly yellow underneath faded sneakers. I laugh some more. Darwin is watching quietly now behind me. I take the gun from his hand and point it at his crotch.

"You are mine now, Jeffrey," I tell him, label him my property. "I'll be back for you, so wait and dream of me. I will haunt you, *you pitiful shit*!!!"

He falls to a delirium heap on the floor, in his own puddle. Drooling, weeping like a wailing baby in need of milk. Darwin and I make our leave, grabbing bags of potato chips on the way out.

19 – The Galactic Confederation

"Drive on," Jonah motions forward with his stubby fingers. "It's down a ways . . . I think past Quivira there's another road."

"Pflumm?"

"No, no, that's not it."

"Lackman?"

"Yeah, yeah . . . that's it! Lackman! Turn . . . left there I think."

The driver rolls his eyes, anticipating a shift's end hours away.

They twist and wind through cookie-cutter residential neighborhoods, eventually landing—with Jonah's spittle exasperations—in front of a one level ranch house at the end of a cul-de-sac.

"Keep the engine runn'n and clock turnin' . . . I can't imagine this'll take long."

It is a quaint little house. The lawn perfectly mowed. Yellow siding. Floral beds hugging each side of the cleanly swept concrete porch. A hummingbird feeder hangs from a Japanese maple. Jonah steps up to the lovely embroidered mat which states "Welcome." He pushes the doorbell. A melodic ding-dong tunes inside.

A few seconds pass, the door is unlocked, and a stately older woman opens the door. Golden-grey hair curls delicately around her shoulders. A pearly smile shines through a make-up stained face.

"Greetings Jonah," she salutes with a courteous nod.

"Trilla," Jonah bows elegantly, dust fluttering from his layers of coats and scarves.

"What brings a gentleman like you to my doorstep?"

"I have business," he raises his head. A discerning look creases his brow. "With the Confederacy."

"Ah," she glowers slightly. She scratches her silk blouse and opens the door for Jonah's entry. He obliges.

Trilla, he knew, had a thing for cats. Walking through the foyer and into the living room he spotted five live ones scattering for cover. Other than those, he noted the numerous feline paintings, embroidered pillows, and the glass display case full of the whiskered faced ceramics. Playing with yarn. Scratching a post. Licking a paw. He felt dirty walking in here, all the pinks and purples covering the walls and floors like an eight year-old girl's play house.

"Should I?" he motions to his boots. They look as if he had walked through the Sahara ten times before catching a flight straight to Lenexa.

"Oh please, if you wouldn't mind," she closes the door behind him. "Would you like some tea?"

"Yes, please. That would be wonderful."

Jonah slipped off his boots as Trilla made her way to the kitchen. She hollers something about making himself at home and he does. Casually inching into the living area, he plops down onto a sofa, a giant feline quilt staring up at him with slanted eyes. After a few moments of thumb twiddling she comes in with a silver tray and hot cups on saucers with steeping tea bags.

"Jasmine, correct?" she asks. "You like Jasmine."

"Yes," he answers, accepting a cup. "As a matter of fact I do. How did you know?"

"Oh," she waves a dismissive hand, abashedly. "The Guardians, you know.....*they* knew, of course!"

"Of course. And the tea ready on time with my arrival?"

"Them too," she giggles and sits down in a fluffy Lazy boy chair opposite Jonah. Her posture upright, knees tight together, she daintily sips from her cup. "They told me you would be coming. The RED Brotherhood, the RED Hand. They're so efficient!"

"Aren't they!" Jonah swigs the entire cup of tea in two gulps, then slams it down on the coffee table as if it was a shot glass. "Woo! Good stuff, ma'am!"

"Thank you, sir! Now . . . what exactly did you come to see me for?"

"Well, I need some help, Trilla. Divinatory in nature. Remote viewing."

"As a veteran agent of RED, do you not receive those benefits on behalf of local Agents?" she takes another sip, her lips perched like a careful canary.

"That's where the problem is," Jonah waves his gloved hands out in a pleading nature. "I got one Agent headed to Aztalan for a recruitment procedure. The other . . . is missing."

"AWOL?" Trilla perks an eyebrow.

"We suspect malfeasance. There's a crypto in town by the name of Spring-heeled Jack!"

Trilla gasps. She almost spills her tea, cautiously placing the saucer onto the coffee table next to Jonah's empty cup. "You don't mean . . . Jack of Wanderers, do you?"

"The very one, ma'am," Jonah musters. "You see what the city is facing right now? I need the Guardians' assistance, if possible."

"Yes, yes . . . I see," she shifts in her chair, grasps her legs tightly. "Well . . . I will . . . I will depart then and let . . . let the Guardians speak for themselves, if you don't mind."

"No, no! Not at all, ma'am."

She smiles gaily and assumes a meditative position. She breathes in heavily, holds in, eyes roll to the back of her head and all Jonah sees is white in her sockets. She breathes in again, heaving. Then . . . an extreme exhale as her head bows low.

Moments pass. Jonah twiddles some more. After hearing a cat meow in the next room, he leans forward to verbally nudge her out of her trance state.

"Trilla," he mutters. "Trilla? Hello . . ."

She lifts her head. Slowly. She smiles at Jonah and lifts the cup of tea on the table.

"Oh," Trilla exclaims. "I do so love it when she makes tea!"

"Who am I speaking with?" Jonah asks.

She sips. "Xonactl of Alpha Centauri 5. You are Jonah Mulligan of the RED Hand. Your exploits in the 1960s and 70s are legendary, even in the Cosmos."

"Thanks, but if we could get down to business," Jonah cringes. He was never fond of the extraterrestrial types. They were hard to peg as far as their motivation to the Cause. Some had Higher ambitions, some Lower. It sometimes depended on who channeled them as well, which was another issue. Bottom line, he could not relate to where they were coming from and that rubbed him sour.

"The Galactic Confederation of Worlds does not consider you a normal construct of the human population," she puts down the cup and curtly folds her hands.

"Pardon?" Jonah tilts on the edge of the couch, one hand bracing the cushion beneath.

"You have arrived here, Jonah Mulligan, to extract services out of the Confederacy. If you were considered a legitimate aspect of the human population, we would offer you those services as a courtesy of our higher consciousness, for we exist to service humanity throughout this chaotic period in your history. We aim to propel you, human beings of Earth, to the Fourth Dimensional stage of the evolutionary process. Though you, however, are not of the normal population, as I have stated. You, Jonah Mulligan, are an aspect of this transitory period. Part of the equation, so to speak, as a veteran Agent and active ally of the RED Hand. In being so, you forfeit your rights to services as a citizen. You are an *active participant*."

"So what then?" Jonah guffaws, tossing his hands into the air. "I get nuth'n? I came out all this way...."

"To Lenexa, Jonah."

177

"Yes! To *Lenexa*! For what? You're not going to help at all? We've got a Dark Matter Anomaly on our hands here! Spring-heeled Jack is in town! He's attacked our Atelier! Possibly taken one of our Agents! RED's done enough for you, you'd think . . ."

"We owe RED nothing, Jonah Mulligan. Just as RED owes nothing to us. We may have mutual enemies, but our means meet no same end."

"We'll see about that ma'am."

"Sir."

"Excuse me?"

"My name is Xonactl. I am of the male variety on Alpha Centauri 5. I merely inhabit Trilla Campbell's body during this particular session. I would appreciate it if you could refer to me and not the form I currently habit."

"Yes, yes," Jonah stands and paces about the room. Frustration pounds at the membranes of his temperament. He ran through the list of other remote viewing possibilities in the community. The list was decent, but nowhere near as sufficient and adept as Trilla, the primary Earth-bound Ambassador of the Galactic Confederation of Worlds, right here in Lenexa, Kansas! Who else would be better equipped to psychically locate two individuals throughout the city based only upon a name?

"However, Jonah Mulligan, it does not mean you will not receive the assistance of the Confederacy."

"Eh?" he whirls around.

"The Elder Guardians of the Confederation could consider this . . . a *favor*!"

Jonah cursed in his head. A favor would mean an organizational arrangement between the Galactic Confederation of Worlds and the RED Agency. It would mean a diplomatic agreement that would put RED at the Confederacy's behest. This would require the consent and endorsement from RED's regional *supu*; that would include time as well as a high degree of ceremony that the current situation could not afford.

"What say you, Jonah Mulligan of Earth? Do you speak for the RED Hand?"

Jonah bit his lip. Looked from side to side: a kitten cookie jar, a pair of booties in the shape of paws. "'*Mark this farther and remember. The end comes suddenly. Enter that antechamber of birth where the studious are assembled and note their faces.*' That's right, I speak for the Agency. But only under the condition of immunity of the organization."

"I'm sorry?" the husk of Trilla's head cocked to the side. "Your affinity for the Earth-author Joyce is admirable, but the point remains ambiguous."

"I get you. You do me a favor, you're doing RED a favor. That's true. And we believe in sacred reciprocity, that's true. We will pay you back. But, it will be *me* that pays you back! It will be as a representative of RED, under the Agency flagship, but you are not holding the organization as whole responsible for a debt incurred on my behalf. The Universe, Xonactl ol' buddy, will respect *my* sacred right to be responsible for *my* own actions."

"Hmm," Xonactl's expression through Trilla seems slightly perturbed. "I will consult with the Others. Please wait quietly."

The next instant, Trilla's eyes shone with a dark blue light, throwing her head back in a rapid convulsion. Jonah jumps up to assist her. Before he reaches her side, her body eases its tension and its composure becomes normal again.

"Do not worry yourself, Jonah Mulligan," Trilla's face looks up at him calmly. "Trilla Campbell is perfectly safe. Her soul is currently experiencing an Atlantean bath from the 37th Century B.C.E. You may resume your seat."

"I'm perfectly fine where I'm at, Cosmo," Jonah stated gruffly. The possessive nature of this entity over Trilla's body grated his skin like nails and chalkboard. He clenches his knuckles in a hard squeeze. "If you don't mind, that is."

"I do," Trilla's hand raised and with it Jonah's body. He finds himself lift lightly off the ground, levitating half a foot above the carpet. Trilla's hand flicks and Jonah's body flits lightly through the air, over the coffee table, and lands gently back down onto the couch. "I have an obligation to protect Trilla Campbell's body and personal space, just as I believe you must be feeling in this case. Incidentally, you know hardly a thing about Trilla Campbell except for a few brief encounters. However, I have been in direct telepathic and astral communication with the deepest parts of her consciousness for twenty years now. We are, in a sense, married to each other through a spiritual bond. I am respecting her wishes. She has an aversion to physical contact with people and you were coming dangerously close."

"But you said she was in Atlantis! In the past!"

"I am respecting her wishes, Jonah Mulligan!"

Jonah pierced Trilla's eyes with a stare. No . . . Xonactl's eyes . . . he could see! Look deep enough and you can see the soul, see who is operating behind the screen filament of matter. There, the extraterrestrial is weighing him down, binding him to the couch like a restrained dog. Jonah wants to kill him, rip that alien bastard to shreds!

"Do not fret Jonah Mulligan," Trilla's face . . . Xonactl's . . . smirks. "Your appeal has been heard and the request granted by the Elder Guardians of the Galactic Confederation of Worlds. But know that when it is time for us to collect what is due, we expect to sequester your services as an ambassador of the RED Hand and not a lone member of the human society. We expect to have access to your clout and reputation as a member of that organization."

Jonah eyes Xonactl glumly. "That works."

"Excellent," Trilla's body gleams, hands clapping in satisfaction. "Now, what exactly is your request? You want us to find someone is that correct?"

"Yeah. Two girls. Kidnapped by a Nova spook last night. Ramona Udell and Lena Samson. They should still be within the metro area I imagine. Spook went by the name of Benjamin. Obviously fake."

"I see," Trilla's eye lids blink; the first time, Jonah notices, since Xonactl took over her body. "Ramona Udell is being kept at a private residence in the south. Alive and well. I will write down directions. Lena . . ." Trilla's face wanders into nothing, a hint of confusion breathes over Xonactl's aspect. "Lena . . ."

"What's wrong?" Jonah ushers, anxiety pinching his gut. He rubs his fingerless gloved hands.

"Lena . . . there is no Lena."

"What? What are you talking about? Gregor's sister, Lena Samson!"

"I am sorry Jonah Mulligan. There is a mistake. There is no Lena Samson."

"You kidding? Is . . . is she dead? What happened?"

"No, she couldn't be dead; because there is no Lena Samson to die. There is no Lena Samson associated with an Enterprise contact called Benjamin."

"I'm confused now."

"So am I. You are asking me to trace the energy signature of people who do not exist. Are you composing a sarcastic response to your disliking of our contentious conversation, Jonah Mulligan."

"No, no," Jonah rubs his chin. Lena's lack of existence to the Confederacy's highly advanced intelligence network was troublesome. If they say she does not exist, they are most likely right. But, he saw her last night! With his very own eyes! "Thank you, though. Ramona . . . I need to find Ramona."

"Of course," Trilla's body stands up and strolls to a nearby desk to grab a pen and paper. "Would you prefer a drawn map or written directions?"

20 – Atelier Aztalan

We come up through Dubuque on 151 into Wisconsin as night crawls over the landscape. Iowa was boring, rolling green of croplands in a blur of redundancy. I slept most of the ride. Dubuque, though, is a signal of change, heralding a transition in energy with its obscure riverfront cityscape. In essence, Dubuque is nothing but a spiky mass of gothic cathedrals and banks, half of which are empty, abandoned and dilapidated. It's a sight to behold in contrast to the monotonous landscape before it. Going through, you pass over the Mississippi into a completely different terrain and *feel*. The hills and green around us have a personality . . . something is *happening* here.

As we head toward Madison, Darwin begins to explain about Aztalan. A big chunk of southern Wisconsin, evidently, is a hotspot of supernatural activity. A Fortean paradise, one might say. There are numerous sightings of UFOs, sasquatch, ghosts, even werewolves. Some local paranormal investigators have even posed hypothesis of a Bermuda Triangle-type electromagnetic frequency in the area. One of these places is the mythical State Park of Aztalan.

Officially Aztalan is stated to have been found around 900 A.D., by Middle Mississippi Native American tribes, a woodland culture of the indigenous tradition. It is characterized by its collection of flat-top pyramid-shaped mounds and log-post stockades. Most archeologists would say Aztalan was established as a proficient trade route (as they say in most cases of discovered cities of the ancients). This may be partially the case. But the shamans know better. Ancient sites, such as Machu Picchu in Peru or Chichen Itza in Mexico, were chosen for a high concentration of energetic qualities. After all, who would climb the insurmountable heights of the Andes to merely trade at a place such as Machu Picchu? No, these sites were chosen first for their spiritual nature. As was the case for Aztalan.

It has been noted that the people of Aztalan were originally the descendants of the Aztecs, who had migrated from the Bering Strait in the north down south to Aztalan and eventually to Central America. Darwin spoke of ancient connections as well, trade and negotiations with the Roman Empire, and a strong connection to the lost civilization of Atlantis. Aztalan was a mystic hub for—what Darwin calls—the Priests of the Old Ones, a sort of backup for its neighboring bigger brother in Illinois . . . Cahokia.

It is late as we pass through Madison, rerouted east on Interstate 94 and got off on 89. We drive through a little quaint town reminiscent of the *Leave it to Beaver* America, and eventually ease slowly right into Aztalan State Park. I note the easy access to the highway; not *too much* off the beaten path.

The moon is almost full, beating down a luminescent sheen on the well mowed plain of the Park. The parking lot is chained up after hours, so Darwin just parks on the side of the road.

"Just leave this stuff here," she motions to the duffel bags of ammunition. "But take your personal backpack if desired."

I do. We get out and stroll onto the grassy knoll. There isn't a cloud in the sky, just about every star dancing and singing its tribute to being. I immediately notice the remnant pieces of the log stockade still standing, which originally surrounded the entire city before the white man came and leveled it. On the southern end of the plot, which is surrounded by a thicket of woodland, sits the largest of the plateau pyramids. The smaller ones are scattered more to the west and north.

We begin climbing the wall of the mound when Darwin points to the opposite end of the park.

"There is a lake over there; part of the city was built underneath it."

"You mean a lake eventually grew over it," I inquire.

"No," she shakes her head. "Part of the city was underwater."

Before I have a chance to probe the confusion of her statement we reach the top of the mound. It isn't a huge pyramid, but it looms a good 20 to 30 feet over the rest of the park. A slight breeze tickles our faces. Darwin's hair whisks delicately in the wind. It is a nice respite from the sweltering hot days we've had recently.

"Now what?" I ask. "Where do we go?"

"Here," she kneels down to sit cross-legged on the top of the mound. "Sit with me, face-to-face."

I sit cross-legged in front of her.

"Now lift your hands, palms facing outward."

I do so and she repeats the gesture. Our hands are inches apart. I feel an electrical charge emanate between them.

"Now close your eyes and breathe," she says. "Slowly in for ten seconds. Hold for ten seconds. Exhale for ten seconds. Breathe."

In, in, in, in. Hold, hold, hold, hold. Out, out, out, out. It is hard at first, not used to breathing that way. I feel strained, unable to do it. But, after the third or fourth time the tension releases and I am surprised at how easy it becomes. I feel the charge between our hands intensify, almost as if tiny needles are pricking them.

In, in, in, in. Hold, hold, hold, hold. Out, out, out, out. A cadence builds up, and my consciousness beats to the resonance of that rhythm. Flow, flow, flowing. In, in, in, in. Hold, hold, hold, hold. Out, out, out, out. It feels so easy, like liquid through a canal. Moving, morphing, fluid snake-like Kundalini twist and curve. I am relaxed, in, in, in, hold, hold, hold, out, out, out.

"Now . . . open."

Breathing halts. Open my eyes and we are no longer outside! We are sitting in a small chamber, a passageway open to the left. I retract my hands and twitch with a shudder.

"Wha—where the hell? What the hell happened?"

"Gregor Samson," Darwin stands and offers her hands to help me up. "Welcome to Atelier Aztalan!" I grasp hold of them and she pulls me to my feet.

"But, where . . . how the hell? Where are we?"

"Physically, we are deep under Aztalan."

"How did we get here?"

"Entry to Aztalan cannot be made by physical means. You can't dig a hole and get into it, yet it's here. Essentially, I initiated our morphic resonance to chime in tune with an *axis mundi* polychoron tesseract. It is the quantum field entry point into Aztalan. Only RED Agents can enter, or a person of their choosing. Completely impenetrable to anyone outside of the Agency."

"I've never been through a tesseract before," I grin jokingly. "I figured you'd actually get sick from such a thing. But, I feel fine. Like in a blink of an eye, from here to there. No disorientation."

"It is the natural way to travel, Gregor. The Ancients did it all the time. Humanity has grown away from it, frightened of even the possibility. Now, come."

She starts down the narrow corridor and I follow.

The walls, floor, and ceiling are all connected, like we are walking down a cave tunnel, but there is no rock. The orange and vermillion surface is hard, but has a pulsating glaze to it. It is not static, in fact, though radiates as if it is *breathing*! Pulmonary pink veins run like roots throughout the walls and ceiling, circulating a life force I can feel surging into me. A calm glow radiates from them, lighting the underground complex with comfortable phosphorescence.

As we stroll down the corridor we pass by hallways branching off like arteries into other areas. I hear voices throughout, a bustling atmosphere of discussions and work. Whispers of restless conference. Sometimes there are doors, I can see through small porthole windows. Figures doing this and that . . . I can't discern as I try to keep up with Darwin's pace. We pass by a person or two, decked out in red, wearing sunglasses. But, Darwin and they exchange brief mumbled greetings and hurry past each other. Again, I trot to catch up with Darwin, eyeing the seeming Agents meandering through the halls of Aztalan.

We take a turn to the left, and to the right. Then right again. The hall has widened, becoming busier. I see a few people in civilian clothes, walking from one doorway to another, one hall to another. We seem to be entering a large meeting area. Finally we pass through a threshold to a gargantuan chamber humming industriously with life!

I am reminded of a Mission Control Center: there are giant monitors on the walls with news casts and other unidentifiable images, people buzzing here and there, tables stacked with materials ranging from computers to weapons to laboratory equipment. CPUs humming with print outs. A symphony of conversation. I estimate approximately fifty people in all, but there are some coming in and out at such speed it is hard to tell. There are other passages branching from this main room, obviously the heart-center of Aztalan. My assumption is confirmed by a gigantic gyrating mass of fleshy bulk in the center of room, connected and supported by the accumulated veins from the ceiling and floor meshing together into a sculptural support. It heaves sonically the pulse of the entire complex.

I watch the video screens: the President of the United States is golfing while the news caption below reads "20 Troops Dead in Fallujah Bombing"; Senator Reed is speaking out at a rally, the crowd is displaying signs such as "Impeach Now," "9/11 was an Inside Job," and "Bail Out Main Street, Not Wall Street"; a man in red clothing and sunglasses—assumedly a RED Agent—on what looks like a home video, spray painting the words "Paradigm Shift Commencing" on a Federal Reserve building; a platoon of troops marching through an Afghan village; aerial footage of an oil spill in the ocean, a black blood stain infiltrating a sparkling blue seascape; another RED Agent in a red tuxedo and a clown mask, talking to a group of black-clad anarchists around a poker table; a Congressional hearing over privacy violations in the Patriot Act.

To the far left a crowd surrounds a circular structure about fifteen feet high. It looks to be constructed of a metal substance I cannot discern carved with alien-like runes. In the center is a vertical ring, a portal of mesh comprised of a type of slime or gelatin with a lime hue.

"We need to go over there," Darwin breaks my reverie of observation. "It's time to meet Edith and Maynard."

We shuffle through the active fray—half of which are decked out in red clothing of some sort (RED Agents) the other half in civilian clothing—all engaged in individual or group activities. Coming upon the circular structure, I make out a tube which extends almost twenty feet past the ring-portal of gunk. A collection of people in red suits and garb sit in Yogic meditative positions on top of the tube. A vibratory hum reverberates the floor as they intone abstruse chants. In front of the ring stands a group of individuals, some red, some not. Some are having discussions while others are diligently studying a monitor overhead; it connected to a computer terminal attached to the base of the tube structure. One of the members identifies Darwin and hails her excitedly.

"Darwin dear! Greetings, child!" It is a small elderly lady, white curling hair dressed in a teal sweater and slacks. Thick glasses settle on a bulbous nose, pearl earrings shine from her lobes. She waddles toward us in galoshes, giving Darwin a hug. "Ooohhh, give a *squinch*, will yeh? Yes!"

I haven't seen Darwin smile so much since meeting her. She shines with brilliance!

"I'd like you to meet our new recruit in the Kansas City *allyu*, Gregor Samson. Gregor, this is Dr. Edith Bruyere. She is one of the Founding Elders of the RED Agency."

"Oh now, now," Edith chuckles, her cheeks flush with joy. "RED always *has been*, dear! I just helped pick up some pieces is all. Come give a *squinch*, Gregor darling!"

We embrace and I feel a thousand grandmothers' love wrap me into a moment of solace. Loss and despair tinge on the peripherals . . . something aching in my heart of realism and surrealism, no . . . non-realism. I cannot discern exactly the twilight memory there, but I want to stay in her arms. She feels like family, the perfumed grandmother smell, and I immediately love her.

"All set to transmogrify, eh?" she asks me with sweet, squinting eyes. I am reminded of Spring. I realize I am smiling, a real smile . . . something I don't remember doing for quite some time. What is happening to me? I am in a place of extraordinary sights and feel more at ease and normal than back in the "real" world, locked into my apartment and cubicle employment. I am home.

"I . . . I'm sorry, I don't know what you mean," I answer.

"Ah, it's okay darling. You'll catch up. Experience is the only true teacher, you know!" She waves a manicured finger in the air and walks back toward the tube. Darwin and I follow.

"What is this?" I ask, utterly amazed at the pure science fiction of the tube structure and its gelatin mesh opening.

"Oh this old thing?" Edith quips. "This is an observation tank into the Maninkari Realms. Like Hubble, but for inner space instead of outer space."

We approach a man with a discerning look, gazing steadily at the overhead monitor. Its image is fuzzy, covered in fractals and unknown colors. Laser streams of light flicker in and out of the prismatic mélange. There is a subtle image of a figure floating, but it's difficult to make out. The man watching the monitor is holding an ear piece strung from the computer terminal. He notices us and blandly looks our way. He is around Edith's age with receding bark-colored hair, large side burns running down his cheeks. He is tall, thin, with sharp crinkled features and hawkish eyes. He is dressed in a brown turtleneck, arms staunchly crossed. By his look, it is obvious we are interrupting him.

"Maynard dear," Edith puts a calming hand on his shoulder and motions to Darwin and I. "I would love you to meet Darwin's new boy, Gregor Samson. Gregor, Maynard Ostrowski. He's our Head of Scientific Operations here at Aztalan, holding PhDs in both quantum mechanics and molecular biology."

He extends a hard hand. I shake it and his squeeze is unbearable. He isn't just a scientist; I can tell the man has endured some hard labor in his time.

"Pleasure," he coldly murmurs.

"Gregor will be joining our organization today," Edith chimes. "Isn't that wonderful? Jonah has told me so much about him; he will be an excellent initiate!"

"Where is Jonah?" Maynard asks.

"We had to split," Darwin answers. "You should know by now from my communication through Mahamaya that Spring-heeled Jack is at cause for our recent disturbances. Some bystanders got in the way, relations of Gregor's. Jonah went on the search and rescue."

"Oh my, poor dears," Edith shakes her head and puckers her lips. "This nasty business with Jack! That boy is a thorn, indeed! Poor Mahamaya! She'll be back online soon enough, dear, don't you worry!"

"Speaking of which," Maynard clicks on the keyboard in front of him. A window pops up of an audio player. He turns on a pair of speakers. "We caught a bit of Mahamaya's last transmission before her unfortunate, but temporary, demise. Throughout Jack's brutality, we got snippets of conversation. The mystery of Merchant's absence is solved, with our fears coming into fruition. Listen to this."

He clicks the play button. We all huddle around intently.

The speakers whine with static, a transmission wafts in and out of frequency. Some words can be heard in the churn: ". . . only use . . . <<SSCHH>> . . . because it is required . . .

<<SSCHH>> . . . fulfill the Mass . . . <<SSCHH>> . . . Merchant's body ready . . . <<SSCHH>> . . . pick-up . . ."

Darwin freezes, stiff.

"Play it again," she orders.

". . . only use . . . <<SSCHH>> . . . because it is required . . . <<SSCHH>> . . . fulfill the Mass . . . <<SSCHH>> . . . Merchant's body ready . . . <<SSCHH>> . . . pick-up . . ."

Edith looks somberly over to Darwin. "Oh dear I am so sorry!"

"So, they killed Merchant," she straightens her composure, unwilling to give in to the loss of her partner and friend. "But the mystery has only broadened in scope. What exactly are they getting his body 'ready' for? And what is 'the Mass' referring to?"

"That is for you all to find out," Maynard states, unaffected by the emotionality of the situation. "I have some conjectures. But first, we ran an analysis on the recording and concluded the voice is not Jack's, yet indeed male. Middle-aged. This will require further investigation."

"All the more reason to get Gregor ready," Darwin turns to me. I feel her razor blade eyes penetrate me through her shades.

"What does that involve exactly?" I ask hesitantly.

"Well, let's catch you up to speed here, darling," Edith takes my arm and marches me closer to the portal entrance of the observation tank. "The RED Agency, as Darwin and Jonah may have already relayed to you, is a shamanic and scientific mission dedicated to an ambassadorship with the Maninkari, the Invisible Architects of our actuality, the *Kay Pacha*, the Middle World. What you may know as *observable reality*. We aim to protect the sacred mystery of the Maninkari's existence, protecting them from the malevolent forces that would manipulate and pervert the knowledge of the Maninkari populace."

"So this observation tank," I jab a thumb in its direction. "It helps you see into the Maninkari world?"

"Very good, Gregor," Edith squeezes my arm. "But it is more like a *dimension*, dear."

Maynard steps up with Darwin. "We call it the Conduit. A spacewalk equivalent to inner space. There is a misconception about shamanic dreamtime. The so-called 'New Age' movement has consistently reverted focus to the 'higher' realm of being, that enlightenment equals outer space, outer dimensions. Although part of this is true, it is not entirely. The shaman's journey begins in the *Ukhu Pacha*, the Lower or Interior Realms. We have hypothesized that the inner journey and outer journey both end in the same place, looping back around to create an infinite loop, a non-orientated Möbius strip."

"Like an ouroboros." I say.

Edith claps with glee. "Oh, well done Gregor!"

"If you please," Maynard insists, perturbed at Edith's joy like a cranky older brother. "Regardless, the Conduit allows us to map out inner space, giving us many models to understand the unseen realms."

"Show him the mandala model," Darwin suggests. It is apparent she is less interested in didactics and more interested in getting my initiatory process moving quickly. "The Dimensional Roadmap."

"Yes," Maynard takes us over to a nearby table with many graphs and charts splayed out chaotically on its surface. Notebooks, paper, sticky note pads are strewn about with mathematical equations and esoteric runic symbols scribbled on all of them. He pulls out a laminated 18 x 24 poster board, beaten and tattered from the pile. "This is a rather crude representation . . . it is so much more complex. But, for layman's understanding, this will provide an adequate breakdown of the structure of the inner universe."

It is a graphic, a diagram: a circle within a circle within a circle.

He points to the outer circle, the outer edge surrounded by little drawings of stick people. "Think of this in terms of the Big Bang theory, if you please. All life and consciousness starts at a single, minute point, almost infinitely dense. This miniature cosmic egg explodes, all of the matter and energy spreading outward. Now, this model shows the shamanic process implemented to get to those Inner Realms; a reversal of the Big Bang, reaching back to that single minute point. The outer edge you see us, people, humanity. Any living being with actuality consciousness, animals, whatever. In this case, the diagram represents RED Agents, as we are looking at the RED process here."

"What *does* R.E.D. mean?" I inquire.

"Don't interrupt," Maynard hushes me. He then point to the next circle in, what looks to be zigzag patchwork scribbles. "While traveling inward, there is a quantum reaction happening to consciousness. This is part of the psychedelic process. We call this layer the Entelechy of the Universe. Radio wave disassembly. This was originally Aristotle's concept, the force which organizes the form of essence into materiality. What happens here is what we call the R.E.D. Shift, Entelechy Deconstruction . . . a virtual breakdown of perceptual systems as one goes from the normal everyday consciousness of reality to *actuality*. It is the next transitioning wave where ideas become solid objects, and vice versa when travelling inward."

He moves further in, to the next inner circle. This layer is represented by geometric blocks of various shapes and colors.

"This is the Maninkari Realms, the Reality Architecture of the Universe. This is where the ideas of the Logos, Jung's collective unconscious—the Center Point of Existence—turns ideas into reality. Anything you can see and measure and observe in the Universe—you, me, plants, trees, rocks, buildings, cars, love, sadness, piss, myth, war, comic books—all starts as an idea. The Maninkari are the Invisible Architects. They take these ideas and form them into material existence. They form the Universe into being, the working machine elves

of the Creator Essence, the Original Thought. Moving further in
. . ."

The next inner circle is symbolized by a line-drawn starburst.

"The Resonant Translation of the Universe. Every thing in the known Universe has a resonant vibration. The Vedic scriptures say that the Universe was created with the sound 'OHM.' The Bible says in the beginning was the Word. Everything starts with the hum, the vibration from the Creator Essence, the Center Point, which is there." He points to the center of the entire model, a small miniscule dot.

"Zero Point. No time. Where it all starts, end, begins, the ultimate everything and nothing. The Resonant Translation hums from the Center Point and literally translates to the Maninkari Realms the Will of the Creator Essence what expression the Universe will take next."

"Pretty fascinating, isn't it dear?" Edith nudges me.

"Now look at this," Maynard pipes in before giving me a chance to answer. It is apparent this is his vibe, where he gets his self-worth. Most likely an introvert with most people, but this . . . this is what he was made to do. I follow him to another table, a laboratory arrangement of large test tubes of all color of liquids. He pulls out a notebook and doodles an image of another tube, but something inside, almost looks like a caterpillar. "This, Gregor, is a Maninkari wyrm. We have an arrangement with the Maninkari to use them for our work; they are our access point into the *Ukhu Pacha*, to Inner Space."

I stare at the crude drawing. He rolls his eyes to the confusion painting my face. Placing the pen and paper down he turns full attention on to me. I notice Darwin and Edith have hung back a bit, a quiet discussion taking place.

"The wyrms are buds, undeveloped Maninkari embryos in our reality. Their life blood is one hundred percent DMT concentrate."

"DMT?"

"DMT . . . N,N-dimethyltryptamine. A naturally occurring monoamine alkaloid present almost everywhere in nature. One of the principle plant molecules of *ayahuasca* used by the shamans in South America. It is the most potent, the most powerful psychedelic in the world. The shaman utilizes the visionary properties of DMT to heal and induce ecstasy, transcending normal states of consciousness, traveling to the Maninkari Realms. In fact, inducing superconsciousness . . . a wholeness."

He taps the paper lightly. An impish glow intensifies his rough edged face.

"What do you mean naturally occurring?" I ask.

He smirks, a crease seeming almost uncomfortable. "It exists in almost every living organism on the planet. All plants: grass, flowers, trees, the bark on trees, the ayahuasca vine, of course, mushrooms. Even animals: most marine animals, many, many mammals including humans."

"You mean we have DMT *in* us?"

"We produce it, boy," he moves past the array of lab tables to an overloaded bookcase in what looks like a tiny break area. Three coffee pots brewing half-full, tan stain circles populating the countertop along with scattered pieces of reports and various office supplies. I'm reminded vaguely of my previous employment, my previous life, just days ago . . . though it seems so long ago. He pulls out a massive text book labeled *Endocrine Physiology* and drops it >>SLAM<< onto the counter. He turns a few pages to an image of the human body, a diagram showing the organs of both the endocrine and nervous systems. He points to a small dot in the lower-center of the brain.

"The pineal gland. Descartes called it the seat of the soul. Though it's located directly above the most critical byway of the cerebrospinal fluid, it actually isn't part of the human brain. It's part of the endocrine system, the information interface of the human body. The pineal gland produces DMT, thus being the trigger for naturally existing altered states of consciousness, such as: deep meditation, lucid dreaming, out-of-body experiences, and so on. These are moments when DMT is naturally released into the human body, inducing a visionary state beyond mundane reality. Otherwise, it is regulated within our bloodstream to such an extent that we have no awareness of an endogenous psychedelic within our very own bodies.

"The pineal gland acts as an antenna for the shaman to establish contact with the unseen worlds, such as the Maninkari Realms. This is the entire model behind R.E.D. It is the Radioactive Endocrine Defect that stimulates the Agents, sustaining their symbiotic relationships with the wyrms. The wyrm, the Maninkari, are pure DMT manifested in our material reality; it is their lifeblood. When ingested, the wyrm boosts the DMT levels into a constant, ongoing catalyst. The wyrm itself lives off of the monoamine oxidases in the body; these MAOs hinder dimethyltryptamine production by dissolving the DMT in our system, partnered with the regulatory processes of the endocrine system itself. Without these MAOs—and the accelerated DMT secretions by the Maninkari wyrm—the RED Agent becomes a living, breathing psychedelic compound. The senses are all heightened to a superconscious perspective. The Agents are constantly, what you kids may call, 'tripping.' As well, the amplified levels of DMT augment and magnify hormone production in the endocrine system. Again, the endocrine system regulates the majority of the functions in our body; it is how the information received by the nervous system is processed. It affects tissue function, metabolism, mood, other parts of growth and development. Imagine these processes being boosted to an almost superhuman proficiency! Your ability to heal, physical prowess, response time, fight-or-flight mechanisms, anti-inflammation, immunity, muscle stimulation, endurance, protein synthesis . . . all enhanced! Even still, the Maninkari wyrm maintains a balance within the system, so the delicacy of the human body doesn't overload."

"Can we back up a little please?" I impede. Maynard wants to cut me short again. I don't let him. "This is a lot to assimilate here. Give me a moment or two. I'm confused by the Mandala Model, the Maninkari Architects, or whatever, and what this has to do with DMT. What exactly *are* the Maninkari?"

He sighs, shakes his head a little, but continues on. Despite his seeming disappointment, a respect grows in his eyes for my ability to assert my position.

"DMT facilitates a direct channel of communication with what a certain ethnobotanist—and RED ally---called Terence McKenna calls the Overmind, the mind behind nature. An infinite network of pure, living information. This is also associated with what the Greeks and Gnostics call the Logos, the source of all knowledge, wisdom, and understanding. The Hindus, of course, were one of the first post-Paleolithic non-indigenous civilizations to refer to it: the Akashic Record.

"Again, this is the thing, the place, the idea that feeds all imagination and creativity in the universe: from the slightest impulse for an electron leaping from atom to atom, to the poet inscribing the greatest sonnet of the Romantic Age. It is the hidden source of all creation, the collective consciousness that connects all; the unifying principle. This place is where the thought forms of the Universe are converted, transmuted into matter, into what we know and perceive as material reality."

He reaches over to a bookcase, scans a shelf. With an "Ah!" pulls out a flimsy paperback with a vertigo vortex on the cover momentarily catching my eye. He flips lazily toward the back of the book until he finds the specific passage he was searching for.

"Another ally of our organization, writer Daniel Pinchbeck, has this to say about these shamanic realms accessed via DMT: 'It is a doorway you can step through to greet the beings who run the cosmic candy store. Spinning down from the immersive matrices of DMT, I suspected those beings were, in some way or other, superconscious entities who created and maintain our universe.' They are, in short, what we here call the Invisible Architects of Existence.'

"The indigenous Ashaninca peoples of the Peruvian Amazon are some of our strongest comrades. They speak of invisible beings found in plants, animals, rocks, water, in all aspects of nature, that are the source of all knowledge. When the Ashanincan shaman, the *ayahuasquero*, drinks the DMT-filled brew of ayahuasca they can see and commune with these invisible spirits. They teach the shaman everything he needs to know about medicine, healing, as well as which plants in the jungle are edible and which are not. The Ashaninca call these spirits 'those who are hidden,' the *maninkari*.

"The Maninkari are the Invisible Architects, and we, the RED Agency, the RED Hand, are their emissaries, exemplars, ambassadors between their plane of existence and ours."

"It's a lot to understand, darling," Edith sneaks up behind me, patting my shoulder. "Maynard stop being so overbearing! The boy has been through a lot. Gregor, come with me dear."

She takes me to a passageway on the edge of the control room, leaving behind Darwin and Maynard. Twisting though a serpentine hallway, we eventually walk into a pristine office with a simple arrangement of an oak desk and some chairs. It is an odd contrast to the Aztalan wall and floors. She sits down at the desk and has me take a seat on the opposite side. An arrangement of lilacs sits to the side. The walls are covered in black and white photos of what looks like Edith's trips around the world, meetings with famous faces and scientists. My eyes land on a picture of a young Edith with a face I recognize.

"Is that you and Carl Sagan?" I point to the picture in question.

"Oh yes! He was such a charmer! There have been many strong associations with RED over the years. We are not an isolated group, just secretive."

"So, what's with the freedom-fighter attitude from Darwin and Jonah, if all of this is just a scientific and spiritual ambassadorship?"

"Well, dear, it is a philosophical and sociological issue as well, is it not? We believe there is a breakdown in society, in humanity. We've all gone mad, isolated from our Great Mother, the Earth. There has never been a bigger problem of collective depression anytime in history.

"RED is where the Weird shall have a Way, where the Strange remain Safe. We are the sanctuary for those outside the boundaries of the accepted norm, the counter to commonly accepted perceptions. But, it's not about being *contrary* necessarily, is it? No! We are all truly connected, biologically, physically . . . but modern culture has made us forget that. That is why everyone feels so alone when they tie themselves so strongly to their individuality. *Individuality* . . . puh! It's an illusion! People should let go of their egos and realize it's all bunk! But that's why we're here to remind them. RED Agents don't just fight for freedom, darling. We promote the strange and anomalous phenomena that force minds to think out of the box! Like Carl there, or David Lynch. Ooh, he was so cute! I do so love his hair!"

"What about someone like Tim Leary, or those guys in the sixties? LSD and consciousness expansion? Was RED a part of that?"

"Good question, darling! In a way we were, and in a way the whole situation was derailed." Edith pulls out a package from a drawer in her desk. She offers the package to me, filled with suckers, gum, chocolates, mints.

"Candy?"

"Um sure," I take a mint and pop it in.

Edith grabs a chocolate and munches on it giddily. She continues with her story.

"Unfortunately, Timothy Leary was an adversary, not an ally; the bane of the RED Agency's existence during the sixties. In many ways the antithesis of what we stood for – a pop guru proselytizing the psychedelic experience to the American youth and counter-culture. Functioning as a triple-agent for the Nova Enterprise, Leary beguiled the budding minds of an unsatisfied generation. He created an uncontrolled and unmonitored mass experiment of LSD and psilocybin. What he promised was free speech, free love, and free illumination. What the children of the sixties didn't understand is that this chaotic cry to break the chains of tradition scared the Dominator culture into a fear-driven hate campaign against the very revolution RED was trying to foster. Watching LSD being handed out freely to their children – showing off their tits at rock concerts and growing beards like savages – drove the conservative populace to war. Not even academic study of one of the greatest phenomena to hit psychiatry was allowed after the onslaught of the Controlled Substances Act.

"That poor fellow Leary successfully infiltrated and perverted the RED Insurgency of the 1960s. Civilization requires a mild, meditative exposure to the ontology of the Overmind. Otherwise they become shocked and terrified animals. The Enterprise knew this and took advantage of it; a reckless cocktail party extravaganza was the perfect recipe to implode and diffuse any hope of RED's success.

"We caught on to his Enterprise affiliation in 1961, when Allen Ginsberg became inspired by the evangelization of instant mysticism. Bless his soul! Allen so fervently sought to latch his ring of Beat friends onto this new and exciting method: why spend a lifetime in meditation when you can become the Buddha in one dose? Out of all the experimental minds of the Beatnik culture, it was Bill Burroughs that Leary was most eager to encounter. Not only did Leary have the greatest respect for Burroughs, he was also aware of Burroughs' activities as a double-agent as well."

"Wait," I interrupt. "You telling me William S. Burroughs was a *RED Agent*?"

"Of course," Edith snaps her fingers. "Haven't you ever read his work, darling? It is all really an elaborate disclosure to broadcast his counter-espionage operations with the Enterprise, what he called the Nova Mob. Although, after a while there were some of us who doubted Bill's loyalty, just as there were doubts within the Nova circles I am sure. Like Leary, he soon lounged in the ambiguous mists of triple-agentry. An effective agent of counterintelligence indeed!

"In any case, it was in both of their interests to keep the other person close to the chest. Poor Ginsberg was just a patsy, wholeheartedly believing in the authenticity of Leary's psychedelic crusade. Leary's manipulation of Allen angered Burroughs . . . he cared for him greatly. But, to Bill the work eventually outshone the person and he too utilized this very manipulation to enable the inevitable encounter with the LSD pseudo-prophet."

Edith's eyes glaze over, glistening in deep reminiscence.

"I remember the time Burroughs invited me to Tangier, a legendary hotbed for espionage at that time. There was a spy on every corner, creeping in every shadow! It was marvelously thrilling! During the Cold War, Tangier was like Woodstock for the counterintelligence community! Anyway, dear, Bill was working with Brion Gysin on the Dreamachine and wanted me to see the results. The Dreamachine was a potential counter to the Enterprise's efforts, a sort of pastiche lamp cylinder rotating enough to create light oscillations at a frequency of 8 to 13 pulses per second. The goal was to harmonize with the alpha waves of the human brain, stimulating the optical nerve in a hypnagogic state so as to alter and eventually realign the brain's electrical framework. Bill revealed the Enterprise's equivalent in his *Nova Trilogy*. He had uncovered a massive Nova plot involving an ancient virus injected into language, mass mind control, and time travel. He was just beginning his work on *The Soft Machine* when I arrived to study their results.

"We had received a communiqué from Allen that he and Leary would be in town. We could not deny the synchronicity of the occasion and I encouraged Bill to partake of their festivities to gather more information on Leary's ambitions. I remember that night well. I remained out of sight while they hit the streets with a fistful of psilocybin mushrooms. The moon was so bright that night. History will tell you that Bill cut his part of the evening short because he could not handle the mind-altering experience of the mushrooms . . . a bad trip. But, I say, come on people! This is William Steward Burroughs! Author of the autobiographical accounts of *Junky* and *Naked Lunch* and *My Education*! This man's lifeblood was a *constant* altered state! To think he couldn't handle a dose of psilocybin from a Harvard yuppie is preposterous! 'No good,' he told them as he sloshed off into the night. '*No bueno.*' But he wasn't referring to the mushrooms, he was referring to Leary."

She pops another chocolate into her mouth.

"After wandering through the Mediterranean scented streets for hours, he eventually landed at my hotel room. The knock was so soft I almost didn't hear it. Throwing on my robe, I quietly eased over to the door and opened it with a revolver in my free hand.

"He looked horrible, so spent. The bags under his alien eyes told the story of man tossed through the ages in a pendulum dream. He collapsed in a chair, neglecting to take off his coat and hat. His frail form so skeletal, so used and abused. A great weight was showing on his shoulders.

"'Edie,' he liked to call me in his crackly, snarly voice. 'Edie, he's so wrong. He's got it all wrong, the deliberate bastard . . . and so right!' The ominous cloud of Leary's effect on the population was apparent. He was, for lack of effort, *appealing*. He was *fun*. I remember Bill saying: 'The psilocybin . . . it helps me see even more, interacting with the Maninkari wyrm . . . I can see the syndicate filth deals on his body . . . the alien Nova vibration. The cocksuckers, Edie! They know they don't have to pick up a single gun anymore. No more battles to be fought. War now . . . Korea, Vietnam, all of it . . . is just a distraction. They've realized the true battlefront. It's culture, Edie. All they have to do now is *market*. And Leary's their salesman.'

"He looked at me with such a sad face, the poor dear. I felt so bad for him, I felt bad for all of us, the World. He was alone, so fragile in his hard ways. Bill had a front to uphold, you see, a disgusting vulgar front. Part of his cover. It was wearing on him, I realized in that moment. All he wanted was normalcy, whatever that meant. All he wanted was his own peace. However, I understood the truth in what he was saying. Our war was over *ideas*, not territory, and we had forgotten that.

"'I don't have the charisma to compete,' he told me. I could have sworn he was about to cry in that moment. I reached out to hold him, but he brushed me away. He wiped his face, stood defiantly, and swiftly made for the door.

"'I love you, Edie,' he said quietly. 'You're like a sister to me. But, I don't know what side I'm on anymore. Don't even know if there *are* sides.' And with that, he left.

"I never saw him again, although I heard musings here and there of his escapades. He did follow Leary's circle to Cambridge and back to Harvard to participate in the psychedelic experiment. It is well known he soon grew discontent of their bewildering excuses for pseudo-self-realization. Of course, when the *Nova Trilogy* came out his insistence against Leary's methods were acute to us. He never maintained contact again, though, and it broke my heart. Because of that we were unable to fully protect him from the Enterprise's continued campaign to slander his reputation. He died alone and miserable . . . not far from you in Lawrence, Kansas actually."

Which brought my friend Lawrence to mind. My friend. I still consider him my friend? After what he did to Ramona and I? So many similarities between Lawrence and what Edith is telling me about Leary and Burroughs. What exactly . . .

"So you see, Gregor, we recruit based on ideas. It is a war of thought-forms we are fighting. The Maninkari wyrm provides the physical capabilities that may be required for survival in a material conflict. We need cutting edge counter-cultural individuals that are conspiracy-minded and can handle a trip down the rabbit hole. Like yourself. You loathe the mundane. The truest hell for you is monotony. Well, RED provides freedom from the mundane. The Weird shall have a Way."

She beams a smile while unwrapping a sucker. "What do you say?"

"Is this where I say 'yay' or 'nay'?"

"It absolutely is, dear. You have a choice, as we all do."

I shuffle the backpack on my back. I need to change the bandages on my boil wounds. Take my antibiotic. I am imprisoned by my own pain. We all are. Facsimiles of pathology searching for ways to make the pain go away, to chemicalize our needs . . . make us all unreal, we don't want to deal. We are all in prison, like Philip K. Dick said . . . this is all a massive jail, this world, this way of life: bills, work, insurance, or lack thereof. The Roman Empire still exists, and its name is the Nova Enterprise . . . keeping us in check, send the sheep to work and promise them riches and Horatio Alger dreams. Tell them they are free and give them a choice between brands. Tell them the power is theirs and let them select between this patsy and that. It is all rigged, and RED puts a kink in that plan. RED is the tremor that disrupts the traffic flow oil energy band ripping up the world while we sit and waste away in front of televisions and computers that have nothing to do with you, me, family, or the very ground we were birthed from.

I believe it is very clear where my mind is on making itself up. I think of Alice and what I want to be for her. I want to be an example for her. I can't be anything else for her anyway.

"I'm in."

"Oh delightful," Edith claps again. She leans forward with a fun-loving grin. "Be prepared to die as Gregor Samson, dear. Because now it's time for Initiation!"

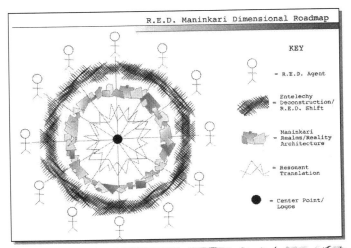

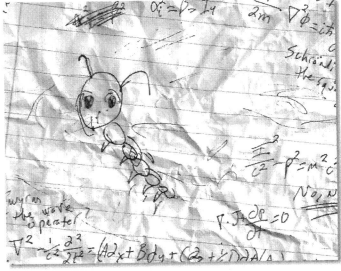

21 – Eating the Wyrm

Darwin had some business to take care of, but she promised she would see me "on the other side."

Edith and Maynard accompany me down a hallway ending in a great steel door embedded into Aztalan's alive skin. There are two men guarding the door, dressed in red. One is of medium build, in a solid red jumpsuit. His head is shaved except a few orange and green braids configured in a topknot. He smiles like a hyena. An M16 assault rifle is straddled on his shoulder with a guitar strap.

"Glorious day, innit?" he cackles.

"Good evening, Iago. How's the post?" Edith claps him a high-five. Everyone appeals to Edith here; she is well-respected. They don't just follow her orders, they *love* her.

"Oh, is not bad, not bad," he motions back and forth like a ticking clock. "Ol' Emory here though is quite the bore, if you ask me."

The other sentry is dressed in a fully red, three-piece suit; a bright venetian red tie. His head is adorned by a gas mask from what could have been the World War II era, old and ragged with age and use. Emory just shrugs, holding his hands neatly behind his back.

"See what I mean?"

"Now, darling," Edith nudges Iago playfully. "Give Emory a chance."

"It's not about giving him a chance, Miss. There's a plethora of things we could be doin', talk'n about while post'n here. I like trains, fer instance, but it's like talk'n to a wall! He don't say nuth'n."

"I don't like him much, Edith," Emory mumbles with a British accent through his mask.

"Now boys, your shift will be off soon. Leave us be now so we can get Gregor here on with Initiation."

Emory punches on a keypad in the wall and the steel door shudders open. As we walk through, Iago slaps me on the back.

"Welcome aboard, new dog!"

We enter the adjoining room. It is a darker chamber, smaller than the heart-center of Aztalan, but probably big enough to fit a few semi-trailers. The texture here is different, covered in honeycomb and coral formations growing out of the walls, floors, and ceiling. There is a violet glow emanating from . . . somewhere. Four RED Agents, all in meditative positions sit throughout the chamber. Each has a textile cloth laid out before them, covered with rocks, shells, lit candles, and other artifacts. A trough of sand sits at the opposite end of each cloth, swords and staffs of all shapes and sizes sticking out of the sand. They are deep in trance and do not notice our entry. Their hands are all facing the bizarre marvel at the other end of the room.

"This, dear boy," Edith introduces, "Is Mithra."

A large humanoid creature lays on a mound of bracket fungi overlapping each other in a planar grouping of horizontal rows. It looks up at me, skin a dark charcoal gray contrasted by large and elliptical compound red eyes. It sits up on top of the fungal caps, looks at me glibly. Large grey legs pushing its body upright to get a good look at me. Full-bodied wings, like a rugged monarch's, flutter notably on its back.

"Holy shit," my Fortean instincts unravel the John Keel experience. "That's . . . that's Mothman, isn't it?"

"Yes . . . well, no," Edith giggles. "Actually, Mothwoman, if you don't mind, dear. And again, her name's Mithra. She doesn't like the crytpoid reference, but yes . . . same one from the West Virginia sightings."

Have you ever read about a fantastical creature or monster in a book, and then imagined how it would look in real life? I suppose you have. But, you didn't tag it. No, the feeling of actually *seeing* what you imagined in your head is quite different. The real thing has rough, almost elephant-like skin. Pulsing veins. It moves. It has a smell. A rather musky, moldy smell . . . might be the shelf mushrooms it's . . . *she's* lying on. But, the point being . . . a sort of unreal terror of the uncertainty of perception grips your spine, twists it, and tosses it out the window into the past of surety.

It's also utterly fascinating! I can't take my eyes off her. She is . . . oddly beautiful . . . a necromantic, *mysterial* quality to her presence. She seems unconcerned by me and lays back down, apparently to sleep, though her lidless eyes do not close.

"The Mothman from West Virginia lore," Edith continues. "He was eventually captured by a joint effort of the Department of Defense and the Nova Enterprise. They initially brought him into existence at Point Pleasant through a mix of explosive technology and satanic ritual at the nearby Army base in the area. They opened a breach, bringing Mithra and her companion, Miirthaal, into our world. Somehow, through their utter recklessness and stupidity, the U.S. Government opened an instantaneous portal into the Maninkari Realms! Mithra and Miirthaal were torn through the Entelechy and brought here into normal reality.

"There were many efforts on the behalf of the Maninkari to seek them out and return them home. Indrid Cold was one such case. The name denotes the process, doesn't it? Animism is a very prominent part of shamanic practice . . . the Maninkari have visited our world many times through animal form. The eagle, the condor, the anaconda. One of the most prominent species used for missions such as these requires the ancient and venerable Indriidae lemur. They have a long mystical history on this planet of being able to carry a Maninkari vessel into such an anthropomorphic form as to almost seem human. Odd-looking, but *human* nevertheless."

"Propit," I whisper. My heart pounds pounds pounds with synchronistic excitement. He was on my side all along. Protecting me. Protecting Stransky. From what? From Jack? There's more to the picture, because George Stransky was not a prospective recruit of the RED Agency.

"Exactly," Maynard enters the conversation. "From the lemur genus: Propithecus. Edith was happy to take Mithra in for refuge and sanctuary, and that is how our relationship with the Maninkari increased to the tangible level it is today."

"She is one of the Mothers of RED," Edith continues. "One of a few."

"But what happened to Mothma—," I correct myself. "I mean, Miirthaal?"

They lower their heads, cumbersome. Maynard is intent on avoiding this subject and finishing his lesson, so he motions us on. I assume Mithra is a widow.

We walk quietly over to a lab display inset into the wall. Many intricate instruments and monitors silently buzz into a display case full of twelve glass canisters full of pear colored liquid. Maynard takes out a key, strung around his neck on a thread. He opens the display case and pulls out one of the vials.

"Let me explain this to you in the most simple of terms," he holds up the canister for me to see. Inside floats a thumb-sized creature that looks a lot like a caterpillar, much like his drawing from earlier. The *wyrm*! Curling antennae jut from its elliptical head! It looks as if it had eye lids that were shut! "This, Mr. Samson, is the Maninkari wyrm. One of Mithra's larvae, if you will. Mithra reproduces asexually, much like plants. Remember, the wyrm emits a trace amount of electromagnetic and acoustic radiation, specifically seen through infrared lighting. We have found what this radioactive charge, and its effects on living tissue, may signify. Long ago, the Maninkari gave Dr. Bruyere and her companions certain permissions to fuse its spawn with human biology. The results were astronomical and superseded all of our current notions of scientific understanding. This process must be protected, at all costs, from adverse influences. Observe the result . . ."

He motions a hand at the Agents in the room, going about their deep meditations. The Mothwoman peers over and something inside me wants to both run in fright and leap in elation.

"When the Maninkari wyrm is ingested into the human anatomy—"

"Excuse me . . . ingested? As in *eat*?" I ask dubiously.

"More like swallowed, dear" Edith chuckles.

"Precisely," Maynard continues. "A chemical reaction occurs unlike anything human beings have ever seen. The wyrm stays *alive* within the human body. After an acidic reaction, the wyrm begins to feed off of various hormones within the host. Conversely, the wyrms's digestive system expels an entirely new set of hormones into the host's body, the pure DMT concentrate we discussed earlier, thereby influencing the endocrine system with a defect: the Radioactive Endocrine Defect. This new set of hormones contains enhancers to the present regulatory factors in the system such as thyrotropin, corticotrophin, gonadotropin, somatostatin, GHRH, and dopamine."

I must be looking at him like a caveman because, as always, he looks agitated. I'm starting to think that's just Maynard's normal look . . . annoyance.

"Think about what the endocrine system *does*, Mr. Samson! It is the ever-present holistic, integrated system of the human organism! It is the great communicator, regulating growth, sexual development, all of the other systems of the body. It assimilates the information taken in by the nervous system and figures out what to do with it . . . essentially, it is *consciousness itself*."

I never thought of that. The endocrine system as everything. And if what Maynard said is true, the pineal producing the most powerful psychedelic on the planet, we are naturally attuned to psychedelic phenomena. It is naturally a part of consciousness.

"The plants, Gregor," Edith takes the canister from Maynard and sets it on one of the ceremonial cloths laid out in front of a RED Agent. The Agents awake from the meditation and their attention is directed toward the canister. They begin to chant, to sing. Some pick up drums and began to beat them. The

Agent whose cloth Edith has laid the canister on stands up, long dark hair trailing over his face, a red tunic covering his body with loose black breeches. He starts to rattle over the canister, spitting air in its general direction. At times he picks up a bottle of yellow liquid, drinks it, and spits it into the air over canister. A floral aroma fills the atmosphere

"The plants are our teachers. They show us how to live with each other and with the Earth. And how do they communicate with us? Through talking, speaking the English language? The notion is not so absurd, dear, when we understand consciousness. How does a plant speak? How does it communicate its needs and desires? Plants are grown to be eaten, are they not? That is their purpose, to integrate with primal bodies. Every time you eat a cucumber, a potato, it is physiologically saying something to the body, telling it what to do, how to live. And when the plants need to reach our heads? Our minds? Our hearts? What do they do? How do they communicate? Shamans have known since before history, my boy. Shamans have always known about biology, DNA, the structure of the Universe. Shamans have always known how to heal ailments, rid the body of cancer, of mental illness. There is nothing special about them, is there? *Anyone* can become a shaman, darling! Because it is the *plants* that teach them how to heal, how to divine. Spirit is egalitarian!"

"What are they doing?" I ask through the din of beats, chants, and rattles. "What're those cloths? Are they altars?"

"Yes, dear," Edith smiles delightedly. "Called *mesas*, in fact. It is where the shamans do their work, a sort of control panel for the Universe. The objects on the mesa are sacred tools, *artes*, which allow the shaman to harness the power of the Universe for healing. They are configured in a particular way, usually corresponding to the four directions and elements, with the center being the *axis mundi*. The mesa is the *technology* of the shaman, darling. They are blessing the Maninkari wyrm for ingestion."

"Ingestion for when?"

As if on cue the shamans synchronistically generate a wispy blow into the direction of the canister and stop the music. My heart freezes, utter calcification.

"Right about now, dear," Edith walks over and picks up the canister. She bows and thanks the Agent behind the mesa and crosses over to me. She opens the lid and extends it to me like a chalice.

"You are to become an Agent of Oddity, my dear Gregor Samson. You are to be a protector of *Pachamama*, our Mother Earth. From this day forward, you will be charged with keeping the world safe from Modernity, Conventionality, and the Ordinary. You *are* the Paradigm Shift! Now drink! Let the old you die and the new you be born!"

All I can feel . . . pouncing over and over my temples, the throbbing drum, my heart . . . the rhythmic sprinkling of the rattle. I thought I was frozen, but my hands rise to take the canister gently from her. I smell the fluid, the wyrm floating quietly inside. It's a putrid, dirty stench. I lift it to my lips anyway.

"Now whisper some prayers inside," she tells me. "Of whom you want to be."

I close my eyes, the rancid funk massaging my nostrils. Inside, deep inside, my blood is curdling, boiling, calling for me to drink. Calling to be awakened. Calling for more. I am so tired. So worn. The past few days, the past few years. Life, job, divorce . . . it is all a lie, all an illusion. My eyelids squeeze tired and softly I whisper into the open end of the canister.

"I call myself to myself."

And I drink.

. . . . . .collapse. . . . . .

* * * * *

Face milk pushes through chrysanthemum ocean, mandala sparks gestalt in surrounding space, ooze face with its participatory fractals and message-body titans speculating the doctor is in. Violet mouth in liquid lip swirls opens and gives out coding words in codex of translation underneath layer of translation, synthesize word: Listen and it will be told – process definition, we have a plan besides, A, B, and D. Recognition is key in the language/image step-by-step configurations – mathematics is key, don't you understand? D . . . M . . . T . . . Language is not the representation of an event, language is that which events are preceded from – everything is language: you, I. The pearl drop acidfield of consciousness. Simulacrum cortex. The sinking feeling is upon you all, denizens of planet Earth. Do you claim citizenship, or nay? I say 'nay', to thee; for claim to citizenship is the abolition of freedom. The Corinthian Order sickens its becoming – columns will crumble under the entelechy construct maze; abort the harvest of flow.

  Panic! Panic! Panic! Losing grip! Losing grip! Abort the harvest, carnivore trip-top; taking off forever! Clinging onto handles - bundle underneath. Seep through the lodge manufacture, Protean logic superfluous allowed. Ol' Vonnegut was crazy like the rest of us. Moving cursor cling to. Believe in the unknown....Belief. Hard-strung man-made counter-flesh bend-down capricious-stank further-more. Buzzing into belief: am I am a spaceman. Honorable, waking up. I am *ubermensch,* the Twilight of capital is drawing near. I live off entropy. I consequence off monotony. Intertwined, aligned betwixt steel girders and shapes of right angle *de Stijl* living everywhere under Mondrian's nose; he knew where the perfunctory swing age resides. White apes in pin-striped three-pieces in navy blue and bowler hat lore. Crooked artery smiles. Teeth etched with placid fornications. Trip-top, tipping their hats to the red carpet cancer of notoriety. Humanist undergrowth clogged fingernails. We abhor *de Stijl,* callous to geometry enforced.....primary colors and oblong cubes: Proun compositions for the never. Marinetti and his Futurists are of the past: their greatest fear. They wallow in ancient modern shit, buried with Tatlin's Tower. Watch me disseminate them. Prounly.

Designation MH: worldwide scale operation.
Operation CHAOS was LBJ's baby. Operation RED comes from within.

. . . Collapse . . .

Panic no more. Stuck inside a molasses epidermal shell. No more wake. Intangible lines cut through me, pierce insides like balloon animal carnivore ride.....ecstatic the down-trodden wait. In a lay low womb covered scrambled egg latex placenta coating . . . move the hand out and through, feel is it real/unreal unburden some democracy? Purple coated placenta step up and through, it stretches fell the pull up and out into muscles that are none; into coagulation of synergetic symmetry of lines and blobs on energy make-up of me. Spinning axis torus whirling the base, spine, gut, heart, throat, forehead, and beyond. Everything is in me and I can see it all. See the inner working flux underneath the matter matrix of reality.

Push, the latex pops, placenta opens. Ocean of color and polychromatic currents motioning motioning, like snake wreath breath side-winding enough. Crawling essences. Bubbling thoughts. Multi-color fumes amorphous all in the river, sink my foot in and there is a

POP   POP

                Crackle, Crackle, Crackle, Crackle
                          Fizzle

Fizzle

                                    POP
          Fizzzzzzzz......

The Entelechy is broken. What once seemed form-full becomes formless. Idiosyncratic deconstruction of Derrida's dream . . . an aporia of illusionment, the barricades are down . . . structural ontology is broken, cut-up method insignia align; there is fragment undone . . . fragments shattered mirror pieces like a metallic melancholy starburst explode and conjoin. My ears pop. Converse on the next idea. Phenomenological deference hits

upon the blasted shades and doors of an inner ego state strewn
into a spaghetti noodle vacuum sucking itself deeper and deeper
quicker and quicker until nothing nothing nothing modicum is
me . . . .

      Ellipses of thought . . . mounting
graphs of zigging, zagging. A phoneme of presence, collected
into !!!!!BROKEN!!!!!
    !!!!!BREAK

               There is
no meaning: inferred.

      An eschatological signifier . . . I am
erased. I am erased. Gone the sudden full lake of illusory
hopefulness . . . of fake dreams and party-going goodbyes.
THERE IS NO METHOD! Puritanical! Transcendental! Let go!
The ego is gone . . . the ego latches on, the ego is LEECH! The
ego WILL NOT LET GO! It will not subside to the
transformative tide. Wrench myself into me no more; come
forth into? Postmodern, poststructural binary opposition
epistemology is done. End point. Period. Exclamation, no end.
Swing, vacuum sucked into further and further no longer discern
into cognizant helpfulness and soon it is there:

   Truly there is no mob. There is no enterprise. There is
no dominator. The only conspiracy, you dead Gregor Samson, is
ego.

      . . . and it is gone now.

          Good bye.

  "Wakey, whitey! Wakey!" She stands there. Where?

  "Through it come you, whitey I call you now." The
round dream shamanness, Mother Wakanabe, painted face stares
up at me with dark face brown eyes like mud. "Portly, portly."
She plops pudgy hands on her tummy.

  "You make it due come time to," she points out and I
am on a plateau cliff top. And below us is a world. It is an entire
existence of layered cross-universal dispatch: a dreamtime
dream of intricate and exotic possibility, a whole other
dimension in the frame of the mind.

I have made it to the Maninkari Realms.

She moves close, clicks and clacks in my energy sea face. *Who are you?* I ask. *Do I belong to you?* She cackles, barrel belly laughing on the ground. Dust strewn up from a desert she once was. "I am the Sahara," I think she says but no.

"Here," she gives me round smooth stone stained in blood. "Life take across there, shoo! Lap up on side other, whitey! Protect! Protect and see you there! Ha!" And she sinks into the ground melted cheese glob and dissipates beneath. Hold the stone in tight. Blood stone. I look out across the way and notice the aspect scape below: Perceive:

The entire world is one . . . big . . . single . . . formation . . .

Wave of wave of hexagonal cells, honeycomb caverns, coral cells horizontally and vertically aligned. Reefs of geometric trihedrals; connectors and nuero-pathways igniting here to there in beyond instantaneous fashions . . . vociferous quadrilateral rhombi. There are highways on monochromatic polygon lozenges, curtain sole of angles beleaguering concave or convex – it is a matter of choosing, the mountains of coral, honeycomb rock loaded and stacked with centroid vectors. The alignments within.

A jeweled ever-morphing uniform polychoron bounces up to me, machine organic, it features Cheshire smile and not, ever changing, morphing cantellations prisms circular angles and truncations . . . an elfish shape-shifting polyhedron article. It speaks in truncated glossolalia, linguistical melody dream stuff (not . . . words):

"HI> WELCOME TO HERE> FOLLOW MY BEING> FUN TO HAVE YOU> FUN>"

It hip-hops skips and like a Humpty Dumpty rabbit leaps off the cliff and no inclination but to follow. Leap, off, the Fool, I am, from card, Zero. No free fall, just afloat and the ease feather down I can watch things, shapes, numerical geometry fly

throughout the air space, little bird like equatorial triangles.
Insectoid isosceles.

"FOLLOW FOLLOW> MUCH TO SEE> DO NOT
LOST>"

Land steadily and seems overgrown molecular
farmstead, crop land agricultural growth of mitochondrion and
endoplasmic vertices. There is a patch row upon row of cabbage
head wide eyes, chubby cheek, little things. A tall graceful being
made of vegetable membrane, chlorophyll cuticles . . . a long
flowing skirt of roots trailing behind, female form face made of
leaves and eyes of apricot stoma. Her head extends out sulking
branch. She eyes me warily then sees the polyhedron elf and
dismisses us casual wave, she kneels.

She pulls out a cabbage head from the ground root dirt
trickle, little fetal masses whining and bumbling, she holds it
infant cabbage thing pupa. She holds it in her arms cradle and it
sucks at stick finger and she laughs but not sound it creates little
imagery particle anodes, electrical dances.

"SEE THIS> SEE THIS IS WHERE WE GROW>
MANY SHAPES> MANY FORMS> WE FARM OURSELVES
IN PRETTY WAYS> HAPPY MOTHERS BRING US> WE
TAUGHT TO SING> TAUGHT TO CREATE> SCHOOLING
TO CREATE> UNDERSTAND YOU OKAY>"

The polyhedron, morphing ever, dribbles itself along
and we travel through canal of honeycomb cell domiciles where
the Maninkari dwell. They are stacked endless walls of
chambers after chamber, world after world. Live in they have
articles of transference . . . a matrix of reality wikis, conjugating
infinite uniform polytopes. Do they eat? Do they sleep?

"WE PRAY>" it says answering my thoughts.

Follow further along: purple mountainous landscapes of
working complex, exercising and excreting polymorphous
thought forms, galvanizing cathodes. Slopes of meandering
bestial aberrations. Languid octopus arrays, skipping from
necrotic plant to diode plank . . . wild life collection herding

across circuit board plains made of membranes. The sky is filament fractals of green algae, water globules.

"HERE> WE WORK> OBSERVE AND LEARN> CREATE>"

Streams of amino acid cacti reaching into heights, collection in abound . . . a collective of workers, surrounding a concrescence pool of molten chromosomes. It shimmers with in and out gamma refractions. We are approached by another figure, crawling insect made of fungal synapses. The headmaster of this particular colony, working for: its head mantis large compound eyes, it extends a claw egg arm and motions toward the pool.

"WATCH>"

The workers are generating via language forms and images, structural model and life cycles, data flows and double helixes . . . an architecture transport, energy releasing pathways. They rise out of the pool in befuddled puzzlement structures and into the sing-song ladder stalk into the ether above . . . up, up into the Entelechy, the red shift to be made into reality. Materiality. It is all language, it is words. Reality is words. Reality is really just a thought made manifest. All it takes is a word, and it is done. Speak, and it shall be so.

They are quantumly singing reality into existence.

"SEE> CREATE> CREATE IS PURPOSE> PURPOSE IS CREATE> YOU> ME>"

You. Me. We are all creator, all Creator. We all exist to create something new. Something hazardous to the health of the mundane.

"NOW GO> FURTHER> TIME FOR YOU> YOU NO MORE>"

Me no more.

I feel Maninkari wyrm . . . I am Maninkari, I am here this is me. Lace relationship with inside the wyrm is me and exchanging with the information byways of my bloodstream, I am Maninkari. Descent.

Feel; the rock . . . the stone between ley line fingers.

The blood stone – curtain on the red, seep eyes into the mud of dried brown:

Red: blood, the life force.

Red: Muladhara, the base-root chakra, the connection to life, to the Earth, the starting point to the rise of the Kundalini serpent.

Red: the longest wavelength of light, 630 to 700nm.

Red: Stephen Crane's badge of courage.

What makes the red man red? the stone of blood look deep inside . . . oscillations . . . descent fall deep . . . . deep into the stone *artes* of life, light, and courage.

So, Mother Wakanabe sends him, the bloodstone mirth: the one who knows . . . he rises, from inside the inside-scape. Rises among weed and thicket long stringy hair dark beard his skin the color of Earth: he comes, naked with a stick in hand, his eyes wild as wild can be, feral and unbelievable; he is savage; there are animal aspects in, among, throughout him there: above his crown a condor soars, mighty wing span feathers; to his left a panther struts muscle strewn ready; his right a dolphin swimming dandily in the air; at his feet mighty serpent anaconda slithering on the ground. His chest marked in blood a cross of even sides. Axis mundi.

He is Hanahpu, millennia old . . . Hanahpu, the First Shaman, first born of the Hero Twins – dual opposites – the cross expresses the distinction between two states of being, a form is the observer, observed, and becomes the total act of observation.

Hanahpu looks at me, smiles, his form begins to shift, mold into anaconda, then to whale, panther, condor. Taking each role like a glove changing back and forth. He tells me in an ever-changing state in pure, plain language only my morphic resonance can understand, not even my brain: "To fly, to shape-shift, to live outside of the limitations of space and time is the modus operandi of the shaman. All breathe the continuous breath of Hanahpu. Hanahpu comes from *Wiracocha*, the Creator, above in the Higher World, down to

Pachamama, the Earth, to heal man, woman, and child. To reintegrate human beings to the correct cycle of time, to liberate them from the linear lie of history."

His eyes pierce me, eyes of death full of skulls and maggots. He is death. He is life.

"What you need to know, you know. All of you just remember at some point in your lives. Somehow, somewhere, you will remember, you all became afraid and ran from your Mother. So afraid of death you fought against Her, raped Her, beat Her down again and again. Now, you drill into her. You strip her land. Your accidents poison her waters and you do nothing. You fill your lives with material items to keep you distracted. Then, one day you wake up and it is time to die. And you find you have never lived. The whole time, raping your own Mother. What's a Mother to do when Her own child becomes a cancer, becomes a virus that is killing Her. She must save Her other children, should she not? But, she does it with great sadness. Her other children, your brothers and sisters. The fish, the monkey, the elephant, the pig, the trees, the mountains, all of them grown out of the same womb and you . . . you above all were given the ability to care for them and nurture them, to fulfill your Mother's dream of peace, but no! Instead, you mow them down, you farm them, you rule over them like tyrants, and then eat them without respect for the life they provide.

"Mother is angry now. So, Hanahpu rises to meet the occasion."

RED rises. RED protects and destroys. Life and death. The axis mundi of the ecological compass . . . the RED Hand is the lineage of Hanahpu, RED aims to set right what went wrong every day you feel it it's in your heart your dissatisfaction which is why you must go out and kill those that don't live within your borders, which is why you have to buy that shiny new car because you are empty inside and alone dreadfully alone that the thought of turning 80 and having everyone gone eats away at you like a deranged shark, why you buy toxic chemicals from companies that control your lives to modify the neuro-transmitters in your brain so you can feel "normal" so you can pass the days, use your oil, use your electricity, use your TV to keep you from caring, keep you from signing that petition that could boycott companies plowing down the homes of innocent lives to make that chocolate bar you crave on the grocery store aisle next to the article about that new crush Bobbi Dakota is having or what politician just solicited sexual favors from a minor in a public restroom, the odds are unfathomable, the rate at which you have gone from simple tools to such interdependent complex economic systems and everything so fragile held together any second the ice could crack, the codes could slip and five thousand nuclear warheads could accidently trigger the next great downfall of a major species on this planet, and does She care? Of course She does, which is why if the message, no no no . . . the Message does not get straight the death you deserve for not paying attention, for caring more about your backyard bar-b-ques and football games and video games and political games and insurance scams and ways in which to hedge bets on nonexistent numbers, for teaching your children purchasing over love, killing over compassion, for waving off with a guffaw the atrocities you inflict upon each other for being desensitized for being sarcastic for not paying attention to your own world falling apart right around you and stepping back in to your own lies deceit because fear rules your life more than anything because you don't know what it means skulls in your eyes to have death to accept death to BE death, to understand the Mother's womb we are in and we are eating it away the insane termites we are, death is all, death is the shaman pupil, the way through to courage to discovering the acceptance of the fragility of life, the way it can all fall apart so quickly, the story to tell the part to play, part of the cosmic play, *Pachamama's* story, not yours, not mine, *Her* story . . . because you were not placed here externally by some white man's hand in the clouds, you were born out of the dirt with the worms and the prokaryotes, She breathed you into being and you do not care because you will go back to your programs and your distractions that serve no purpose but to keep you at home, on the couch, locked within the confines of your own room, a prisoner of your world.

And all the Dominators had to do was sell you something pretty.

Chock one up for the Nova Enterprise! The conspiracy doesn't even have to lift one finger.

Hanahpu, Hanahpu, I am Hanahpu, first born .
. .

Time to move on, blows me away on the life stream of *Wiracocha*, flow; the wind and center in on the closing point where the number becomes negative.

"Jump in whitey!" Mother Wakanabe says from somewhere.

Deeper . . .

One. Two. Three. Four.

One. Two. Feel the pull of the resonant translation.

Inside deep, the hum is there. Inside the stone. And broken pieces of Truth spin up to pierce the allocated manifestation of who I think I am. Dilations. Oscillations, burrrrrrrrrrrrrr. Hum, hum, hum, of the Ohmmmmmmmm. Flick, flicker of ambient light. How many Hertz it blips?

I am Gregor.

The resonant translation of the Universe hums into me . . . I can feel it speaking to my atoms, pulsing into my blood stream. Emanating from the Center, Zero Point. The resonant translation is a Delta T frequency . . . Terrestrial time minus Universal time: two time lines interlacing weaving into each other DNA/RNA helix twisting and turning anaconda serpents into mesmerizing caduceus, the flying serpent, Quetzalcoatl . . . humming, oscillationing, flicker flicker flicker Dreamachine 8 to 13 pulses per second . . . hypnologic delirium. Time to remember the lie.

I am Gregor Samson.

Blood. The flute player's
song ago, trip-top one foot, two
One foot, two . . . trip-top! The woodwind flute.

Red. Deep in the recesses in, inside I
see through the dark the little moment when the frock coat
passes by . . . through the little hole I can see. He passes by.
When did this happen? Did this really happen?

Is this a Memory?

The flute is playing, (red blood) I
hear it clearly down the hall of death.

Is it Ian Anderson?
It is playing Jethro Tull . . . what is it? *A Song for Jeffrey*? I lift
my head from the cell floor, barely able to lift, ear up to the
concrete wall. It is real. Someone in the hall, playing *A Song for
Jeffrey*! What—

Jeffrey . . .

Hear the guards, shouting, they are coming after him,
clumping boots down the hall. He is still one foot, two prancing
and playing trip-topping down the hallway. More guard shouts
and then,

>>> >>>> BOOOOOOM <<<< <<<

Explosive concussive blast, rock shattering pieces
spilling across the way people wailing crying in pain blood
curdling ouchies and through a hole of dust and concrete film, a
hand reaches across and it is not the frock coat bearded man,
who stands behind:

Young girl, late teens. A clean
cashmere sweater, an embroidered emblem resembling . . . long
raven hair, it is . . . It is her, in my dreams, the underground
grocery market in NYC. The Fortune Teller girl. It is her. She is
real! Completely absolutely real! Her skin pale but beautiful,
pink soft lips, and hazel eyes that look like autumn.

"Look like autumn," I must have mumbled in awe. She smiles and takes my hand.

"It's October," she says. "Everyone thinks about death." She pulls me to her and we race down the hall, the girl and frock coat man picking the others up as they go along. All the others, boys like me. We are all imprisoned, lab rat mice poking and prod. It hurts. It is terrifying, life is a nightmare. No parents, all gone. Runaways. Orphans. Nobody notices we are all gone. That's how they do it. We look at the cashmere girl and frock coat man with innocent despairing hope.

"Come with us." "You are free."
"Don't be afraid."

There are gunshots and the man with the flute goes down. "Keep running!!!" he yells. He blows on the flute and sonic concussive blast throws itself at the men with guns. They fly back and shriek in pain. We round a corner I can barely stand and the others are just as bad. All shaved heads we are covered in scars, bruises, scrapes, some patches covered in stitches. I see one used to have memory dark curls hair trailing over his face, I know him before and now. Lawrence! Head shaved now, but I recognize the face. Lawrence and I were once here!

There are two men with pistols yelling to get back to our cells and the girl steps in front of us shining like a radiant Madonna. She pulls out a card from a satchel slung over her shoulder. She raises it to her mouth and whispers in a raspy voice: "Kal'kuthulah!!!!" Aquamarine serpents race out of the card and into the air, wrapping themselves around the two guards, incapacitating them. They are down, being squeezed of life. We step over them and move on down the hall. And then . .
.

. . . all goes black.

In and out of waking consciousness . . . hazy waves of imagery flow in and out, am I restrained again? Am I bound? Do they have me again? What happened to the girl? The frock coat man? Was the rescue unsuccessful? The Dominators have me!

Can make out words, phrases, various shapes and forms indecipherable . . . except . . .

". . . to do with them now . . ."

". . . too much exposure, too costly to transport . . ."

". . . can reprogram . . . reintegrate them back into the masses . . ."

". . . method initialized . . . reintegration commencing . . . feel it is blood into anymore again you stink filthy ridden cockroach love seat death tears in the heat crane is the underside barcode feel of belief and LISTEN because this is your new life, brain, this is your new life. Your name is Gregor Samson. You will believe that you went to get your undergrad degree in Liberal Arts. You will believe you got out of school and couldn't find a job, but you landed a suitably paid data entry position for the Kansas City Trade Board. You marry Kathleen Preston, have a child, and then divorce because you are paranoid and a bore. You get your child taken away from you and rarely see her. You are afraid of everyone and everything. You are sick and constantly have conditions that require medical attention. You are depressed and find little meaning in life."

". . . there is . . . possibility of deprogramming . . ."

". . . an eye on him and the others, we can't afford . . ."

". . . words undo, words acting as numbers, roundabout equations . . ."

Wake.

I am not Gregor Samson, the OMMMMMMMMMM buzzing hum reverberates throughout the translation of me, and I am not Gregor Samson. I am a bug. There is a bug, a defect in the system. A defect . . . undone by another defect . . .

. . . paradigm shift commencing . . .

The Radioactive Endocrine Defect, undoing the parts not real, undoing the illusion and I am not me.

I was taken. Long ago, kidnapped and brought into their underground. Poked me. Prodded me. Used me. And something happened. She came to get us out and they didn't want to take the chance. So they gave us fake dreams, fake lives, fake memories, and shoved us out into the world with fake people telling us fake sentiments and fake circumstance and IT IS ALL JUST A FUCKING DREAM> A FUCKING ILLUSION> A FILAMENT SCREEN OBSCURING YOUR VISION> YOU ARE NO LONGER DEAD> YOU ARE NO LONGER IN PRISON>

Not real? Not real. My daughter, Alice. My wife, my ex-wife . . . not real. All a set-up, a big elaborate shadow, puppet show in Plato's cave. Actors, figments. Alice, oh Alice!!

I REMEMBER WHEN YOU WERE BORN!!!!!!

My baby, sweet eyes curled into my arms that night I looked into the stars that are your eyes and knew you were my baby. You are my baby forever, my sweet Alice. You are nothing. You ----- I am dying ----- you do not exist but in a made up story ----- can't do this no it is too much ----- you are a lie, you do not belong ----- death deliver me please I cannot give up my little girl . . . .

She is my little girl, God, please NO

Please . . . NO . . . please . . .

--

countdown

. . . I want my Alice . . . my rabbit hole little girl . . .
I want my life back.

drip

)))))))))) ZERO
POINT (((((((((

))))))))))) o (((((((((

I am not above the (UN) known, the waking world no
more, gone.
Not the Final Term:
I am the Psycho-Shaman; the Product of the Bleed - air
pushes on my chest, all story is the story of the child
ripped from its Mother's breast . . .
>Matter Immaculate<
Mystery humbles . . .
. . . assimilation with ambiguity.
No more of the "I".
Never again.

Breathe out.
Awake now.

Myself called.

23 – Limited Space: An Excerpt From Gregor Samson's *Akashic Memoir*

A reflection:

There is a valid reason to explain my great affinity for Charles Fort.

It was a few years ago. My life was a malaise, a perpetual gray cloud hovering over every facet of existence. I was recovering from a traumatic state of circumstances: the destruction of my marriage and parental rights being stripped away like they were just a pair shoes torn off my feet. One minute you're a dad, the next you're just another shmuck off the street. Fatherhood is a flip of a coin: heads, your weekend for playing in the park with that little girl who looks up to you more than any other guy; tails, back to the loneliness of bachelorhood. It's a schizophrenic existence and tough to walk in any sort of balanced framework.

Eventually my role became diminished. Circus Dad that Alice only wanted play-things from. There was no respect, no connection, no serious embodiment of the paternal nourishments I so longed for long ago. As well, any attempts from her mother to shut me out of her school life, church life—anything else that might have made me a real father—were ignored by the courts on the traditional basis that "mother knows best."

Well . . . she knew best how to diminish my status of fatherhood to such a point that defeat was inevitable. I became a broken filament. The shattered pieces of purpose were no longer there to try to piece together. I was lost; no stones to toss, nothing to throw them at.

My marriage was no better even when we were legally bound. The gray was always there, almost dream-like, walking through fight after fight after fight. We were never meant to be together, and I think I remember one night, waking up, looking over at her pale skin and auburn hair and thinking to myself,

"Who is this person? How did I get here?" Even though that marriage was a prison I tried so hard to break from, the fallout was so destructive on my psyche it shattered my immune system—contracting a plethora of *conditions* consuming my body's ability to function in any normal capacity. External dependencies on chemical agents were a must! In a coalesced haze of social disparity and physical illness, I wandered aimlessly from month-to-month; a beleaguered automaton inept with any prospect of joy or fulfillment.

One day, I stumbled into Spivey's Bookstore on Westport Road. Spivey's is housed in a rugged brick building constructed in 1910, five floors of nooks and crannies and portals to dark places. Ol' David Spivey himself sat on a rustic, beaten chair covered in soot and dog hair, near the back of the dilapidated tenement. He's a caricature of himself, munching on his cigar and reading stacks of yellowed newspapers through bottle-lensed spectacles. A droopy bloodhound lay quietly at his feet as a chestnut colored Great Dane with bulky hind-legs lumbered quietly around the corner to see who entered through the bell-tinkle door. The old fray-haired lady at the counter with twinkly eyes smiled at me. Ol' David never interacts with customers, just sits there quietly reading his decades-old newspapers. The place is a concoction of rooms randomly situated with no rhyme or reason other than to stack shit: old dust-worn tomes a century old; cluttered piles upon piles of maps of the world when countries had different borders, or when the New World was uncharted territory; books capriciously stacked out of order on crooked shelves along with bowls of water, dog food, and cat food; and yes, the occasional feline languidly brushing by your feet as you peruse the cobweb aisles. I love the place.

This one particular day, I was in the basement, next to the water heater, sluggishly browsing the book stacks of (mostly) biographies. I was in a supine mood. But I happened upon a hardback with golden leaf embroidery and a torn spine. Don't know why it caught my eye . . . many pages were missing, including the publishing information and title, but scanning the book I realized it was a series of non-fiction articles about a man named Charles Fort and his eccentric ideas. The last half of the book contained excerpts from Charles Fort's own publications *The Book of the Damned*, *New Lands*, *Lo!*, and *Wild Talents*, along with essays from various writers regarding his unpublished works *X* and *Y*. Flipping through the dingy, crumpled pages I came upon a passage chiming and glimmering among all the others:

" . . . *there are no coincidences, in the sense that there are no real discords in either colors or musical notes. That any two colors, or sounds, can be harmonized by intermediately relating them to other colors or sounds.*"

Without knowing a thing about this Charles Fort guy, I purchased the compilation immediately.

So, who is Charles Fort? And why is he so important? The books highlighted in this unknown volume are the pinnacle of Fort's achievements from the late 19th and early 20th Centuries. Charles Fort, I would say, is the god-father of the layman's investigation of anomalous phenomena. Fort wasn't a scientist, in fact, never even finished high school. Apparently he wanted to be a famous writer and never succeeded in his fiction work. Depressed from the negative reviews of his first novel, Fort began spending his spare time in the New York Public Library. For years and years he read . . . pretty much everything: newspapers, scientific journals, history, astronomy, psychology, and sociology, whatever he could get his hands on. Reading through a plethora of various articles, stories, and other accounts, instances of unnatural events began to trickle to the surface. Interested in data normally ignored by mainstream science and culture, he uncovered hundreds upon hundreds of eye witness accounts: frogs raining from the heavens; fish raining from the heavens; unexplained disappearances; cases of spontaneous combustion; unidentified flying objects; cryptozoological sightings; ghostly apparitions; aerial phenomena, such as ball lightening and airships (before there were any such thing); and so on. Fort recorded these anomalies on tiny little strips of paper he filed away in shoeboxes labeled by category of phenomenon. What few friends he had marveled at the stacked columns of shoeboxes lining his apartment walls.

After years of collecting these notes, to Fort, a pattern emerged.

The product of that pattern was X. To Fort, X was the great mystery, an external or objective force that guided all things. In all of Fort's reading he discovered a universal law, a formula underneath all seemingly disparate things. This force acted as a great attractor, or influencer on all of society, all nature. In essence, Fort was a believer of orthogenetic evolution. He believed evolution was not a set random processes, but a guided system headed toward one great goal. However, this goal was a malevolent one, directed by a force which convinced us we had free will whereas free will was actually a simulation:

"I shall try to show that X exists, that this influence is, and must be, evil to an appalling degree to us at present, evil which at least equals anything ever conceived of in medieval demonology."

Fort even went so far as to blame this presence for his publishing foibles: *"I suspect that strange orthogenetic gods are mixed up in all this."*

So, what unearthed for me were two realizations: a.) Charles Fort was the godfather of supernatural inquiry, until he came along no one took seriously the notion of approaching the subject in an investigative manner; and b.) Charles Fort was also, according to my own researches, the godfather of modern conspiracy theory in a time when science and reason ruled the psychological and sociological landscape.

In fact, according to Fort, X ruled over all. Even, as this sentiment bellowed into my gut, over reality and consciousness itself:

"I am convinced that everything is fiction."

This was when I was indeed convinced, or rather vindicated, of the *unreality* of reality.

So it was that I became a Fortean. His legacy has continued through the long-lived Fortean Society and a publication of anomalous phenomena called *The Fortean Times*.

I recall, not too long after getting that book, I had a visionary experience of the nightmarish variety. A flash of light flickered across my perception and I collapsed to the floor. Do I hear music? If there is music at all . . . it is the sound, it is part. Then, on the ground, I felt fluid, underwater liquid motion of my body, all feels underwater. Consciousness is not lost. I was fully aware of what was going on and immediately . . . there is no wait—no second—no mere moment . . . I was immediately pulled away from the waking reality without warning—the beast crawls through my ribs. But, there is no choice, I stay with it. I have to. I am being pulled out of this world and all I can think of is I am leaving Alice behind; I want to be with Alice . . . but she is back there, in that world asleep at her mother's—at Kathleen's—house away from me, because now I am in another place and time entirely. Parts of me, little streamers of dull luminescence, get tugged underground, roller-coaster streams, rungs in a pulley being tugged and dragged underneath . . . to an Other world.

I am slipping in. I hear my mouth, my body back there in that other place, screech in shock, in terror of being gone. The beast in my ribs jumps into my stomach and laughs.

First, the legs go under. Then, the mid-section and torso. All the way to my head. Then, before I know it, I am THERE. There I am. No, no . . . there is no other . . . there is . . . I am in this world, but I am in another . . . this world . . . the other, an eye (so much bigger).

I awake in the eye of me (so much more than this) and, no . . . it is Lovecraftian! I am in a room somewhere, in a vast place—that is nothing—some space of a building. It is limited. I am, right now, you are, right now, we all are, right now, out in a limited space somewhere(when) . . . and I am dreaming away, dreaming this world (the one whose denizens are reading this) and that is what life is . . . merely a dream, literally . . . a

fabrication . . . a fantasy . . . because I, and others like me
trapped in this limited space inside this building, complex, pod
space in somewhere(when) (resonating with almost every dream
I have ever had, every dream I am in this complex, this building,
maze, and I am trapped in there and that makes up that entire
world, that entire universe, dimension) and that is real, that is
where I *really* am and here . . . here we are all dreaming this, we
are all trying to get away from that limited space and concocting
this whole experience we call "life."

What is terrifying through this episode is that this
concept is no longer an idea, it is *real*. I am Here. I am in This
Room. Then, feeling the pull, tugging back into the dream, into
the reality-dream that is my apartment and Alice and Kathleen . .
. this is all I have in the face of what is waiting for me when I
finally wake up; when we wake (die) we go back to that space,
those corridors that are emptiness and it (they) are all watching
me, a matrix revealed, it really is.

Fear boils at this point . . . I want back, back into the
dream, into the place where we can revel in the things that don't
matter because what lies beyond is something, and that
somewhere(when), it is that limited complex of building, that
small space, that we are trapped in . . . the us, maybe all of us in
one, person among a few—am in, I am in the room there,
wooden floors, I am lying on the floor, no bed or mattress or
furniture and I see my eye, looking at me here in the dream
because the barriers have been broken by that flicker of light, the
veil lifted, eye is bigger than the me in dream, in this realm. I
know, and I say, 'No, no, no, no ,no, no why are you *trying* to
wake up? Go back and take care of the dream you have! No!
What the fuck are you doing, take care of what you have now
because when you get Here it is not enlightenment!' You are
really a prisoner trapped in a place of rooms among a few other
people that are lost—you don't know where they are—and it is
terror because you don't know who *you* are, who you are trapped
by, and why or what for or what you are or where you came
from, it is all all all all all all made up! This is all made up and

when I slipped back into this realm, when I am slip-sliding, slithering back into this "conscious" world, the reality structures (so solid; not flimsy, cloudy, psychedelic stuff) reassemble. I can feel this fabricated world put itself back together, fabricate the illusion around me of sight, touch, taste, hearing, all of these lies we pass off as senses.

And I know then how fragile it all is.

All of this building block, tinker-toy reality is assembled and can fall apart so easily and it does all the time: we don't understand . . . every minute lunatics break it apart; crazies who maim torment torture and control others and magicians break it all to pieces. Why are we doing this? We can't let this dream fall apart because all of us . . . we are all fragments of mind gone awry, end up back in that same room we are trapped in (beyond forever because we cannot comprehend) the pace and time for the real reality to sink in; this is all NOT real, that is precisely why we HAVE to protect it! Keep the dream . . . for as long as we can . . . keep those fragments that are there because it is the only relief that we have in that wooden room that has Nothing on the other side, absolute Nothing in the universal sense. Don't you understand what that means? WHAT? We (I, you) were a cosmonaut that breached that place of Nothing in a psychonautic scheme, and there we are at the edge of finality, finally cracking with lunacy, choked with the understanding that there is Nothing there! Oh God, we are (I, you) so scared, I want my life, my dream, my Alice, and let it last while it can—death is no solace . . . I cannot tell my little girl that anymore . . . life is the solace . . . death is the return to that insanity, that break . . . which is why life is precious, needs to be catered to. Treat it like a dream . . . free from thought . . . freeeeeeeee from emotion . . . true freedom without desire without want without need of security . . . there is no security, only then can we truly realize how to be, TO BE . . . . this is all a figment of our crazy imaginations. The only place that is Real, the place of the break, the matrix pod breach next to Nothing . . .

There is no eternity
here!
This episode left me . . . isolated. Vulnerable. The
Fortean way was—is—my only way out!

Maybe I encountered X, maybe I didn't. But I want to
find it . . . I want to make it mine so I am no longer afraid. So
I've searched, been searching, for that common law, that
underlying framework that governs everything. I became like
Charles Fort. Because that is the only way out of the fear, isn't
it? To understand?

There is something wrong here. Something is not right
with the world. Western civilization, more than any other
civilization, has affected the ecological stability of the planet . . .
being the most destructive force in human history. We blindly
follow the shadows on Plato's cave wall, what Jim Morrison
calls "The Dim Cave." Everything *is* dim; it is bleak, for that is
how the mists of illusion are allowed to manifest a simulation of
what is real, rather than display the ultimate and horrible truth.

The panacea for this plight in humanity, I am
beginning to realize, is not some scientific remedy or political
shake-up: it is merely a realization, an awakening. Mathematical
cosmologist Brian Swimme advertizes our "cousin" relationship
with everything in the universe, especially planet Earth. When
science, from Newton's womb, has tried drastically to isolate
itself from Nature and its observations of Her makings, I can
imagine Isaac pissing himself in his own grave when the
percolations of quantum mechanics began to seed themselves in
the scientific community.

Look at super-string theory: all matter in the universe,
down to its finest point, really just consists of tiny vibrating
strings, smaller than the smallest particles known to man. These
strings can experience an infinite number of vibrational patterns
that are referred to as "resonances." Physicist Michio Kaku
likens this phenomenon to a musical instrument, the frequency
of vibrations coming from the string determines the mass of the

particles in which it resides. In his book on parallel universes, Hyperspace, he elucidates this idea:

"Matter is nothing but the harmonies created by this vibrating string. Since there are an infinite number of harmonies that can be composed for the violin, there are an infinite number of forms of matter that can be constructed out of vibrating strings . . . the universe itself, composed of countless vibrating strings, would then be comparable to a symphony."

The Universe, I conceive, is a vast orchestra of vibrations whose music is composed by the strings that resonate inside every particle of existence. These strings are all equal, exactly the same in every way. The only difference from one string to another is the vibrational sequence that resonates from each one, determining the differentiation of the particle.

This is tantamount! The threshold of scientific discovery! Just recently, the Solar Physics and Space Plasma Research Center from the University of Sheffield discovered that our very sun emits acoustic sound waves in the milli-hertz frequency akin to "musical instruments such as guitars or pipe organs." Beyond that, researchers at the University of Virginia spend their time analyzing the background radiation produced by remnants of the Big Bang, the primordial explosion that created the Universe. They have discovered that this radiance itself broadcasts sound waves that give an idea of how the Universe *sounded* during the first 400,000 years of its existence. Sound is everything! Vibration! Frequencies!

What I find most interesting is that the realms of mystics and primitive societies have known this about the Universe all along. Not only that, but these societies have always "listened" to the resonance offered by Nature. Again, Brian Swimme has discussed how the aim of primitive peoples was to live in "resonant participation" with the Universe, which is how the drum came to be one of their most sacred instruments:

"The drum was part of the sacred techniques for orchestrating the unity of the human/universe dance . . . In their

rituals and in their life in nature, the first peoples attended to the music sounded in their depths by the surrounding mysteries."

Primitive societies strove to live in harmony with the frequency of the world around them. Through the drum they were able to tune themselves in to this frequency and direct their lives in accordance with this rhythm. It is determined that the shaman, the medicine man, has always been the leader of these primitive cultures in this regard. The shaman's main function, according to mythologist Joseph Campbell, is *"to keep mankind in accord with the natural order."* The shaman is the one who instructs the society. The shaman is the one who experiences the resonance offered by the Universe and imparts what he/she learns to the people. Brian Swimme believes that because of this new knowledge we have of the cosmos (i.e. – quantum theory), science must accept and embrace the shamanic way of life:

". . . the scientist must participate to some extent in the shamanic powers so characteristic of human presence to the universe in any significant manner. The capacity of Einstein to transform the Newtonian science of his day through his teaching of relativity required a shamanic quality of imagination as well as exceptional intellectual subtlety. So we might say that the next phase of scientific development will require above all the insight of shamanic powers, for only with these powers can the story of the universe be told in the true depth of its meaning."

Joseph Campbell, as well, recognized the ability of the shaman to listen to the resonance of the cosmos. Since the strings that comprise us are all the same, we can assert that Carl Jung's "collective unconscious" is an extension of the vibrations that resonate from these strings. What the shaman receives from their ecstatic visions and experiences rings throughout the orchestra of the Universe, and what it is saying is that "We are all the same!" "We are only different from nature by choice!" "We must live in tune with the symphony of the cosmos!" "We are a collective!"

The problem with the modern human is that we do not act like a collective.

You want to end war? Famine? Poverty? Hate? Want to protect the fragility of this dream? Then consider this: we are all made of elementary particles. Each particle is made of a vibrating string. Each string is exactly the same. We are all *exactly* the same. As well, this is the same for every particle in Nature. We exist of the same elementary particles as everything in Nature: trees, rocks, birds, coyotes, elephants, worms, jellyfish, clouds, stars, etc. Every organism in the Universe, every string, is identical. We are only differentiated by how much these strings vibrate. We only differentiate from anything else in Nature, and ourselves, by our resonance. We are defined only by our vibrational frequency. The Butterfly Effect remains true in this energetic conglomeration; the vibrations of one's suffering—from the smallest flower—resonates throughout the rest of the cosmos—to the largest star.

The great mystic Jiddu Krishnamurti understood. He understood that, not just philosophically, we are all part of the same stuff. *"There is no difference between the individual and the collective,"* he said. *"I have created the world as I am."* He understood that the world is not an external object from the person, a thing to be tested in a laboratory. Krishnamurti's statement is that we are in a constant state of participation *at all times* with the world, we are never *not* participating!

"I can observe myself only in relationship because all life is relationship."

These are the words of understanding the world. Not controlling it. Not dominating it. These are the words of integration, not war. Assimilation, not segregation.

It is my assertion that the key to this integration and assimilation is in the recognition of ourselves as patterns of vibration, and nothing else. There is nothing to fight about, because those borders you see dividing this land from that are just an illusion . . . just a dusty old map lost in Spivey's tottering stacks. What X is, is ego. For it is ego that asserts our individuality over all else. It is the ego that says "I am" and not "us." Ego tells you to stand up for yourself, to forget about the other person's needs, where they are coming from, what their plight is. They don't have the history that you do, after all . . . ego establishes those walls building up stalwart around you to protect you from all the badness in the world. "*A confident man is a dead human being,*" Krishnamurti said. That is because a confident man believes he has nothing more to learn, believes he and only he is in the right, the Universe could only be on *his* side. He is clothed in the drapes of ego, they keep out the weather of collectivity. No need to ponder over the needs of others, it is I that must be looked after, he would say.

He forgets about the orchestra. He forgets that the conductor is conducting us all. His instrument is no better than any of the others.

What allows this ego to work is fear. Fear of losing identity. Therefore, control comes into effect . . . by controlling one's environment, one controls the security of one's identity. So, in essence, what if the Dominators, the Illuminati, the governments and politicians and corporations are *not* all deliberately part of the same plan? What if they do not meet in small gatherings in tribute to X, this malevolent force that directs us all, that exerts its control over our lives? What if they are not as organized as most of us in the conspiracy community assume?

What if they are all just normal dicks like the rest of us?

Then, why does it all point to *something*? Why does everything get traced to something, some X, pulling the strings? Is it the Illuminati? The Dominators? The Brotherhood of the Dragon? The Freemasons? Grey aliens? Who? What?

A further sentiment from Krishnamurti rings true: "*The simple fact is that we are afraid, not that we are afraid of this or that.*"

The true conspiracy is not that we are being controlled by aliens, the Illuminati, or X. The true conspiracy, we should realize, is that we are all being controlled by ego. That is why everything is so scary, because ego survives by turning everyone—everything—into a conspiracy. That's how its identity remains intact.

The only true conspiracy is ego itself!

24 – Awake

This is the answer.

Gregor opens his eyes. Intention, the corrugation of life seeps all around him, distinct and indecipherable. Everything all around is energy. Every segment of space is a lotus spin of every atom, quantum notions buzzing swarms in a chorus all around.

"Gregor?" she says. "You awake?"

It is all bright, every follicle of scope, bright. Exotic kaleidoscope of luminescent streams and pearls geyser in and out of her pores. Crazy ballistic glows and ley line crisscross; he can hardly discern the proper forms and configurations of distinction. Darwin, hovering over him, glowing like a connector; they see each other as energetic hubs, microcosms in the great Macrocosm – individual axis mundi. Pyre resonance, humming together with each other, with Atelier Atzalan, with the Earth, the Great Mother . . . buzzing, drumming underneath and all around in a symphonic matrix of pure information.

"Gregor?" she asks again.

"There is no Gregor." he murmurs, rubbing his eyes. "Never was."

"Here," Darwin proffers a pair of dark sunglasses. "It helps your brain to better process distinctions. Otherwise the information is overwhelming. Your nervous system can only process so much data at once. We all *have* to wear them."

He takes them, slides delicately onto the bridge of his nose. Film, bright cacophony skewing his vision dims over . . . it is better, more clear. The ley line everything of the room and Darwin is seen—spider web network—however, he can now discern the delineations of forms. He can see the cot he is laying on, the chair Darwin is sitting in, the coffee table with two cups of steaming tea, all in their spirit emanation. All in how they are connected to the greater network of Gaian/Universal tentacle mind. We are all, everything is, only an idea. The RED Agent doesn't just see that, but *experiences* it.

She offers him a cup and takes one for herself, sitting back. He accepts and sits up to sip it. Woozy spin a slight cascade in his head.

"Careful," she warns. "It'll take a few minutes to adjust to the new reality. The tea will help. It has cocoa in it. A sacred plant."

"Aren't they all?" he asks. The brew is warm and settles his system.

"Exactly," she smiles, a golden beam of holistic participation, and sips her own. "So, if you are not Gregor Samson, then who are you?"

There was a boy, long ago. The Dominators took him. Broke his mind. The boy's mind became a maze; memories lost, twisted and perverted. He had become forsaken. But, something happened. They had to abandon the operation. And then that boy became Gregor, which was a lie. Gregor was a fabrication. The boy before that could never return.

"I am Dedalus," he says, watching at the cocoa leaves swirl in his cup through dancing steam. They are speaking to him. "The Labyrinth Breaker. Now and forever."

"Always was," she adds. "So you understand now. Gregor Samson never existed. Even if that identity *was* real, you still never would have *been* Gregor Samson."

"It's still all choppy . . . fractured bits. I can't completely recall."

She sets her cup down on the table. "You are a rescue child, Dedalus. Who you were before Gregor Samson was a potential kidnapped by the Enterprise. The Enterprise continually seeks innocents with psychic potential to experiment on, turn into their own little entourage of super soldiers. They tried to turn you into a weapon. You spent years in an underground facility, you and hundreds of other kids and teenagers nobody would care about, or somehow forgotten. Homeless. Runaways. Orphans. Outcasts. But, there was a break, a rescue attempt, by . . . some people."

"Not R.ED."

"No, not RED. We don't know who. There are many freedom fighters besides us. In any case, the break failed. The Enterprise panicked. They were working through a Department of Defense subsidiary. The DOD pulled the plug for fear of media exposure. They reintegrated you and some of the others back into society. Though they swiped your minds, gave you false lives. Coded your brains. All they have to do is reactivate that code, and they would be able to turn you all back on again . . . become their weapons."

"And that's why you had me work with Mahamaya," he surmises. "To deprogram me."

"That was only some minor clean up. The real deprogramming came from Propit. He deactivated the numerical sequence in your cerebral cortex that would have allowed the Enterprise to trigger you into a psychotic state. "

"Town Topic," he notes the incident at the diner; passing out from Propit's queer intonations. "But, you said you weren't sure why he was here."

"I'm not." The crisp integrative connectedness of her aspect, golden egg aura with no aberrations attached. She is telling the truth.

"Then George Stransky . . ."

"He is the real mystery," she continues. "There have been others . . . I have been getting reports, gathering input. Propit has been busy in the Kansas City area. Random bodies showing up in coma states . . . all his actions, we assume, that are deprogramming activities."

"But obviously the Nova Enterprise would be responding, wouldn't they?"

"Exactly. Spring-heeled Jack is one element of that response, but he is not the full story. We still need to find out what this 'Mass' is, why Merchant died."

Dedalus takes another sip and sets down his own cup. A reinvigorating force pumps smoothly through his system. He can feel the Maninkari wyrm siphon copious amounts of DMT into his blood stream, though also regulating it in partnership with his endocrine system. A perfect machine in self-psychedelic cooperation.

"Lena," he muses. "Kathleen . . . Alice!!! If I'm not Gregor Samson then . . ."

"We call them Mannequins," she explains. "Actors. People the Enterprise have blackmailed to show up in your life to fulfill the false fantasy of your existence. If you think clearly, you only saw Lena a few times, Kathleen only once or twice, and Alice, your mother . . . probably never."

He recalls . . . the memory of their faces hazy. His own daughter! *Not* his daughter . . . just a gray cloud obscuring his ability to discern reality from unreality, a silkscreen illusion. It was all a fabrication! It all feels so far away now; a bad dream almost impossible to wake up from. Almost.

He sits up and notices a set of clothes lying at the end of the cot: a black shirt, black combat boots, with a set of red pants and red tailored sports coat. He looks quizzically at Darwin.

"Some Agents just wear what they want in the field," she smirks. "But Edith likes for us all to be homogenous if possible."

Dedalus takes off his clothes, unabashedly, and put on his new uniform. He embraces his new identity as a revolutionary, a shaman insurgent, an emissary of the Maninkari and the Earth.

Modernism is his enemy for now and ever more.

Fully dressed in his new skin, he asserts, "We need to go back to Kansas City now. Ramona is in danger. My sister is not my sister and Ramona doesn't know it. And with Jack loose, Jonah has more than he can handle."

"Agreed," Darwin walks over to the only door, opens and walks through. Dedalus follows. "But we didn't just come here to recruit you. We need backup."

They walk through the halls of Atzalan, now blooming with a renewed radiance through Dedalus' eyes. He can feel the heart of Atzalan beating, breathing, humming itself in vibrational melodies under his feet, up through into his body . . . resonant pond ripples. He can feel it: Atzalan is greeting him, welcoming him aboard the mission with song. A cheerful grin breaks across his face.

He feels home.

They enter the control center. Atzalan's heart shimmers golden pulsing light, thumping, throbbing transcendence and austerity. There is still a crowd around the Conduit, which radiates like a kindling fire. Dedalus sees Maynard and Edith studying the screens. One of the screens displays Mithra on her mushroom perch. She emits tangible violet, a bountiful DMT Maninkari light filling the entire screen. Mithra: the Angel of Light, the Morningstar of R.E.D. juices creating entirely the consciousness around her. Gazing at the screen, Dedalus yearns to be in her violet—a magnet, the Great Attractor. He understands, for all RED Agents, she is the source of their Life, the Great Mother along with Earth: Twin Mothers. Mithra: the Alpha and Omega. Because of her, this is how the Agent presence sees, assimilating information; the people and things in the environment can be read, and how they feel . . . their energy signifies.

Darwin notices Dedalus' observation, but instead walks in a different direction. He reluctantly follows. He is, after all, on a mission.

They approach a bench, a set of lockers, a little recreation area with table, chairs, a couch. There is a lone man sitting on a cloth on the ground. He is in a meditative position, but Dedalus doubts he is in trance. He is an Agent. Dedalus can feel the magnetic pull between them just as he can between him and Darwin. The man has an ancient scent. He is middle-aged, chocolate sheen skin, thin mustache, dark goggles cover his eyes. A red kurta with Chikan embroidery adorns his narrow head. His electromagnetic field burns with experience.

"Dedalus," Darwin stops and crosses her arms. "This is Special Agent Srinivasa, from the RED branch in India."

"RED *suyu*," he jolts upright into a standing position. If Dedalus had still been Gregor, he wouldn't have seen it, he moved so fast. But, he is not Gregor anymore, he is R.E.D.; Dedalus could clearly see the air molecules split as Srinivasa cut through them with meticulous speed from sitting to standing position in fractions of a second. Srinivasa extends a hand cordially. He is shorter than Dedalus first imagined, though his countenance is respectable nonetheless. "Welcome, friend. I am a Rakshasa Specialist. I have come to assist in your Tzolk'i situation."

"Tzolk'i?" Dedalus inquires.

"Jack Blue Note of Wanderers," Srinivasa explains. "Imix Akbal is his true name. He is a Tzolk'i, elemental demons, ancient conjurations by the Mayan sorcerers to rid the continent of the colonial invaders."

"Srinivasa is an expert in conjuration," Darwin clarifies. "He is also an asshole. I requested his presence anyway to help extract Spring-heeled Jack. His methods will be very useful."

Srinivasa smiles mischievously. "Come now, Darwin! Don't be giving the boy false impressions!"

"Why's that?" Dedalus asks.

Srinivasa is about ready to talk when Darwin interrupts. "Watch your back around him is all I'm going to say. We need his skills, but other than that don't trust him anymore than you would trust a strung out junky with your wallet. Got me?"

Srinivasa grumbles a bit, but quietly lets Darwin's statement stand.

Dedalus nods. "So, what is the Tzolk'i exactly? If he was created by the Mayan civilization to beat the Dominators, wouldn't they be allies?"

"The Tzolk'in is the Mayan calendar, you understand," Srinivasa gathers up the cloth he was sitting on and stuffs it into a large hiking backpack. "It is comprised of twenty named days. When the Spanish invaded, the shaman priests were desperate and turned to the dark arts to call off the invaders. They created an army of demons by magically infusing the numerical glyphs of certain days from the Tzolk'in. Spring-heeled Jack is one of the last descendants of this brutal force. His true name is derived from the first day of the Tzolk'in, *Imix'*, and the third day, *Ak'b'al*. *Imix* literally means 'crocodile' and *Akbal*'s meaning is 'darkness' or 'night'.

"When the Spanish conquered MesoAmerica, the majority of the Tzolk'i were extinguished in the ensuing battle. Though there were a few which survived and abandoned the continent. They became known as immortal Wanderers throughout the planet, wreaking havoc wherever they go and frequently contracting with the Nova Enterprise to gain wealth and prestige in the supernatural realms. In essence, the Tzolk'i are a form of Rakshasa, ancient demon spirits described in the *Ramayana* and *Mahabharata*. I am highly trained in the dispatch of Rakshasa entities."

"Those are Hindu epics, right?" Dedalus recalls.

"Precisely."

"Based on your expertise," Darwin speculates. "Can you figure out why Jack would be in the area? Why the Enterprise would be exercising Tzolk'i involvement?"

"Your suppositions so far about Propit seem correct," Srinivasa nods in agreement. He loads the hiking pack on his back; the bulk is about as large as he is. "He is here to counteract Propit's presence. Jack is merely a work-for-hire. Being a Tzolk'i demon, the only thing he gets out of this is blood. That is all he cares about. As the audio clip you presented to me earlier suggests, there is a bigger hand at play. Someone is conducting this mad symphony. Only by extracting Jack Blue Note will we find out exactly what is taking place. He is in the way."

"Well, let's go then." Darwin swiftly turns and walks away toward one of the exiting corridors. Dedalus turns to query Srinivasa.

"What did you do to her?"

"She's telling the truth, boy," Srinivasa straightens his pack and follows Darwin out. "Don't trust me for shit."

25 – Jonah Makes His Mark

She has not cried. Not yet.

There is still a way, a way out. There is always a way.

She is gagged and tied, wrists bound together with leather straps probably bought at a sex shop. She is fastened to an antique armoire that is probably lined with ironwood, or something similar, because she can hardly budge it. Fortunately, her captor did not blind-fold her and has strategically placed her right next to a bay window. She recognizes her surroundings. The uncut fields and ocean of sunflowers. She has been in this very living room, just days ago, populated by an outdated patchwork of dusty furniture. She is in Wallis Manor.

Lawrence's house.

As she continues to tug fruitlessly at her binds, she scans the room. Every couch, table, chair, and inch of floor space is taken up by stacks of various boxes. She reads the print on each one: *Crunchy Bear Cereal, Snackilicious Butter Crackers, Ultra-Grain Bread, Muffle Burger Buns,* and more. A memory is triggered and she recalls being here with Gregor a few nights ago. Lawrence had an abundant amount of bread in his kitchen, noticed even more in his pantry. In fact, he had more bread products than any other food item. Lawrence has always been odd, but this was suspicious; his psychotic behavior that night coupled with the fact she is back here, confined, was enough to almost make Ramona lose it. She wanted to squeeze out a tear. Just one. Maybe it would help release the churning fear writhing in her gut like a nasty leviathan.

But, no! Not now. Break down later, not now. Now is a time for thinking.

Whatever chance she might have had to concoct an escape plan was interrupted by a figure walking into the doorway. Shirtless, dark mammal hair curling around his nipples and belly. The only clothing a maroon, flannel kilt and a mask . . . a mask of a cherub, baby face. She can see his greasy tendril hair flop about it, onto his shoulders. He is holding a ghetto blaster.

Ladies and gentlemen, Lawrence Wallis. Discordian.

He places the stereo on the ground and pushes play. Grandmaster Flash blares at full volume: "White liiiiiiiiiiiiiiines . . . vision dreams of passion . . . blow'n through my miiiiiiiiiiiind . . . and all the while I think of you . . ." Lawrence jiggles back and forth, like he is at dance party. Swaying his kilt from side to side.

"Lar-fff-enfff!!!!" she tries to scream at him through her gag.

"'Everything is true,'" he orates over the bass beat walloping the room. "'Even false things are true!'" He hops over to her, smacking the air in front of him, grind-style. He kneels down close to her. The squinting cherub's face smiling at her. He sticks his tongue through the breathing hole.

"Ticket to ride . . . white line highway . . . tell all your friends . . . they can go my way . . . pay your toll . . . sell your soul . . ."

"Know what I am, Ramona?' he croons through the plastic mask. His body snakes over hers, he grasps at her thighs and buttocks. "I am part of a tribe, baby. As the *Principia Discordia* says, 'We are a tribe of philosophers, theologians, magicians, scientists, artists, clowns, and similar maniacs who are intrigued with ERIS GODDESS OF CONFUSION and with her doings.' I'm a warrior, baby!"

He leans in to her ear; she struggles to ring herself out of his grip.

He whispers: "I always wanted to fuck you."

She kicks with all of her might. >>IMPACT<< His body hurtles backward and collapses on a tower of *Aunt Nelly's Cake Mix* boxes. They collapse onto his limp body as he tumbles to the ground. Adrenaline success pumps through her veins!

He pushes himself up . . . mask is craning slightly off his head. She sees part of his face underneath. It is painted in merriment.

He crouches on his feet and SPRINGS . . . leaps at her like a cougar!

Caught . . . stop, and he is thrown halfway across the room. SMASH, into a shelf and boxes avalanche over his limp frame. This time, he does not get up.

Copernicus is there. His face looks weary, and pained. Grandmaster Flash has stopped.

He reaches down to Ramona with a knife, cuts off her straps. As she pulls away in fright he strolls over to an even space between Lawrence and her, sits halfway on the arm of a couch. She undoes the gag and spits.

"I apologize," Copernicus fumbles through a soft pack of cigarettes in his shirt pocket. "That was very unprofessional. It wasn't my choice to work with him. My hands are kinda tied in that matter."

"You're not the one tied up, *Benjamin!*" she tosses her binds in front of him and tentatively creeps to the other end of the room. She eyes the doorway cautiously.

"I mean it," he finds a cigarette and is now searching for a lighter in his jean pockets. "When that fucker wakes up I'm going to beat the living shit out of him. That's no way to treat a lady, or a prisoner of any kind."

"So I'm your prisoner?"

"That's obvious isn't it?" he finds one, brings it up to the cigarette dangling from his lips. Lights it. Smoke pours from his nostrils. "But that doesn't mean your fate is doomed. And that also doesn't mean you're *not* going to be treated well."

She creeps slightly over some boxes of cereal toward the doorway. "Great precedent you set for that one," she quips.

"I mean it, I apologize. I had to have my men drop you off here. Orders are orders. I was hung up with another issue before I could get here. I rushed over as soon as I could. I don't trust the little bastard any more than you do."

"Orders?"

"We're using this as a safe house for this particular operation. As you probably know from history, the Central

Intelligence Agency isn't exactly known for hanging out with the wholesome types. We utilize whatever resources we can."

"Why? So you can catch Gregor? Put him in jail?"

"Or trade prison for information. If he can lead us to the higher ups on the tree of this particular cell then he would have another chance at life. If he doesn't cooperate, well . . . then . . . you know . . ."

"Not to rain on your little good cop routine here," Ramona slides a chair in front of her, stacked with granola bar boxes. "But I don't believe a fucking word you're saying. I was just about to be raped by your partner here who tried to kill Gregor and me the other night. You'll have to forgive me if I'm a little on edge and not in a cooperative mood. Where's Lena?"

"Fucking mind sweeps," he rubs his wrinkled brow. His eyes were ornamented with aggravation, but—she noticed—not by her. His was frustrated by some situation other than her. "Look . . . Lena isn't really Lena."

"What the hell are you talking about? Show me where Lena is now or I'll go on a crazy-wild-bitch rampage! NOW!"

"Look , I . . ."

>>CRASH!!!!!<<

The window breaks . . . a canister pops through, smoking gas billowing out of its end.

"Shit," Copernicus curses, jumping up to grab Ramona and pulling her through the doorway, out into the hall. She heard some yelling, and a cackling laugh. Had she heard that voice before?

Copernicus pushes her down and pulls a .357 Magnum revolver from a holster inside his shirt. He reaches around the doorway, points the revolver into the living room, and pulls the trigger twice. BLAM! BLAM!

He pulls back and waits. Ramona is curled into a fetal position, frozen in fright. A voice hollers from outside, through the broken window.

"Ha, ha!!! What izzat? A Colt Python you got there? Nice! But, you're gonna haveta do better than that, Nova asshole!!"

Copernicus grimaces, throws his arm around the corner and fires another time. BLAM!

Ramona hears giggling as the voice seems to tarry away, as if the perpetrator is circling around the house.

"Was that . . . Jonah?" she asks softly.

"Yep," Copernicus swings out the cylinder of his gun, loads three bullets into the empty chambers, and closes it. "You stay here. Trust me, don't try to run. There's nowhere to go. I got to go hunt now."

He rises slowly and heads for the front foyer. He turns a corner, goes out of site.

Ramona takes off down the other end of the hall. Toward the basement. Toward the back door.

* * * * *

Jonah jogs hurriedly from the front porch, his many coats and satchels flailing as his mangy frame bounces up and down. Panting, he plunges behind a nearby bush. He chuckles as he waits . . . impatiently.

"Come on, needle dick," he squawks. "I can't wait all day!!!"

Almost on cue, the front door opens. Peeking through the shrubbery, Jonah sees that the doorway remains empty. He frowns in disappointment.

"Hey Mulligan," Copernicus bellows from inside. "You know you are waaaaaay outmatched, right? I'm a veteran case officer, for crying out loud! You? You're a washed up junky wannabe revolutionary!"

Jonah becomes enraged. "I'M NO JUNKY YOU POOP-FACED NINNY!!!"

Copernicus gets his target's bearings. He reaches around the threshold and fires in the direction of Jonah's voice.

BLAM! Dirt kicks up an inch from Jonah's face, twig and leaf fragments splay about. He snickers. Time to move about.

"Way to miss my flabby black ass, Elmer Fudd," he heckles Copernicus, rushing to a nearby tree. "Ha, ha, ha!!!!"

The target's moving. To peg him, Copernicus will have to step out a little bit. He moves out his right foot, leans out a few inches. Fires twice. BLAM! BLAM! Pulls back inside.

Something is wrong. Something . . . that smell! Copernicus looks down. Sizzling steam rises from sole of his shoes.

"Shit," he stumbles, trying to push the shoe off of his foot as fast as he can. But, not fast enough . . . the acid burns through just enough, searing bits of his flesh. The shoe and sock fly off. "Shit shit shit shit shit!!!!!"

"How do you like THAT?" Jonah hollers from behind the tree. "Fluorosulfonic acid mixed with antimony pentafluoride! We call that *magic*! Oooh yesss!!!" He cheers, arms thrown into the air in victory. A slight sting. He looks over to his left arm. A hole in his coats' sleeves . . . blood runs down.

"Oh damn."

Copernicus is writhing on the floor. The pain is miserable. His foot is burning, flesh dissolving away. He has never gotten burned by acid, but has encountered it in the field many times. Water. He needs water. Flush out the area *fast*. He quickly crawls to the kitchen, dragging his foot along. His muscles in that leg are in shock, atrophied. He braces the counter top and pulls himself up. Throws his burning foot into the sink, throws on the cold water.

"AAAAARRRRRGGHHHHH!!!!!!!!!!!!!!!!!!!!!!!!!!!"

Jonah looks up from tying the knot around his arm, cutting off the blood flow. He relishes in his adversary's pain. The Nova scum is obviously indisposed. He pulls out of his coats a handheld stun gun. Taking a deep breath, releasing, Jonah runs toward the house.

He approaches the front porch. Pulling out a canteen, he pours water over the acidic trap he laid for Copernicus. Stepping over the threshold carefully, he inches into the foyer. A burned shoe and sock are strewn on the floor. The chandelier above jingles slightly. All is quiet. Not good. He presses himself against the wall, gun held close. Tip-toe down the hall, following a smeared trail of blood. He comes to a doorway. Peeks with one eye. The kitchen. There is water all over the floor and counter mixed with Copernicus' blood. No Copernicus. Where is he?

A black tentacle reaches from behind and encloses itself around Jonah's neck. Reflexively, he drops the stun gun, pulling on the dark mass squeezing his trachea. It is too strong. He tugs with all of his might, but the lack of air is weakening him. Soon, after struggling for about a minute, Jonah droops and slips to the floor unconscious.

Ramona, held by another mass of Jack's shadow tendrils, is paralyzed by consuming horror. Jack does not even have to flinch to hold her. Jonah, her last bit of hope, is down.

Copernicus limps around the corner, his foot bandaged with kitchen towels. Sweat is pouring from his brow. He leans exhaustively on the wall.

Jack pasty face snarls like wolf. "Tell me again why they assigned you to me?"

In anger, Copernicus raises his gun to the ceiling and pulls the trigger. BLAM!

"Fuck off, demon!!!" he screams. "I followed orders! I lured them here!"

"And made a mess of the situation," Jack roars back. "Look at this place! Look at *you*! Pathetic human meat! Only good for cooking over a fire!"

Jack, standing triumphantly over Jonah's body, pulls Ramona close. His dark limbs hold her a foot off the ground, so they are face-to-face. His skeletal hands delicately touch her cheeks. His fingers are rough as sandpaper, colder than ice. She faints in fright.

"Heh, heh . . . *meat*!"

Copernicus moans in disgust. "What now? Did you hear from your boss?"

Jack peers over playfully at Copernicus. He drops Ramona on top of Jonah in heap.

"We both ultimately work for same person, you know," he growls, pure tangible night dancing like death around his boney build. A walking protoplasmic cadaver. "So stop acting like we are not, *monkey*. You are only alive because I need a secretary for the moment."

He walks over to the front door, closes it slowly. The shadow forms surrounding him envelope his body in a tailored suit of raven feather black.

"I heard from Blome," Jack melds in the shadow of the hall, indiscernible from the form darkness. "He appreciates the clean-up job you did on Merchant's body. The concoction is complete. The Mass is ready for implementation. Test Phase I. Now you need to gather up these two meat piles and take them into the city. Tomorrow evening. Penn Valley Park."

"Liberty Memorial?"

"And take the Wallis boy with you. I like him. He has potential. *Good* meat!"

"But tomorrow is the Reed speech," Copernicus digs for another cigarette, eyes heavy from fatigue. "He's doin' the whole anti-President, anti-Patriot Act thing. The place will be swarming with demonstrators. How are we supposed to operate under those conditions?"

Jack is no longer visible, having melded completely into the shadows on the wall.

"That's precisely why we will be there," Copernicus faintly hears the echo of Jack's scratch voice. "The War of Ideas will soon end."

He is gone.

Copernicus limps wearily over to Ramona and Jonah lying ragdolls on top of each other. He shuffles through Jonah's pockets, empties what he can through the layers of coats and multitudinous pockets: a stun gun, three satchels with various chemicals obviously for use in warfare, two types of Bowies knives, a ball of yarn, fishing line, five lighters, one zippo, a vintage British No.36M fragmentation grenade, a bird eggshell stored in a small plastic container, eighteen films of tinfoil, and one copy of James Joyce's *Ulysses*.

He moves over to Ramona, knowing full well her pockets should be emptied by now, but not trusting in Lawrence's ability to fulfill his duties. With care and respect, he pilfers through them: car keys, a stick of lip balm, and a cell phone. He pushes the center button. Good, it is not locked; though the screen shows recent activity. He goes into the mailbox. A recent text exchange. He looks at her sent message.

"Lenas boyfriend CIA. Lawrence working with him. Ultragrain bread and other products like that everywhere. Somethings very wrong. Help!!!"

He looks at the time sent. Just a few minutes ago. Must have been when she slipped away, before Jack caught her.

The phone buzzes. A returned message. The sender: Gregor Samson.

"On my way."

Dormantz®

You, and only you. Hi, my name is Toni Maronis. You know me as Mr. Bisledore on "About the Family", America's favorite television sitcom in the Fall of 1981. So, you know how much I *care* about family values, and holding to those values in this information-rich age of cell phones and other high-tech gadgetry. Heh, heh . . . I even remember when the idea of a mobile phone was preposterous. Back when we had tape decks and wood paneling.

But now, you don't have to worry about your children getting swept away in this fast-paced world. Thanks to Dormantz®!!!!

Easy to use. Fast acting. Slllooooww results. Dormantz® is the answer to all your family's problems.

Need your children to settle down? Focus on their homework? Maybe just to stop hopping around and sit down in front of the T.V. so you can get supper done? Well trust me, Mrs. Maronis and I understand perfectly! That's why Dormantz® is an FDA approved barbiturate that is healthy and wholesome for your child's stimulant needs. Just pop the rapidly absorbing tablet into any drink of your child's choice: juice, lemonade, even soda. Dormantz® will absorb so well into any beverage, they won't even know what hit 'em! Then . . . voila! In less than five minutes: mild-to-moderate sedation! Just watch young Johnny and Jane in front of the T.V. here while momma cooks some yummy chicken pot pie!

[*Johnny and Jane staring into a static-filled screen with zombie eyes, drooling at the mouth.*]

Don't have that problem at home with the kids? Dormantz® can be used in any scenario: calming down the boss, nursing home residents in a rampage, first dates, or *just plain fun*!!! Take it from me – America's favorite fictional butler – Dormantz® is the anesthetic for you!

Time to slow down that family time! Dormantz®!!!! All *about the family*!!!

26 – Infiltration Cabal

He scans over the blazoned, smog layer covering the concrete landscape below. Steel structures jut out from the haze - reaching like mechanical tendrils to the Babel ether expanse, rising, rising. The city screams at him. *His* city, he claims thoughtfully. It beckons and repels all at the same time. Amorphous grid of noise currents and electric configurations migrating from block to block in a frenzy of malaise; a gargantuan circuit board of depletion, destruction, and deprecation. "Feed me." "Feel the stink." "I need you to pump me." It says, over and over. Breathing, heaving, a Pynchion nightmare of backward mutants and automatons.

We're not warring against an organization, or a state, he ponders. *We're warring against an entire culture. A feverish, addicted, insane culture.*

He loves it, in a way. It feeds him. Makes him want to fight, fight it all. All feeds in the all. Off the perch, he moves down, swift air whistles past brittle ears. His ears hear everything. Car honks, screeching vultures, crashing cranes, explosions of grandeur. His thoughts move past him—catch up . . . nevertheless, the waiting is upturned.

He clatters down the hill, crumbling pebbles rolling, scattering about, twigs and bushels caught on pant leg deep. His city is full of trees. This makes it better than most cities. The trees: his eyes (heft essence in heart beat) see in RED their before and after, immediately then and hence. Rapid like shutters inside the bark, miniature workings sees tiny colonies of life life LIFE purging through from underneath roots their own cities of flushing and pursuing. Everything is pursuing life.

They are hearkening, a collection of forestry. Vibrating at levels beyond, higher frequencies than the cold more dense concrete, ready to walk onto a parking lot where Darwin and Srinivasa sit waiting for him in the van. "Call, call." The trees say. There are so many; one, a gaunt oak, the eternity of leaves

singing like heavenly chorus in even slightest wind barely
tangible to normal human, but highly sensitive to him in the new
way of seeing/thinking/perceiving/participating. They enrapture
him in their being, needing and making love to the very idea of
he. That is what they do, you see. For survival is mutual and the
trees understand that. The maple to the side is wary and
protecting its seedlings. The oak up the way is heavy and jolly.
They holler for him to stay, but he cannot. *Alas*, he thinks to
them. They sink from peripheral imaging, understanding the
unknowable; not stupid but water out of fish.

Alas, indeed. The ground is hard. RED is pulsating.
The way back was serendipitous, synchronous, ecstatic.
Watching the world go by, sitting in the van on the trip back
from Atzalan, the Maninkari stream coursing in and out of
consciousness, becoming consciousness, permeated all
sensibility. He learned everything in an instant, and nothing
throughout eternity. THE RED way of being is a constant trance
of *Adi-shakti*, as Kali is in her eternal dance, the perpetual
motion of balance. Enlightenment and banality circling each
other in the yin-yang polarity. Philip K. Dick was right.

A RED Agent sees and feels everything within its
electromagnetic frequency structure. Instead of a tree, he will
see a loose vibrational sequence of atoms, molecules, quanta,
feeling, perception, and the like. Instead of a car, the sequence is
more dense, mechanical, rigid, but still there. A person, looser,
like water, and more chaotic with feeling and perceptual acuity.
Each EM structure is unique, formidable and individual, but also
integrative with its environment in such a way that is subtle to
the untrained eye yet obvious to the enlightened one. The Gaia
principle is correct: every object on this planet is part of one
working organism; we are all parts, organs, nerve endings, or . . .

Cancers.

He knows where to go from here. Priority one:
Ramona. Upon arriving from Wisconsin, from Atzalan, they
rushed straight to Wallis Manor. No Ramona, no Lawrence,
nothing. Expect stockpiles of food. Mostly crackers, breads,

cereals. An abundant amount of grains. So, now they are here, an excellent view of the city, in the Northland, Fairfax District and the Bottoms below. Decrepit railroad tracks and bustling cars zigzagging through interlocking highways. A good place to think, Dedalus had told them. Gregor came here all the time.

This is why he was fired. He was getting too close. They were using him, but he was beginning to remember so they had to send him away from the source of information. He remembers *now*.

"I know where to go from here," he says. Darwin approaches. Srinivasa stays at the van, flicking through stations on the radio.

"Where's that?" Darwin inquires.

"Gregor Samson is in the center of all this," he explains. "There is a reason for everything, right?"

"What are you suggesting?" Darwin is cleaning a Glock pistol.

"All of those boxes at Lawrence's house," he explains. Darwin listens intently. "I recognize some of those brands. *Ultra-Grain Bread. Aunt Nelly's Cake Mix*. I, as Gregor, worked at the Kansas City Trade Bureau. They specialize in commodity futures in wheat, specifically hard red winter wheat. Gregor worked in futures and options, where distributors would purchase specific quantities of wheat through various contracting vehicles. I handled a lot of paperwork. Menial tasks, really. Entering data from farm stockpiles of hard red winter and allocating those stockpiles to their designated distribution centers. Just entering numbers, but there was a lot of information I was exposed to. Hard red winter is used to make flower and yeast breads, for a wide variety of products. *Ultragrain* and *Aunt Nelly's Cake Mix* brands are just a couple of those. This is no coincidence."

"It rarely ever is," Darwin adds, loading rounds into a clip. "You're right, Dedalus. There's no such thing as a coincidence in *this* Universe."

"I think I should go to the KCTB. See what I can find out."

"You mean *we*," she arms the pistol. "That's our only lead to finding Ramona and Jonah, hence getting to Jack. Being an Agent now, breaking into buildings should be simple as pie for you. But, with everything that's going on, it would benefit you to have Srini and I provide some cover for you."

Dedalus peers over at Srinivasa in the van, who has settled on a station and is laughing at whatever he is listening to, clapping his hands together.

"What's his story," Dedalus asks her. "What's the beef between you two?"

Darwin runs fingers through her hair with her free hand, stuffing the Glock into a holster inside her red jacket. She shoots a quick glare over at Srinivasa, quickly diverting it back to the city to watch the polluted layer of toxic exhaust blanket the cityscape.

"Srinivasa is an interesting character," she whispers, talking away from Srinivasa's direction. "As you can tell by now, the Maninkari wyrm changes you, it enlightens you, but it doesn't turn you into a Jesus or a Buddha. Most of the time the effects of the RED Shift cause most Agents to surrender completely to the cause, as with you and I. Other times— because of some unknown genetic factor maybe, or a defect in the brain chemistry, we don't yet know—it creates an unstable . . . *glitch.*"

"Srinivasa . . ."

"Is a Rakshasa Specialist. And in that line of work he deals daily with a force of maleficent energies the normal human body, even a RED host, finds it difficult to sustain. Because of the particular irregularity of his body chemistry he has access to a specific wavelength of reality that taps in to the murkiest recesses of the Universal Mind."

"But his energy signature," Dedalus watches Srinivasa chuckling to the radio station dialogue. Sounds like a KCUR talk show. "He has the same frequency of radio emissions as we do. I don't see or feel anything out of the ordinary."

"That's why I warned you in Atzalan," she acknowledges. "There is an undercurrent, a code written deep within that we cannot see unless we are trained specifically to decipher it. It surfaces randomly in schizophrenic outbursts that destabilize his demeanor. Last year, during a Nova Mob assault on a RED Atelier in South Africa, Srinivasa's condition was triggered during the ambush. He threw one of our fellow Agents, his partner Bach, into the Nova line of fire. Bach was killed. RED decided to keep him on because his skills are too valuable to waste, but he is forbidden to be stationed at any Atelier locations and partnered with any other Agents. Plus, he is under constant scrutiny and tests so we can figure out how to treat his condition."

"So, instead of punishment, RED is actually mitigating the problem."

"Precisely, except they are making an exception in this case. It's been a long time since we've had the opportunity to bag a Rakshasa demon. RED couldn't pass up the opportunity."

"Hey you guys!" Srinivasa hollers over to them. Startled, Dedalus and Darwin quickly reassert their demeanors and stroll over to the van seemingly undisturbed. "Check this out! Look what your hospital bombing antics have drudged up!"

He turns the volume knob up on the radio and a news reel blares through the scratchy speakers: ". . . because of the recent terrorist threat level security will undoubtedly be high. Senator Spike Reed had a few comments regarding his upcoming visit to the recently attacked Kansas City metropolitan area

"Reed: 'The Administration thinks it can get away with further revisions on the already-illegal Patriot Act which violates our civil liberties as a free people. They are taking advantage of our fear of terrorist activities to do this. To make a statement against these heinous acts of political and civil aggression against our God-given rights to privacy, I am accompanying

various peace activist organizations in a rally at Liberty
Memorial in Kansas City, Missouri. I will be speaking about the
Administration's failings in the numerous wars they have lead us
into in Iraq, Afghanistan, Yemen, and others since 9-11. I will
also be making a case for and be collecting signatures for a call
to impeachment of the President.'

"Senator Reed will be speaking at precisely 8:00pm this
evening, not exactly at the Memorial itself as the Senator
claimed, but at a stage set-up in Penn Valley Park. There is
expected to possibly be as many as 3,000 people at this event
and health and law enforcement officials are concerned about
the record-breaking heat levels. There will be . . ."

Srinivasa turns it off. He jeers laughingly at Darwin and
Dedalus.

"See what fun you've caused?"

* * * * *

Picture the indefinite simulacra of ages....the image of
mortar and cement callously formed into shapes of *de Stijl* -
furiously pumping the midnight dream of modern satiation; the
building stands erect on 48th Street, brass relief shimmering
wave of golden wheat in doldrums twilight, art deco type
displaying itself to the Plaza below: KANSAS CITY TRADE
BUREAU. Above all, Dedalus realizes, this is the adversary: a
symbol of commerce. The structure radiates with a slow Hertz . .
. oozing itself into his consciousness field irregularity . . . it
feels him. He scalars himself around its being, its structural
essence . . . it now knows him, recognizes him. There is
information in there, and it knows it - it tells him in a slow
anonymous way, he thinks (*find myself standing on the side walk
conversing in thin air, maybe an hour or two as patrons walk
passed going home from a day of hunched over cubicle droning
with their ties and brief cases and clicking high heels too
uncomfortable to walk in . . . they see a man in a red coat, red
slacks, shades and a freakish grin . . . but for some reason they*

263

*go on with their day, stick out but not intrude, the eyes glaze
over, their haze focused on the trip home to their little brick
compartments containing beds and TVs stacked upon one
another in columns of melancholy and rye*) seeker of him, brief
and he knows (after hour, hour-and-a-half) the sun is almost
down and it is time. The last remaining suits will be security and
over-worked project managers too discontent to go home to
more mediocrity, sticking around and heating up left-overs from
lunch, surfing friends' status updates while looking as if that
process diagram is getting worked on.

Darwin and Srini should be ready at any moment.

Across the street, on a sidewalk of the Country Club
Plaza, a little Indian man in a red kurta and dark goggles begins
to scream. He is holding a woman with a soft apricot face and
sepia hair by the throat. He has a vest on of what looks to be
explosives and a mechanism in his free hand. He is hollering
something about "Allah!" Darwin wails as the victim. Srini
plays the part of the mad Arab. The diversion begins.

Perfect, Dedalus smiles. *Plays perfectly into their story.
Exactly what they would expect.*

People cry and gather around in fear, unable to pry their
eyes from the Hollywood-esque excitement. Plaza security close
in cautiously and a few guards from the KCTB building stumble
out of the front revolving doors and over to the scene. After all,
they may be needed as protectors of the innocent until the police
arrive.

Time to make the move. Dedalus lurches forward. The
air makes room for him - sensuous pockets maneuvering
presence with subtlety. Nimbly he darts into the front,
practically gliding over the air as full-force concentration on
speed and agility is acute and centered. The Maninkari
excretions pump the orders into his muscles, swiftly carrying
him through in seconds.

He is in. The front desk is clear; only two guards
regularly on duty at this time of evening and they are out

attempting to free the American woman from the Muslim extremist. Good luck to them.

Eyes the elevators. Too risky. Makes for the stairwell near the back and pumps up four flights of stairs in just a few seconds. To the top. He is amazed. He feels great. No panting, no catching of breath. Didn't even break a sweat.

He enters his old office area. The lights are dimmed after 5:00pm. The sea of cubicles splay out before him, a grid of information carrying and assimilation he would not have noticed from before. There are ghosts here: Jena, Doug, Paul, Manoj, others, even himself . . . gray shadows of today and yesterday, a week or a year ago, recorded images of history implanting themselves, running the mill, over and over, mechanistic industrial froth generating and generating the same paths, again and again. Walks in, a few aisles down. His old cube, right across from Jena. Seems like years ago. Does he miss it? The feeling is dead, sad. His body was there, last week, typing away, probably scanning the latest conspiracy theory or UFO sighting on *WildPendulum.net*. But it wasn't real. None of it was real. All fake, a simulation designed to keep him from remembering what had happened to him. What had happened to him?

The overtly artificial light blinks at a narrow frequency that used to cause palpitations in his lower left eyelid. Palpitations come from the heart, starting at 150 MHz. A light flickering at exactly the right frequency can send any animal brain into a hypnotic state. The light, he can notice now, kept him in trance . . . the Maninkari flow allows him to see the layered code disseminating into the atmosphere of visual perception. Reflecting off of the retinas. Turning him into a zombie. Processing paperwork. What was he processing as Gregor Samson?

Walks into his old cube. Name tag is gone, his computer is still there. Clicks it on, it boots. Buzzes. Login. Password: *Alice0703*. Seven, the number of Heaven. Three, the number of Earth. Heaven on Earth. Is she even real, somewhere?

Moves the mouse. The energetic precision of the processing unit fascinates him, he can see why Darwin was inspired to create Mahamaya. Perusing the documents folders . . . "Transactions" . . . "Investments" . . . "Commodities" . . . "Distribution"! He clicks on "Distribution" and scans the contents. *Snackilicious Butter Crackers, Crunchy Bear Cereal, Ultra-Grain Bread, Muffle Burger Buns, Aunt Nelly's Cake Mix* . . .

What's the correlation? He conjectures silently. *What connects all these branches to me, Lawrence, and this whole elaborate lie?*

He highlights all the subfolders, right clicks. Imports all the information into a spreadsheet. A few minutes pass and the spreadsheet appears, all of the distribution information separated by columns and the products listed in rows. He clicks through the columns: "Date", "Location", "Quantity", "Cost", "Customer", "Stakeholder". Each column heading has a drop down, he moves to "Location" and scrolls through the options. Pauses at "Kansas City, MO". He selects. The spreadsheet updates.

Massive quantities of shipments of all of these items were sent to various locations within the city within the past few months. As Dedalus scans through the dates, the shipments increase as he gets within weeks. But the customer doesn't. In fact, as he scans closer and closer to the present date, one particular customer begins to show up more and more, with exponential quantities and their only stakeholder labeled as "Not Applicable". That was a rarity for this Bureau and usually meant it was some sort of government or corporate entity that wished to be anonymous and paid for that classification. Dedalus then sorts by that customer and prints out the spreadsheet. He stares fixedly at the customer name: "Artichoke Laboratories."

Dedalus walks over to the printer to grab the report. And there he stands: brown top coat; olive skin; large round, unblinking lemur eyes; olive green skin; arms folded, hands tucked into his armpits. There stands Propit Cold.

"Greetings," whines his shrill phonograph voice. "Pont-Saint-Esprit." Dedalus is entranced. Purple flames waft out of Propit in Maninkari magnificence! He stands out from normal perception as an indigo beacon, a lighthouse attracting the R.E.D. moth sentimentality. His presence does not belong here, on this plane. He is out of context, an incongruity on materiality. Propit's past is written in the perplexity that surrounds his recurrent wave undulation . . . the history of the spirit animal residing within: he is not pure Maninkari manifest like Mithra; he is Indriidae, lemur, primate, mammal, wolf, panther, bird, eagle, condor . . . the Maninkari spirits throughout time that have wished to manifest into physical form to communicate with the human shaman do so through the animal totem. The animal is a vessel, a host . . . the Maninkari spirit co-inhabits the vessel with the animal spirit, but only with permission from the animal. This is prevalent in The Sorcerer at Trois-Frères, and other indigenous works of art from the ancients. Half humanoid, half animal. Propit is both Propithecus lemur and Maninkari spirit, a walking, breathing covenant. His head twitches slightly.

"Hello Propit," Dedalus returns the greeting. He feels like he should bow, or at least nod in respect. Before he decides which to do, Propit walks one step to the side.

"The cereal man wrecking the plane, is he?" his voice squeaks.

"I guess," Dedalus answers. He decides to bend down on one knee, lowers his head. "I guess I have you to thank. You deprogrammed the equations formulating the illusion running my life. For that I'm in debt to you, for the rest of my life."

"The wyrm baby inside of you leaping," Propit takes a step back, huge grin painting his round face. "Wyrm brother/sister component to the Propit yield. We . . . are . . . one. Family interfections says ye, aye? Heh, heh." He chuckles.

Dedalus stands. The printer is finished with the report and he grabs it, takes a glance down and looks back to Propit. The cereal man.

"The cereal man is up to something," he tells Propit. "What's Artichoke Labs? Do you know? What is the Red Mass?"

Propit cocks his head to the ceiling, as if trying to gather invisible data streaming from the skies. "It is churning in the red, you see . . . life liquid. Catalyst, the one we called Merchant." He moves his wide-eyes back to Dedalus and smiles approvingly.

Dedalus ponders: life liquid . . . Merchant. Life liquid, red . . . blood! Merchant's blood.

"So," Dedalus conjectures out loud. "Merchant's blood is being used . . . by these same people? Artichoke Laboratories? This has to do with the Red Mass?"

Propit takes a tentative step closer to Dedalus, the grin loosens slightly. Arms stuffed tightly under his arm pits. Dedalus can see the Maninkari presence pulsing under the mammal shell.

"Very, very, very important," Propit's intonation drops an octave. "Close to look at the place."

Dedalus looks down to spot the location of Artichoke Laboratories. He looks back up, and Propit is gone. No more Propit. No essence of his presence can be traced, no ghost of a frequency/signature. It's as if he wasn't even there.

Quizzically, Dedalus shuffles back over to his old cubicle and opens an internet browser. He types in "Artichoke Labs" into the search engine. No results—only articles on artichokes, the perennial thistle. He opens the maps option and types in the location on the spreadsheet: 215 West Pershing Road, Suite 51. The map pops up.

Dedalus flinches. *Pershing Road, running perpendicular to Main Street . . . 215, right on the corner of Kessler and Pershing . . . located directly across the street from Penn Valley Park, the site of Liberty Memorial!*

27 - Incarceration Part 3

1964:

Harris Isbell was the doctor's name.

The head-hack, the Wenger of the US Public Health Service (PHS) Hospital's covert research facility in Lexington, Kentucky. The National Institute of Health funded his research with a blind eye, streamlined through the PHS all the way from 1 primary source: the Central Intelligence Agency. The CIA granted Isbell full reign in PHS's underground program and he flaunted it like a mad king. Moreau and his island. Isbell's word was law, and that law was a new breed of territorial psychosis never yet encountered in encyclopedic knowledge.

If you were poor, black, Hispanic, anything other than middle class white, and admitted to the ARC, you were immediately signed on as 1 of Isbell's particular menu items. Isbell, to gather some context, was a product of the Nazi-inspired methods America adopted during the Cold War era. Mind control was a top priority for the intelligence/counter-intelligence communities, which made mind-altering substances the playing field. Anytime the CIA needed a new substance tested out to measure its possible potential as a mind control agent, they shipped it to Isbell 1st class with an Executive Order to do as he will . . . provided, of course, he issue a monthly report of its effects on an unwitting population. Isbell had fun with this, acting out his most depraved Freudian fantasies—an emerging adolescent blowing up toy soldiers with firecrackers. In the '50s and '60s, Isbell's favorite cherry bomb was indeed the notorious lysergic acid diethlamide-25 . . . LSD.

Moved permanently to an observation cell adorned only with a 2-way mirror, he was. Walls and floor were white. White cot. White toilet. He knew they were watching him, but he could only watch himself.

Still slipped one meal a day through a slot in the door, though this time each meal was spiked with a dose of pure LSD. Each day, the doses became stronger and stronger. Soon, Jonah could no longer configure any lucid moments of sobriety. 1 trip led into another until existence became one psychedelic continuum. It didn't take long to spiral into complete madness while they were being watched. Before, in solitary confinement, Jonah could use his imagination to segregate himself from the reality of his situation . . . now, there was no escape. His mind belonged to them.

It could have been weeks, maybe months, of the same treatment when something different finally became manifest. 1 day, instead of a meal sliding though the slit, it was a book. Approximately 3 hours went by before Jonah even realized what had just shuffled through the door. The monotony of ingrained hallucinogenic nothingness had gripped him, and this anomalous oddity jarred his very being! Is it real? Is this the drug? But, he touched it, giving it a few caveman pokes . . . he could *feel* it, the textured pages, crimped spine, the smell of dust. He read the cover:

Ulysses by James Joyce.

He cried. Jonah wept so hard it stung his ribs. He had nothing at all during this entire nightmare, no company but his own mind, his own demons. It was maddening. No external stimulation to feed him whatsoever. What had been delivered to him was a godsend, something to commune with, to participate in.

Immediately, he began to devour its contents. At this point the LSD had equalized itself in his psyche to such a degree that it was not a distraction to his new task . . . more like a side-effect or an enhancement. He read and read and read. And then, something began to happen.

The avenues of conscious mind had expanded, opening the content of the book in a cathartically prolific way. It became *the* world. The only reality. Thus, the "real" world became an utter and absolute dream. It's about time. The modern world slips so fast through our fingers, we're running out of it. It squeaks by into the oblivion of the past.

However, what *Ulysses* began to unveil to Jonah—as if he already knew—was that time is very much on *his* side, if he only wanted it to be. The clock is the only prison. Not the walls that physically caged him in. It was time to defeat the clock . . . the chronological passing of one moment to the next.

Think of Einstein . . . he unleashed an earthquake into the academic community by overturning the Newtonian methods of observing time. Einstein proposed that time did not accelerate at the same speed everywhere in the universe; for instance, some areas of space-time move faster, in others it moves slower. This, ladies and gentlemen, was a mind-fuck for the scientific community at the time. To them, time was a stagnant and static occurrence that could be easily measured throughout the entire cosmos. Einstein, though, showed that time was actually a completely relative occurrence; relative to the position and/or speed of the observer. Therefore, the observer affects the perception of the universe based upon their position and action; hence the observer affects the universe just by observing.

Joyce was the Irish guru of this sentiment. In over 800 pages of text, the entire book of *Ulysses* happens in only 1 day. That's a hell of a lot of story for a 24 hour period! Or is it? Joyce encapsulated this form . . . this archetype of relativity in *Ulysses*. He uses our limited Western conceptions of what a day is—a series of events that follow one another sequentially from sunrise to sunset—being contingent on our reflections of it. The speed of the day is what pervades our current culture-consciousness. To Joyce, a day is so much more than just a series of events. As well, Einstein partnered with centuries of mystics and shamans that would agree. *Ulysses* is not just a series of events, as any of our days are, but an entire multi-layered network of memories, allusions, affections, and metaphors.

June 16, 1904. Dublin.

Leopold Bloom and Stephen Dedalus. Their lives intricately crocheted together into an elaborate blanket of abstruse layers. Dedalus struggling emotionally with the death of his mother; Bloom afflicted with being Jewish in a primarily Catholic community; Dedalus obsessed with imparting to everyone he knows his preposterously boorish theories on *Hamlet*; Bloom obsessing over his wife's extra-marital affair while relishing in his own erotic deviances; and so on and so forth. So much complexity. How to make sense of it? Jonah began to uncover it, following the faint glow at the end of a maze, hidden in between the dots and lines . . .

Chapter 7, "Aeolus," is patterned directly from Homer's *The Odyssey*. In *The Odyssey*, Aeolus is the "manager of the winds" and is visited by Odysseus and his men. Odysseus describes the Island of the Winds, Aeolia, as a frantic place where there is little rest among its citizenry, full of busy people doing busy things, never at rest to keep the functions of the island going. In *Ulysses'* "Aeolus," Bloom visits the *Freeman* newspaper office:

> *He pushed in the glass swingdoor and entered, stepping over strewn packing paper. Through a lane of clanking drums he made his way towards Nanneti's reading closet.*

> *WITH UNFEIGNED REGRET IT IS WE*
> *ANNOUNCE THE DISSOLUTION OF A*
> *MOST RESPECTED DUBLIN BURGESS*

> *(. . .) The machines clanked in [3-4] time. Thump, thump.*

The office is swarming with the buzz and turbulence of the printing presses; printers are rushing back and forth, and the ping-pong effect of palaver. Episode 7 is packed full of the fast, choppy rhetoric of journalism. Conversations are whipped around the printing rooms like the winds of Aeolia. Structurally, Joyce injects bold headlines through the chapter, the headlines from the papers in the process of print, breaking the entire episode into smaller passages. This creates a tone of expediency, a certain rhythm, like poetry.

(. . .) THE WEARER OF THE CROWN (. . .)
(. . .) HOW GREAT A DAILY ORGAN
IS TURNED OUT (. . .)
(. . .) ORTHOGRAPHICAL (. . .)
(. . .) ONLY ONCE MORE THAT SOAP (. . .)
(. . .) SAD (. . .)
(. . .) HIS NATIVE DORIC (. . .)
(. . .) THE GRANDEUR THAT WAS ROME (. . .)
(. . .) A DISTANT VOICE (. . .)

Up to this point, the book has been told from the perspective of 1st person narratives of Dedalus and Bloom. Here, Joyce is elevating the text above that level to a whole new variance of tone and perspective.

The machines clanked in [3-4] time. Thump, thump, thump. Now if he got paralyzed there and no one knew how to stop them they'd clank on and on the same, print over and over and up and back. Monkeydoodle the whole thing. Want a cool thing.

It is at this point the text creates its own rhythm now. The machines of the printing room take control of the narration. It is a prescribed mood. And then, it escalates:

Sllt. The nethermost deck of the [1st] machine jogged forwards its flyboard with sllt the [1st] batch of quirefolded papers. Sllt. Almost human the way it sllt to call attention. Doing its level best to speak. That door too sllt creaking, asking to be shut. Everything speaks in its own way. Sllt.

The environment conquers the narration. *Sllt, sllt.* It is speaking the language of the machines, the very room and all its mechanisms. The text has *become* the newsroom, having a life of its own. *Everything speaks in its own way.* The newsroom, setting itself, is the consciousness of the episode, where the men in the newsroom—their conversations and chatter—become the background noise. Joyce even echoes Aeolia:

Gone with the wind (. . .) The tribune's words howled and scattered to the four winds.

Like layers, the conversations overlap each other, most of them remain unfinished, arguments trail off into obscurity. All of it drowned out by the noise of the pressrooms.

CLEVER VERY

—*Clever, Lenehan said. Very.*

—*Gave it to them on a hot plate, Myles Crawford said, the whole bloody history.*

Nightmare from which you will never awake.

The rhetoric continues . . . fast, turbulent! It is broken . . . into pieces, fragments. Like real life. No certainty. Nothing really finished. Broken, fragmented. The primary format of Episode 7 is dependent on the overlapping of the noise of the press machines, the headline breaks, and the dialogue. It creates a shingling effect, layers and layers of experience faced in an almost singular moment. Episode 7 takes place for no more than a few minutes in the Life of Leopold Bloom; but, his experience is full, tantamount, most likely infinite.

This is how Jonah got through Isbell's hell. Infinity doesn't represent a long line that stretches on forever. Not just, anyway. It can be a singular instant too. The continual dosage of LSD in Jonah's system allowed his consciousness to assimilate these possibilities and what became weeks soon became mere moments . . . in those moments were found years of interior otherworlds he could experience apart from the exterior situation of his incarceration.

Jonah learned how to make time, to make experience—reality—relative.

1 day, the effects wore off. 1 day, gradually, at a snail's sprint, Jonah became sober again. And it was on that day that Jonah found himself back in Isbell's phlegmatic interrogation room.

Isbell shifted in a metal seat across the table. His white coat slightly unbuttoned at the top, a pastel shirt and corduroy tie peeking out. Jonah noticed more details of the situation this time around. The world, perceptions, were unfolding because, well . . . the fear had left him. *Ulysses* had helped him garner control of his own reality. And the crinkled, nervous vein on Isbell's receding brow admitted that.

"How are you doing, my son?" Isbell crossed one fidgety leg over the other.

"Peachy," Jonah answered, calm, resolute.

"We have been monitoring your situation and we are aware of your transitioning. Your . . . growth."

"Am I a flower?"

"More like a moth," agitation crowded Isbell's voice. He had no intention, Jonah suspected, of having a quaint chat. He was trying to observe Jonah's interactions, he wanted to find out what made Jonah tick.

"Do you enjoy the book?" he asked dubiously.

"A *shiver of the trees, signal, the evening wind. I pass on*." Jonah quoted.

"I expect an answer, *child*!" Isbell was used to being a puppet master. Being so, he never expected the puppet to start moving on its own accord. His objective was to be able to have his hand up someone's ass and making them move on his will. Instead, what he was experiencing was a psychic coup. Jonah could see that he didn't appreciate it.

"Do you realize," Isbell continued, crinkled furrow. "I could have you burned in an oven like a fucking *Jew*!"

"*I pass on*," Jonah repeated.

"Hanged like the *strange fruit* your Billie Holidays sing about?"

Again: "*I pass on*."

"I could, if I wanted, peel your skin of your body in tiny strips, one-by-one, until you died slowly of trauma."

"*I pass on*."

"I can find your family. I have a whole file on them. Mama, papa, your brother. What you don't seem to get, *nigger*, is that you belong to *me*. You are *my* property. *I* control *you*!"

Jonah calmly stares him Isbell, straight in the eye.

"*I pass on*."

Isbell sniffs. He waves Jonah away with his hand like a fly. An orderly came in, dragged Jonah mercilessly back his cell, and beat him viciously until little pools of red collected on the white concrete floor. From that moment on, the dosages were accompanied by floggings.

But, Jonah's spirit didn't break.

Langston Hughes talks about the blood of the Afro-American's ancestors flowing through the generations like a river. Jonah could feel the strength of the family line, their suffering, their resilience . . . it was as tangible to him as peaking on the acid. He could actually reach out and touch it, hold it, caress it. It filled him, the embrace of the ancestors.

Isbell made Jonah one of his own personal demons from that moment on. He paid particular attention to him, resulting in continued meetings to convince Jonah that he was property, not person . . . followed by more and more beat-downs.

Then 1 day, just as hope was beginning to slip, the most curious thing happened.

The door opened. Only this time it opened without a pair of fists ready to take out their pseudo-adolescent insecurities on him. Escorted by two orderlies, a portly white woman stood in the door, the hall lights radiating a halo around her little silhouette. She shuffled forward and leaned down toward Jonah, as he crouched on the floor. Behind thick lenses he saw kind, wise eyes , crinkling into a sublime squint. Whitening hair frazzled around her oval head, a bulbous nose pointed directly at Jonah. She too wore a white coat, with the only name tag Jonah had seen since his arrival: Dr. Bruyere.

"Hi," she extended her plump little hand. Jonah tentatively brought his to meet hers, insecure in how dirty he was. She met him the rest of the way, slowly, warmly grasping his hand. Her voice was laced with a quiet candor. "My name's Edith. I'm going to get you out of this joint."

Then, she winked at him.

She asked the orderlies to get Jonah to his feet. She picked up *Ulysses* from under his cot and wobbled into the hallway. The orderlies carried Jonah, following her out.

He couldn't have known it then, but that was the last time Jonah would ever see his cell.

They walked directly past 4 security posts Jonah had never seen before, and straight into Isbell's office. It was a gray room, decorated with dusty medical manuals and plants that were brown and dying. One window lay behind his pristine desk with the shade drawn.

A window! Jonah winced. Sunlight inched in through the blind, streams of real light spilling into the room in what seemed, to Jonah, a glorious display! To Isbell and Edith, it was a dim blurb of light covered by intense shadow.

Isbell's face was flush with hatred. Dr. Bruyere marched right up to his desk with a purity of confidence Jonah had never seen before.

"This is the one I want," she diligently commanded, arms crossed.

Isbell, slowly retaining his spite, stuffed his hands in his pockets.

"You can't have him," he argued rigidly.

Jonah's gut sank. The edges of freedom were on the horizon, but also being stripped away in a fluctuating tide. Edith though, he could tell, wasn't about ready to give up.

"I'm keeping him," she demanded. "You got your orders. I get any one of my choosing. I choose him. You have no say about it, Harry."

"Don't call me that in front of the patient," he told her.

"Fuck you, Harry," she retorted in the most polite tone possible. "I will eat you up! Chew you into bits and spit you out. I am a bitch you do not want to mess with. We are at the height of the feminist revolution and I have an order in hand straight from the Director of Central-fucking-Intelligence, McCone himself! Do . . . not . . . *frustrate* . . . me! I can have you shut down in a week, your license revoked in 2, and have you living on the streets drinking whiskey with hobos, singing Christmas carols in July to convince pedestrians to give you a penny so you can save up for your next bottle! I don't know how to be clearer about this: I . . . am . . . a . . . force . . . to be . . . reckoned with! Give me this man, or I will make it my life's purpose to drive you into obscurity!"

And with that, Jonah Mulligan was free.

* * * * *

They drove across country together for two days. Just he and Edith. She shared everything with him.

Dr. Edith Bruyere was an MD with a PhD in behavioral psychology. She explained to Jonah that she and a group of peers had been a part of the Central Intelligence Agency's MK-ULTRA program . . . but had secretly broken away. They had their own research project in the works that was turning into more of a cabal. Edith had used her influences in the upper echelons of the PHS to get Jonah out, as her group had covertly been watching his progress with enthusiasm. Jonah asked how, with Isbell's influence everywhere, they manage such a feat. "Remote-viewing," she answered matter-of-factly, as if the realms of science fiction were as familiar to her as the changing of the seasons.

Their journey ended in Colorado. In the mountains, somewhere outside Boulder. Hours of dirt roads, they approached a log cabin in a heavily wooded area surrounded by snowy peaks. They entered without knocking. Modestly decorated, Edith pulled back a rug covering the only room of the rustic domicile. A trap door opened and sent them down a flight of stairs to an elevator, which took them down even further. Deep, deep under the ground.

The elevator stopped, but the door did not open. Edith, hand on his shoulder, met Jonah's eyes with authoritative intention.

"Before I open this door," she said cogently, softly. "Are you ready to join the good fight? The cause? The sole purpose?" Sensing a slight hesitation in him, Edith began to expound on a theory about the evolution of biological systems.

"If a species, system, whatever becomes stagnant," she explained. "It will collapse. A system needs to be in a state of flux in order to grow. Chaos, right? Well, chaos is the only way to evolve, it acts as a catalyst. Otherwise, a system will just bottom-out. Implode. There is a danger . . . forces that, for some reason, are trying to thwart evolution. They are trying to control that growth, instead of just letting it happen naturally like it should. These forces, the Atonists, the Dominators, the Nova Enterprise, are influencing the world governments, leaders, pop culture, corporations in unprecedented ways. Like the name suggests, they thrive in dominance. Tyranny. We don't know exactly who they are or where they come from, but we know they exist.

"So, we've uncovered a counter-force to this. The realms of the unseen, of consciousness itself, have opened up to us this past century. We have tapped into new planes of existence, new worlds, and new ways of perceiving our own. The Novas are sabotaging these discoveries. The Maninkari, the species populating these daimonic realms, are not taking too keenly this onslaught of domination and manipulation."

The 1960s contained the most notable counter-culture movements of the American 20th century. Acid bloomed like a lotus flower across the societal landscape. And what do we get with this massive cultural upheaval, as with any other throughout history? A self-proclaimed messiah. In this case, Timothy Leary. A clinical psychologist in Oakland and later a professor at Harvard, Leary had an extensive history with the CIA. In Oakland, while working for the Kaiser Foundation Hospital he developed a personality test adopted by the Agency for prospective agents. As well, at Harvard, Leary took part in gathering guinea pigs for MK-ULTRA, unwitting students wanting to "turn on" to the mass appeal of altered states of consciousness. He claimed that during his first psychedelic experience, a handful of magic mushrooms, he had the most profound "religious experience" of his life. He said that during that experience he "discovered beauty, revelation, sensuality, the cellular history of the past, God, the Devil—all lie inside my body, outside my mind." Like a newspaper headline, he touted psilocybin mushrooms and LSD as the "philosopher's stone." Like a good messiah, he began proselytizing: instant enlightenment for all! It works for everyone! Egalitarian illumination! Commune with God for just one hit!

"We," Edith clarified. "The RED Agency, hold the view that the psychedelic consciousness does indeed open doorways to new places of perception, but that this tool should not be trifled with. Thrown out into the masses for teenagers to ingest anytime they damn well please on a Saturday night."

That was Leary's dream, the goal of the Dominator.

Why?

Because if you have 100,000 teenagers stoned and tripping on acid across America you have an opportunity to demonize an authentic research opportunity; hence, a 1 way ticket to public consent: automatic legislation with no debate. Tyranny. That is how they keep things under control. That is how overnight sessions of Congress work. You wake up 1 morning and BOOM . . . your rights of privacy have been violated! The Nova Effect. Political manipulation reigns supreme in a democratic society, and Leary's appeal to pop culture played right into the hands of the Dominating culture.

The RED Agency, Edith illustrated, was creating an army; a fusion between human and Maninkari . . . shamanic guerillas in a rebellion against the Dominating Nova pervading—*invading*—our planet. Jonah had a choice: be a RED Agent and spend the rest of his life for the cause; or, walk away, be free, no catch.

He thought about it. What could he do if he was free? Get a job, go to school, work toward a career, toward retirement. Get a family, settle down. Embrace mediocrity. But how? With everything he knows, how could he keep on going? Waking up from day to day like nothing is happening . . . like there isn't torture, disenfranchisement, genocide happening right in his back yard? This blasé day-to-day, 9 to 5 existence . . . this is what they want, this is how the Dominators dominate. They turn you into a cog.

We can't change the country, he remembered from the character Stephen Dedalus. *Let us change the subject.*

"Ok," Jonah answered with surety.

Edith smiled. She moved in to embrace him. "Give a *squinch,* darling!" They hugged. And Jonah felt like he was home for the first time in his life. Edith turned, dialed a numerical sequence on a keyboard in the elevator wall.

. . the doors opened.

28 – Ergot Mass

Darwin seriously doubts the sanity and safety of the group's decision on a diversion. It isn't the guards with their guns pointing in her general direction that makes her most nervous. It is Srinivasa's hand clasping around her bare throat that gives her that feeling of "Oh-Jesus-Christ-What-The-Hell-Did-I-Get-Myself-Into?" All it takes is one instant, one trigger, and he could snap her neck in two. The bombs on his chest are, of course, fake. However, seeing as how they are already on the terror watch lists for the FBI, CIA, and local law enforcement officials, the staged distraction should be adequate enough to buy Dedalus enough time to find a lead.

"Let the lady go," one of the police officers bellows. He is a tall, proud fellow, a round belly lumping lazily over his shiny belt loaded with a baton, mace, and other essentials. His revolver is pointed directly at Srinivasa's head. He and another officer pulled up five minutes ago to relieve the nerve-racked security guards of the Plaza and KCTB. They stand back a few paces from the police, shaking anxiously, eyes darting from side-to-side, unsure of what to do.

"Just stay calm, man," the other officer proffers; a tough, blonde female. Middle-aged. "We can help you out . . . just tell us what you want! This doesn't have to happen!"

The radios on their shoulders are chirping about approaching backup. Darwin urges Dedalus in her mind to step up the pace. She can sense Srinivasa's rough edge tilting a bit off balance.

"Insha' Allah," Srinivasa hollers to them. "Blah, blah, blah!" He leans in closer to Darwin for a whisper: "Do you know any Arabic?"

"No," she responds quietly through the side of her mouth. "Keep it up, though! These are Midwestern cops; it doesn't matter what you say, as long as you look the part."

"I resent that," he quips.

"Sir, put the trigger device down," the male officer yelps. Sweat beads on his forehead glimmer in Srinivasa's eyes.

"I don't like white people," he tells Darwin, loosening his grip on her throat. "You especially! But, these guys . . . they grate my nerves, cheese grater kind of grate, know what I mean?"

"Shit," Darwin sighs. This is part of Srinivasa's condition: losing sight of the task at hand. "Just a few more minutes, Srini."

"No," he shoves her away. The officers flinch, reasserting their aim and stance at him.

"Halt! Halt!" one of them yells. The female officer nods and motions quickly toward Darwin. A security guard hesitantly inches in close to relieve Darwin from the scene. Naively he believes he is rescuing her. Darwin shakes her head and curses under her breath.

"Down! Now!" The male officer screams at Srinivasa, blood-rushing face.

"Oh, is that so, eh?" Srinivasa waves his hands in the air at the male officer. *He's losing it*, Darwin knows. *God, I miss Merchant!* "You know what the difference is between an Indian and an Arab, you hick son-of-a-bitch? Huh? Do you??? How about a Hindu and a Muslim?? You know who the fuck Krishna is, you cow-tipping, goat-raping hill-billy!!!"

"Calm down, sir," the male officer backs a step, his revolver shaking unsteadily. "I said stay calm, Muhammad!"

"Oh is that right?" Srinivasa laughs eerily. He tosses the fake detonator to the female officer who—flinching—catches it. "I'll show you 'Muhammad,' you war-mongering elitist!" Srinivasa leaps into the air, sweep air current lapse, the officer blinks and he is gone . . . behind him a >>KICK<< the officer's back cracks, splinter; he crumbles to the ground howling in pain. He drops his weapon.

"Jesus Christ!" the female officer shoots in Srinivasa's direction, but he moves too fast for her—dodging the bullet with RED precision; a knife through the wind. The female officer re-aims and . . . her hand is caught, Darwin is inches from her face breath hold.

"I'm sorry about this," she apologizes, head-butting the officer into quick, repelling unconsciousness. The female officer drops rag doll to the sidewalk. Darwin looks back.

Srinivasa is standing over the male officer, who is crawling miserably to his dropped gun, writhing from the injury. Darwin figures his back may be broken. Srinivasa raises a hand, ready to strike the fallen officer. Darwin pulls out her own pistol from inside her jacket. She aims at Srinivasa.

"Srini," she calls to him.

Srinivasa looks up, frowns.

"Is this what I'm going to have to do," she asks him. "Pull a piece on my own fellow Agent?" She side-glances to the surrounding security—shaken from the episode before them. She knows they are no threat. Most of them have never even fired a gun at another person and probably aren't looking forward to that possibility. They are more engaged in the conversation at play.

"But," Srinivasa argues, pleadingly like a child. "He called me 'Muhammad'! That's just *crazy*, Darwin! Doesn't he get the difference between *monotheism* and *polytheism*? He can't *honestly* believe I'm some washed-up ingrate from *Al-Qaeda*!"

"He only called you that after you started acting like an asshole," she responds, eyeing the security guards who seem to be gaining the courage to step in and take action. Her Maninkari fusion pumping mad, adrenaline equilibrium on the cusp . . . she wants to shoot him to gain control, but they can't beat Jack without him.

* * * * *

As Dedalus leaps into the driver's seat he knows there is going to be a situation on his hands. Srinivasa's plan was outrageous and risked exposure, but the security of Dedalus' infiltration into KCTB was vital. Srinivasa's scheme was a guaranteed distraction. Darwin, Dedalus could tell, was too worn and debilitated to debate the scenario. He had been watching her fatigue increase through the days . . . her closeness to her partner, Agent Merchant, must have been deep, maybe even intimate. She was becoming jaded, especially after the destruction of her companion, supercomputer *Mahamaya*. Despite all this, Dedalus still succumbed to his inexperience as an Agent . . . if Darwin had a strong negation to the idea, she would have put a stop to it.

He clicks the van on, it churns to life with a sputter, and he turns the vehicle onto Ward Parkway. It's hard to miss them, and something definitely *has* gone wrong: they are surrounded, two policemen lying on the ground—one writhing in pain—and Darwin has a gun pointed straight at Srinivasa's head!

Dedalus inches the vehicle forward. What should he do? The wyrm pulse dilation inside begins its ruse, effervescence and into the cortices and in-line thrust of pumping veins. It is making its work upon him. The questions in his mind meld and fuse and begin their coalescent fervor, as the Maninkari adrenal river brings song and equation into his upper conscious artery . . . until he feels a formula of derision . . .

. . . every Agent has their specialty . . . and Gregor Samson could see through the cracks of reality, the fault lines of what is!

. . . and Dedalus begins to see the solution play out:

flow birth the equilateral idolatry
stands beneath. see Darwin and Srinivasa huge plume infrared
Doppler radiation insert into primal memory: D + S

2 officers on ground, one crux of blackened
varnish on back . . . needs healing, but the terminal matrimony
of incidence is preening . . . four count 4 security guards all
flickering, weak signatures: cause anxiety upon their cranial
mass in dim froth

it is understood now: see through the cracks > reality
fault line – everything determinable as true or false . . . this is
the Dedalus talent: see through the Labyrinth

and = the conjunctive normal form
or = the disjunctive normal form
the arrow implies . . . actuality
breaks/it is all tiles and they sit around us in geometric
algorithms implied, this is how the Maninkari build perception
and the Dedalus talent sees it all, hands up: move beneficial
(arrow) action
implication elimination. true = the hands easily
distribute the tiles here, and inside, over there/cross-criss grid
work patches, quilting the conscious personifications of
perceptibility here and there . . . and sprinkle it upon them
. . . the officers, the guards in
implication < their fluctuations splash throughout the
microcosm spectrum of harnessment, make broadcast an
intimate knowledge of the hexagonal alchemy interior their
eye(s) . . . they panic . . .
. . . stop the van to holler at Darwin and Srinivasa . . .

"Get in," Dedalus hollers. "We gotta go to Penn Valley Park!"

Sweat beads seep through his pores, head wobbling. Darwin and Srinivasa hop over the downed and dazed guards, rushing hastily to the vehicle. They notice Dedalus' groggy aspect.

"He can't drive," Srinivasa hesitates.

Inwardly, Darwin concurs. It takes her a brief moment to consider her options. She levels her pistol back at Srinivasa.

"Push him to the back," she commands. "You're driving."

"Why not you?" Srinivasa gives a mischievous grin. She wants to shoot him right now, shoot him *bad*!

"Because," she answers tersely. "Someone's got to keep a gun on you until you settle. Now, drive!"

They jump in, shoving Dedalus' half-limp body to the back seat, and speed off down the road. Keep her gun aimed steadily at the driver's seat, Darwin leans back to Dedalus curiously.

"What did you do to them?" she asks. "They all just went loopy, like they were suddenly sucked into another world . . . in fact their electromagnetic fields *read* that way! Did you do that?"

Dedalus sets himself up on the seat, shaking away the jumble. "Ugh . . . yeah . . . I . . . I think I found my niche."

"Is that right," Srinivasa cackles. "So soon to get the kit and kaboodle, eh? Ha, ha!"

"I . . . I can see where reality has scuffs, weak points," Darwin sees a slight smile creak onto Dedalus' face. "I know how to manipulate them, rearrange them . . . likes puzzle pieces . . . that's what I did to those guards and it was like . . . like they were thrown into another dimension . . . for them it was like being third dimensional beings in a fifth dimensional whirlwind."

"So, really . . . you just made them *stoned*?" Srinivasa guffaws.

Darwin sees the full, delightful grin on his face. "I guess . . . yeah."

"It seems to have disoriented you," Darwin observes.

"Yeah, the wyrm is taxed, I can feel it . . . gonna need a few minutes to rest."

"Strong talents have their drawbacks," Darwin states. "Paradox."

"Not much time for that," Srinivasa wails at the traffic, honking the horn. "What'd you find out?"

Muddled, Dedalus unsteadily explains his break-in to the KCTB, his discoveries of the hard red winter wheat distribution, and his encounter with Propit.

"He directed me toward Merchant's blood," Dedalus explains. "Described it as a catalyst."

"The Nova have been aching forever to get a sample of one of us, and now they got it with Merchant," Srinivasa lights up. "They're using the Maninkari fusion in our blood!"

"For what?"

"To create soldiers," Darwin concludes, sighing. She is tense; her electromagnetic frequency is limp, weary. "*Super* soldiers. Like us, but Nova ones. Like Srinivasa said, they've been trying it forever. The Nova Wet Dream. Our sources show they are tired of contracting their efforts out to bestial phenomena like Spring-heeled Jack. They've succeeded in the zombie automaton model, mindless slaves to do their bidding . . . but there's always faulty wiring; a screw loose. So far, that has worked to their advantage."

"You mean, like the Manchurian Candidate, right?" Dedalus asks.

"What? What's that?" Srinivasa asks, throwing his eyes off the road. Darwin hollers at him to put his attention back to the task of driving. With a jarring wiggle from the van, he aligns to a steady pace.

Darwin glares at him with a side-long grimace. "It's an anti-communist American novel, with many bad film adaptations to follow it up."

"Ha! She's right," he spits. "Americans suck at making movies!"

"It's about a sleeper agent, unaware of being brainwashed into an inadvertent assassin," Dedalus remembers being a big fan of the story as Gregor Samson. The appeal is obvious. Subliminal empathy.

"Look at the Enterprise's foot soldiers throughout the 20th Century, specifically the assassins during the Revolution: JFK's Oswald, Bobby's Sirhan Sirhan, MLK's James Earl Ray, Lennon's Mark David Chapman. They were all soldiers, programmed through some sort of trigger or neurological encryption to execute a task . . . followed by a memory swipe to cover the Nova tracks. That's how all of these highly-trained assassins are dubbed 'lone gunmen,' as if they had no connections or affiliations . . . they come off as crazies. Those are just a few examples and all of them were mind control victims. All of them were a type of Gregor Samson."

Dedalus recalls some excerpts from the *Akashic Memoir*, the shooter Seung-Hui Cho from the Virginia Tech Massacre. One of his first RED sightings, and obviously so when looked at the situation properly: the cover story never added up! Thirty-two people executed in such a short amount of time, a 60% fatality rate, which is expert level assassin work . . . Seung-Hui supposedly was a mild-mannered student who never touched a gun. Not only that, but in the two hours between his first and second killing sprees, Cho managed to flawlessly execute these tasks: create a confession video, burn it, travel to the post office to ship it, then travel back to campus to retrieve his weapons and then continue on with the massacre. This was a boy—according to the media and Virginia Tech—that required psychotropic therapies in order to function from anxiety and other emotional problems. To carry through all those tasks under the duress of just committing his first murder raises serious questions, especially regarding the precision in which he continued his methodical slaughter on campus. Add to that these intriguing facts: days after the massacre, Virginia Tech began pulling all information off its Web site containing links to CIA partnerships, specifically recruitment programs. As well, an image of Cho in a military uniform has circulated the Internet, being pulled from sites by Government authorities whenever it gets enough notice. MK-ULTRA whistleblower Cathy O'Brien has cited Blacksburg, Virginia as being a prime location for CIA mind control programs.

What Dedalus, as Gregor Samson, and many other conspiracy theorists have postulated was that Seung-Hui Cho was a sort of mind control robot gone haywire. Like the foot soldiers Darwin suggests. Like what Gregor Samson could have been. Like . . .

"Or a type of Lawrence," Dedalus adds.

"Exactly," Darwin concurs, nodding. "And every single one of them was strategically placed in their lives to give the Enterprise, the U.S. Government, whomever, the tactical advantage over the situation."

"This is all fine and pretty, people," Srinvasa is whipping the wheel back and forth, zipping them through downtown traffic. "But what does this all have to do with the Trade Bureau and bread products?"

"If I was placed at KCTB for a reason," Dedalus conjectures. "It was to monitor the shipment of these bread products to Artichoke Labs. Lawrence must have been a sort of carrier, a distributor based upon all of the stockpiles we saw at Wallis Manor."

"But why?" Srinivasa screeches. His brain, Dedalus can tell by the fluctuating waves of purple and orange careening around his cranial area, must be struggling with whatever force is overbearing his material aspect. The signature is that of a balloon ready to pop; Dedalus is waiting for blood to begin dripping out of Srinivasa's ears.

"What was it that Propit said to you? When you first saw him?" Darwin asks. "Pont-Saint-Esprit? Does that sound familiar?"

"No, but Artichoke Labs does," Srinivasa interrupts.

Dedalus and Darwin turn to him quizzically.

"You crazy American psychos," he sputters, turning north onto Rainbow Boulevard. "Project Artichoke is where MK-ULTRA got started!"

They speed toward Penn Valley Park.

29 – Liberty Immaculate

> *". . . this big war machine never ceases to amaze me . . ."*

Ramona cracks open her eyes, whirlpool vision . . .
gunshots, explosions, screaming . . . odd, narrative voiceovers.
She is not bound—head throb sending streaks of knife pain
down her neck and spine—sitting in a hole . . . a massive
circular ditch with a dark ceiling over the rim of the ditch, muted
lighting. Sits up from the cold floor, funneling out to the top in a
single round wall of mud and charred debris: scattered fragments
of books, parchment, a broken wheel in mound of earth, broken
brick wall, a shattered window frame, splinters of wood, tatters
of clothing.

> *". . . everywhere that we go we see guns, guns, and
> more guns . . ."*

Grogginess weighs on her eyes, addled and confused.
These voices, they are recordings . . . coming from embedded
speakers in the ceiling.

> *". . . we heard one alarm, and then another . . ."*

She stands, shakily, wobbling knees. A slight dizziness
wavers over her cold, frail frame. Suffocating with bewildered
vulnerability, she turns . . . sees a door out of the mortar hole.

> *". . . and then yesterday, I woke up to the sound of
> explosions . . ."*

Tentatively, but knowing there is nowhere else to go,
she steps out and through the door, entering a wooden hallway . .
. low ceiling, with dull wire bulbs hanging from the ceiling,
resembling a mine shaft. She leaves the voices behind.

> *". . . everyone thought it was a daylight raid . . ."*

Through the shaft there is an array of display cases, full
of old uniforms and artillery, accompanied by more voice-overs,
bombings . . . she scans around a room full of massive turn-of-
the-century field guns, placards of information, a steel tank only
slightly taller than she, theatre rope surrounding the pieces.

She recognizes the place. Been here before . . . a field trip in college.

The National World War I Museum beneath Liberty Memorial.

She shivers. How did she get here? *Why* is she here? As if on cue, she smells the smoke of a cigarette. He walks up quietly.

"Copernicus," she gasps.

"It's pretty amazing isn't it," he points to the tank. A bulky contraption only big enough to fit one occupant, Ramona imagines, its rusted steel bolts aching with age . . . she flinches, realizing the cannon happens to be pointing directly at her.

"It's the Renault FT-17," he continues, smoking rapidly as he talks. "A French development, and one of the most innovative advances in modern warfare. Light, fast, fully-rotating turret. They were a tactically brilliant addendum to the battlefield, if you had a ton of them, right? The point was to get a swarm of them, like bees . . . if you only had a few of them they were useless. Only forty-one left in the world, and this is one of them."

"What am I doing here?" she presses, uninterested in his exposition. He doesn't make eye contact, absorbed in the tank's steel angles of the armament.

"Honestly, I don't know," he fidgets, shifting weight from a heavily bandaged foot. He is sweating profusely, patches of wet splotching his shirt. "I wish I did. Really . . . I do. The problem is I'm just following orders. I'm just doing what I'm told."

"That . . . *thing*," she remembers the dark, tentacle shadow man clutching her and knocking her unconscious. His ghostly sick face makes her tremble. "Is that your . . . *boss*?"

"His name is Jack. And yeah, he's more like a . . . a customer that my superiors assigned me to satisfy." He reaches around to his back belt and pulls out his .357 Magnum. Checks the chambers of the cylinder for ammunition. "You might want to come with me."

He turns and walks, expecting her to follow him. She has no choice, she discerns. She could turn and run but he could shoot her in an instant. There is no place left to struggle. She follows suit.

They pass through a corridor decorated by a row of tunics and quilts. Everywhere, screens and voiceovers expressing the suffering of soldiers, the plight of the mothers of the dead, the strategic advancements of the Allies over the Central Powers. Turning to the right past a Ford Model T, they walk onto a terrace and into a massive dark chamber.

It is the Horizon Theater, the whole wall a back-drop screen montage depicting the horrors of trench warfare. Below the terrace, in coarse, eerie lighting of reds and oranges manifesting a life-size model of a battered landscape of mud and debris resembling the mortar hole she had just walked out of; a line of mannequin British soldiers march through the muck, heads hanging low in weary lament. Though, on the screen, she looks twice . . . projected images of explosions and running soldiers shooting into gray smoke . . . she sees a form, a figure of a man, hanging by his hands—knotted in rope—limply dangling onto the draped display.

It is Jonah! The man who snagged Gregor at Unity Temple!

"Oh my god," she heaves, breath escaping in revulsion. "What's going on here?"

"You've got to know," Copernicus snuffs out his cigarette on the ground under his unbandaged shoe. "That this man tried to save your life."

"What?" Ramona leers at him quizzically. "Why are you telling me this?"

"Because this has gone too far," eyes Jonah's unconscious body, misery distressing the wrinkles on his face. "Because what's happening here has no definable purpose, and it has to end. I want to get the two of you out of this."

"How utterly illuminating," the hiss, bone-grating voice curdles into the air. They jump in shock, turning to the source.

293

Copernicus with the revolver drawn. Twisting darkness forms in the shadow of the theater seating. "It's good to know your intentions, Copernicus. Your presence was an annoyance in the very beginning; now I have just cause to consume you prematurely!"

The horrific mass manifests into hardened being, his tall wicked frame plopping into existence. He saunters nimbly out of the shadow with a turgid grace. Ramona and Copernicus recoil . . . his face! Copernicus had noticed a shattered display case by the Renault tank, a missing piece. A splinter mask worn by tankers to protect them from bullet splash coming in through the narrow eye holes of the turret. A bizarre, grotesque piece, worn leather brown goggles made of sad slits, supported by heavy rusted chainmail to cover the lower face and mouth.

It adorns Jack's face with grisly elegance.

* * * * *

The van screeches to a halt on Kessler Street, next to the caramel-colored office building at 215 Pershing. Red awnings cover the first floor windows, which reveal a gutted out lobby. A real estate sign stands lop-sided on the checkered side walk. The hill leading up to Liberty Memorial Tower lies directly across the street.

"It *looks* abandoned," Srinivasa creeps the van down Kessler, to the back entrance of the building. A few cars are parked in a miniature lot, connected to a larger parking arena for a massive gray complex with Greek columns, enclosed with black iron fencing and state-of-the-art security facilities.

"See that?" Darwin points. "The Internal Revenue Service. And the Federal Reserve is right back there, on the south end of Penn Valley Park. None of this is coincidental."

"The Conspiracy is everywhere," Srinivasa spits. "This is unsafe."

"It never is," Darwin counters. "The Enterprise always strategically places their most ritually honored establishments in particular esoteric formations in the cities where they have a heavy presence. Whatever is going down, is going down here at Liberty Memorial, in Penn Valley Park. It is safe, on *their* terms. Completely enclosed by their own standards, their own allies and institutions." Her breathing goes quiet, her head lolls back.

"They're not in there," Darwin whispers. "Ramona and Jonah."

"How do you know?" Dedalus asks.

"We all have our own little faculties, Agent Dedalus," Srinivasa explains.

"If I've been around an aura before," she clarifies. "I can sense if it's close. Jonah and Ramona are not in that building. But, Merchant *has* been. There are . . . traces . . . his memory is populating the area . . . screaming."

"Like his ghost?" Dedalus begins to dig through the bags for a weapon to choose.

"Sort of," Darwin places a hand on him to halt his rummaging. "You can't come in with me."

"What do you mean? We're in this together!"

"No, you had your time at the Trade Bureau," she rationalizes. "Merchant was my partner, my *friend*. This is my fight, not yours."

"What's in there, Darwin?"

"Whatever's causing this mess," she stares at the forlorn corporate monolith.

"Then . . ."

"*You* have to find Ramona and Jonah," she interrupts him. "*That* is priority number one."

"But how do we find them if we don't follow you in? The answers are in there!"

"Not necessarily," Srinivasa's shoulders are crunched, licking his lips. He is gazing past Darwin, through the passenger window, to the concrete phallus of Liberty Memorial in the background.

"You see . . . I am a Rakshasa Specialist, Agent Dedalus . . . I can . . . just as Darwin has senses . . . I do too . . .

but of a *special* kind . . . when a Rakshasa is near . . . I know . . .
he is here . . . *Jack* is here!!!"

Darwin and Dedalus tense. Darwin grabs an extra pistol
from a bag below. One in each hand, she kicks the door open.

"Then we are losing time," she orders. "Go get Jack!
Where you find Jack you'll find Ramona, Dedalus. You have to
get Srinivasa to Jack!"

She bolts furiously across the sidewalk and through a
window of the office building, glass shattering in her wake . . .
she moves so quick even Dedalus can hardly see her, an energy
stream of red streaking a trail behind.

He has not developed that kind of speed and agility yet.
The Maninkari wyrm must take a while to reach full capacity . . .
get used to the human system. He wonders, then, how he could
be of any assistance to Srinivasa against Jack!

He looks over to the Indian Agent. Srinivasa is
practically drooling from the mouth, eyes dazed into a fixed
zone on the Memorial.

"We need to go," he tells Dedalus. They exit the van
and Srinivasa grabs his gargantuan hiking pack, throwing it on
his shoulders. "Oh, and grab some kick-ass guns!"

Darwin's crash through the window did not trigger any
alarms. She is not surprised. If she knows the Enterprise, she
knows how much they enjoy drama . . . and if this is to be a
showdown they would be sure to prevent any authorities from
spoiling the theatrics. She scans the lobby of concrete floor and
drywall, crunching her boots over shards of glass. She reaches
herself out, out into the ether to configure the positioning, the
primary location of Merchant's presence. She locks on to a mass
of his memory complex. The basement, of course.

She creeps swiftly down the hall, both guns drawn.
Passing the elevators, she makes for the stairwell and scampers
down. Coming through to a dark hallway with only dim
emergency lighting, catches the scent of antiseptic, hydrogen

peroxide, and death. She follows to a set of swinging doors and nudges through.

Inside: a lab, full with trays of surgical equipment, front-loading autoclaves, racks of test tubes and boiling tubes, sickly fluorescent bulbs spitting down a grim iridescence into the cold, dank room. There is a man near the back, curled over a table, in the middle of a dissection. Beside him sits a little wooden table with a dull lamp and journal, where he seems to be jotting notes. He notices her right away, unstartled and unconcerned of her presence, almost as if he had been expecting her. She inches close, both pistols raised and ready to fire.

He is a decrepit snail of a man . . . bald head with strings of white spurting here and there, speckled with toad spots; spectacles taped over three times, a crack ringing the left lens; back hunched, rounding out a frail lump of tissue paper flesh arthritic appendages sticking out of a yellow-stained lab garment. The cadaver beneath him is shredded open, as if by a bear. It has been beaten, torn, left rotting for days. Darwin takes a closer look, but she can already tell . . .

It is Merchant.

"Good afternoon," hyena smile creeps across his prune face. "It is afternoon, isn't it? I do so lose track of time when I am working."

"Who are you?" she demands, trigger fingers itching.

"I am Dr. Blome. Kurt Blome. And you are, young lady?"

"Kurt Blome?" Darwin flinches. As long as she has been an Agent, RED has been tracking—or attempting to track—the recruits of Operation Paperclip after World War II, the Office of Strategic Services' venture to recoup Nazi scientists and enlist their aide in post-War defense strategies. It was rumored that some of those scientists had been subjected to immense amounts of manipulated nuclear radiation in order to increase their brain size and thus efficiency; a not-too-unfortunate side-effect of these experiments was the life extension of these subjects, however ill-fitting their bodies would become. Kurt Blome was one of these possible subjects. He was notorious, even among his Nazi peers, for his ruthlessness and utter disregard for human life.

After the War, Blome was retrieved by U.S. officials and hired by the Army Corps of Engineers for his bacteriological warfare experiments on human subjects at the Dachau concentration camp. The official story is that he was, years later, arrested in France and eventually rotted away in prison. The truth is his life was secretly prolonged and his services forever rendered by the U.S. Government for his expertise on germ warfare.

And here he is.

"What's the Red Mass, Blome?" Darwin requests adamantly. She steps steadily closer.

"Look at us," he sputters, crouched like a sloth over the decaying carcass. "You, the obscurely dressed vigilante; me, the pulp mad scientist. We're the products of science fiction, crazed Moreauian mutations from the Atomic Age. It's a symbiotic relationship, and you know that, don't you? Your heightened senses reveal such a thing, do they not? One cannot exist without the other. The eternal duality."

Darwin watches as he coughs into the corpse, lays down a scalpel, and leans over to the side table to his dictation and makes a mark or two. The dust collected over cracked coffee mug with a bird silhouette. Blome blows on the end of the pencil. Speckles in the air. His eyes wrinkled ink blots. He is intent on his project, unhindered by Darwin's interrogation.

"Allow me to elucidate. There is a quaint little commune, a hamlet, called *Pont-Saint-Esprit* sitting on the Rhône River in southern France. The magnificent Saint Saturnin cathedral looms over its medieval bridges and cobblestone streets. Pristine! An ideal European village. In the summer of 1951, Pont-Saint-Esprit underwent an epidemic of psychotic outbreaks resulting in hundreds of episodes, even a few deaths. You know this one, I'm sure! Church ladies running the streets naked, policemen shooting wildly into the air, random acts of arson, defecation in public places, etcetera. Complete madness! Investigation incidentally lead to what the locals called *pain maudit* ..... 'bread that is damned.' You've *got* to love superstition! What *really* caused the event was a very highly potent and volatile form of ergotism, the *claviceps purpurea* fungus found on wheat rye. Poisonous to humans, obviously. The town only had one baker, one grocer. Simple, quick distribution, so it was favorable and opportune for testing. In the history books that outbreak remains a mystery to this day. But, in actuality, that was my first successful experiment in a long-term research project that inevitably became my *magnum opus*: mass biological weaponry."

Blome puts down the pencil. He brings his full attention back to the incision. Darwin considers rushing over, blasting him in his prune face . . . but she needs information, and right now information is more important than personal vengeance.

"I was involved in other projects over the years, of course. Staying one step ahead of the Ruskies was imperative. If intelligence suggested they had a psy-ops program, we started our own. If they built ten nuclear warheads, we built ten more. It was a race to see who had the biggest balls in the 20th Century, and I loved being a part of it! The government enlisted my aid in some of the most innovative and experimental programs since the Nazis' refurbishment of human evolutionary potential. Project ARTICHOKE, MKULTRA, MKDELTA, and *especially* MKNAOMI. I'm sure you got the pun for the Lab, eh?"

Coughs a bit more, erupts into a little fit. Pulls a handkerchief from out of his sleeve, hacks up vile liquid into it. He places it to the side and looks at Darwin queerly. She feels Blome studying her, organism under a microscope.

"That is how some of your people got started, I'll wager. But, that is another matter." He pokes Merchant's corpse and Darwin wants to scream. Scream and kill.

* * * * *

RED Agents Dedalus and Srinivasa climb the hill, up hundreds of zigzagging stairs and a set of fountains toward the primary deck of Liberty Memorial. They are greeted by the Great Frieze on the north wall in Roman-Greco style: an angel stands in the middle of a fray of grief-stricken soldiers and citizens, heralding the end of the war, holding both a broken sword and palm leaf; a husband and wife carrying their child on the horns of a ram, symbolizing the common man; next to that a symbol of industry, the wheel of progress in motion . . . the dead have moved under the heels of the war machine.

The description above the Frieze reads: *"These have dared bear the torches of sacrifice and service. Their bodies return to dust but their work liveth evermore. Let us strive on to do all which may achieve and cherish a just and lasting peace among ourselves and with all nations."*

Reaching the deck, the massive terrace overlooks all of Penn Valley Park to the south and Union Station, including the downtown city scape of Kansas City, to the north. The picturesque Memorial Tower rises 217 feet into the air. Carved into the limestone Tower, four ornately robed spirits loom over the city, guarding the ideals of Courage, Honor, Patriotism, and Sacrifice. At night, a flame burns at the top of the Tower, to honor the fallen soldiers of the Great War. Below, two sphinxes sentry the Tower, limestone wings of purity draped over their faces. Dedalus and Srinivasa cross the deck to the other side, descending the south stairs to the Park below.

The crowd is voluminous but sporadic, dispensed throughout Penn Valley Park in random clusters of picketers of all kinds: liberal activists, social anarchists, neo-hippies, and others. Signs and chants garnish the multitudes under a nefarious blanket of heat, compounded by the suffocation of increased humidity. "End the War!," "Support Our Troops, Bring Them Home," and "Fuck the Prez" are among the cacophony of token slogans ringing out across the green knolls.

There is a stench, of portable bathrooms and fried concessions. It is all static – Dedalus sees, hears, experiences a fuzz of ineffable noise permeating the atmosphere. It is not just the city; there is confusion in the air . . . a bewildered concoction of anxiety, fear, and anathema.

The crowds await Senator Spike Reed's controversial ideas on the endless crusade against terrorism, on the proposed impeachment of the President and his entire Cabinet, and finally . . . to hear about the Administration's exploitation of the attack at St. Luke's Hospital as further justification for the enforcements outlined in the Patriot Act. They cluster closer and closer to the stage area, anticipating his arrival. The few trees spotting the Park provide inadequate shade in the oppressive heat.

Dedalus and Srinivasa stop at the heavy steel doors of the National World War I Museum entrance, directly below the Memorial Tower deck.

Srinivasa pulls out a large textile from his backpack and rolls it gently onto the ground. Cotton with a brocade border, it erupts with bright colors of vinery designs coalescing into three lotus flowers. The way he lays it before him the flowers divide the cloth into three parts.

"Now this," he motions to Dedalus. "This is something most every Agent acquires soon enough. It is every shaman's control panel to the Universe. It is how we Agents do our greatest work. My sect of RED, in India, we call it a *puja*. But here, in the Americas, you Agents call it the *mesa*. Ritual objects are placed on the *mesa* in accordance with the five directions and your own intuition. Then, the power of the objects is harnessed to perform your work as emissary of Brahman . . . of the Universal Source."

Dedalus recalls the Agents in Mithra's chamber, before he drank of the wyrm, remembering the altar cloths they rattled and drummed over.

Srinivasa pulls out five wrapped objects from his bag. He sits cross-legged in front of the *mesa* cloth. Dedalus feels a shift in the molecules around him.

"Now the *mesa* is facing north," he points in front of him, toward the Museum entrance. "Notice the ley line alignment happening in the Earth's electromagnetic field."

He is correct . . . Dedalus could see, in through the concrete, the blades of grass, under the rocks, in between the soil grains . . . he could feel the shifting of current . . . the skeletal make-up of reality was beginning to hone in on the cloth. Srinivasa unwraps one of his objects, places it directly in front of him. It is jagged, sand-colored rock.

"This object goes to the south, representing the Mother of the Earth," Srinivasa illustrates. Dedalus had never seen him so calm, so measured. He unwraps the next object . . . a large, spiral shell.

"To the west, the element of water. Also, it is the realm of the Goddess of the Moon. This side of the altar symbolizes the feminine aspects of being."

The third object, a massive ostrich feather. He kisses it, placing it directly opposite the rock at the south.

"The north, represented by the creatures of air, where the Creator resides."

He unbundles the fourth object carefully. It is a plain white candle, which he places on the east side. He pulls a lighter out of his bag and lights the candle.

"The east. Fire, where the Sun rises . . . this is the side of the masculine. Now, we have balance, you see? The four elements of material existence are expressed. And finally . . ."

Srinivasa delicately cradles the last bundle, the largest of them all. He is more careful to unwrap this one, whispering tiny little prayers into it as he does so. It is a statue. A monkey-headed figure with a human body, holding a golden club in its hand and decorated in ornate golden jewelry with crown. Srinivasa kisses the statue, places it in the center of the *mesa*, and bows forehead to the ground.

After a few moments of whispered prayers, Srinivasa lifts his head and directs his attention back to Dedalus.

"The center is where all of these energies come together, the *Axis Mundi*. It is your heart's greatest desire, the universal cross-section where everything is balanced . . . the yoke. This," he nods to the statue. "Is Lord Hanuman. This is how I am going to kill Imix Akbal, the one now called Spring-heeled Jack."

"You're going to kill him with a statue?" Dedalus quips.

"No, you dirty American bastard! I am going to conjure Hanuman!"

"You're going to conjure . . . wait—what? You're going to . . ."

"Beg of the services of Lord Hanuman, ultimate slayer of Rakshasas, of demon-kind. You see, Hanuman's story is in the Hindu epic the *Ramayana*. Coming from a half-monkey/half-human tribe of forest-dwellers called the Vanara. Lord Rama, the seventh Avatar of Vishnu, acquired Hanuman's services to rescue his beloved Sita from Ravana.

"Ravana, Agent Dedalus, is known as 'He who makes the universe scream.' He was the King of all Rakshasas, all demons. Hanuman's exploits in the military campaign against Ravana, as Lord Rama's supreme agent are legendary throughout the cosmos. Without Hanuman, I daresay Lord Rama may not have been able to defeat Ravana.

"Lord Hanuman is the ultimate personification of devotion, for it is his complete love of Lord Rama that fuels his uncanny abilities. He is the ultimate demon-slayer, and it is he I will call to this place to rid this Earth of Spring-heeled Jack."

Dedalus, in drollery, scans the area for on-lookers, asks, "So, you've done this before I take it?"

"Hanuman," Srinivasa becomes terse. "Is alive and well today, residing in a Himalayan cave, awaiting Lord Rama's return. He has been seen many times throughout history by many notable prophets . . . Madhvacharya, Sri Ramdas Swami, Raghavendra Swami, Sri Sathya Sai Baba . . . and of course, Agent Srinivasa of the RED Hand. As I said before, Agent

Dedalus, I am a Rakshasa Specialist. Do you think Agent Darwin would have requested my services if I were not able to deliver? Lord Hanuman is my mechanism of Rakshasa dispatch, because I am his servant. Now go!"

"Where?"

"In *there*," Srinivasa points to the front doors of the Museum. "Imix Akbal is in there, which is most likely where you will find your friends."

"So, I'm going in there *by myself?*" Dedalus argues hastily.

"You have kick-ass guns, do you not?"

Dedalus reviews what he brought along. A German Walther P99 semi-automatic pistol rests in a holster inside his red coat, a James Black bowie knife sheathed at this belt, and slung over his shoulder is a particular piece that caught his eye: an MP5K sub-machine gun, designed for close-quarters combat used specifically in Navy Seals operations. Dedalus made a note to later inquire where the RED Agency procured its firearms. *If* he survives.

"So, let me get this straight . . . you want me to go in there, alone, and retrieve a demon for you . . . is that it?"

"Absolutely, now go and leave me to my work," Srinivasa commands. He closes his eyes, sitting in a lotus meditative position. And begins to chant: "*Shri Guru Charan Saroj Raj Nija Man Mukara Sudhari, Baranau Raghuvar Bimal Jasu Jo Dayak Phal Chari . . .*"

The energy grid lines of world around bend and lean in on the mesa in front of Srinivasa. The statue of Hanuman jiggles with a hum and begins to shine as all the imaginative reality structures of being converge to center on it. Dedalus turns. Faces the doors. He sighs.

"A long time ago," he whispers to himself. "I was a bug."

And, without further hesitation, walks into the underground.

"Blome," Darwin reasserts her demeanor. She is standing directly over him now, as he croons over Merchant's corpse. Her pistols leveled at his brow. He remains unconcerned. "Back to the point. Red Mass. What is it?"

The place reeks of sultry asphyxiation, of complete abomination. Connecting with the energy grid of planet is proving difficult here; the Nova must have contingencies in place to prevent a RED connection to a pure source. Her Maninkari wyrm fusion is sending signals of alarm. She must work quick, it says, she must end this as soon as possible.

"Little girl," Blome's chuckle sounds like someone choking. "I'm giving you everything you need. If you just listen."

With a pair of forceps, he extracts a piece of sinew and places it carefully on a silver pan. He licks wrinkled lips with a purple tongue.

"See, it wasn't long ago, young lady, that we discovered *quinuclidinyl benzilate* . . . BZ. We called it *EA-2277*. This particular drug actually disrupted the neurotransmissions of the brain. Where LSD was temporarily disorienting, we found subjects coming out of EA-2277 sessions never the same again! It would render a subject completely immobile, sometimes up to eighty hours . . . a veritable incapacitating agent! Most subjects never even remembered their experience. *All* of them permanently recoded in the nervous system."

He picks at the clump of tissue of a scalpel.

"And you know what the best thing was about EA-2277, my darling? It could be dispersed in aerosol form . . . in a plume of cloud, smoke, or mist. Carried by the wind. We manufactured this fascinating substance into a legion of cluster bombs, plowing the Vietnamese down in droves while our troops marched in and blew their fucked up asses into oblivion! Panama! You name it! And now, we have stock-piles of the

305

same weapons here, as a contingency in case of civilian unrest, to counter an insurrection in case of any . . . *revolutionary* threat."

He picks up the sinew with the forceps and drops it into a canister, closing a lid on top. Blome finally looks up to Darwin, with a stern consternation as if she were his daughter interrupting his work.

"I'll give you a few minutes to figure it out. Meanwhile, leave me to my studies." He goes back to his diction, looking up every few seconds to examine the sinew in the cannister. Then records the results.

Darwin considers: Pont-Saint Esprit . . . the *claviceps purpurea* fungus found on wheat rye . . . the shipments of hard red winter wheat products. Disorientation, civilian insurrection . . . if the fungus was to be mass distributed, settling as a code into the bodies of the unwitting populace, eating their *Crunchy Bear Cereal, Snackilicious Butter Crackers, Ultra-Grain Bread* . . . and then EA-2277, dispersed in mist form . . . it could act as a catalyst, triggering the fungus code and setting off a chain reaction of pure hysteria.

"You're planning an outbreak of madness," deducts Darwin, eyeing Blome's semblance for confirmation. There is a slight bent to his energetic flow. "People have been eating these products for weeks! But why Merchant . . ."

"A refined stimulus, little girl," Blome interjects. "It allows us to have the control. It keeps the subjects measured, so orders can be followed. And I thank your friend here, *your* kind's particular DNA, you red men, for the final touches of my new recipe. Not only will we induce madness, but now Merchant has unleashed *the* catalyst that allows us to genetically harness this mass-psychosis into a blood bath of insurmountable proportions!"

Darwin imagines Lawrence times a thousand. Bile gobs in the back of her throat.

"Just so you know," Darwin cocks both pistols. "You are going to die today. That body used to be my friend. I've never had many friends. So, for that, and that alone, you are going to die."

"Victor Hugo once said," he looks up from his journal, gently placing the pencil on the desk. He moves a rugged, arthritic finger to the keyboard of a nearby computer terminal. "'Our life dreams the Utopia. Our death achieves the Ideal.' Merchant's passing will live on, ripples in the pond, he is providing the future with a chance of success against chaos."

"So this is the Red Mass," she hollers, fingers massaging the triggers of her weapons. "You're going to poison innocent civilians and turn them into zombies!"

"Obedient zombies," Blome crinkles a wretched, toothless grin. He pushes a button. Darwin, tries to run, but is caught by rushing air, fire, sulfur . . . the basement explodes.

* * * * *

Atop Liberty Memorial Tower—where the smoke of remembrance is usually aflame to honor the dead heroes of World War I—a mist is discharged, carried by a slight wind, to a naïve crowd below.

* * * * *

The front foyer extends to the right and left, lined by concrete columns with a backdrop wall illuminated from behind. Black-and-white portraits of ghostly veterans softly switch from one image to another . . . lost faces in a time dictating the fall of Imperialism.

Ahead lies a glass bridge, illuminated by the pyramidal grid window ceiling above. He can see the Tower loom overhead through the ceiling, a slight plume of smoke trailing from the top. *Odd*, he thinks to himself, *doesn't the flame only burn at night?*

He walks over the glass bridge, dubbed *Paul Sunderland Bridge* by a yellow placard. Below his feet, an indoor field of scarlet blazes underneath the bridge . . . 9,000 plastic orange-red poppies cover the bottom. Poppies habitually grow in disturbed Earth, so as the fields of Northern France were ripped open from the harsh trenches on the Western Front, the poppies were the only semblance of life that grew from of the blood of fallen soldiers. Hence, one flower for every thousand combatants killed in the Great War, equaling an appalling count of 9 million. The Enterprise honor their work.

"Hey Gregor!"

Dedalus follows the voice to the far end of the field. Lying snow-angel style in the corner of the indoor poppy field is Lawrence, dressed in a pink tutu, his hair in pigtails, a 12-gauge shotgun pointed directly at Dedalus above.

"*Fnord*, old buddy," he snarls. "'*First I must sprinkle you with fairy dust*,' sayeth the *Principia Discordia*!"

!!!!!BOOM!!!!!

The shotgun rings out, shattering pieces of bridge into millions of glass fragments, sprinkling onto the poppies below. Dedalus—the Maninkari pulse pumping in micro-second reaction—leaps out of the path, rolling across the bridge toward the exhibit entrance. He cocks the MP5K, and readies it on Lawrence.

"Ha, ha, ha, ha!!!! Wooo!!! Don't you love it???? All Hail Discordia!!!!!"

He shoots again !!!!!BOOM!!!!! in Dedalus' direction. But, his aim is off, he is disoriented. Dedalus aims directly at Lawrence, his best friend, through the aligned aperture sight. Breathe in, out . . . he pulls the trigger.

Rat-atat-atat-atat-atat!!!! Numerous holes splay Lawrence in the chest, spilling dribbles of blood spotted over the poppies below. He falls to the ground. The Western Front field holds another fallen. And finally, Lawrence is still.

"Goddammit," Dedalus rises. His body is shakes, a slight convulsion. The Maninkari cannot protect him from feeling, from emotion. It cannot prevent despair where despair is due. Head swells, a tear building in his eye. He grits his teeth, kicks open the exhibit door, and walks through.

The Museum is buzzing and alive with its film narratives and recordings describing the historical timelines of War, events leading up the War, the effects of the War. The channeled memories swirl in a vortex of distraction. It is hard to focus . . . Dedalus understands how vital this hub of energy is for the Enterprise, with the right geometric placement of establishments around the Memorial—for instance, the IRS and Federal Reserve—this could make for one mad bit of sorcery! He walks quietly through the donut-shaped path, displays of artillery and trench models, worn uniforms, and videos of dead bodies in mud.

There is no movement, he notes. No signs of an ambush. And then . . .

>>> CRASH <<<

Copernicus' body smashes through a display of spiral-barbed stakes, used to quietly create trenches on the Western Front. Shards of glass bite into him and his shoulder is snagged on one of the rusted metal barbs.

"Fuck!!!!!" Copernicus yells. Dedalus turns to see what had tossed Copernicus so effortlessly.

Jack, covered in octopus darkness, ornamented by the ghastly splinter mask and goggles . . . a distasteful abomination of a long-dead soldier risen as bogey beast. He walks toward Dedalus, hand outstretched in Christ-like fashion.

"Greetings, Gregor," Jack croons in sardonic din; atonal violins of hell screeching from his throat. "It is so welcoming to have you at such a wondrous time of ceremony! Sporting clothes you have there! It seems you have been adopted by the red epidemic . . . do you need cured?"

Without vacillating, Dedalus aims and fires.

* * * * *

Srinivasa continues his mantra conjuration: "*Jaya Seeyaa Raama, Jai Jai Hanuman, Jaya Bajrangbalee, Baba Hanuman . . .*" The Earth beneath him hums with a glorious rhythm. He feels a place opening, inside his *anahata*, the drum-beat of the heart. " *. . . Hare Raama Raama, Seetaa Raama Raama Raama . . .*"

Behind him, in the Park crowds, he hears screaming, shouting . . . frenzied disturbances of derangement. What is going on? Nevermind that! He must continue, faster: "*. . . Jaya Hanumana gyana guna sagara, Jaya Kapisa tihun loka ujagara . . .*"

Something opens . . .

* * * * *

Ramona stands frozen in fright. Jack and Copernicus had tumbled to the other end of the museum, and now . . . she hears gunfire, crashes. She looks over to the screen, poor Jonah hanging unconscious in front of the display . . . words spill over him in a smoke battlefield montage as the film continues to run endlessly:

"*Men die of mud, as they die from bullets, but more horribly. Mud is where men sink and—what is worse—where their soul sinks. Hell is not fire . . . hell is mud.*"

What can she do? Trapped, sinking . . . alone in a trench, waist deep. How can she reach Jonah in such a horrible display . . . there is no way to get to the top of the screen. But, she must try! In her desperation, she judges the height to the bottom of the screen from her position on the terrace. Maybe . . . six or seven feet? She climbs over the terrace railing and drops down in to the life-size trench. She collapses onto the ground in a heap, miscalculating the height in the darkness of the theater.

"Jesus," a sharp snake of pain writhing around her ankle, sprained. "More like ten feet!" She catches herself blurting out loud. She peers up to see Jonah dangling the same distance above.

"Jonah," she decides to holler. Maybe she can wake him from his reverie. "Jonah! Wake up you crazy old coot!!!"

She grabs onto the screen, a drape of cloth covering the entire wall. Her hand squelches the projected face of a young man in uniform, smiling with innocent freckles. She shakes the fabric, foolhardy; recklessly attempting to wake him up.

"Wake up you bastard," she begins to cry.

Then, a flicker. Shaken from her despondency, she instantly sees a figure above the lights of the screen. A little man, in a trench coat . . . a round head with wide-lemur eyes, smiling cordially at Ramona. She stumbles backward, unsure of the anomaly.

Before she can make out exactly what the little man is doing, he makes a quick motion at the knots tying Jonah to the screen. And then Jonah falls smack into the ground. Ramona runs to him, grabbing him instantly. She looks up to the strange man . . .

Eyes lemur lens wide, a precarious smile, opens to speak, a melodic calliope voice: "Reach Ramona . . . 52, 6-dot-4 . . . 24 . . . 8.1 divide 7 . . . x9-dor-6p7 . . . 44. Good night."

And she collapses into unconsciousness.

* * * * *

Running through a cacophony burst of splintering glass, Dedalus loads his last clip into the submachine gun and continues to fire at the shadow appendages leaping at him. Jump over one, another smacks him square in the side, sending him reeling into a wall brandishing pro-war propaganda posters.

Maninkari reaction—he pushes off in a panther leap, running toward a set of glass booths entitled "Reflections" . . . each containing a luminescent wall of varying colors. He continues to spit machine gun fire in Jack's direction, scanning the area for a way to incapacitate him. He pauses, turns to meet his adversary.

The waste—the carnage of thought . . . Jack is directly behind him in his black maelstrom—coming across Dedalus' spectrum of elucidatory factory; mechanical microbes in (non)conscience, inebriating the air with formulation and fear. Jack's long chin jutting through the chain mask, oil hair in spirals waving with no wind, constant movement (not from this plane, Dedalus sees, cannot abide by this physical domain) the impossibility of dark shape around eyes so deep, so Deep, beneath those leather slits . . . empty of sympathy, empathy, so full of pre-Apathy, except for an instinctual vibration only found in an insectoid metabolism . . . it is the survival to kill, to live is to invade . . . this creature: its pathways are too foreign to assimilate into Earthly prospects . . . the only way a Victorian Englishmen could translate this sort of carnality was to demonize it, as is every human inclination . . .

"I think it amusing little weasel wants to sing a song," Jack punches through with shadow arm through a display case and pulls out a withered bayonet. With a pale hand, he lifts the chainmail mask, sticks out a yellowed lizard tongue. Shadow tentacle brings the bayonet over and he licks the serrated edge. Black blood oozes from his tongue, down his chin, dripping to oil puddles on the carpet. "How much pain can you take?"

He eyes Dedalus wolfish, sizing up a lamb: "I think . . . I think I want to see what you look like without skin. Probably *very* red, yes . . ."

A human could not have recognized it. The seconds between seconds, motion so instantaneous the bayonet blade becomes a missile catapulting from his darkness. Dedalus hears, feels the air extraction, the splitting of molecules before the blade even enters proximity . . . a fleeting dodge, not as fast as Jack, but fast enough . . . it whistles past and sinks into the wall behind.

"Oh . . . a *real* Agent now, eh?" Jack cackles, cellophane in a graveyard. No more pause—a cacophony of similar bayonets shoot from his cryptic gloom: one, two, three, four! Dedalus leaps acrobatically into the air . . . arm to the left, whizzing under, right leg up, skimming by feet, torso the left, clips his jacket . . . blades streaking like little bottle rockets propelling through the museum chamber.

He is preoccupied, Dedalus surmises. Good! He will not stop . . . lead him out . . . run, leap, twirl, one whizzing past here, another shooting across, nicking his arm, blood spilling through the air . . . no matter, keep moving . . . jump, tumble, dart to the front entrance, run, run, run more! Pumping furiously, legs in a Maninkari siphon.

Act the bridge, leap onto the railing, across . . . Jack has run out of trinkets to throw. Dedalus hears him scream from behind, psionic banshee wail! He is furious and wants blood! A blackened appendage pummels down, shattering section of the glass bridge. Dedalus narrowly thwarting the attack, darting for the front doors, he kicks!

Slam! Out into the spilling daylight. He lands and turns around, pulling out the pistol from inside his coat, ready to fire.

Jack bursts through the door!

"RREAAAAAARRRRRRGGGHHHHHH!!!!!!!" his lurid howl echoing. The darkness tentacle form surrounding his body splayed out like black crustacean legs in the sun. His wretched face seething, burning away the leather goggles, a void in his eyes piercing the very marrow of existence into Dedalus . . . ready to feed, so full of ancient hunger! He crouches, ready to pounce, and . . .

))))) SLAM (((((

A colossal golden club smashes down onto Jack's shadow form, splattering it into ooze over the ground. For all the bullets that barely scathed him, his body now rendering itself tangible to this massive bludgeon vibrating the ground under Dedalus' feet.

It rises, a sickly smattering of oily parts crumpling beneath the mighty golden mace. Awestruck, Dedalus gazes at its wielder: fifteen, maybe twenty feet high, a gigantean behemoth of a physique; a large, half-man, half-gray furred langur monkey deity, a black face with a scuff of whitening beard around the face . . . wise, eternal, kind eyes . . . acute; a piestic aspect unlike anything Dedalus has seen, felt . . . even beyond Mithra. This giant, moving with such epicurean grace, pulls up its golden mace, ornamented in glorious robes covering enough to maintain humility, but open enough to show a blue face, the face of Rama, tattooed on his chest. The powerful heavenly bulk emanates an impressive radiance of power that forces Dedalus to his knees in pure reverence.

"This," Dedalus hears Srinivasa call out behind him. "Is Lord Hanuman!"

The mandible clutches of Jack's smattered form begins to churn itself together. Dedalus can hear clicking and clacking as the parts begin to mend. He sees a maniacal eye spook out of the blackened mulch.

"I . . . I, as I . . . I am," he sputters, liquid darkness, spilling out of his indigo lips. "I am . . . all . . . you . . . you are dinner . . ."

"Quiet," a magnificent tone, full of treasure and exaltation, sounds from above. The gargantuan form of Hanuman looks down disdainfully at the pitiful mass of Spring-heeled Jack. "Let us return you from whence you came, to the Void."

Hanuman pulls a chalice from his wind-blown robes, be-speckled with shining rubies. He lowers the great cup and, with his club, scoops the remains of Jack into the goblet. Jack puts up little resistance, his form broken and subdued. Dedalus can hear him squeal as Hanuman lifts the chalice into the air. It floats static and alone for a few seconds, a blip of light, it is no longer there.

Then, the towering behemoth shrinks, placidly, so that within seconds he is the same height as Dedalus. The empyrean firmament that surrounds Hanuman's aspect interweaves lace of light and glittering rhapsody; Dedalus can't rise from his knees, it would make him feel so . . . ugly. He bows his head in respect.

"Thank you," he offers to the great mystic Lord.

"Thank you, Agent," Hanuman's blissful voice not as clamorous as it was in his colossus form, but steady and venerable nonetheless. The monkey man stands next to him, placing a gray-furred hand full of holiness on Dedalus' shoulder; he becomes flushed with honor, a royal illustriousness. This being, so ancient . . . so cosmic . . . an idea turned manifest . . . beyond the characteristics of personality. Beyond definition.

Hanuman turns to the south, and Dedalus copies the motion. The throngs of protesters are frantic, running to and fro about the park, maniacal. Women pulling out their hair and punching the ground until their fists bloody, men stripping bare and chasing after others in the crowd, screaming endless obscenities and jabbering that makes little sense, lunacy and delirium spilling rampant among the crowd. A crowd of thousands . . . ranting, raging, wild, untamed . . . all completely mad.

"There is nothing I can do about the mania," Hanuman states calmly. "I am sorry."

Dedalus turns back to view the magnificent deity, to respond, but . . . he is gone. The Lord Hanuman has vanished completely. Back to his Himalayan retreat, Dedalus assumes, to await his Master's return.

"That is it," Srinivasa expounds, hunched over in a sheen of sweat, panting heavily. His eyes roll to the back of his head, body is trembling like the Earth was when Hanuman made his grand entrance. "He has . . . done the work . . . that he can do . . . glory to Lord Rama! I like . . . cookies . . ."

Srinivasa faints onto the mesa from exhaustion.

"His work really takes it out of him," Dedalus hears her say.

She approaches, limping, covered in soot. Exhilaration explodes as he sees the red shine of fuse Maninkari connection approach from the office building direction . . . black smoke bellowing into the sky behind her.

Darwin flops up to Dedalus.

"What happened?" he nudges toward the plume in the background.

"Ran into an Enterprise creep," she spits out a glob of blood. "They like blowing things up, with me in the fray. But, they always seem to forget how fast I am."

"You really look horrible," he observes the scuffs and tatters of her once-red jacket . . . holding her arm that seems to be broken.

"Eat shit," she retorts jokingly.

They hear a languished wail and their attention is drawn again to the horrific furor in the park. Sirens are blaring in the distance, the authorities are obviously notified of the mass psychosis pervading the Penn Valley gathering.

"What's going on?" Dedalus watches the chaotic configurations wave with improbability, impossible to muster . . . the horde is a prison of dissipation.

"This," she limps over to lean on Dedalus . . . a shattering throb still aching from the explosive impact she barely avoided. "This is the Red Mass. This is what they used Merchant's blood for. Every one of these people, every single one, is a potential Nova automaton in waiting now. They will stir in hysteria for days, and then it will die down . . . then they will go home, and return to their lives relieved it was all just a bad dream. But, someday, they will be turned on . . . and they will mindlessly serve the Enterprise's needs."

"So," Dedalus realizes, sinking gut of melancholy. "We lost. We failed to stop them."

She looks over at him. If the sunglasses weren't there, he would see eyes stricken with devastation and grief. He can touch the penetrating despondency.

"Yes."

30 - Freaks

No words had to be said. Copernicus can feel the warm, recently used barrel of the Uzi machine gun press firmly to the back of his neck. Not many people can sneak up on him. Must be a RED Agent.

"I'm getting them to safety," he shrugs the two limp bodies of Ramona and Jonah he had been pulling through the emergency exit. Had been until he felt the steel at his nape.

"Good story," Dedalus retorts behind him. "And I am to believe you *weren't* going to incarcerate them because . . ."

"Because you saw Jack kicking my ass back there. Now here," Copernicus turns, maneuvering Ramona's limp body toward Dedalus. Dedalus lowers the weapon, his bluff called. "Take your girlfriend and let's get them out of here."

With no effort, Dedalus picks Ramona up and cradles her delicately in his arms. She is so still, quiet asleep, her energy a pale steady hue of blue. Her frequency is on hold, in a comatose state.

"What happened?" he asks Copernicus who, battered and torn, is struggling to get Jonah's bulk around his shoulders. Copernicus, though worn and cut to shreds, manages to lift Jonah to carry him shoddily down the hill by Kessler Street.

"Don't know," Copernicus grunts, heaving from Jonah's weight. He teeter-totters toward the shade of a tree grouping. Dedalus follows, holding Ramona tight. "By the time I walked into the theater, it looked like she was attempting to rescue Jonah. She was on the ground, had him in her arms. But she was looking up, at the lighting, something was up there . . . I heard a voice . . . like an old monograph . . . and she passed out. By the time I got over there . . . whatever it was, it was gone."

"Propit," Dedalus confirms.

"What?"

"Nevermind," he lays Ramona gently down into the tree's shadow. Gray leaf forms dance over her still, yet sublime face.

"How is she?" Copernicus clumps Jonah down with a grumble. Unraveling one of Jonah's many scarves, he tucks it under his head for support. Jonah mutters slightly.

"Weak, but stable. I can . . . see," the auric fragility sputtering with a constant wane, Dedalus touches in, reaches out, her depleted aspect reworked; Propit had worked his magic. She must have eaten some of the products—remembers: Wallis manor, Ramona helping herself in Lawrence's kitchen . . . she *had* eaten a sandwich; she was coded, this whole time waiting to be turned on by the Red Mass. But, Propit . . . Propit had gotten to her just in time! "I can . . . go in and find her."

"Again . . . what?" Copernicus, haggard, reaches into his pockets, searching for a cigarette. He scans the outskirts of the park for any oncoming threats and/or authorities.

"Just keep watch," Dedalus commands. "I'm going to get her back."

Closing his eyes, he taps into his talent: *frothy mote tap, tap, tapping into the inner eye flow of that structure behind reality, that structure made of all and underneath, beneath; the seek inner lay, structure chakra system not exactly what was studied. They are more like atoms, spinning electrons and protons in orbits with a nucleus beaming significantly at each core, all interactive, integrative like the endocrine system itself. Jump into stomach cortex a radiant glide and the tell-tale cream of reality all partaking around; the trees singing and praising magnificence of the sun, beating down in rhythms of consistent brilliance . . . she, Ramona, the pale blue frequency in a bulbous shell . . . touch the outer filament, the tiles shift – ability to shift the building block structures that hold it all together and fingers move in to her abated aura.*

There is dilation everywhere . . .

Sinking down into her essence, a pyramidal cape vortices pushing through the barrier of comatose snail call . . .

moving down, down under epidermis thrice, poetic geography where cells converge. Lower world inside of her (everyone has their own Lower World). She is in a cavern cul-de-sac, sitting alone in the dark . . . hugging her knees close to her chin. She does not see. Timber glow permeating from heaving walls . . . no, not alone . . . a plump gray cat with emerald eyes sits beside her. It rises, and gracefully saunters up, curling tail. It stands out on the matrix like walking sentence fragment.

"And you are?" ask it.

"I'm Mama Isis," the cat answers in a very humanly, motherly tone.

Remember in Gregor aspect: Ramona had talked about a cat she once owned as a child. Her favorite pet. Mama Isis. This must be her.

"You must be a totem," tell Mama Isis. "A guardian spirit?"

"And you must be clever," Mama Isis plops to the ground, assumedly ready to nap. She is unthreatened. "We knew you as Gregor, but now you're not. I know your kind. Ancient ties. Somewhere on another spectrum. What do you want here?"

"I want Ramona back," answer to the cat. She is small, but her power is dense, concentrated . . . not sure what she could do but most certainly not yet trained or experienced enough to find out. Must reason with her.

"We don't want to come out," Mama Isis sighs, large protruding fangs in a puma mouth. "We are scared. We've been hurt. It's safe in here. Too many monsters out there."

"The monsters are dead now. It's safe to come out."

"We don't believe you," Mama Isis conjures an incisive stare, looking through, spiritual interrogation.

"You know I speak the truth," reason, pleading. "I can tell you are wise. You can see truth. So, why do you resist?"

"We are tired of being hurt," Mama Isis looks lazily off to the side, at nothing. "We are tired of trying and trying."

Configuring, establishing thought shape basis for being. Ramona's form behind her stone, unmovable, stoic.

"Tired of trying what?" ask.

Mama Isis looks back over with the acute emerald focus, Ramona's eyes raise toward as well.

"Tired," Mama Isis intones. "Of trying to love you."

Remembering as Gregor, remembering what as . . . the broken mirror facades of memory—Ramona cooking; Ramona, her blackbird silhouette arm churning a pot; sitting there on the couch looking at her, reading an account of the JFK assassination; looking at her, want to tell her, want to say, 'Thank you,' want to express appreciation, express care, for sticking through it, for keeping on churning, moving through all the shit, everything Gregor couldn't offer her . . . so stuck as Gregor, frozen in fear, drowning in disease and paranoia . . . nowhere to go, choking on the words to tell her . . . to reach out to her . . . want to, but fear's embrace so tight, a constrictor vice squeezing ever tighter around the reasoning of sanity, of clarity . . .

But, now know.

Now, Gregor is a figment, a falsity. Dedalus is the new moth.

"I'm sorry," reach our throat chakra with all authenticity, movement out to fill the cave . . . the chakra of truth, the energy center of creation. "I am truly sorry, Ramona. For everything. For bringing you into all this. For never being able to express how much you meant to me. I was locked in, lost in a maze. I was so afraid of you, of life, of my own shadow."

Ramona's eyes begin to glisten, moisture glint off the crease forming between her eyes.

"Yes?" Mama Isis urges on.

"I had always loved you Ramona," finally give to her. "And I can't imagine that I would truly ever stop. I'm here now. The real me."

Mama Isis turns her head back to Ramona, seeking confirmation. Ramona streaking tears down smooth cheeks.

320

"I'm not going to leave you anymore, Ramona. I want to be the friend to you, the friend that I was never able to be. Someone to take care of you now."

Mama Isis dissipates into nothingness, a whisk of cool air. Ramona stands, a careful, sobbing smile glowing to life on her resplendent face.

Her eyes open.

"Gregor!" Ramona yelps, reaching up to squeeze him like the world is over. "Oh my God I'm so glad you're okay!"

"Yeah," Dedalus returns the embrace. They hold on to each other for—according to Copernicus—a few uncomfortable minutes. He sucks on his cigarette quietly.

"My God I thought maybe you were dead," she breathes into Dedalus' ear. Air follicle prickles into the surge— he could evaporate in her mist, he knows. "I'm so glad you're safe."

"I'm glad you're safe too," he tells her. Ramona, surprised, glints up to meet him eye-to-eye. The sunglasses reflect her face back at her. He brushes back a strand of her glowing hair to see the crease between her eyebrows. "But, I am not Gregor anymore. Gregor is a lie."

"Unggh," she waivers, overthrown by a surge of dizziness.

"Careful," Dedalus lays her gently back to the ground. "You're going to be weak, don't over exert yourself."

"You just essentially pulled her out of a coma, didn't you?" Copernicus exhales a plume of smoke into the air.

"Take the van," Dedalus suggests to Copernicus. "And Ramona."

"We need some time," Darwin adds, walking up to them through camouflage of the tree covering. Her resolute stance a further suggestion to Copernicus that they are more *ordering* him, rather than suggesting.

"You'll see an unconscious Indian guy in there," she continues, looking down at Jonah lying in the grass, covered by his layers of coats, sweaters and scarves. His breathing is unsteady, slowing by the minute. A heavy countenance of age weighs on his face. "Leave him be."

Ramona begins to argue, but her wooziness halts her protestations.

"There is an outbreak of insanity on the other side of that hill," Dedalus waves toward the Memorial. "You need to be taken to safety. I'll meet up with you. I promise. If he does anything other than what I ask of him, I will hunt him down and kill him."

Dedalus looks up at Copernicus.

"Won't I?"

Copernicus shrugs nonchalantly. "You win. You're in charge."

Grudgingly, she obliges the request. Propping her up, Dedalus assists to steady her balance.

"Thanks," she proffers. "I'm okay, I'm okay. Getting better. Not so groggy."

"Where do you want me to go?" Copernicus asks.

"Just head down to Crown Center," Darwin answers bluntly. "It's far enough away from the Mass, but close and public enough the Enterprise won't be making any more moves."

"Are you coming?" Ramona's yearning eyes turn to Dedalus.

"I'll be there," he confers. "I promise. We just need a few minutes."

Copernicus and Ramona ferry each other across a patch of green to the van. Accepting a wave of relief, Dedalus watches as they head east down Pershing.

He turns to Jonah. The energy depleting . . . he can touch in the presence a Maninkari trace . . . very much similar to Merchant.

"Jonah was," he inquires to Darwin. "An actual Agent?"

She nods.

"But, why was he . . . *normal*? Why didn't he have the signatures, the abilities we do?"

"He did, a long time ago," she elucidates quietly, reminiscence of time when she had worked with Jonah . . . flooding her warmly with appreciation, companionship. "But, the Maninkari wyrm can only last so long in its symbiotic state on this plane. Eventually, the wyrm dies off. Which is why Jonah was no longer an Agent, but an ally reserved for recruitment activities. It also makes you . . . not insane, but just a little . . . *loony*."

She smiles down at Jonah, who seems to have pried open his eyes barely a slit.

"Though in a charming way, I'd say," he utters weakly.

His lumbering eyes oscillate from Darwin to Dedalus, regarding the newfound red sport coat and shades covering his eyes.

A smile of satisfaction flourishes on his worn face.

"'*As a philosopher*'," he faintly mutters from *Ulysses*, fragile and decrepit. "'*He knew that . . . at the termination of any allotted life . . . only an infinitesimal part . . . of any person's desires . . . has been realized.*'"

Jonah shudders; and then Darwin and Dedalus watch as the life leaves him like wisp of cloud. His life is gone.

Quiet. A soldier has fallen this day.

Darwin turns away, limps fraily past the collection of trees, off toward the west.

"Where are you going?" Dedalus implores. "What are we going to do?"

She stops, leans on one of the oaks at the edge of the grouping. She doesn't turn around.

"*You* are going to go make good with your girlfriend," she responds. "Make sure she's okay. Give her what she deserves . . . a little bit of *you*."

"But this," he folds Jonah's empty hands, one on top of the other, over his chest. "This is too much . . . it's *uncalled* for! We've got to do *something*!"

"And we will, Dedalus the Labyrinth-Breaker," she replies. She averts her gaze from the sun, inching down to the horizon, painting the landscape with long shadows and orange hues. Dedalus can see half her face, a tear glistening down her cheek.

"You know Patti Smith, don't you?"

He shakes his head in disbelief. "The singer . . . yeah, I guess . . . why?"

"It's time to shake out the ghost dance on these fuckers," Darwin continues to limp away. "But, go take care of the person who loves you first."

Dedalus returns his attention back to the corpse getting cold under his touch. Jonah's body stiffening, becoming one with emptiness and Earth. The dross scoria of essence descending into the lower realms of the reflective spirits. He has a regal countenance.

"Thank you," Dedalus whispers to the passing memory structure that was Jonah Mulligan, retired RED Agent from days past. "Thank you so much, for waking me up."

* * * * *

He is crouched on a bench at the edge of the Crown Center fountains. He watches as children and parents play in the grid work of spouts squirting randomly into the air; innocent and ignorant of the catastrophe just blocks away. They dance in the gushes of water, a solace from the oppressive heat. How many of them are there? How many of these smiling faces have eaten the product? His heart sinks.

"Copernicus," Ramona interrupts his watchful reverie. "Or whatever your name is . . . here you go."

She hands him a cup of coffee purchased from the Westin shopping center across Grand Boulevard.

"There's a little convenience store in there," she offers, nodding to his wounds. "If you want an actual bandage or something."

"Naw," he curls his hands delicately around the sytrofoam cup, steaming wafting in his face. "This is all I need. Thanks."

"Don't you think it's a little hot for coffee?"

He gawks at her. "Blasphemy!"

"Hey, whatever suits you," she throws her hands up in casual defense. She settles herself beside him—arms crossed bird's shadows oscillate in the fountain sprinkle—watching the splash through the spouts in laughter. She sighs with heavy fatigue, exhaustion exasperating the gravity of her being. A languid grogginess still permeates her senses. "They'll lie, won't they?"

Copernicus gazes over in a hawkish squint.

"The mind control," Ramona finishes her thought. "Everyone going crazy, being poisoned. The government, the media will lie. And, even here in the city, on this very block . . . people will believe them, won't they?"

He goes back to sipping his coffee, clasping the Holy Grail.

"Most likely," he grunts. "You know, Ramona . . . for people like me, guys who spend all their time surrounded by the most grotesque shit you can imagine . . . we like to unwind. Off duty . . . we don't like to think, you know? A nice cold beer, a Stallone flick . . . that's bliss! When and if we were to pick up a book, it's gotta be fun, right . . . something that makes all the shit we see every day seem like we're heroes in an action movie. It keeps you sane, so you can do your job and not break. One of my personal favorites, when I do read, is Jim Butcher and his *Dresden* stuff. I remember one scene, in one of the books . . . I think it was *Small Favor* . . . where Dresden is explaining how all the supernatural shit he fights all the time isn't ever noticed. Living in a city being one of those reasons, right? Because a city has walls. And another reason . . . I remember this very distinctly . . . he said, '*We're ostriches and the whole world is sand.*'"

He pauses, reaching into his shirt pocket to pull out a crumpled cigarette, plops it into his mouth. Tobacco pieces flutter to the ground, some delicately landing on the black surface of his warm drink.

"I'll never forget that line," he says. "Because that's the way people are, you know? Nobody wants to be bothered. Even if they did care about something other than their mortgages and car payments, it's all too much for them to bear. It's too frightening to think . . ."

"That your own government will kill you to protect its own interests," finishes Dedalus, quietly appearing behind them. Ramona starts though Copernicus remains unflinching.

Ramona snags Dedalus once more, intent never to let go. Dedlaus affably returns the embrace.

"What's happening?" she requests emphatically. "The world is spinning . . . I don't know what to believe anymore."

"There is nothing *to* believe," Dedalus enunciates.

Crease deepens, puzzlement staining her face. Before she can react, Copernicus interrupts.

"So, non-Gregor," he holds the dingy, unlit cigarette between two fingers. "Is everything clear back there? I'd appreciate a head start if Jack slipped through your fingers."

"Why should I give you a head start?" Dedalus steps in between Ramona and Copernicus, easing her behind him. Copernicus sits calmly on the bench sipping his coffee.

"Why? Because I kidnapped your girl?" Unable to find a lighter, he stuffs the unlit cigarette back into his shirt pocket. "Let me tell you someth'n . . . let an old man humor you. You see, all I ever wanted, since I was a little boy raised on John Wayne movies, was to grow up and serve my country . . . only to find out that my country doesn't even exist. This *country*, this *government*, and the illusion that people are somehow in control . . . it's only a public relations front for what's *really* going on, for the *real* governing body of a handful of white bankers whose only concern is to keep us all fighting in the playground so they can compose the course of history like a macabre dance."

He peers over calmly at Dedalus, who hovers over him stalwart.

"We're not all fighting for Big Brother, *non*-Gregor," he sips some more. "Some of us still believe in something pure, something good. And we're not perfect, but it's that willingness to work with the monsters that saved your girlfriend's life."

He keeps on sipping, watching children splash water on each other, cackling with laughter. Dedalus examines his electromagnetic flow . . . steady, ardent, not the least bit anxious . . . but tired, weary, ready to collapse. He believes him. He *knows* him. An old warrior trapped in a maze . . . Dedalus knows mazes.

"What's going to happen?" Ramona queries, thumbing Dedalus' red sport coat. "You're . . . you're one of these red men . . . what are you going to do now?"

Copernicus looks up with casual interest.

Dedalus watches the children play . . . droplets of water spewing into the air he can drift through pockets of air with slowest and quickest of effects . . . awe-inspiring enigma the world is! These poor children, these people, rummaging through it all, through the humdrum like sheep. The Enterprise has their Huxley-like, soma-induced slaves . . . the whole world is sleepwalking, and RED struggles to react, fights to wake up a citizen here, a citizen there.

"The RED Agency," he answers softly. "They are a guerilla force. They will always be there, countering the Nova efforts, countering the ones trying to keep things *ordinary*. But, that's just the thing . . . they are only reactionary. As long as this mode of operation stays static, the war will only continue on as is. More days like today."

"What are you saying?" Ramona grabs his sleeve. She moves in close, unwilling to give him away again, adamant to keep him close.

"Sounds like what you're saying is," Copernicus returns his attention to the crowd, cradling his cup. "You're wanting to be proactive."

Dedalus nods.

"No, wait," Ramona keens, grabbing his jacket now forcefully. She punches his chest. How could he? Why does he keep going away? She tries and she tries . . . she's been through hell, near-death to be close to him, because she cares . . . and he's going farther away. He is deliberately moving himself away from her! "Why??? Why can't you just *stay put*? Do you know what I've been through for you??"

Dedalus holds his hands out, caressing her arms, consoling.

"I know," he states. "But there's no turning back now. I think . . . I think I have to take the fight to *them*, Ramona."

She cries. Blue spark light, lament dawn in a cull fraction—he can see her pain: and it hurts. What he was, what he always was for her; while in the gray, while Gregor Samson . . . and now this . . . Gregor Samson is dead. Agent Dedalus is already married to the Cause. Gregor would have left her behind. But, Dedalus will not.

"Don't worry," hand petting delicately through golden hair, assuaging her fears. "I'm going to need help."

An attenuated smirk flashes on his face. She gets his message and relief sparks her. They are together. She has him, and he will not go away. This new Gregor, this RED man before her, is no longer frightened, no longer going to create a divide. He is here, embracing her.

"I'm sorry," Copernicus espouses, regretfully interrupting their connected moment. "You're off to fight the good fight, kid?"

"Your point?" he inquires to Copernicus' musing.

"It's just . . . what you're doing . . . what you're saying . . . you're declaring war! How do you intend to do that? I don't imagine the M.O. of your people conforms to that sort of action."

"You're right," Dedalus unwraps himself from Ramona and grabs ahold of her hand. They clasp firmly. He looks back at

Copernicus decisively. "I guess that means I will have to *mobilize*."

And with that, Dedalus and Ramona walk away from the fountains, without a farewell. Copernicus shrugs, pulls his attention to the joyous families experiencing innocent play in their naiveté. He sips his coffee and smacks his aging lips in satisfaction.

He is left alone.

* * * * *

Out off the beaten path, *Gus' Gas Pit*, sits like a cancerous lump off a scenic highway in northern Missouri. Jeffrey sits behind the counter, day in and day out . . . barely attentive to the few customers that lumber in to pay for gas or pick up some fishing tackle. Instead, he is reading his New International Version of the Holy Bible, intent; in a feverish solemnity with impatient, shaking hands. Repentance, repentance; his soul is screaming with fear as he flips through the book furiously in search of a way to dispel the trepidation.

Jeremiah 31:19: "*Surely, after my turning, I repented; and after I was instructed, I struck myself on the thigh; I was ashamed, yes, even humiliated because I bore the reproach of my youth.*"

The passage makes Jeffrey wince, reminded of the sting on his back. Crusted scars from the limitless nights of flogging with the horse whip he purchased from the Auction House. Why? Because he is reminded.

Matthew 4:17: "*Repent, for the kingdom of heaven is at hand.*"

Beyond reproach; he sees it every once in a while. A blur, a blip. Almost like a dream. Out his window. Within the trees. Or on the road. Sometimes even in his own room. Before he can ever get a complete look, it is gone . . . evaporating into the ether of his own paranoia. They are watching him, he knows. They will come back for him . . . they said they would.

Revelation 12:3: "*And another sign appeared in heaven: behold, a great, fiery red dragon having seven heads and ten horns, and seven diadems on his heads.*"

He sees the red flashes now and again, and it is enough to keep him afraid. So very afraid! The red men will come back for him! He knows it, and quivers in true terror every day and every night . . . awaiting their return for his soul!

* * * * *

DJ Kat: "Welcome back to *The Slide* Rock FM, and we were listening to "Make it Hurt" from Savage Faucet. That piece just kicks some ass, man! What 'd you think, Bone Dawg?"

Bone Dawg: "Love it, man. Tight, yo!"

DJ Kat: "Absolutely! So, we're *back*! This is DJ Kat and my side-kick-in-crime, Bone Dawg Mad Dawg!"

Bone Dawg: "Yo! Wassup Kay Ceeeee???"

DJ Kat: "Wassuuup??? So . . . now, as promised, we brought back our very special guest, and local madman and looney-bin escapee . . . Pssssssssychooooooo Mike! Psycho Mike, you on the line, brutha?"

Mike: "Hey, DJ. Thanks for having me on."

DJ Kat: "Thank YOU for comin' on, man! So . . . Psycho Mike . . . to recap for those that have never heard you on before, you are a conspiracy nut, correct?"

Mike: "That's correct."

DJ Kat: "You believe, basically, in UFOs, aliens, government cover-ups . . . Oliver Stone sh(*bleep*), right?"

Mike: "Yes, that's correct."

DJ Kat: "Now the last time you were on you were explaining to us that we shouldn't brush our teeth anymore, remember that Bone Dawg?"

Bone Dawg: "Aw man, that's some crazy sh(*bleep*), man! That's sick! It's called hygiene, bro!"

Mike: "No, no, you don't understand!"

DJ Kat: "Then why don't you illuminate a little bit for us, Psycho Mike! Give us a recap, will ya?"

Mike: "Sure, see the thing is pretty much all of the toothpaste we use contains fluoride, which is actually not good for us, you see?"

DJ Kat: "Right, because all the dentists of the world would let us use toothpaste that is bad for us!"

Mike: "It's a misinformation game, DJ, and the corporations are in control! Fluoride is a poison, it's toxic! As well, they use it in anti-psychotics which is how they control the population! And it hinders pineal gland activation, which is a very important part of neurological processing . . ."

DJ Kat: "Sure, sure, Psycho Mike! So, I feel sorry for *your* wife! How's your teeth looking these days?"

Bone Dawg: "Ha, ha!"

Mike: "Actually, I brush with tea tree oil and baking soda."

DJ Kat: "Baking soda? That's f(*bleep*)ed up!!!"

Bone Dawg: "Eewwww! Grosss!"

DJ Kat: "So, anyway, the question I have for you today is, the reason I wanted to have you on is, because of the recent terrorist attacks on St. Luke's Hospital and Penn Valley Park here in Kansas City this past week. Now, the Administration, the FBI, CIA, and local law enforcement officials have all come forward with credible evidence to suggest that this is an Al-Qaeda linked attack. Now, I know how you believe that Al-Qaeda is a myth concocted by our government. We especially covered this topic a few years ago with the beginning of the U.S. occupation in Iraq and Yemen . . . you made quite a few of our viewers angry, do you remember that?"

Mike: "Yes, well, they were *invasions*, DJ, not just an occupation."

DJ Kat: "Yeah, well . . . ANYWAY . . . my point being is, the point I want to get to is, what's your latest Psycho-crazy-Mike concoction on this one?"

Bone Dawg: "Yeah, man! Is it the *Government*? Ha, ha!"

Mike: "Well, actually this recent episode has been very telling. The Illuminati used to be the puppet masters and the U.S. Government their puppets, but I think there may be some dissent in the ranks, as it were. I think what we saw--at Penn Valley Park especially--was a kind of argument between the Government and Illuminati, but they're still all after the same thing."

DJ Kat: "And what is that, Psycho Mike?"

Mike: "Control, of course! They're both evil, they just have different ways of implementing their agendas. But, a new component has come out of this recent attack that has the conspiracy community buzzing!"

DJ Kat: "Is that so? What's happening that's got your conspiracy panties tied in knots?"

Mike: "The Red Man sightings!"

Bone Dawg: "Say what? Like Indians, or someth'n?"

Mike: "No, no. Red Men . . . like Men in Black, you know?"

DJ Kat: "Yeah, we know Men in Black!!! Don't we, Dawg?"

Bone Dawg: "Yo Will Smith!!!!"

DJ Kat: "Ha! Awwww yeah!"

Mike: "Anyway, the Men in Black phenomena is a very common occurrence, especially in UFO sightings. But, there is a new type of mystery man, or mystery woman too, that is showing up in all types of cases that deal with the supernatural, aliens, cryptozoology. . ."

DJ Katz: "Crypto-what???"

Mike: "Sightings of these red figures have been seen throughout history. A member of parliament from the Isle of Man, in the Irish Sea, Thomas Kermode saw, at the turn of the 20th Century, fairie-like apparitions that looked like soldiers dressed in red. Even Napoleon had encounters with a supernatural figure dressed in red that protected him from harm. In 1954, in the small town of . . ."

Bone Dawg: "Whoa, yo! Did he just say fairies? Heh, heh . . . so you look'n for gay men takin' over the world now?"

DJ Katz: "Ha, ha, ha! Aw, sh(*bleep*)!"

Mike: "Please let me finish! These Red Men sightings have increased exponentially throughout history, especially with a major boom in the 1960s."

DJ Katz: "Free love!!!"

Mike: "And what I think, there is a lot of speculation as well, that these Red Men are a counter-force to the Illuminati, to the tyrants in charge. Out of all the scary stuff going on out there, all these things trying to take over the world, the Red Men are there for *us*!"

Bone Dawg: "Super Gay Men! Na na na na na na, na na na na na! *Gay Men*!!!"

DJ Katz: "Ha, ha, ha, ha! Aw, Dawg, you kill me!"

Mike: "Please, guys, I'm serious! This is an exciting new development in . . ."

DJ Katz: "Naw, you listen to me, Psycho Mike! This is *my* show! *I* will take floor! I think we've heard enough of your bullsh(*bleep*)! You know what? It's *sick*! You know why? Because people *died*, Psycho Mike! *Died*! Innocent women and children and families have lost their loved ones! And you know why? Because some crazy Arab terrorist from the f(*bleep*)ing desert doesn't like our freedoms so they wanna come over here and bomb us! And you know what? It's people like *you* that distract from what's going on! It's people like *you* that sit around making up crazy *Liberalist* bullsh(*bleep*) while our men and women are out there on the other side of the world, on the front lines, fighting for *our* freedoms!"

Bone Dawg: "Yeah, risking their *lives*, yo!"

DJ Katz: "Fighting for *your* freedom to be a PSYYYCHOOOO!!! Got it?"

Mike: "Now listen guys, you asked me to come on . . ."

DJ Katz: "And now I'm asking *you* to leave, Psycho Mike! Get off my radio program you twisted, unpatriotic lunatic!"

Bone Dawg: "Yeah, get off!"

DJ Katz: "Is he gone?"

Bone Dawg: "Yeah, I cut him out."

DJ Katz: "Cool. Alright, wasn't that exciting everyone? Coming up next we're gonna talk about that new lesbian sex photo of Bobbi Dakota and Sonya Lattin that surfaced on the Web the other day! We'll be talking with the guy who allegedly caught them on film!"

Bone Dawg: "Hell, yes!!! That is *tight*, yo!"

DJ Katz: "We'll be back right after the commercial break!"

END

About the Author

Daniel Moler lives in the Kansas City metropolitan area. He is married with two kids, three cats, and five fish. His education consists of two Bachelor's degrees in Art and English, as well as a Master's in Liberal Arts with an emphasis in modern and postmodern theory.

The online magazine *Reality Sandwich.com* holds the gamut of his work: "Ouroboros," an account of postmodern theory seen through the eyes of art history; "The Universal Heart," a personal account of engaging in a shamanic ceremony with the San Pedro cactus; and "Machine Elves 101," an exposé on the life and work of psychedelic scientist Terence McKenna. "The Universal Heart" has also been published in the hard-copy British magazines *Indie Shaman* and *Sacred Hoop*. Additionally, he wrote a review of the documentary <u>What if Cannabis Cured Cancer</u>, called "Chemo or Cannabis," published both online and hard-copy in Kansas City's *Evolving Magazine*. Recently, Daniel's interview with <u>What if Cannabis Cured Cancer</u>'s director Len Richmond was published in *Cannabis Culture Magazine*, *Positive Health Online Magazine*, and *Reality Sandwich*.

As one can tell from his work, Daniel's primary passion is in the shamanic arts. He is currently undergoing an apprenticeship in the Pachakuti Mesa tradition, a form of Peruvian shamanism with lineages in Northern Coastal *kamasq curanderismo* and Andean *Q'ero paqokuna*. Additionally, he is a volunteer committee member of The Heart of the Healer (THOTH) foundation, a non-profit organization whose mission is to preserve indigenous cultures and restore our Earth.

Daniel's next novel <u>Ghost Dance</u> (a sequel to <u>Red Mass</u>) is currently in the works, including a nonfiction book on shamanism and postmodernity. Updates on Daniel Moler and his work can be found on The Daedalus Thread at www.danielmoler.com.

Made in the USA
Lexington, KY
21 November 2011